Liturgical Liaisons

Princeton Theological Monograph Series

K. C. Hanson, Charles M. Collier, D. Christopher Spinks, and
Robin Parry, Series Editors

Recent volumes in the series:

James L. Papandrea
Novatian of Rome and the Culmination of Pre-Nicene Orthodoxy:

Aliou Cissé Niang
Text, Image, and Christians in the Graeco-Roman World:
A Festschrift in Honor of David Lee Balch

Sara M. Koenig
Isn't This Bathsheba?: A Study in Characterization

Gale Heide
Timeless Truth in the Hands of History:
A Short History of System in Theology

Koo Dong Yun
The Holy Spirit and Ch'i (Qi):
A Chiological Approach to Pneumatology

Stanley S. MacLean
Resurrection, Apocalypse, and the Kingdom of Christ:
The Eschatology of Thomas F. Torrance

Brian Neil Peterson
Ezekiel in Context: Ezekiel's Message Understood
in Its Historical Setting of Covenant Curses
and Ancient Near Eastern Mythological Motifs

Susan Marie Smith
Christian Ritualizing and the Baptismal Process:
Liturgical Explorations toward a Realized Baptismal Ecclesiology

Liturgical Liaisons

The Textual Body, Irony, and Betrayal
in John Donne and Emily Dickinson

Jamey Heit

With a foreword by David Jasper

PICKWICK *Publications* · Eugene, Oregon

LITURGICAL LIAISONS
The Textual Body, Irony, and Betrayal in John Donne and Emily Dickinson

Princeton Theological Monograph Series 189

Pickwick Publications
An Imprint of Wipf and Stock Publishers
199 W. 8th Ave., Suite 3
Eugene, OR 97401

www.wipfandstock.com

ISBN 13: 978-1-61097-770-8

Cataloguing-in-Publication data:

Heit, Jamey.

Liturgical liaisons : the textual body, irony, and betrayal in John Donne and Emily Dickinson / Jamey Heit, with a foreword by David Jasper.

xxii + 202 pp. ; 23 cm. Includes bibliographical references and index.

Princeton Theological Monograph Series 189

ISBN 13: 978-1-61097-770-8

1. Donne, John, 1567–1631—Criticism and interpretation. 2. Donne, John, 1567–1631—Religion. 3. Dickinson, Emily, 1830–1886—Criticism and interpretation. 4. Dickinson, Emily, 1830–1886—Religion. I. Title. II. Series.

PR1191 H33 2013

Manufactured in the U.S.A.

for dad

Contents

Foreword

THE BEST TEXTS, AND WE COULD BEGIN WITH THE GOSPELS THEMSELVES, are perfectly simple and infinitely complex, or, to put it another way, they have a crystal clarity which has the capacity to reflect the profoundest depths. Jamey Heit's *Liturgical Liaisons* has precisely that clarity and capacity. It is essentially an extended conversation between literature and theology, or perhaps of theology in literature, the literature endlessly and restlessly disturbing and destabilizing, the theology, in Heit's words, "an exercise in stability which . . . is not the text's province." The reader who seriously engages with this book is drawn into a world in which one is left teetering on precipices, confronting betrayal, on the edge of death in moments of seductive eroticism, tragic irony and blinding insight. In short, one enters into and experiences those moments of real presences in a Christian "liturgical poetics" in which light is shone in brilliant flashes on Jesus' eschatological presence, known first in the demonstrations, the words and actions of the Last Supper as they draw attention to the body which is insistently present in all its particularity, on the brink of death, and present also in a universal future that is yet to be realized: *hoc est enim corpus meum*—"for this is my body."

Heit begins his text, which is a kind of act of remembrance, by remarking that "what follows is neither a strict literary analysis nor an exercise in theology." Don't be too quick to take him too seriously—for he is far too serious a writer for such simple literalism. He is, of course, seriously engaged in both of these things—literary analysis and theology—though in his own way. Heit's writings are, very precisely, an enactment of liturgical moments (and nothing can be more theological than that) through brilliant conversations and exchanges with the love poetry of John Donne, priest, and his reclusive nineteenth century American poetic heir and disciple, Emily Dickinson. Theology, like literature, at its best is never rude, but neither is it shy or coy. If we begin on the first page with St. Bernard of Clairvaux in the place of humanity's displaced condition, that is, with fallen humankind, then it is only through honest, and yet also somehow dishonest and transgressive, seductive and paradoxical encounters with the body that finally an eschatological vision begins to be revealed and anticipated through that body and in the encounters between bodies.

This book is writing within a distinguished tradition of scholarship in the field of literature and religion which found its voice among some scholars in Britain and North America in the later years of the twentieth century as it absorbed and transformed the unsettling insights of postmodernity and deconstruction. Above all the figure of Robert Detweiler in his now classic work *Breaking the Fall: Religious Readings of Contemporary Fiction* (1989) is heard frequently, its insights on the community of readers transposed into the world of the poems of Donne and Dickinson. But scholarship and literature never stand still, and Heit develops and sharpens this tradition further for his own time through voices from contemporary continental philosophy—from the slightly earlier Blanchot, to Nancy, Marion, Lacoste, and others, in their toleration and finally their embracing of infinite deferral and displacement as the only possible "places" for true religion.

The reader of this book must be bold, and must be prepared to participate as well as to listen and be instructed. It is about more than simply understanding. That is of the nature of all liturgical practice. Its community of voices are many, though through them the singular vision of a liturgical poetics shines with clarity, with its focus on the body, erotic, betrayed, broken, triumphant. It is a body known at first only through the ironies and paradoxes of the poetics, but felt in exchanges both illicit and hospitable. Like the literature of the gospels, such a poetics is utterly simple—when the penny has finally dropped, as Ian Ramsey (another unseen and rather Anglican presence) would once have said—but it is precisely then that the difficulties and complexities begin. No action of the body is without its consequences. For a true poetics is finally and insistently irreducible to any minimum, for it must be lived with and recognized, but only through careful reflection and the closest attention. Heit demands both of those of us—but the reward is great. This book takes the study of literature and religion onto a new plane, an enactment of what it says and a theology found in the very heart of the poetics of Donne and Dickinson.

David Jasper
Glasgow and Beijing

Acknowledgments

I OFFER MY DEEPEST GRATITUDE TO MY SUPERVISOR, PROFESSOR DAVID Jasper, who from the beginning guided the research behind this book with a steady (and steadying) hand. His endless suggestions were always challenging and welcomed signposts to keep me headed in the right direction. Even during the frustrating moments, his commitment, patience, and humor never waned. I could not have asked for a better supervisor, mentor, and friend.

After my supervisory meetings, my colleagues at Glasgow University's Centre for Literature, Theology and the Arts were always ready to head to the pub for a calming pint. Some of the best ideas in this thesis can be linked to the conversations I've had with those around me. What follows is a better piece of writing thanks to the influence—intentional and unseen—of Dr. Elizabeth Anderson, Dr. Bryan Dove, Dr. Brian Nail, Dr. Sam Tongue, Anna Fisk, Jennifer Reek, Dr. Mark Godin, and Dr. Alana Vincent. Professor George Newlands deserves thanks for sharpening my ideas over frequent cups of coffee.

Sections of chapters 2, 3, 4, and 5 were presented at Durham University's "Interdisciplinarity in Theology and Religion" conference (2009); "The Erotic: Exploring Critical Issues" conference in Salzburg (2009); and the International Society of Religion, Literature and Culture's International Conference in Oxford (2010). I would like to thank the organizers, delegates, fellow panel members, and those who listened and offered feedback on my nascent ideas for the opportunity to present my work in its unpolished state.

Harvard University Press kindly provided reprint rights for all of the Emily Dickinson material in this book. I am grateful for their help and generosity.

My family continues to be a wellspring of support in this and other endeavors. I want to thank my dad in particular for encouraging me to think daring thoughts. Each page of this project reveals the depth of his influence on my thinking, a legacy for which I am eternally grateful. Likewise, I could not have asked for a better companion than Amy with whom to wander these last three years. As always, she goes before me.

I want to thank my daughter, Isla, for the final burst of energy to finish this book in its first iteration as my dissertation. I look forward to teaching you about John Donne and Emily Dickinson.

A final word of thanks goes to my father. He was my first teacher and continues to inspire me to stretch my mind to places that liturgical poets dare to wander. It is only appropriate, then, that I dedicate this book to him.

Prologue

As he examines the Song of Songs, St. Bernard of Clairvaux describes in erotic terms how the journey towards God unfolds: "You will love with greater ardor, and knock on the door with greater assurance, in order to gain what you perceive to be still wanting to you. 'The one who knocks will always have the door opened to him.' It is my belief that to a person so disposed, God will not refuse the most intimate kiss of all, a mystery of supreme generosity and ineffable sweetness."[1] This passage highlights two essential features of this project. First, Bernard speaks to humanity's displaced condition, which can be summarized as the absence from God. This dislocation occurs when God expels humanity from Eden; as a result, humanity seeks to be restored to God's presence. Though Bernard offers what can be considered encouragement in response to this expulsion, there remains in his description an obvious barrier; the door reiterates humanity's displacement because it maintains the separation from God. Moreover, Bernard's anticipated response—that God will open the door—belies that this act has not yet occurred. God remains absent. As a result, humanity can only gesture towards God, who awaits behind the still-closed door.[2] The second salient feature in this passage is the distinctly erotic capacity in which Bernard conceptualizes both the journey that seeks a reunion with God and the act by which God's presence will be known. The ineffably sweet kiss counters Jesus' erotic betrayal[3] and, in so doing, consummates humanity's passing through the doorway into a restored, Edenic stability.

Bernard's description makes clear that texts[4] are seductive in how they speak to the human condition. For Roland Barthes, this erotic energy places

1. Bernard of Clairvaux, *On the Song of Songs*, 19.

2. The theme of the door as marking a continued separation is an important feature of the Song of Songs. I discuss this image in chapter 5.

3. I discuss the implications of the kiss in chapter 6.

4. I use the term "text" to indicate what Ricoeur calls "any discourse fixed by writing" (Ricoeur, *From Text to Action*, 106). In conceptualizing a text as a discourse, I highlight Ricoeur's stress on the exchange between something written and the act of reading (see Ricoeur, *From Text to Action*, 107). This exchange experiences a significant rupture

particular demands on how the reader engages the text: "it is this flash itself which seduces, or rather: the stating of an appearance-as-disappearance."[5] The paradoxical quality that Barthes cites explains two important features that will be discussed below: the text's possible meanings and the impossibility of structuring the text's meaning into definitive hermeneutical conclusions. As Barthes explains, the instantaneous flash constitutes a "Text of bliss: the text that imposes a state of loss, the text that discomforts . . . unsettles the reader's historical, cultural, psychological assumptions, the consistency of his tastes, values, memories, [and] brings to a crisis his relation with language."[6] The text's blissful properties deconstruct what it suggests. The consequent crisis indicates a way to conceptualize the analysis below by accommodating through an erotic construct the latent instability that all texts exhibit.

The flash leads the reader across the text. This progression eventually reveals, however, that the text is a hollow space. Consequently, the flash's absence becomes apparent: "writing is the destruction of every voice, of every point of origin. Writing is that neutral, composite, oblique space where our subject slips away, the negative where all identity is lost, starting with the very identity of the body writing."[7] The text's allure proves to be deceptive; that which suggests presence begins the deconstructive process that the text cannot resist. Maurice Blanchot explains the consequences of this disjunction: "this all powerful imagery does not represent the truth of a superior world, or even its transcendence. It represents, rather, the favorable and unfavorable nature of figuration—the bind in which the man of exile is caught, obliged as he is to make out of error a means and out of what deceives him indefinitely the ultimate possibility of grasping the infinite."[8] Blanchot identifies a paradox that is crucial to the analysis below: to anticipate a reunion with God based on what the flash promises is to undertake a task that cannot be completed.

---

insofar as the author is absent from the text and, therefore, shifts hermeneutical responsibility to the reader. In turn, the reader enters this discourse in its displaced capacity. The text, then, alters "the relation of dialogue, which directly connects the voice of one to the hearing of the other" (ibid.). This disjunction is one of many factors that indicate a latent instability in the text as the locus for the discourses that I examine in this project.

5. Barthes, *The Pleasure of the Text*, 10.

6. Ibid., 14.

7. Barthes, "The Death of the Author," n.p.

8. Blanchot, *The Space of Literature*, 80.

A consequence of this brief discussion of the text is to unhinge specific authors from normative labels and to complicate the exchange between the author and the reader. As such, Barthes' claim that "The author is a modern figure, a product of our society insofar as . . . it discovered the prestige of the individual"[9] is a helpful stepping off point for understanding the text's impossible errand as it unfolds in a dislocated capacity. In releasing the text from the author, Barthes pinpoints two important concerns within the specific framework that Bernard exhibits. By virtue of its expulsion from Eden, humanity's condition is decidedly not prestigious. Rather, it undermines any claims to privilege the individual. This is a crucial distinction. Bernard exhibits a late medieval understanding of humanity that differs significantly from the modern paradigm that Barthes cites as untenable when considering the individual's lack of prestige.

The consequences of Bernard's analyses link together the two central authors in this study: John Donne and Emily Dickinson.[10] Whereas both

9. Barthes, "The Death of the Author," n.p.

10. There exists a strong literary and thematic link between Donne and Dickinson, which clarifies why these two poets are a central feature of this thesis. Both develop texts that embrace the deconstructive effect that pervades the Last Supper narrative. Textually, this emphasis emerges in the displacing images, narratives, and other literary devices that undermine their work in its anticipation of a fulfilled liturgical promise. Like Tertullian, they expose the latent, destabilizing features that preclude definitive—which is to say stabilizing—conclusions. Donne and Dickinson highlight, for example, how the body is an ironic sign of a coming eschatological condition. Images of sacramental feasts that occur in other poets (or even other readings of Donne and Dickinson) gloss over or fail to realize the purposeful irony that, as a liturgical locus, the body generates. I emphasize, then, the mis-reading of the Last Supper that occurs in Schwartz's analysis of Donne in making this claim. The distinction I am making between a liturgical poetics and a broader use of the Last Supper narrative—its signs, its theology, etc.—is precise. However, the accent that characterizes a liturgical poetics is crucial and it is this particular textual and theological feature that brackets Donne and Dickinson from other writers who appear to undertake similar projects.

Donne's presence in particular warrants a brief explanation. In establishing Donne as a textual cornerstone, I stress that he occupies a unique place in the development of English Literature. His writing establishes a new tradition—a public balancing of literature and theology—that did not exist previously (see Alvarez, *The School of Donne*). Subsequent writers in the English canon who exhibit similarities are, then, considered derivative of Donne's innovation. Moreover, Donne's unique position as a prominent clergyman and a literary presence in courtly circles enabled the criss-crossing of significant theological fault lines that emerged following the English Reformation.

By yoking these two figures together, I am not claiming that they exhibit exclusively the textual and theological characteristics that I stress throughout this project. Other poets—both their contemporaries and those in the intervening years—adapt imagery

fit chronologically within the epoch that Barthes describes, their writing mirrors the assumptions that inform Bernard's work. As a result, a common eschatological trajectory—one that resists emphasizing the individual as a stabilizing feature of the text—provides the basis for the argument below. Donne and Dickinson exhibit a shared tone in their writing and this resonance reflects the latent dislocation that affects both the human condition and the texts that emerge therein. For both, any notion of unity lies in the anticipated "destination"[11] that the text cannot reach. The kiss is still to come, a closure that the text must endure.

The absence of textual stability provides the point of entry into the liturgical tradition that emerges out of the Last Supper narrative.[12] In Matthew's Gospel,[13] Jesus describes his eventual, eschatological presence in terms that cannot be contained within the text and, moreover, signals the text's inevitable closure. Jesus tells his disciples: "For as the lightning comes from the east and flashes as far as the west, so will be the coming of the Son

---

from the Last Supper, utilize irony, or reflect on the body's death. The distinction between such figures as George Herbert and Christina Rossetti and the liturgical poetics discussed in this thesis is the capacity in which the poets like Donne and Dickinson situate their texts squarely within the destabilizing space that the body's irony outlines. The effect is to acknowledge the antecedent failure of identifying and sustaining hope in a promised eschatological condition. The capacity in which Donne and Dickinson draw upon the Last Supper's irony to indicate a possible condition that must, in the end, remain a textual impossibility is the subversive reading of this narrative and theological tradition that characterizes their work as a liturgical poetics.

11. Barthes, "The Death of the Author," n.p.

12. Throughout this project, I will use the phrase "Last Supper narrative" to indicate the eschatological arc that frames the Gospel accounts of Jesus' impending death. Consequently, I include as important to the specific Last Supper story the events that prefigure the central promise that Jesus makes in the Upper Room: through the signs of his body, Jesus promises that humanity will experience an eschatological return to God's presence.

13. The displacement that frames this text is symptomatic of the narrative trajectory throughout Matthew's Gospel. Matthew's text emphasizes repeatedly the displacement that Jesus brings to bear on the temple as a liturgical foundation. This consistent textual feature explains my decision to focus primarily on Matthew's Gospel in this project. The displacement embedded within the entire Gospel literally shakes the text and rips apart the temple's most sacred space (cf. Matt 27:51). Moreover, the symbolic and actual destruction of the temple mirrors the eschatological presence that Jesus' new liturgical paradigm—located in his body—enables through his death (cf. Matt 27:52). The initial decision to root my analysis in Matthew's Gospel instead of John's Gospel (which will become important later in this project) emphasizes, then, the symbolic shift that Jesus' body marks in establishing the promise during the Last Supper.

of Man."[14] Efforts to parse this phrase cannot keep pace with the immediacy of the image that Jesus offers. These words are certainly meant to be instructive, but the image of lightning—an effect that mirrors what Barthes describes—forces the disciples (and thus the reader) to grasp (at) a meaning that has already disappeared. This flash dislocates the text as it illuminates briefly the stabilizing presence to come. To use Barthes' language, the state of bliss that Jesus suggests must be anticipated as discomforting; the promise is experienced as a loss because the text cannot keep pace with the flash's eschatological implications. Clarity can only come later; the disciples are left to anticipate the Son of Man's stabilizing arrival as Jesus' departure shatters their expectations. Through the text's displacement, then, Jesus announces what is not yet realized. Importantly, this dynamic prefigures the more detailed promise Jesus makes when he establishes his body as the locus of this promise during the Last Supper.

The crisis of language that emerges in this brief passage cordons off what this book will and will not attempt. What follows below will be neither a strict literary analysis nor an exercise in theology. With respect to the former, lightning's simultaneity is instructive; it departs as it appears. As such, the textual examinations below will not engage in close, extensive readings in hopes of shoring up tentative interpretations. In the Matthew passage cited above, the implications of this flash clarify a central textual problem that this project addresses: the text's latent properties dictate that the promise can *only* be anticipated. The text cannot stop the flash's necessary and immediate departure. Consequently, close, sustained readings are untenable, as they require a sustained presence that the text does not permit.

In characterizing Donne and Dickinson as liturgical poets, the deconstructive approach below conceptualizes what is at stake in the promise Jesus speaks during the Last Supper. The text can only continue its progression towards the stabilizing other, the divine lover who will fulfill the promise he made to his disciples. This extension belies the text's unstable identity; the desire for this lover's embrace has already been rejected. This concluding ambiguity captures the essence of a text that embraces a deconstructive arc. Valentine Cunningham stresses the text's refusal to sanction a definitive reading as characteristic of deconstruction's critical effect: "The

---

14. Matt 24:27. All biblical quotations come from the New Revised Standard Version (NRSV), except for those found in chapter 5, which come from the King James Version (KJV).

great good of deconstruction has been to make readers all at once uneasy about easy meanings, and relaxed about polyphony, multiplicity, puzzle, and meaning over-spill."[15] As liturgical poets, Donne and Dickinson add ballast to Cunningham's broad claims. In the particular reading that this thesis offers, the refusal of any reading, much less an easy one, plunges Donne and Dickinson into a puzzle that exhibits the consequence Cunningham ascribes to the ability of deconstruction's ability to unhinge even the most well-trodden critical pathways. The result, in Cunningham's words, is that the text keeps "yielding meaning but also seems to keep withholding it."[16]

The limits that language imposes on a text cannot be avoided and, therefore, an intertextual conversation becomes a necessary methodological undertaking. The point of suggesting this model is to account for the different capacities in which the texts below strain under the indefinite nature of their anticipation. As an ongoing discourse, this conversational methodology embraces Blanchot's guidelines for engaging the text: "One must never be done with the indefinite; one must never grasp—as if it were the immediate, the already present—the profundity of inexhaustible absence."[17] Acknowledging the anticipated presence's inexhaustible absence produces a cyclical effect; different points of emphasis converge upon the limit that no text can transcend. Consequently, a critical analysis of such texts will frequently arrive at similar—or perhaps the same—conclusions. Practically, this means that at times the analysis below will appear repetitive as it explores the spaces that emerge from its analogous readings. This cyclicality is intentional insofar as it reflects the endless re-readings that a text must undergo in its anticipation of an eschatological stability that will never arrive. What can be considered a repetitive argument becomes in this capacity a critical analysis that remains open to indefinite re-readings, which, in turn, ensures that the discussion below minds Blanchot's caution: one is never done with the text's indefinite character. As a result, this project suggests an analogous relationship between the late medieval assumptions that Bernard exhibits—particularly the reading of the (human) body as displaced from Eden—and the Continental tradition's emphasis on Deconstruction. Both traditions emphasize that the text advances towards a presence, which, in the end, can only be recognized as absent.

15. Cunningham, *Reading After Theory*, 39.

16. Ibid., 40.

17. Blanchot, *Space of Literature*, 79.

Importantly, this project is specifically an intertextual conversation. In his article "The Best Stories in the Best Order? Canons, Apocryphas and (Post)modern Reading," Cunningham stresses that intertextuality—especially when incorporating biblical voices—resists hermeneutical clarity. Because a text's linguistic properties ensure that it remains open to further and therefore different readings, the reader faces multiple interpretive possibilities. According to Cunningham: "Interpretation and ways of interpretation do not stand still. There is, and there will be (as there has always been) a continuous up-dating of readerly responses to the Biblical texts."[18] This claim does not relativize the analysis below so much as emphasize the particularity with which writers establish their own intertextual relationship with biblical material. Cunningham's caution encourages one to avoid critical bias based either on what texts an author draws upon, or on the specific links they develop between biblical material and their own writing. Consequently, this project suggests a further particularity, which should not be read as excluding necessarily other analyses. Plural hermeneutical points of entry[19] encourage sustained—and therefore different—readings in response to the text's allure. The analysis that follows, then, is one of many possible readings.

These introductory remarks clarify both why the argument below is not an exercise in theology and, moreover, how traversing the boundaries between literature and theology can enrich what could be dismissed as a hermeneutically dislocated exercise. Theology demands specificity and a point of emphasis that is untenable in light of the methodological concerns discussed above. The Last Supper's anticipatory implications necessarily displace the text, which in turn resists the kind of tidy readings frequently found in theology's storehouse. Consequently, efforts to conceptualize the presence that Jesus promises must fail by virtue of the textual parameters that enable these anticipatory gestures.[20] Theology is an exercise in stability, which Barthes makes clear, is not the text's province. The analysis to follow thus stays within the textual boundaries, so to speak, insofar as it can only reach for the flash that is already gone.

---

18. Cunningham, "The Best Stories in the Best Order?," 72.

19. On this point, David Jasper offers an important reminder: "there is no privileged 'innocent' point of access to a text" (*The Study of Literature and Religion*, xvi).

20. Jasper offers a helpful summary of this point: "to write of 'ultimate truth' is to deny it in writing—for such truth, if it were ultimate, would never suffer the process of textuality" (*The Study of Literature and Religion*, xviii).

Tracing this absence begins in the "Introduction" by defining the concept of a liturgical poetics. On the basis of this definition, a close look at the paradoxical character of the Last Supper opens into the specific instability that death brings to a text, which in turn helps to stake out important methodological considerations. In chapter 1, this framework enables readings of Donne and Dickinson that highlight the specifically erotic implications that both draw out from the Last Supper. Irony's presence is a particular concern insofar as it is an important feature of how a liturgical poetics unfolds.

Chapter 2 sounds the textual instability that irony creates in more depth by drawing on significant figures from Continental Philosophy. The result is a focus on the theme of exile as a structuring metaphor throughout this book. Exile captures both the text's latent displacement and the implied return to stability that underscores a liturgical poetics' textual and theological identity. Chapter 3 brings these methodological considerations into conversation with the specific theme of the lilies as symptomatic of a liturgical poetics' dual identity. This image provides the basis for drawing on Derrida to articulate how deconstructive readings are crucial to a liturgical poetics. Moreover, the as a symbol the lilies emphasize how the body functions as a coordinating and displacing presence in the text. This paradoxical influence clarifies the link between Donne and Dickinson while simultaneously bracketing Romanticism from the argument at hand.

In chapter 4, an extended textual analysis situates Donne within the scope of a liturgical poetics that has been established in the previous chapters. Specifically, his concern for the separation of the body and soul at death informs his specifically erotic texts. By stressing the need to balance Donne's theological and literary identities, this chapter highlights specifically how Donne draws on the erotic body to anticipate God's presence after death despite the rupture that death brings. In a similar vein, chapter 5 examines Dickinson's frequent use of death as a signpost that extends her texts to the limits of displacement. This feature of her liturgical poetics manifests itself most clearly in how she draws upon biblical gardens to articulate a liturgical anticipation of God's presence after death.

Having discussed the primary authors in this study, chapter 6 discusses in more detail the specifically theological implications that the readings of Donne and Dickinson generate. The emphasis on the erotic body thrusts the text into a necessary betrayal, which both extends the liturgical promise spoken at the Last Supper and calls attention to the risks of a text that emerges when considering any erotic body. In its risk this betrayal allows the text to endure the necessary closure that the body must experience as a liturgical symbol, a further paradox that the Conclusion examines. In the end, the inability to outrun the body's displacement ultimately extends the bodily promise made in the Last Supper towards its eschatological fulfillment.

This brief outline makes clear that the ridge between literature and theology can be difficult to traverse. Despite this challenge, this book relates to each of these domains intimately. In holding the two disciplines in appropriate tension, the goal is to enable readings that enrich both domains. The specific instabilities that characterize the threshold between literature and theology—what Christopher Norris calls the "element of undecidability"[21]—confound any effort to suggest definitive readings. The eschatological implications of Jesus' promise demand an indefinite re-reading of the text, which cannot transcend its latent dislocation. No critical project can bring about what is and must remain absent from the text. Insofar as Jesus' promise cannot be fulfilled textually, the flash must linger as the already absent suggestion of what a disruptive bliss might be: a presence that cannot be experienced but can be anticipated.

21. Norris, *Deconstruction*, 28.

Introduction

To our bodies turn we then, that so
Weak me on love revealed may look;
Love's mysteries in souls do grow,
But yet the body is his book.[1]

SHORTLY BEFORE THE ACCOUNT OF THE LAST SUPPER, MATTHEW'S GOSPEL describes an ominous moment in a journey that will soon end decisively. "As Jesus came out of the temple and was going away, his disciples came to point out to him the buildings of the temple. Then he asked them, 'You see all these, do you not? Truly I tell you, not one stone will be left here upon another; all will be thrown down.'"[2] Jesus offers a complex and confusing response to the disciples' gesture. The temple—a fixed place of religious identity—recedes into the background as Jesus literally walks away from it. In so doing, he distances himself from what the temple represents for the disciples, namely the space that symbolizes God's presence. Jesus' actions, then, convey a destabilizing narrative that subverts the disciples' wider liturgical framework. Throughout this vignette, the disciples do not speak; they merely gesture towards that which they understand to represent stability. In response, Jesus asks and answers his own question with a vaguely prophetic but certainly unsettling displacement of the temple that orients the disciples' actions. Every detail in this short passage fractures the temple's symbolic foundation, which foreshadows the total displacement that will occur during the Last Supper. Even though the temple's final destruction is yet to come, Jesus' actions and words begin to deconstruct the stable liturgical paradigm it anchors.

The above passage anticipates a symbolic shift from the temple to Jesus' body, a transition that Jesus clarifies during the Last Supper. Two chapters after he turns his back on the temple, the significance of Jesus'

1. Donne, "The Ecstasy," lines 73–76.
2. Matt 24:1–2.

1

actions becomes apparent when he describes a new liturgical framework during his last meal with the disciples:

> When it was evening, he took his place with the twelve; and while they were eating, he said, "Truly I tell you, one of you will betray me." And they became greatly distressed and began to say to him one after another, "Surely not I, Lord?" He answered, "The one who has dipped his hand into the bowl with me will betray me. The Son of Man goes as it is written of him, but woe to that one by whom the Son of Man is betrayed! It would have been better for that one not to have been born." Judas, who betrayed him, said, "Surely not I, Rabbi?" He replied, "You have said so." While they were eating, Jesus took a loaf of bread, and after blessing it he broke it, gave it to the disciples, and said, "Take, eat; this is my body." Then he took a cup, and after giving thanks he gave it to them, saying, "Drink from it, all of you; for this is my blood of the covenant, which is poured out for many for the forgiveness of sins. I tell you, I will never again drink of this fruit of the vine until that day when I drink it new with you in my Father's kingdom."[3]

Jesus punctuates the substitution concerning the temple when he relocates liturgical hope in his soon to be broken body. Unlike the temple building that houses God's presence, Jesus' body provides a liturgical locus predicated on an absence. Jesus offers a promise that rends and replaces the temple's liturgical significance insofar as it initiates a displacement that delays the promise's fulfillment indefinitely. The betrayal that begins the Last Supper narrative thus parallels the narrative momentum that builds throughout Matthew's gospel, a development that deconstructs the established liturgical paradigm that the temple sanctions. The new paradigm rests upon a promise that refuses fulfillment within the text, a paradox that Matthew privileges throughout his narrative. This indefinite displacement constitutes a crucial textual effect that Jesus intensifies when he locates the liturgical promise in his body.

As a symbol, Jesus' body functions in a particular narrative and liturgical capacity. It conveys the foundational displacement at work in the Last Supper. Represented as bread and wine,[4] his body signals an eschatological promise that is not yet fulfilled. This substitution defines a traditional

---

3. Matt 26:20–29.

4. Already the disjunctive nature of symbols is apparent insofar as the body is a symbol twice removed from the thing it represents. I discuss this point in more depth in chapter 3.

mode of discourse wherein one thing represents another (absent) thing. In addition to this basic textual property, Jesus' body indicates a second mode of discourse: that death marks life's physical finitude. These two discursive strands intersect during the Last Supper narrative, which generates the particular context that this study examines. Specifically, in substituting his body for the temple Jesus enriches the symbol's capacity to respond to the finality that death marks. The reality of the second mode of discourse informs the first, a textual joint that through the first mode's substitutive linguistic function enables Jesus' body to function as a specifically eschatological symbol.

In its capacity to accommodate simultaneously these two modes of discourse, Jesus' body exhibits a distinctly paradoxical quality, which in turn displaces the promise that it conveys. By virtue of death's finality, the body cannot fulfill the promise because the body cannot escape the closure that death brings. Death's reality, then, subverts the symbol's capacity to articulate the crucial eschatological point at hand. Consequently, Jesus' promise enables its own deconstructive denial, an unavoidable effect that characterizes necessarily the dual concerns that the bread and wine accommodate. Importantly, this paradoxical effect is the dynamic that both Donne and Dickinson recover from the Last Supper narrative. Both authors recognize the dual discursive modes at stake in the body's symbolic role within this liturgical context; their mutual recovery of this particular paradox links their writing as thematic derivatives of the Last Supper's symbolic framework.

Defining A Liturgical Poetics

Defined broadly, the term liturgical anticipates Jesus' eschatological presence, which will fulfill the promise he locates symbolically in his body during the Last Supper. This definition indicates that the following salient features characterize the texts that this project treats: the absence of that which fulfills the promise; a consequent awareness that the paradigm denies the stability connoted in the presence that the promise anticipates; the inescapable reality of death as a part of the human condition; the possibility that through remembrance death can be transcended symbolically; a pervasive sense of displacement that results from the boundary death establishes between the promise's anticipatory component and the (possible) condition that results from the promise's fulfillment; and, finally, the promise's inability to excuse those who anticipate its fulfillment from having to encounter their own deaths. Within a liturgical context, these characteristics indicate two concerns that affect the eschatological implications that emerge out of defining liturgical poetics in this capacity: spatiality and temporality. Jesus' command establishes parameters that define the promise in a way that forces the disciples to recognize an unavoidable condition: the reality that their own deaths will always subvert any anticipated fulfillment. That is, a liturgical context demands recognition that death frames the promise and, moreover, that this promise is not an exemption. As Jesus makes clear, his body must be absent through its death if the promise is to be made. Consequently, to speak of the liturgical is to speak of a response from within a condition, defined by death, to a possibility wherein the reality of death ceases to be human life's final feature. Put another way, the promise outlines a context that anticipates fulfillment as a condition beyond the limit that death marks, both actually and symbolically. This boundary affects necessarily the capacity in which a liturgical symbol functions within a text.

For Donne and Dickinson, the way in which death influences spatial metaphors becomes a stepping off point for the text to consider the eschatological implications that the promise offers. Death (and its effects) opens into alternative images and possibilities, which serve as the basis for deconstructing theology's sterilized readings of the Last Supper. Death displaces this text, but this instability enables a necessary shift to the body as the primary liturgical image. Both Donne and Dickinson draw on the displacement that they perceive in the Last Supper narrative. More specifically, the body's necessary encounter with death provides a basis upon which to account for and transcend imaginatively the body's finitude. The body, then, becomes the point at which their respective writing transitions from a purely literary context to the border between the literary and the theological.

Death also marks a temporal boundary that affects how a liturgical text functions. Death is the moment at which any person's embodied life ceases, a non-negotiable end that affects necessarily how any spatial images will unfold within a particular text. As will become apparent, the reality of death ensures that any hope articulated through an image—be it spatial or temporal—cannot override the definitive conclusion to life that death constitutes. Because it marks a literal cessation of ability to experience something as embodied, death is a disruptive force within the text. In the Last Supper narrative, the effect is obvious in each of these capacities. Jesus' impending death will separate him necessarily from the presence of his disciples. Moreover, that departure creates a gap that the disciples cannot cross insofar as any hope they find in Jesus' words cannot traverse the absence that Jesus' death will bring. As a result, the symbol's promissory function generates a temporal consideration; the promise's fulfillment can only occur in an eschatological capacity that is necessarily beyond the temporal parameters that inform the text.

Based on these salient features, The concept of a liturgical poetics can now be clarified. In the argument that follows below, this term indicates a text that acknowledges and responds to the human condition by anticipating the presence that fulfills the promise and, in so doing, transcends death's limit. Such texts are poetic insofar as they respond to the instability that death imposes through thematic and imagistic features. The hallmark of a liturgical poetics is to re-imagine the human condition in a capacity wherein death ceases to be the final reality to which the text can speak. With this definition in place, it is important to identify several caveats. The definition of poetics in use during this project is not the only possible way to understand the term. In this project, a liturgical poetics indicates a particular kind of textual space that responds to a particular (though generally accepted) characteristic of the human condition. An awareness of this condition is present, always, in texts this project will examine. Variations in tone, theme, metaphor, or any other textual property do not affect the underlying dynamics that govern the text.

The Limits that a Liturgical Poetics' Paradoxical Character Imposes

Having defined these key terms, the significance of the paradox at the heart of the Last Supper narrative becomes apparent. This is a story that establishes a liturgical poetics' parameters; it outlines how to anticipate death and, moreover, it suggests how symbols that occur within this context imagine a condition that extends beyond death. More simply, a liturgical poetics envisions a possible condition wherein death is not the final word on human experience. Such texts articulate hope that death can ultimately be transcended, even if this release cannot occur within the text. This "latent possibility"[5] is a liturgical poetics' paradoxical, symbolic backbone; that which does not appear in the text ultimately sustains its promise. As Richard Kearney suggests, "it is divinity's very potentiality–to–be that is the

---

5. Kearney, *The God Who May Be*, 1.

most divine thing about it."[6] By "rethinking"[7] this narrative in terms of the possibility that despite an indefinite delay emerges during the Last Supper, the analysis offered below coheres with the implications of the liturgical promise's denial. Significantly, such a reading accepts that the eschatological implications present in the text must remain unrealized, as the text cannot provide more than an unfulfilled promise. Consequently, Kearney argues, there must remain "a free space gaping at the core of divinity: the space of the possible."[8] This possibility in its promise and absence marks a crucially important feature that both enables and subverts the capacities in which a liturgical poetics draws upon the Last Supper narrative.[9] To counter the absence at the core of Kearney's possible space, the text enables an alternative response: anticipating a presence that will fill this gap.

The stress on anticipation distinguishes a liturgical poetics from theology. Another tradition, the *Ars moriendi*, provides an example that, in turn, clarifies how the latent paradox of Jesus' body affects the liturgical paradigm that emerges out of the Last Supper. Articulated most fully in Jeremy Taylor's *The Rules and Exercises of Holy Dying*,[10] the *Ars moriendi* tradition conceptualizes death optimistically as the point at which (eternal) life begins. As Nancy Lee Beaty notes, contrary to its role as the definitive end to humanity's embodied condition, in the *Ars moriendi* death becomes "the first of the Last Things."[11] Though she quickly adds that there exists the possibility that God might reject the recently deceased,[12] Beaty reads Taylor as emphasizing clearly that the eschatological possibility beyond death can be experienced (in part) before death, which consequently diminishes the capacity in which death dislocates the human condition. As Beaty notes, "Properly understood, *dying* is indeed synonymous with *living*."[13] In conceptualizing death in these optimistic terms, the *Ars moriendi* tradition assumes that the eschatological promise is fulfilled already and death

---

6. Ibid., 2.

7. Ibid., 1.

8. Ibid., 5.

9. Kearney offers a helpful summary on this point: "The eschaton is just that: a promise, not an acquisition. A possibility of the future to come, *impossible in the present* where the allure of total presence reigns supreme" (*The God Who May Be*, 16; my emphasis).

10. Taylor, *Holy Living and Dying*, Chapter V Section V.

11. Beaty, *The Craft of Dying*, 216.

12. Ibid.

13. Ibid., 217.

ceases to mark a definitive closure of life. In turn, this conception of death glosses over the displacement and consequent anticipation that defines a liturgical poetics.

Beaty's helpful analysis of the tradition that precedes Taylor,[14] as well as Taylor's definitive literary treatment of the *Ars moriendi*,[15] demarcates an important difference between a liturgical poetics and the theology behind traditions such as the *Ars moriendi*. Her reading of the latter conveys the extent to which such theologies often depict the movement towards the promise's eschatological fulfillment by minimizing the disruption that death brings to a text (a fact that will become apparent in both Donne's and Dickinson's work). The Anglican tradition, for example, embraces the *Ars moriendi* because it "is 'in the world but not of it' in a uniquely tempered way."[16] This gloss sounds precisely the optimistic tone that distinguishes the *Ars moriendi* tradition from a liturgical poetics. In softening death's effect, the former alters the displacement that characterizes the Last Supper. The symbolic mode of discourse is privileged in a way that limits its ability to respond to death. As a result, the symbol no longer represents an absent possibility, but, rather, assumes the promise's fulfillment as present. This approach, which permits the text to understand death as life's beginning, rests on an assumption that the Last Supper narrative does not support.[17]

The scandal of Jesus' promise is that it lacks certainty; the bread and wine permit the reader to anticipate that the promise will be fulfilled because the text cannot overcome death's rupture. As such, death elicits a more sober response in a liturgical poetics, a tone that avoids the theological optimism that characterizes the *Ars moriendi* tradition. This strategy establishes a textual foundation that upholds the dual discursive influences of Jesus' symbolic body. By maintaining the instability that results from the latent paradox therein, a liturgical poetics thus provides a stepping off point to anticipate an eschatological possibility without shying away from the total uncertainty with which death rings life. Though an eschatological release from death is certainly implied in the notion of a liturgical poetics—and

14. Ibid., 32–53.

15. Ibid., 197–270.

16. Ibid., 204.

17. Questions concerning the bread and wine were, of course, crucial points of theological debate during the Reformation. Article XXVIII of Cranmer's *39 Articles* marks a definitive theological shift from the Catholic reading of the bread and wine as actually constituting Jesus' body and blood to the symbolic reading of these images. This point is of particular concern to Donne's liturgical poetics, which I discuss in chapter 4.

clearly so in the Last Supper—the point at stake in this study is that such possibilities exist only beyond the boundary of the texts in question.

A liturgical poetics, then, stresses the utter displacement that death brings to humanity's embodied condition. This is the particular narrative context out of which Jesus' promise emerges, which in turn constitutes an important thematic link between the Last Supper narrative and the liturgical poetics that Donne and Dickinson develop. Contrary to the assurance that the *Ars moriendi* tradition finds in death, Kearney suggests that narratives like the Last Supper imply the opposite of such optimism: "The limit experience of death is the most sure sign of our finitude. Moreover, it is precisely *because* we are beings who know that we still die that we keep on telling stories, struggling to represent something of the unpresentable, to hazard interpretations of the puzzles and aporias that surround us."[18] As will become clear later in this argument, it is only by confronting this total displacement that death brings to bear on humanity's condition that Jesus can relocate liturgical hope symbolically *within* a specifically embodied context. In unspooling this thread from the Last Supper, Donne and Dickinson write as minority voices amidst different Christian conceptions of death. However, their emphasis on displacement affirms the anticipation at the heart of their respective faith traditions and, paradoxically, constitutes the basis for their respective recoveries of Jesus' body.

Recovering the Last Supper's Latent Scandal

When discussing the specific contours of a liturgical poetics, one cannot stress enough the extent to which the notion of displacement affects the Last Supper narrative and, moreover, the importance of recovering this uncertainty. An early example of affirming the scandal at the heart of the Last Supper occurs in Tertullian's *Apology*. Reflecting on the images that convey Jesus' promise, he writes:

> Eternal life is promised in return. Believe it for the time being, for argument's sake. And then I ask you this; whether, although you believe it, you think it worthwhile to attain it at such a cost to your conscience. Come, plunge your knife into an infant, harmless, innocent, and helpless; or if this be the duty of another, do you at least stand by while this human being dies before it has really lived; wait for the flight of the newly-entered soul; catch

18. Kearney, *Strangers, Gods and Monsters*, 131.

the immature blood; soak your bread in it; feed freely upon it
. . . Thus initiated and sealed, you will live for ever. I want you to
say whether Eternity is worth all this.[19]

Tertullian recognizes clearly that Jesus' body signals a displacing point
for consideration. The calculus at work in the Last Supper challenges the
grounds upon which theology rests optimistic readings. Jesus' body articulates a promise that remains a problematic mystery by virtue of the complex
interaction between the two modes of discourse discussed above. Tertullian
emphasizes the displacement that characterizes the body's symbolic function in the Last Supper, which must, then, be read alongside the body's
inescapable finitude. As a result, he recovers the scandalous disruption
that characterizes the Last Supper. One certainly finds an eschatological
possibility, a hope Tertullian makes clear by framing his passage with the
promise of eternal life. At the same time, the images used to convey the
promise displace the disciples (and the reader). To believe the promise, one
must engage the text on its deeply unsettling terms and, therefore, resist
the optimistic readings frequently found in orthodox theology.[20] Tertullian recovers, then, the influence of the second mode of discourse—death's
actual and final effect on the body—on the symbols that emerge out of the
Last Supper.

Death's Implications for a Liturgical Poetics

A liturgical poetics anticipates the divine in a way that, according to Jean
Yves Lacoste, "death ceases to be the final reality to which we can reconcile ourselves."[21] Lacoste thus recognizes what is at stake in the liturgical

---

19. Tertullian, *The Apology of Tertullian for the Christians*, 26–27.

20. Tertullian recognizes that death separates the text from any eschatological fulfillment. He highlights, then, the basis for a liturgical poetics' demanding a particular hermeneutical approach that ultimately frustrates the kind of stability that the eschatological
promise implies. By situating hope intimately close to death, a liturgical poetics speaks
from an indefinitely displaced condition, which precludes any hermeneutical certainty.
As discussed in the prologue, no text can extend beyond its own destabilizing limit. The
texts in question, then, require a hermeneutical approach that accepts as a precondition
to relating to the liturgical promise the impossibility of interpreting exactly what is at
stake in this narrative tradition (a fact the disciples' confusion emphasizes insofar as they
do not understand the implications of Jesus' words; cf. Matthew 26:36–46).

21. Lacoste, *Experience and the Absolute*, 60. I find Lacoste's project helpful in emphasizing the displacement that death brings to the human condition and in this respect
he parallels important thematic concerns within a liturgical poetics. At the same time,

promise: an/other possibility in eternity that transcends the finality that death imposes on the human condition. To engage a liturgical poetics is an experience that, if performed in full recognition of the implications and consequences of one's participation, allows one to anticipate the promise's fulfillment in a way that transcends the necessary instability that death brings. Importantly, this space is more than mere possibility; Lacoste is clear that within a liturgical context the image is "not simply a metaphor."[22] As a result, the images utilized in a liturgical poetics hold open the possibility that the Last Supper promise will be fulfilled despite humanity's displaced condition.

The holding open of the text thus permits a response to death, but it also emphasizes the reality that no text can cross that boundary. One cannot, strictly speaking, experience the moment in which the ability to experience ceases to be possible; death alters inevitably and irreversibly humanity's embodied condition. Consequently, the moments that precede death become important, as they bring the text into proximity with the specific moment of death and thus allow the individual to anticipate both death's definitive end of life and, in a liturgical poetics, to imagine possible conditions that lie beyond this boundary. Liminality, then, demands attention as a salient characteristic of a liturgical poetics. As will become apparent in this project, it is often from within these liminal spaces that liturgical hope emerges most clearly. At the same time, by virtue of their proximity to death the images that sustain belief in the liturgical promise soon collapse. Like human life, they cannot outpace the inevitable disruption that death brings.

In his *Apology*, Tertullian emphasizes that the body is *the* crucial image in the Last Supper narrative. Jesus' body faces a definite closure as it establishes a liturgical promise in response to this condition. There must be two theological modes of discourse when examining Jesus' symbolic body: its inevitable death and the promise that another condition is possible after death. The demands that the Last Supper's liturgical implications make on the body thus compound the stress that Jesus experiences as he anticipates his own death. Jesus' command during the Last Supper is, significantly, a poiesis—it must *be done*—a term that stresses the paradoxical role that the

---

his work is largely a self-contained reflection, which limits necessarily the coherence between his project and the specifically literary analysis that I undertake.

22. Lacoste, *Experience and the Absolute*, 37.

body plays in a liturgical poetics.[23] During the Last Supper, redemption becomes possible as Jesus anticipates his own bodily destruction, which in turn provides the metaphor that describes the Christian community.[24] Those who would participate in this community must *do* so; that is, they must commit their own bodies to endure the tension Tertullian describes. In both cases, the body serves as Christianity's central symbolic resource. Consequently, within the Last Supper the body emphasizes that the human condition cannot escape death, regardless of how the text imagines an escape from the parameters that death imposes. The story of the Last Supper makes clear the implications of a liturgical poetics: the space in question demands the literal destruction of the body.

Methodological Implications

Death establishes a boundary to human life and this project focuses on texts that are situated near this limit. These liminal spaces bring into focus the disruption that emerges from the symbolic paradox described above and, moreover, the effects this disruption has when anticipating an eschatological presence. Importantly, the argument that follows does not attempt to transcend this boundary; in limiting this study's critical reach to the eschatological *promise* within a liturgical poetics, the relationship between the argument's salient literary and theological elements come into focus. Consequently, there are two related yet distinct concerns that will not—by virtue of the parameters that death establishes on and in the text—be examined in detail. The first point recognizes that two distinct methodological strands weave through this project: the literary and the theological. In lieu of attempting to separate these concerns, the goal is to balance on the edge between these two discourses. Methodologically, this demands at times the need to elide concerns from either discipline. For example, how to conceptualize the body (in simplified terms) suggests two distinct though frequently overlapping possibilities. On the one hand, the body can function within a symbolic range that stresses the displacement that it generates within a text. This literary concern is, however, distinct

---

23. Kearney's reading of the divine as possible clarifies Jesus' command. He writes, "because God is *posse* (the possibility of being) rather than *esse* (the actuality of being as fait accompli), the promise remains powerless until and unless we *respond* to it" (*The God Who May Be*, 4).

24. See 1 Cor 12:7–31.

from the theological reading of the body in an ecclesial sense, wherein the body constitutes a community of readers influenced through its interaction with the texts in question. To contain the difference, the following statement summarizes how this project holds these two related possibilities in appropriate tension: the symbolic body in a literary capacity orients the text towards the ecclesial possibilities that the theological body implies. Within the texts that this argument examines, the outline of the theological possibility that the literary body implies can only be imagined within the textual boundaries at which this project stops. A realized eschatological condition is, then, outside the scope of an analysis that traces theological concerns only to the moments that occur right before death.

Importantly, the methodological decision not to extend the argument beyond this threshold and, therefore, definitively towards the ecclesial and theological implications that the literary body glimpses affirms a crucial link between the two concerns. A liturgical text enables the theological body to come more clearly into focus as it traverses the textual space that unfolds towards death. The specifically Western, Christian theological tradition that this project addresses posits a distinct eschatological possibility beyond death, which, tellingly, it conceptualizes in terms of an ecclesial body. The body's role as a liturgical and literary symbol implies this eschatological body, which, as will become clear in the conclusion, posits space for a subsequent analysis in line with the argument that unfolds in the following chapters.

1

Ironic and Erotic Bodies

I dwell in Possibility—
A fairer House than Prose—
More numerous of Windows—
Superior—for Doors—[1]

AS THE LAST SUPPER PROGRESSES, MULTIPLE INTERPRETIVE POSSIBILI-
ties emerge. The narrative's textual and liturgical parameters come into
focus and there exists a growing awareness of the pronounced, intolerable,
and necessary symbolic complexity that materializes out of Jesus' body. By
locating a response to death in the place where death manifests itself in
an obvious capacity, Jesus emphasizes that his promise is filtered through
humanity's embodied experience. Consequently, there is no stable point
from which the text can unfold *without* accounting for death. The body
is always displaced by virtue of its relationship as a being-towards-death,
which compounds the sense of instability that comes when attempting to
articulate any possible response to death. The Last Supper's thus exhibits
a paradoxical character by locating an eschatological possibility in Jesus'
body, an image that cannot outpace its own dissolution.

The Last Supper's paradoxical identity cannot be overstated. A discussion of Jesus' body as a temple will clarify, then, how this paradox affects
the notion of a liturgical poetics. During his account of the crucifixion,
Matthew emphasizes clearly that a complex symbolic shift is underway. As
Jesus is dying, his claim to destroy and rebuild the temple in three days
reemerges in the text through the crowd's voice as it watches him die.[2] The

1. Dickinson, J657 ("I dwell in Possibility—"), lines 1–4.

2. Matt 27:39–40: "Those who passed by derided him, shaking their heads and saying, 'You who would destroy the temple and build it in three days, save yourself! If you
are the Son of God, come down from the cross.'"

crowd mocks his claim because the temple stands firmly as they watch his death. As the text shifts the temple's symbolic coordinates, the crowd interprets Jesus' words literally—a misreading that recalls the disciples own pointing towards to temple—and thus fails to recognize the new liturgical locus before them. Jesus' body substantiates his claims from the Last Supper by upholding the capacity in which death affects all bodies and, therefore, it maintains the dual modes of discourse that the bread and wine accommodate. Jesus' death completes the temple's deconstruction; Matthew makes clear that it is the temple—not Jesus' body—that suffers symbolic displacement.[3]

By drawing on Martin Heidegger,[4] the textual mechanics within the current discussion can be brought into sharper focus. Specifically, the symbolic substitution that Jesus' body undergoes requires the paradoxical interplay that Heidegger uses to characterize temples. In *Off the Beaten Track*, Heidegger claims: "It is the temple work that first structures and simultaneously gathers around itself the unity of those paths and relations in which birth and death, disaster and blessing, victory and disgrace, endurance and decline acquire for the human being the shape of destiny."[5] The temple is an image that through its structuring presence orients the text towards an anticipated stability.[6] Specifically, this process unfolds through the text's relationship with death, which in turn reiterates the displaced context out of

3. In the wake of Jesus' death, Matthew's narrative describes the severe disruption that sweeps through the entire earth and finishes in the very heart of the temple—the Holy of Holies—that Jesus displaces. After Jesus' death, Matthew writes: "Then Jesus cried again with a loud voice and breathed his last. At that moment the curtain of the temple was torn in two, from top to bottom. The earth shook, and the rocks were split. The tombs also were opened, and many bodies of the saints who had fallen asleep were raised. After his resurrection they came out of the tombs and entered the holy city and appeared to many. Now when the centurion and those with him, who were keeping watch over Jesus, saw the earthquake and what took place, they were terrified and said, 'Truly this man was God's Son!'" (Matt 27:50–54). Jesus' death thus conveys unmistakably the symbolic at hand. His body's fragility marks the extent to which the new symbolic temple disrupts completely the temple's stability and, therefore, that which houses God's presence.

4. Heidegger provides a constant intertextual presence in this analysis. Though I draw on his work with due caution, the strong thematic links between his work and the displacement that defines a liturgical poetics validate the extent to which I have incorporated him into my methodological framework.

5. Heidegger, *Off the Beaten Track*, 20–21.

6. As will be discussed shortly, Heidegger conceptualizes the human condition as thrown, a label that exhibits clearly the displacement that precludes the text's anticipatory character.

which these temples emerge. However, in relating the temple to the embodied experience's dislocation, the temple simultaneously (and paradoxically) anticipates the recovery of a stabilizing presence. This transition does not cancel out death's disruptive effect, but it does recalibrate the condition that anticipates death in a capacity that transcends imaginatively death's finality.

Heidegger's temple balances an antecedent instability with the hope that it symbolizes within the text's displacement. The temple, then, provides a gathering point that allows readers to confront the reality of their condition.[7] This coordinate approximates stability within a displaced context, not through the denial of the conditions that give rise to the temple, but, rather, through its own dislocated condition. The governing parameters of the experience in question do not change and the temple as Heidegger describes it has no permanence; as a gathering point, the temple's impermanence parallels the body's instability, which is precisely the point that a liturgical poetics articulates. The temple announces to those who acknowledge the conditions of an embodied existence that through that body's experience of moving towards death one can find within that movement the hope that death—the inevitable conclusion to the journey—may not be the final reality to which humanity can reconcile itself. The temple is thus not a presence that fulfills the promise; it does not actualize the condition it imagines beyond death. The temple's role is to provide a momentary signpost that sustains the text as it progresses towards its closure.

Heidegger's temple thus offers a helpful critical approach that clarifies how the Last Supper and Jesus' death condense symbolically the body and the temple. Within this reduction, the relationship between the body and the temple suggests a new way for an embodied experience to relate to its own inevitable death. This process indicates that the body's symbolic capacity—evident in Jesus' substitution of his body for the temple—enables a particular function within the context of a liturgical poetics. More precisely, because the body is the place wherein death's effects are pronounced definitively, the body provides an important image for relating intimately to death. As Jesus' deaths illustrates, the body can through its mortality function as a temple in the Heideggerian sense.[8] These imaginative possi-

7. In *Heidegger: A Guide for the Perplexed,* David R. Cerbone describes the dynamic as "imposing a unity of meaning or significance on the events making up [the participants'] lives . . . so that they are delineated or determined as those discrete events" (117).

8. While discussing Derrida's work (to which I will return in more depth in the following chapter), Timothy Clark recognizes how an embodied experience, articulated through writing, can transcend through its own symbolic possibility its own inevitable

bilities provide a way to articulate clearly from within the displaced human condition a transcendent possibility. Such images are the groundswell of liturgical poetics; it is through a Heideggerian notion of the temple that the body can anticipate a stabilizing possibility beyond the text.[9]

Emily Dickinson's Treatment of Death

In 1862, Emily Dickinson sent a letter to Thomas Wentworth Higginson in which she described a central concern in her writing. She tells Higginson: "My Business is Circumference."[10] Though Dickinson's imagery is not immediately or easily accessible—a density that reflects the Last Supper's interpretive challenges—Circumference at the very least indicates a boundary that affects significantly how humans understand their embodied condition.[11] In J378 ("I saw no Way—The Heavens were stitched—"), Dickinson writes: "—and I alone— / A Speck upon a Ball— / Went out upon Circumference—Beyond the Dip of Bell—."[12] Dickinson describes a journey that moves away from a center's connoted stability towards a

---

decay: the "*récit* [is] an experience that takes consciousness and language to the limits of their possibility; an encounter, either sexual or traumatic, which is too immediate to be mediated by language and thus remains heterogeneous to the very narratives which set it in motion" (*Derrida, Heidegger, Blanchot*, 85).

9. Heidegger's understanding of the sign strengthens my reading of the body's symbolic possibilities. In *Being and Time*, Heidegger states: "[Signs] let what is at hand be encountered, more precisely, let their context become accessible in such a way that heedful association gets and secures an orientation" (quoted in Cerbone, *Heidegger*, 45). Consequently, Heidegger claims that signs afford a resource for understanding the human condition, which is defined by its embodiment: "[a sign] explicitly brings a totality of useful things to circumspection so that the worldly character of what is at hand makes itself known at the same time" (quoted in Cerbone, *Heidegger*, 45). Analyzing these passages, Cerbone concludes that signs, should, then, "be noticed so that [they] might direct our attention in one direction or another . . . [and] thus have a kind of revelatory function, and so serve to make things 'conspicuous'" (*Heidegger*, 45).

10. L268.

11. Albert J. Gelpi anticipates an important feature of Circumference when he notes: "Emily Dickinson's most frequent metaphor for ecstasy was Circumference. Each of the negotiations which consciousness conducted between the *me* and the *not me* established a circumference" (*Emily Dickinson*, 121). Gelpi rightly understands the erotic overtones that Circumference exhibits, but he too quickly frames his consequent analysis as a transcendent spiritualism (ibid.). This characterization ignores the extent to which Circumference is, first and foremost, a metaphor for death in Dickinson's writing.

12. J378, lines 5–8.

destabilizing outer boundary.[13] In its ability to conceptualize and traverse the space in question, Dickinson's geometric imagery extends the text's instability to its outer limit. She thus emphasizes that her speaker must endure the precarious context that the distance from a center implies, which in turn clarifies the symbolic connotation of death that "Circumference" exhibits. For Dickinson, the center's connoted stability recedes as the text moves towards its boundary. As a spatial metaphor, then, Circumference establishes the limit to which the poem can reach and, therefore, the edge that humanity's embodied condition can gesture. Beyond Circumference lies a mystery that is inaccessible, but Dickinson is consistent in her efforts to bring the text to this edge. In J378, this outer limit establishes the displaced, liminal space that structures the poem despite the disjunctive implications that this image suggests.

The claim that Circumference is her business indicates how Dickinson conceptualizes her liturgical poetics. By moving away from a center's implied stability, she incorporates a necessary instability into the text's contours. Moreover, the image of Circumference establishes an intimate space from which she examines death's finitude. By recognizing these features, another use of the term Circumference takes on added significance in describing her work as a liturgical poetics. Elsewhere, she develops Circumference in a way that adds another symbolic layer to the way she imagines death: "Circumference thou Bride of Awe / Possessing thou shalt be / Possessed by every hallowed Knight / That dares to covet thee."[14] Here, the text exhibits a similar motion away from a center towards an edge, but this time the edge is more than just a boundary; it characterizes death in terms of fulfilled desire. The journey towards life's limit becomes a courtship wherein death entices the speaker (and the reader) as the text approaches Circumference. The Bride[15] who awaits at this limit destabilizes the text

13. Dickinson's symbolism can elude attempts to pin down her meaning. In *Dickinson and the Romantic Imagination*, Joanne Feit Diehl offers a helpful guideline with respect to the term Circumference: "As I interpret Dickinson's use of the term, Circumference is the outermost extent the imagination can reach. The space thus created is what the self can explore, a kind of demarcation of imaginative limits and possibilities" (56 n. 6).

14. J1620 ("Circumference thou Bride of Awe"), lines 1–4.

15. I acknowledge that Dickinson frequently populates her writing with distinct gender roles, but in this case the roles are subversive. Moreover, this image inverts other, more famous personifications in which death appears as a distinctly masculine character. The short point to be made, then, is that Dickinson does not utilize gender to suggest that her liturgical poetics should be read through a gendered critical structure. She is playing with the notion of gender, to be sure, but to dwell on this feature directs attention away from her liturgical concerns (see chapter 6).

as she suggests the Knight's desire will be satisfied. Like the Knight, then, those who seek to capture this Bride—and all will eventually be possessed because no one can escape death—will find a disruptive conclusion to their pursuit of desire. The Bride's ability to fulfill the Knight's yearning fractures the entire poetic space in question. Dickinson emphasizes this point with her uniquely barbed way of describing such encounters by playing on the commandment not to covet.[16] In J1620, she makes clear how desire can be a dangerous thing.

Despite the seemingly pessimistic tone in J1620, one can see in this poem the hints of Dickinson's liturgical poetics that will emerge more clearly during a lengthy treatment of her work. At the same time that J1620 suggests the satisfaction of the Knight's desire for a deathly Bride, there exists a faint sense of hope. The image of the Bride/Knight implies mutual fulfillment should the two actually embrace, which sustains the Knight's desire even though the point at which he can meet the Bride is also the point of death. To traverse this poem therefore requires a paradoxical desire for a union that from the outset will be subverted in the end. In one sense, then, the text is clear how the conceit will play out. At the same time, the metaphor implies in its erotic contours an extension beyond the point at which the Knight would finally meet the Bride. In stopping at Circumference rather than trying to cross the boundary, the symbolic logic at work extends the fulfillment of that desire beyond Circumference. Thus, in daring to covet, the Knight can through his own death imagine a transcendent possibility—always a strong desire in Dickinson's poetry and indeed in all liturgical poetics—beyond the limit imposed by/at Circumference. In suffering this death, the Knight will ultimately experience the consummation he desires, which, paradoxically, transforms death's finitude into a lasting union.

A Liturgical Poetics and Irony

This brief analysis of Dickinson's poem identifies an important textual feature that characterizes a liturgical poetics: irony. In J1620, Dickinson very clearly establishes death's presence; the textual boundary marked off by Circumference is definitive and nonnegotiable. At the same time, this image constitutes that which enables the text to anticipate a transcendence of death. Circumference thus exhibits a deep irony in its dual symbolic

16. See Exodus 20:17.

capacity. In *The Alluring Problem*, D. J. Enright discusses irony in a capacity that dovetails with the preceding analysis: "The ironic figure of speech, Kierkegaard noted, is 'like a riddle and its solution possessed simultaneously.' Or, like flashes of lightening, ironies are at once powerful and momentary, and exegesis cannot live up to them in either respect."[17] In J1620, Circumference is the point where life ends, but it through this limit that death ceases to be the final reality to which the text can reconcile itself. Circumference, then, functions ironically. It destabilizes the text as a point of collapse and through this collapse generates alternative readings. By enabling the text to anticipate a condition beyond death, Circumference affords a symptomatic example of how irony functions in a liturgical poetics. As Dickinson shows repeatedly, irony causes the text to unfold and fold back on itself as it anticipates the fulfillment of the liturgical promise.[18]

Irony's textual helix both clarifies and confuses readings of J1620, an effect that reiterates the complex dynamics that define a liturgical poetics. In *Rhetoric, Power and Community: An Exercise in Reserve*, David Jasper offers a suggestive analysis on how irony's paradoxical character "is inherently unstable and destabilising," yet this effect initiates "its theological overturning."[19] As the ironic image subverts the text, the liturgical promise's fulfillment surfaces, which is the flash that Enright identifies. As the governing image in J1620, Circumference does not sustain in the end a definitive (and hopeful) reading, which casts the text in terms that cannot be sustained and, therefore, cannot be fully understood. Irony's effect, then, is felt acutely at Circumference insofar as it undermines the text that imagines a condition beyond death. At the same time, this subversive image is precisely the element that enables the text to anticipate the impossible possibility[20] beyond death's limit.

17. Enright, *The Alluring Problem*, 3.

18. Irony's simultaneous destabilizing and anticipatory properties call attention to the deconstructive activity that characterizes a liturgical poetics. This process echoes the Derridean trace, which marks the point at which, as I discuss in chapter 3, the text glimpses the recovery of the trace's originary absence. This dynamic affects the text not only at the level of the metaphor, but also in a larger narrative context. For example, Moses' experience on the Pisgah Height (see chapter 2) describes the moment at which the text's promised stabilizing presence emerges, though it remains beyond the text's boundaries. This momentary vision extends the narrative while simultaneously reiterating that the fulfillment of the promise will not occur within the text. This dynamic prefigures, of course, the trajectory of the Last Supper.

19. Jasper, *Rhetoric, Power and Community*, 132.

20. Irony functions in a capacity that parallels Derrida's deconstructive approach to

Irony's momentary character reflects its paradoxical effect. Its subversive presence calls attention to a textual absence, which in turn displaces the implied presence that the image anticipates beyond death's boundary.[21] At the same time, this anticipated alternative to death reiterates that death's boundary is impermeable. Irony, then, brings into focus the instability that frames the human condition by denying the hope that emerges within a liturgical poetics. On this point, Enright's analysis clarifies what is at stake: "This is the type of irony that doesn't reject or refute or turn upside–down, but quietly casts decent doubt and leaves the question open: not evasiveness or lack of courage or conviction, but an admission that there are times when we cannot be sure, no so much because we don't know enough as because uncertainty is intrinsic, or the essence."[22] This distinction captures the relationship between the Knight and Death/Bride insofar as this image resists hermeneutical clarity. The crowning moment that implies fulfilled desire is deeply ironic because it can only anticipate this condition. Any desire remains a possible but unrealized fulfillment forever beyond the text. This intrinsic instability serves as irony's reminder: any anticipated stabilizing presence must be erased. The effect, Enright emphasizes, is unmistakable: "the detection of an ironic twist is supposed to make us feel better. In this instance it can only make us feel slightly worse."[23] In a liturgical poetics, the irony is, quite simply, that denial prefigures any anticipation that the promise will be fulfilled.

Irony's presence helps to identify when and how the text opens towards an eschatological fulfillment of the liturgical promise, because, paradoxically, it reiterates the necessary destabilizing of any possibility an image suggests. In J1620 and, more broadly, within the notion of a liturgical poetics, irony pinpoints significant textual, thematic, and liturgical dynamics by calling attention to the simultaneous possibility of the fulfilled promise and the necessary denial of such desire. The ironic simultaneity of possibility and impossibility suggests, then, that there exists a double irony within a liturgical poetics. In J1620, for example, because death is both Circumference and Bride the desired consummation marks a symbolic and textual closure, as well as a liturgical disclosure. For Dickinson's Knight, it is

---

reading a text. I discuss the specific paradox of the impossible possibility below (see chapter 3).

21. In this capacity, irony aggravates any text's latent instability.

22. Enright, *The Alluring Problem*, 6.

23. Ibid., 35.

only through desiring death that the text can configure the (possible) transcendent union that the Knight anticipates. At Circumference, however, the text denies the implied climax between the Knight and Death/Bride, yet a wholly new and transcendent narrative emerges through this denial. Perhaps more than any other salient feature in liturgical poetics, the ironic interchange between closure and disclosure identifies the process whereby a text anticipates the fulfillment of the liturgical promise. Read through this critical filter, the Last Supper is clearly an ironic narrative, which in turn clarifies the simultaneous closure and disclosure that Jesus' body signals. Importantly, the new temple can emerge only after the dislocation of the basis for this anticipation. Jesus must die and that death clearly subverts the promise he lays out in the upper room.[24]

This disruption reflects the intrinsic uncertainty that Enright ascribes to irony. The text's disclosure of an eschatological possibility cannot escape the destabilizing effect that Jesus' death generates. The symbolic promise that the bread and wine convey foreshadows simultaneously an impending textual closure and a liturgical disclosure. The disorienting effect is clear in the disciples' lack of a response, which reiterates the elusive nature of irony's effect. Jasper describes well the dislocation that irony causes: "Irony, inherently unstable and destabilising, happily works against its own narrative discourse and against its own textuality. The best irony is barely perceptible."[25] Irony, then, deconstructs the text with the faintest touch, a dynamic that proves incongruent with the alternative readings into which the text opens. As the groundswell of a liturgical poetics, this rupture sustains through its dislocation the liturgical promise that emerges—and departs—in a momentary flash. It generates and endures a stress that permits the text to anticipate the eschatological, stabilizing presence that Jesus

---

24. The Gospel accounts of the events surrounding Jesus' death are consistent in describing the disciples' initial response in a way that indicates they clearly do not understand the the Last Supper's liturgical implications. It is only *after* a vision (see especially John 20:24–31, which I discuss at length in chapter 6) that the disciples' behavior changes to reflect their awareness of the liturgical possibility at hand. Mark's gospel emphasizes the point at stake here. Mark's gospel ends abruptly (Mark 16:8) when the disciples disperse in confusion. The end of Jesus' life in this account has, quite literally, collapsed the text. The consistent thread in all of the Gospel accounts is the need for the text's closure to disclose the liturgical possibility that emerges simultaneously.

25. Jasper, *Rhetoric, Power and Community*, 128–29. In addition to the disciples' silence in response to Jesus' words, the particular announcement of betrayal is noticeable in its subtlety. I discuss the specific implications of betrayal within a liturgical poetics in chapter 6.

announces. This promise emerges out of irony's wholly destabilizing influence, which traverses the text's closure in order to anticipate stability by virtue of the promise's fulfilment.

A Liturgical Poetics and the Erotic Body

The simultaneous closure and disclosure that unfolds within a liturgical poetics thus depends on irony to hold open the text in order to permit a release into an eschatological possibility. In the examples discussed above, it is telling that the body provides the locus for this process. More specifically, the image that best holds open a liturgical space in order to experience and announce a simultaneous closure and disclosure is often an *erotic* body. The term erotic indicates the ability to relate intimately, a definition that encompasses the human experience as embodied.[26] In his recent book *A Theology of Love*, Werner G. Jeanrond locates this experiential and communicative praxis in the physicality of embodied experience: "All loving relations into which we humans are capable of entering are made possible, but are also limited, by our physical existence."[27] Within the body's physicality lies its erotic capacity, which, in Jeanrond's analysis, affords "a uniting force that

26. I use the term "intimately" to suggest varied readings within the broader notion of the erotic. Intimacy frequently denotes an emotive or sexual condition and I certainly include this common understanding in my definition. At the same time, the term can suggest a variety of proximities that need not be read within these parameters. The erotic can bring objects (bodies) into intimate proximity without exhibiting any qualifiers beyond a close physical proximity. The ability to relate to death intimately, for example, can be understood in terms of the body's condition when death is near. Textually, for example, Jesus' body relates intimately to his coming death when he speaks at the Last Supper. As such, his body exhibits an erotic capacity to relate to death that need not be read in sexual or emotive terms (though as will become clear in the analysis below, these connotations are present) in the Gospel accounts of his death.

27. Jeanrond, *Theology of Love*, 10. Jeanrond emphasizes throughout *Theology of Love* that love must be understood as praxis, which in the context of a liturgical poetics recalls the plural readings of the body in the Last Supper. The symbols offered gather a dispersed community (see chapter 1), a function that identifies nascent ecclesial factors within a liturgical poetics. In its erotic capacity, then, the body provides the basis for the emphasis on praxis that Jeanrond stresses. Of particular note on this point is his argument that Jesus' own understanding of the body emphasizes "great care for the [body's] physical integrity" (12), which in this case applies to the body's function in a liturgical poetics. I discuss the communal implications of a liturgical poetics—an important footnote despite these texts' deconstructive effects on theology's readings of the ecclesial—in the conclusion below.

brings together previously separated beings."[28] The ability to unite in and through the body is precisely the reason that the specifically erotic body offers a symbolic resource for a liturgical poetics. As a result, emphasizing this aspect of humanity's embodied condition exhibits multiple capabilities that fall under the broad definition of the erotic. According the Jeanrond, "The erotic realm includes here sexual desire, cognitive desire, and the longing for union with the divine."[29] Within the body's different symbolic capacities and thus the framework within which to imagine a transcendence of death, Jeanrond recognizes an important thread: reunion. Importantly, a strong desire underscores the capacity in which the body anticipates the divine other's stabilizing presence. Herein lies a crucial component of liturgical hope, namely an extension of the body (or the text as body) towards a destabilizing outer limit. Moreover, this trajectory approaches the point that anticipates other's stabilizing presence in the shadow of its own inevitable closure. In the end, as Jeanrond points out, the desired union therefore includes a divine other that must remain beyond death's boundary. Consequently, this desire and denial coalesce in the image of the erotic body, which in turn emphasizes the eroticized body's unique function within a liturgical poetics.[30]

Within a liturgical poetics, the eroticized body calls attention to the traditional association in Christian thought between sexuality and sin and death.[31] Jeanrond is clear what is at stake in this link: "Approaching love

28. Jeanrond, *Theology of Love*, 14.

29. Ibid., 16.

30. Within the orthodoxies that a liturgical poetics deconstructs, there exists a significant theological point that affects how a text anticipates a stabilizing presence. The specifically divine other exists outside humanity's embodiment, yet this other has experienced embodied condition that death destabilizes. In the context of a specifically Western theology, Jesus issues a liturgical promise while subject to the limit that the promise transcends. This paradox only adds to the complex symbolic structures within a liturgical poetics, but, Jeanrond notes, it is also a critical element of Christianity's liturgical hope: "The belief in God's assumption of a human body does not only present a challenge to any thought of human love without a body, but stresses the participation of the very body in all acts of eternal love" (43). Jesus makes this point clear when he establishes the body and bread as symbols to convey the liturgical promise and, moreover, when his death marks the closure and disclosure that sustains the promise. Here again one can see why Jesus nuances the relationship between the body and the temple; his body is a temple insofar as it provides a gathering point from which the text anticipates the promise's fulfillment.

31. For a helpful discussion of how sexuality and sin have been condensed into a suspicion of the body's erotic abilities, see Jeanrond, *Theology of Love*, 45–65.

through doctrines of sin and original sin cripples our imagination, because it views our finitude and flaws as the insurmountable barriers to the work of love, and reduces our attention to our own ontology of failure. It blocks eros, spontaneity and community development and locates us in negative and self-centered spiritual reckoning."[32] In broad terms, theology frequently associates sin with death, a move that deemphasizes the body's erotic capacity. Moreover, this association neutralizes the irony that the body injects into the Last Supper narrative, which in turn prohibits the text from moving beyond the closure that death brings about. A liturgical poetics, however, absorbs this disruption into the text's deconstructive character. Herein lies an important contribution that a liturgical poetics can make within a theological context. Though death is nonnegotiable, responses to death can be imagined through the very bodily characteristics wherein death is manifest. The eroticized body's symbolic richness becomes apparent as a way to respond to its own finitude. That which is supposed to be the locus for death becomes the point at which the text opens into readings that anticipate a transcendence of this limit. Significantly, the crucial moment in which death ends life mirrors the climactic moment that punctuates human sexuality.[33] Whether one discusses the moment of death—when the body's experiential capacity ceases—or when desire is fulfilled, the same dynamic is apparent. The crucial point that defines the narrative and thematic logic at hand is, paradoxically, absent. One cannot describe one's own death, just as one cannot sustain the instantaneous fulfillment of desire. A liturgical poetics thus treats these critical moments from the liminal space that precedes them, which links sex and death in their mutual collapse. In both contexts, the body encounters an inevitable erasure, which prohibits necessarily a stabilizing presence within the text.

Recovering the Erotic Body in John Donne and Emily Dickinson

Reading Jesus' body as erotic enables the recovery of crucial textual features within the Last Supper narrative. There exists a latent irony that displaces the liturgical promise Jesus speaks, which in turn subverts the

32. Jeanrond, *Theology of Love*, 245.

33. As seen above in my discussion of J1620, Dickinson condenses these thematic parallels to emphasize how the erotic body, like death, is defined by the possibility of fulfilled desire.

body (symbolically and textually) as the mark that the liturgical promise that will be fulfilled. Once recovered in its erotic capacity, Jesus' body enables the kind of alternative readings that Donne and Dickinson offer in their respective liturgical poetics. Irony and its displacement thus underscore several of the salient features at hand in the Last Supper narrative and, therefore, recover a long forgotten (or actively ignored/suppressed) symbolic thread: Jesus establishes a liturgical paradigm that during crucial moments characterizes his body in distinctly erotic terms. Moreover, his erotic body affords through its thematic and symbolic parallels with death a way to escort the text into appropriate proximity with the text's closure. Philippe Ariès argues that relating to death intimately is an important step towards responding appropriately to death's finality: "The old attitude in which death was both familiar and near, evoking no great fear or awe, offers too marked a contrast to ours, where death is so frightful that we dare not utter its name."[34] Because of its liminal relationship with death, a liturgical poetics offers a helpful response to death because, as Aries describes, within such texts death ceases to be a source of overwhelming fear. It stands to reason, then, that recovering an intimate familiarity with death enhances the text's ability to anticipate the fulfillment of the promise that Jesus speaks prior to his own death.[35] This is precisely what the eroticized body accomplishes as a liturgical locus: the text's ability to relate intimately to death and thus to occupy consciously a space dislocated by an impending closure.

In the argument below, this framework will inform how, in the wake of the English Reformation, theological fissures created space for writers to provide alternative approaches to crucial theological concerns. For Donne, this freedom effectively "takes [the Eucharist] to the bedroom,"[36] a shift that constitutes a clear departure from the orthodox theological climate of his day. However, at the same time he deconstructs his contemporary orthodox boundaries, Donne retains a strong personal belief in the very tradition his writing challenges. In recovering the erotic body, he strikes a finely tuned balance between his innovative (and scandalous) liturgical poetics and the deeply ingrained theological beliefs that are frequently obscured in

34. Ariès, *Western Attitudes toward Death*, 13.

35. Interestingly, Ariès comments elsewhere that: "the tomb is also a temple, a consecrated place where the liturgy can be celebrated; later it will be called a chapel" (*The Hour of Our Death*, 39). This point strengthens the analysis above concerning Jesus' substitution of the body for the temple, as Ariès' insight is consistent with the Heideggerian notion that the temple constitutes a textual gathering point.

36. Schwartz, *Sacramental Poetics at the Dawn of Secularism*, 87.

critical treatments of his work. The reading of Donne in this project thus recognizes the intimate capacity in which Donne engages his own personal, social, and theological context, which, through his overtly erotic imagery, recalibrates how a text can anticipate a condition beyond death.

By drawing on and critiquing Regina M. Schwartz's book, *Sacramental Poetics at the Dawn of Secularism: When God Left the World*, the subtlety with which Donne deploys the body in a liturgical context will become clear. Schwartz rightly identifies what is at stake in the post-Reformation literary landscape, but, I will argue, she conceptualizes the shift in terms that do not, in the end, recognize the complex relationship between Donne's literary corpus and the theological context out of which his writing emerges. What is at in stake in questions concerning the Eucharist is displaced more subtly and therefore profoundly than Schwartz suggests in reading Donne's work as a specifically literary development from the sacrament to the sacramental. Donne's writing is distinctly *liturgical*, a difference that hinges on the capacity in which he recovers the body's ironic function from within the Last Supper narrative. By focusing on this simultaneous closure and disclosure, Donne challenges orthodox readings of the body (and the Body), while at the same time maintaining a delicate equilibrium between his theological and literary personas.

After examining Donne's liturgical poetics, this project then analyzes Emily Dickinson's writing in order to argue that she, too, establishes the body's ironic role as the basis for a liturgical poetics. Like Donne, Dickinson responds to death in a manner that utilizes the body's erotic capacity to deconstruct her culture's orthodox milieu. Specifically, Dickinson draws upon the denial of desire in order to bring her work into intimate proximity of death. Moreover, just as Donne's liturgical poetics emerges as he distances himself from institutional frameworks, so too does Dickinson challenge established theological paradigms in her cultural context. Writing in the twilight of the Romantic era, Dickinson rejects the search for hermeneutical clarity and embraces the destabilizing effect that irony brings to the text. In so doing, she follows Donne's lead in moving away from the notion of a textual center—and its consequent hermeneutical precision—in order to extend her writing towards the disruptive limit that death establishes.

In the work of both Donne and Dickinson, then, the argument below recognizes patterns that ultimately derive from the pervasive irony that the Last Supper exhibits in stressing Jesus' body as the mark of the liturgical promise. Both writers recover the extent to which a liturgical poetics requires a specifically erotic body. Insofar as death makes life inherently unstable, Donne and Dickinson recognize in distinct yet related ways the limits of their respective orthodox traditions. By emphasizing the erotic body as the starting point to deconstruct the text in order to open that same text to alternative readings, both Donne and Dickinson recover a crucial but often forgotten component of the promise Jesus speaks at the Last Supper: liturgical hope can occur only by virtue of a doing. As a result, their deconstructive readings reinstate irony's displacing presence within the text in order to allow the liturgical promise to endure its own erasure. Through irony, Donne and Dickinson accept and manipulate a text's inevitable closure in order to anticipate the eschatological disclosure that emerges through Jesus' death.

2

The Text's Indefinite Exile

Then the Lord God said, "See, the man has become like one of us, know-
ing good and evil; and now, he might reach out his hand and take also
from the tree of life, and eat, and live forever"—therefore the Lord God
sent him forth from the garden of Eden, to till the ground from which he
was taken. He drove out the man; and at the east of the garden of Eden
he placed the cherubim, and a sword flaming and turning to guard the
way to the tree of life.[1]

IRONY IS A PRIME EXAMPLE OF THE DESTABILIZING DYNAMICS THAT AF-
fect a liturgical poetics. Blanchot identifies this latent instability as an
"Error," which, he explains, "is the risk which awaits the poet and which,
behind him, awaits every man who writes dependent upon an essential
work. Error means wandering, the inability to abide and stay."[2] The text
is, if Blanchot is correct, engaged in a task that is defined at the outset by
an antecedent failure, as the wanderer's journey cannot reach its implied
destination. A text that seeks stability will inevitably encounter its own closure without fulfillment, as its "error" causes indefinite displacement. As
a result, the text must be traversed in the absence of reliable coordinates:
"where the wanderer is, the conditions of a definitive here are lacking. In
this absence of here and now what happens does not clearly come to pass
as an event based upon which something solid could be achieved . . . what
happens does not happen, but does not pass either, into the past; it is never
passed."[3] Markers that would otherwise guide the journey towards a stable

1. Gen 3:22–24.
2. Blanchot, *The Space of Literature*, 238.
3. Ibid.

conclusion dissolve continually in the text's non-space. Wanderers will therefore find themselves where the text "is not truth, but exile . . . [they] remain separated, where the deep of dissimulation reigns, that elemental obscurity through which no way can be made and which because of that makes its awful way through [them]."[4] Herein lies the error and consequent risk that Blanchot recognizes as fundamental to the text. To traverse the text's exilic space is, in the end, to realize only that which was latent from the beginning: because of the instability that the error generates, every reading is already decentered.

This condition resists definitive hermeneutical conclusions, a negation that within a liturgical poetics demands attention. The error ensures that the text can only anticipate a presence through a destabilizing absence. The text, then, unfolds in a state of endless anticipation, an indefinite dissatisfaction that no re-reading can absolve. When Blanchot emphasizes the error, he is discussing an absolute denial, which underscores the displacement that characterizes a liturgical poetics. Exile, then, describes accurately the condition out of which the Last Supper gives rise to Jesus' promise; the error is present, always, and, therefore, refuses to permit the presence that the text anticipates in the wake of the liturgical promise.

Blanchot helps, then, to clarify the inherent instability within the new liturgical paradigm that Jesus establishes. A deeply rooted error governs the promise that Jesus articulates at the Last Supper; his response to death affords hope, but such hope crumbles beneath the dissimilitude that Blanchot describes. The text's latent error glazes Jesus' promise with an obvious irony, an effect he stresses by signaling the promise with his body. As symbols, the bread and wine emphasize the conditions that define Jesus' embodiment—his death—which, in turn, remind the reader of the error at hand: death *always* threatens life. Consequently, Jesus' body opens the text into an eschatological hope only by acknowledging the antecedent erasure of that hope. The exile Blanchot describes is, therefore, amplified within the liturgical paradigm that Jesus establishes. Death continually dislocates the body from any notion of stability, an unavoidable reality that prohibits the ability of the body to abide and stay. This exilic quality defines the human condition and, consequently, magnifies the instability already present in the text. Through this dislocation, however, the body's erotic capacity enables alternate readings in response to death's undermining error. The body's erotic capacity to relate to death intimately foregrounds the irony

4. Ibid.

that characterizes a liturgical poetics. The image that marks the liturgical promise makes clear the extent to which death disrupts any textual (or actual) body.

Heidegger's understanding of human nature in *Being and Time* lies behind much of the argument in this chapter and underscores Blanchot's point.[5] Of specific interest in the present discussion is Heidegger's notion of anxiety. He writes, "Anxiety thus takes away from Dasein the possibility of understanding itself, as it falls, in terms of the 'world' . . . Anxiety throws Dasein back upon that which it is anxious about—its authentic potenti- ality-for-Being-in-the-world. Anxiety individualizes Dasein for its own- most Being-in-the-world, which as something that understands, projects itself essentially upon possibilities."[6] Such possibilities must be understood as counterweights to the release from the actualized loss of an originary

5. As with the previous chapter, I am drawing on Heidegger in a significant capacity in order to establish a critical *literary* methodology. As such, I will not explore the philo- sophical implications of Heidegger's work in depth and, moreover, I am not trying to force Heidegger's writing into theological categories. Linking Heidegger with Blanchot's notion of exile resonates with the specifically theological elements that exile exhibits in the liturgical paradigm that I am discussing as a result of the body's function in a literary context. I accept that Heidegger would be the first to say that while exile may inform theological concerns within a literary context, exile is not in and of itself a theological issue. Rather, in the context of this argument exile provides a descriptive metaphor that condenses literary, theological, and philosophical concerns when conceptualizing and responding to death's finality. Exile indicates both the necessary considerations when an- alyzing a text and, moreover, the implications of those conditions for possible responses, liturgical or otherwise.

In drawing on Heidegger, then, I am qualifying how my literary analysis approaches (and frequently intersects) distinctly theological concerns. In relating texts in this capac- ity, my methodological approach recognizes in Heidegger a strong theological echo. As Kearney notes, "much of his [Heidegger's] language is deeply resonant with the religious language of Christian eschatology" (*The God Who May Be*, 92). Specifically, Heidegger's conception of the human condition as thrown emphasizes how dislocation from a sta- bilizing origin both unsettles a text and permits an anticipatory function to emerge. Within the instability that defines the human condition, an absence—the not-yet pres- ence that opens the text into eschatological readings—becomes a crucial fulcrum with a liturgical poetics. The critical approach that locates the eschatological element within a literary context not only focuses on this anticipatory element as it affects the text, it also deconstructs the inability of theology's own texts to account fully for the dislocated human condition that gives rise to such texts in the first place. Heidegger, then, pro- vides a valuable critical tool that balances multiple disciplinary concerns as it examines and clarifies what is at stake in the Last Supper's eschatological implications by virtue of understanding the anticipated presence—the not-yet—as that which the text (and the human condition) cannot accommodate by virtue of its latent error.

6. Heidegger, *Being and Time*, 40.

stability; death makes self-understanding (itself a hermeneutical problem) difficult. Subsequently anxious, Dasein will, according to Heidegger, "flee *in the face of* the 'not-at-home'; that is, we flee in the face of the uncanniness which lies in Dasein."[7] Confronted with its inherent displacement, humanity can only run away, a reminder of what is at stake in the event that punctuates the Last Supper narrative: Jesus' own death. The end of Mark's gospel articulates clearly how anxiety reacts when reminded of its dislocation. In the wake of Jesus' death, the disciples flee because they are afraid.[8] Jesus' death subverts the liturgical promise uttered during the Last Supper, an erasure that reiterates for the disciples their own inescapable anxiety (the error, in Blanchot's terms).

Heidegger offers a helpful critical framework that calibrates the effects of Jesus' death on the liturgical promise that his body marks. Any presence anticipated through this image reverberates with the reality that death remains a decisive limit to humanity's embodied condition. Any anticipation thus suffers an unavoidable anxiety. David R. Cerbone summarizes well how this disjointing process affects the text as it conceptualizes the human condition: "Anxiety is revelatory of just that: in anxiety, Da-sein confronts its existence *as* an issue, as something not yet determined and so constituted precisely by a 'not-yet'."[9] Anxiety both prompts and overwhelms any possible presence that a liturgical poetics anticipates. This "not–yet" is symptomatic of the displacement that results from the error, or rather from the lost (and thus absent) origin. As a result, Kearney argues, "our existential anguish before death is experienced as radical *Unheimlichkeit*: a sense of deep disorientation, or not-being-at-home in ourselves."[10] As a defining characteristic of the human condition, death constitutes an error that prevents a simple reading of the liturgical promise that Jesus locates in his body. This body must encounter death, which subverts the possibility announced therein and, as Heidegger articulates, casts humanity into a continually anxious state.[11]

7. Ibid.

8. See Mark 16:1–8.

9. Cerbone, *Heidegger*, 90.

10. Kearney, *Strangers, Gods and Monsters*, 77.

11. In casting the human condition as anxious, Heidegger mirrors a frequent critical approach in literary studies: melancholia. In his famous essay, "Mourning and Melancholia," Sigmund Freud suggests, in Kearney's reading: "Instead of undergoing the painful process of mourning the idealized loved one, the melancholic refuses to accept the reality of loss and turns the grief *inwards* instead" (Kearney, *Strangers, Gods and Monsters*, 165).

Dasein, then, constitutes a corrective response to the dualistic optimism that frequently underpins theology. Whereas the distinction between body and soul affords a measure of stability as the body progresses towards death, Heidegger problematizes this binary as normative within the Western theological tradition. Dasein reiterates the displacement that characterizes humanity as specifically embodied. As such, Dasein is unhinged completely from any originary stability, and, therefore, coheres with the exilic parameters out of which a liturgical poetics arises; any attempt to imagine stability runs counter to the displacement that governs the human condition. The error that Blanchot describes dovetails with this total displacement, a resonance that ultimately enables the erotic body to provide a liturgical locus insofar as it emerges wholly out of its own latent instability.

Building on Heidegger, Lacoste makes clear that the body is a necessary consideration within the human condition because a clear boundary—its own death—substantiates this anxiety. For Lacoste, the indefinite not-yet that circumscribes humanity's condition becomes in death a "never."[12] Death marks life's finitude, yet within a liturgical poetics, this never paradoxically enables a hope grounded in anxiety. Just as death is yet to come, so too might death not be the definitive moment—a there, in Blanchot's terms—that will never become a textual here. As embodied, then, humans must understand the multiform displacement that affects their condition;

This inward turn must confront, then, the inherent displacement that any individual will find in death. For Harold Bloom, this realization provides the genesis of writing: "[it] begins ('however unconsciously') by rebelling more strongly against the consciousness of death's necessity than all other men and women do" (*The Anxiety of Influence*, 10). As a normative concern, death deconstructs all texts, but in so doing it enables an important shift. The not-yet that generates anxiety becomes—when confronted openly—a source for anticipating the eschatological possibility that death obscures. Thus, Kearney argues, "The melancholic moves from destruction to creation by accepting his/her own death. Darkness encountered and traversed becomes a source of new light" (Kearney, *Strangers, Gods and Monsters*, 171). Bloom echoes this transition in telling language: "Freud, in defining anxiety, speaks of 'angst vor etwas.' Anxiety *before* something is clearly a mode of expectation, like desire. We can say that anxiety and desire are the antimonies of the ephebe or beginning poet. The anxiety of influence is an anxiety of expectation *being flooded*" (*The Anxiety of Influence*, 57). The strength of expectation in the face of death is precisely the effect that enables Jesus' body to extend the liturgical promise through death. The body, then, becomes the fulcrum between the anxious awareness of death and the desire—which is distinctly erotic in Bloom's language—that responds to death's dislocating effect by anticipating an/other possibility beyond death. The ability to balance death's displacement with a specifically erotic desire is precisely the dynamic that Donne and Dickinson recover from the Last Supper narrative.

12. Lacoste, *Experience and the Absolute*, 8.

they occupy a physical context, which, haunted by death, effectively constitutes a non-space. Being-in-the-world is simultaneously a not-being at home.[13] Consequently, humanity finds that its natural condition constitutes a state of "house arrest,"[14] which generates anxiety within the very space that would otherwise connote the safety that a symbolic center provides. In humanity's exilic condition, any such center must be read as decentered.

Within a liturgical poetics, this dislocation informs significantly how a Heideggerian temple functions. These images imply an absent stability that belies a text's underlying exilic characteristics. The temple remains, always, built on the text's instability. This characteristic highlights an important distinction between the literary space in which Heideggerian temples emerge and the theological implications that these images convey. The indefinite not-yet that frames the temple prohibits a stabilizing presence, which in turn alters significantly any theological conception of the liturgical paradigm that unfolds on the basis of anticipating this stability. Exile stresses absence as the governing textual principle that frames such temples as they emerge. For Heidegger, the temple functions in an ironic capacity by subverting any notion of a real presence. Exile, then, provides a distinguishing metaphor that clarifies how a liturgical poetics as a literary concept differs from a theological text. The originary stability that underpins the latter counters directly the conscious decentering within the former.

A necessary absence complicates these concerns, as texts simultaneously exhibit an imaginative freedom to respond to their inevitable closure. The consequent instability becomes a liberating denial that enables a particular response to a necessary textual absence: anticipating a presence beyond this condition. This fine distinction between the parameters that govern texts and the definitive presence that theology often assumes when describing liturgy clarifies what unfolds in the specific notion of a liturgical poetics. These textual seams enable an imaginative response to an inevitable textual closure. The result, as Kearney argues, is a disclosure of a possibility that "liberates the reader into a free space of possibility, suspending the reference to the immediate world of perception (both the author's and the reader's) and thereby disclosing new ways of being in the world."[15] The notion of suspension emphasizes the unavoidable limits that govern any imaginative possibility; an anticipated presence must recognize that

13. Ibid., 11.

14. Ibid., 12.

15. Kearney, *On Paul Ricoeur*, 41.

a textual absence is unavoidable. In the Last Supper, this dynamic is clear. Jesus brackets the inevitable textual closure that awaits in order to enable the disciples to anticipate his presence in the future. This possibility does not erase the claims that death makes on their human condition, but it does imagine that death can be transcended. A liturgical poetics enables, therefore, the text to anticipate an eschatological possibility—understood as a presence, the not-yet—without attempting to override the textual (and corporeal) limits that death establishes.

John Donne and Anticipating the Not–Yet

John Donne's "Divine Meditation V" exhibits clearly these exilic themes and, consequently, indicates how the notion of a liturgical poetics deconstructs orthodox theological concerns. Donne begins the poem by establishing the tensions that characterize his embodied existence: "I am a little world made cunningly / Of elements, and an angelic sprite, / But black in sin hath betrayed to endless night / My world's both parts, and, oh, both parts must die."[16] A clear Western dualism frames this poem; the speaker is acutely aware of both his body and his soul within the little world that symbolizes his condition (as created, as embodied). However, Donne does not characterize these concerns as stable. Rather, the poem conveys through the "endless nights" the speaker's indefinite dislocation. The image prohibits the text from opening into a new day, which, though always implied in the governing image's temporal condition, ensures that the speaker cannot transcend his exilic reality. Sin—the crucial, disruptive error—erases the hope that the angelic part—the soul—might feel in the face of the body's inevitable death.[17] The speaker recognizes the endless physical decay that any body knows, yet, because of sin's effect, what would otherwise hope to transcend the little world's darkness suffers the same denial of daybreak that shrouds the text. All Donne's speaker can do is pray to God, who exists beyond this endless night, for comfort *within* this little world: "Pour new seas in mine eyes, that so I might / Drown my world with my weeping earnestly."[18] Because the anticipated morning never comes, the speaker's hope must endure the world's exilic limits; his only option is to mourn

16. Donne, "Divine Meditation," lines 1–4.

17. Donne means death in a dual sense, both a literal physical death, as well a theological notion of sin as death.

18. Donne, "Divine Meditation," lines 7–8.

the night's permanence. Contrary to the normal diurnal rhythms that the physical body would experience, the human-as-world is, Donne makes clear, aware only of the night's denial of a new morning. As such, the text demands that the speaker extend his words through the exile that holds God at a distance; any comfort must be filtered through the endless nights' discomfort.

Despite the exilic parameters that characterize "Divine Meditation V," Donne's speaker articulates a hope that continual tears will extend beyond the text; the speaker weeps/prays to God, a presence that sustain this hope despite the text's limiting parameters. As this cry crosses the poem's symbolic and textual boundaries,[19] it exhibits the paradoxical duality that defines a liturgical poetics. The speaker cannot escape his displacement, but he still anticipates God's stabilizing presence. His tears thus reiterate that despite the text's displacement there is hope that the world's exile can be transcended. Crucially, then, the speaker does not request exemption from the world's textual (embodied) condition. Rather, he endures the exilic condition out of which his tears emerge. This image alludes to Psalm 30:5b: "Weeping may linger for the night, but joy comes with the morning," which signals that the speaker accepts the reality of a world disrupted permanently. This resignation enables the speaker to anticipate a stabilizing presence that (or rather who) is not subject to the text's dislocated condition. Though the speaker cannot escape the night's endless disruption, he can still hope for the morning that will not come. This impossible daybreak is the not-yet that enables the text to anticipate an impossible presence.[20] This is the joy

19. Donne alludes here to the Israelites' famous cry to God at the beginning of Exodus that, significantly, God hears. In this poem, the desire for God to replenish the speaker's dried up tears echoes both the possibility that comes when God hears the Israelites' cry, as well as the exilic journey that follows. See Exod 2:23–25.

20. Kearney is helpful in characterizing the transition that orients the text towards the (possible) fulfillment of the liturgical promise. In Kearney's words, the speaker undergoes a crucial transition: "by accepting his/her own death . . . [the] Darkness encountered and traversed becomes a source of new light" (*Strangers, Gods and Monsters*, 171). Affirming exile's pervasive displacement initiates the cycle wherein the liturgical possibility emerges. This point echoes the Last Supper narrative as it moves into the garden of Gethsemane. Another example of this dynamic occurs in the well-known parable of the Prodigal Son (Luke 15:11–32), which portrays God clearly as this implied other. Having left his father's house, the son enters into an exilic condition wherein he encounters an increasingly dislocated space. Amidst the pigs, the son realizes his exilic condition; another possibility now awaits in the return to his father's house. This anticipated return, which brings hope despite his destitute circumstances, envisions the implied other as a stabilizing presence that exists outside the exilic condition in which this anticipation begins.

that the speaker longs for, even if the poem's governing dynamics prohibit this release.

When Donne shifts metaphors in the latter half of "Divine Meditation V," he reiterates an important textual dynamic within a liturgical poetics. The speaker qualifies sin as "lust and envy,"[21] which burn the speaker's world and make it "fouler."[22] As a response to these problematic conditions, the speaker thus anticipates God's presence as corrective of the latent error that disrupts the little's world's natural cycle. The purifying fire sparks a liturgical hope for God's "fiery zeal / Of thee and thy house, which doth in eating heal."[23] In response to his sinful condition, the speaker imagines God's anticipated presence as a Eucharistic meal. God's house—and here Donne recalls the temple that Jesus deconstructs—hosts the meal (or even *is* the meal) that will sanctify the speaker's sinful condition. Participating in this meal fulfills the liturgical promise that Jesus speaks at the Last Supper and, therefore, constitutes a transcendence of death as a bodily and theological dislocation. In desiring this healing, the speaker in "Divine Meditation V" acknowledges the fragmented human condition as both the locus for these deaths and, moreover, recognizes the paradoxical character of a liturgical poetics. More specifically, Donne affirms through the speaker's anticipation of this meal the text's ironic, subversive contours. By anticipating this meal, however, the speaker reiterates the Last Supper's promissory character, even as an indefinite delay in fulfilling the liturgical promise subverts the moment in which the text opens towards this eschatological possibility. The healing, then, remains a not-yet, a reminder that the text cannot, in the end, step outside the initial dislocation that defines the speaker's little world.

"Divine Meditation V" clarifies, then, how the notion of exile informs the textual dynamics within a liturgical poetics. A crucial notion that underscores any exilic text is the definitive lack of a here, a point clarified in the anticipated presence of the not-yet. Within an exilic text, one can only wander through an endless night; dawn will never arrive. The impossibility of arriving at the text's implied destination emphasizes, therefore, the indefinite nature of exile's displacement. As a result, Blanchot claims: "The poem is exile, and the poet who belongs to it belongs to the dissatisfaction of exile."[24] The inability to satisfy that which the text desires will

21. Donne, "Divine Meditation V," line 11.

22. Ibid., line 12.

23. Ibid., lines 13–14.

24. Blanchot, *The Space of Literature*, 237.

always subvert the implied transcendence of the text's displaced space. Consequently, Blanchot argues that due to its "Exile, the poem makes the poet . . . a wanderer, the one always astray, [s/]he to whom the stability of presence is not granted and who is deprived of a true abode."[25] This denial underscores what is at stake in the speaker's initial tears; it conceptualizes God's anticipated presence—what becomes the stabilizing house, or rather the site of the promise's fulfillment—in terms of a textual absence. This paradox indicates, moreover, the transition that irony marks, namely the moment in which the promise's possible fulfillment emerges only as a not-yet. This delay, extended indefinitely alongside the anticipation of what cannot come, strengthens Blanchot's conception of the text as an exilic space. Any anticipated presence underscores this notion insofar as it acknowledges the necessary absence of fulfillment.[26]

A Liturgical Poetics and Exile

Exile, then, offers a helpful framework for examining the textual features that characterize a liturgical poetics. As a coordinating metaphor, it identifies a liturgical poetics' limit: such texts can do no more than anticipate through their own dislocation a stabilizing presence outwith their boundaries. This is precisely what Jesus does in signaling through his body the Last Supper's indefinitely delayed promise. The bread and wine therefore destabilize the text insofar as they affirm the exilic conditions that govern the liturgical promise they convey. Timothy Clark offers a critical analysis that links the Last Supper and Blanchot's notion of exile. Clark writes that when reading dislocated texts, "The kind of understanding required is not analytic: it must be more a kind of participation."[27] This experiential point of emphasis recognizes the extent to which exile refuses the notion of textual stability and, moreover, clarifies the emphasis Jesus places on doing. The reader must endure the text's instability—the lack of a definitive here—and anticipate a there which is not–yet but which has been promised. The stress on doing orients the text towards its own (via Jesus' death) closure. As Clark

25. Ibid.

26. According to Blanchot: "Here lies the most hidden moment of the experience. That the work must be the unique clarity of that which grows dim and through which everything is extinguished—that it can exist only where the ultimate affirmation is verified by the ultimate negation—this requirement we can still comprehend, despite its going counter to our need for peace, simplicity, and sleep" (*The Space of Literature*, 46).

27. Clark, *The Poetics of Singularity*, 74.

explains: "To preserve the uncanniness of the poetic text is thus to refuse explanations and grounds and to preserve instead the elusive un-grounding of human existence . . . in a realm of discomfort, lack of assurance and uncertainty, but also to keep open the possibility of a . . . non–appropriative relation to being."[28] Doubt pervades the Last Supper narrative, which, in turn, reveals the irony that enables and subverts the liturgical promise. This not-yet materializes in anticipation of and in response to the promise's anticipated fulfillment and simultaneously stresses the necessary delay that follows the announcement of the promise. The body emphasizes, then, the disjunction between Jesus' impending absence and the anticipation of his stabilizing presence.[29]

As an organizing and explanatory metaphor, exile calls specific attention to the dislocation that pervades the Last Supper narrative. The reader finds that the text's language, in Blanchot's words, is "[the] word, yet the word is itself no longer anything but the appearance of what has disappeared—the imaginary, the incessant, and the in determinable. This point is ambiguity itself."[30] The reader, then, realizes that irony amplifies textual displacement, which calls attention to the fact that the liturgical promise must remain unfulfilled. This denial resists the notion of a "central point"[31] as a stabilizing textual feature. To propose such hermeneutical certainty ignores the text's exilic character, which in turn obscures the demand to anticipate the presence that will fulfill the liturgical promise. The lack of a central point, then, indicates the paradox that becomes clear when reading texts as exilic, which, Blanchot explains, "alone makes the work present. But at the same time, this point is the 'presence of Midnight,' the point anterior to all starting points, from which nothing ever begins, the empty profundity of being's inertia, that region without issue and without reserve, in which the work, through the artist, becomes the concern, the endless search for its origin."[32] By suggesting that a text's displacement stems from an impossible search for exile's implied origin, Blanchot points to an anticipated stability that structures any text when read as exilic: such an origin would resist the antecedent dissimilitude that Blanchot mentions. In Donne's "Divine

28. Ibid., 46.

29. Clark is careful to emphasize that despite his seemingly pessimistic analysis he, like Blanchot, maintains a hint of hope: "The 'poetic' in Blanchot bears the mark, or promise, of [a] necessary futurity" (*The Poetics of Singularity*, 109).

30. Blanchot, *The Space of Literature*, 44.

31. Ibid.

32. Ibid.

Meditation V," for example, this anticipation endures the endless nights that frame the text's desire for—and ultimate lack of—stability.

The implied origin's absence lies at the heart of describing a liturgical poetics as exilic and, moreover, clarifies what is at stake in utilizing this concept as critical scaffolding for this project. Conceptually, exile anticipates a return to some place—be it an origin, a conclusion, or a fulfilling destination—that steadies the text despite its dislocated condition. Specifically, a liturgical poetics anticipates this stability as a transcendence of death.[33] For such hope to be articulated, a liturgical poetics must acknowledge prior to anticipating this release that the text can only conclude with a destabilizing absence. This is the deeply troubling irony that lies at the core of the liturgical paradigm Jesus establishes. As the text announces the liturgical promise, it simultaneously reiterates humanity's exile. The promise, then, indicates the text's ever-present displacement—its inherent error—as the prohibitive consequence that the text's necessary absence generates.[34]

Antecedent Exile: Eden and the Pisgah Height

As the locus of the liturgical promise, Jesus' body must be fully embedded within humanity's exilic condition. As a result, the Last Supper follows the specific narrative for explaining humanity's exile: the Fall in the Garden of Eden. There, the body suffers expulsion from its paradisiacal origin, which situates any subsequent text within exile. This predicative story emphasizes the displacement from the origin that Eden represents. In his book *The Trespass of the Sign: Deconstruction, Theology and Philosophy*, Kevin Hart traces how the notion of sin (theologically, a displacement from God) informs the Garden of Eden narrative; sin manifests itself in the role that signs play within language. Hart writes: "The Fall may establish the human need to interpret yet it simultaneously sets firm limits on interpretation. No longer in harmony with God, this world becomes a chiaroscuro of presence

---

33. Overcoming death's limit becomes, of course, the basis for the theological removal of sin, a point Donne's speaker in "Divine Meditation V" makes clear.

34. Blanchot describes this complex dynamic as "oscillating perpetuity" (*The Space of Literature*, 45), a label that underscores the displacement that characterizes exile. The text, then, exhibits "the successive unreality of terms that terminate nothing, and ht total realization of this movement—language, that is, become the whole of language, where the power of departing from and coming back to nothing, affirmed in each word and annulled in all, realizes itself as a whole . . . In the poem, [then,] language is never real at any of the moments through which it passes" (ibid).

and absence; everywhere one looks, there are signs of a divine presence that has withdrawn and that reveals itself only in those signs."[35] Hart's reading of the Fall echoes Blanchot's argument; at the heart of the human condition to which a liturgical poetics responds, there exists an error. The sign itself exhibits this same displacement. Moreover, as Hart argues, the sign's own instability intensifies the displacement that governs the human condition. All signs aggravate an already established instability. There exists, therefore, another irony insofar as Jesus' death anticipates an unavoidable absence, which sanctions the liturgical promise's anticipated presence.[36] This paradox emphasizes the disappointing conclusion that Enright suggests; in conveying the liturgical promise Jesus' body opens the text to an eschatological stability and the denial of that stability. As irony dictates, the bodily signs collapse the text into a concurrent closure and disclosure.

Jesus' body thus condenses humanity's post-Fall separation from God (conveyed through the theological notion of sin) both experientially and textually. This initial error irrigates subsequent biblical narratives that elaborate on the notion of exile. Of these post-Eden texts, the Israelites' journey through the desert offers particular insight into the argument at hand.[37] At the outset, God promises a land flowing with milk and honey as the destination that provides a counterweight to the Israelites' exilic journey.[38]

35. Hart, *Trespass of the Sign*, 4.

36. According to Hart, this tension defines how texts function theologically: "the sign always works with two modes of repetition. The one, sanctioned by metaphysics, allows for the sign to repeat its originating presence; but the other, a structural trait of the sign, concerns its repetition outside its original context. Now when the sign is so repeated, what it signifies will be modified by the chance new context. In being subject to the second mode of repetition, the sign must fail to perform its first and primary mode to the extent to which it does not signify the presence purely and simply" (*Trespass of the Sign*, 123). See also Jacques Derrida, *Of Grammatology*, 283ff.

37. It is important to note that in the discussion that follows, I am aware that some would consider my use of the term exile to describe the Israelites' journey *after* God leads them out of their captivity. Their enslavement is very much an exile, but in the analysis I am undertaking, exilic indicates specifically the displacement that in the book of Exodus clearly forms part of the narrative framework. Exile characterizes the Israelites' journey between an implied origin and an anticipated conclusion, which, in the case of Exodus is Canaan, the Promised Land (i.e., an anticipated destination), a label that emphasizes both the stability this land symbolizes vis-à-vis the exilic journey, as well as the textual absence of this land. By virtue of its anticipated character, the Promise Land remains beyond the text that describes the journey through exile.

38. "Then the Lord said, 'I have observed the misery of my people who are in Egypt; I have heard their cry on account of their taskmasters. Indeed, I know their sufferings,

At the end of forty years of wandering through the desert, Moses climbs Pisgah in order to glimpse from within his exilic experience the Promised Land that he thinks he will enter: "and the Lord showed him the whole land . . . [and] the Lord said to him, 'This is the land of which I swore to Abraham, to Isaac, and to Jacob, saying "I will give it to your descendents"; I have let you see it with your eyes, but you shall not cross over there.' Then Moses, the servant of the Lord, died there in the land of Moab, at the Lord's command."[39] Moses sees the possibility of his release from exile, but this vision ultimately underscores his exilic displacement. At the top of Pisgah, the text calls attention to the space from which Moses views Canaan. The fulfilled promise is, for Moses, still there—a not-yet—across an exilic boundary that the text does not cross.[40] As is the case in a liturgical poetics, the text's ironic closure occurs at the same time that it opens towards the promise's fulfillment. When Moses sees the Promised Land, he dies, which captures the irony that exemplifies a liturgical poetics; the moment of fulfillment collapses into the moment of denial.[41] For Moses, the promise thus

---

and I have come down to deliver them from the Egyptians, and to bring them up out of that land to a good and broad land, a land flowing with milk and honey, to the country of the Canaanites, the Hittites, the Amorites, the Perizzites, the Hivites, and the Jebusites'" (Exod 3:7–8).

39. Deut 34:1, 4–5.

40. George P. Landow characterizes the mountaintop on this point in a helpful capacity: "The Pisgah sight is a coming together, a confrontation of the human and the divine, the temporal and the eternal, that occurs immediately before the death of the prophet who had given life to serving God and his chosen people" (*Victorian Types, Victorian Shadows*, 205). This moment of confrontation establishes the disjunction between the displaced condition that anticipates the Israelites' passage into the Promised Land, as well as the necessary delay of crossing over exile's boundary. The notion of confrontation thus unsettles God's promise, which thickens the subversive effect that Moses' ironic death brings to the text. The source of the promise becomes the source of denial, an inversion that prefigures the encounter between Jesus and Mary in the garden of John 20.

41. Two other features of this vignette deserve mention. First, Moses' death is solitary, which highlights the dislocation that death brings to the human condition. Thomas Altizer describes solitude in terms that echo the argument above. Solitude opens possibilities that paradoxically result from "a loss reversing every manifest or established center or our interior so as to make possible the advent of a wholly new but totally immediate world" (quoted in Jasper, *The Sacred Desert*, 143). David Jasper describes this effect as "a profound decentering," which affects "every true desert traveler" (Jasper, *The Sacred Desert*, 143). The journey that precludes Moses experience on Pisgah thus intensifies the decentering that clarifies the lack of a stabilizing center within exile. The Pisgah experience, then, emphasizes the extent to which irony subverts (as it seemingly reaffirms) the liturgical promise.

remains unfulfilled, which reiterates his exilic displacement. For the text to open towards the stabilizing presence that fulfills a liturgical promise, the text must assert its ironic character.[42]

The mountaintop from which Moses views the Promised Land exhibits two telling characteristics that help to clarify how a liturgical poetics unfolds. First, the Pisgah Height is a liminal space within the narrative, a threshold between the exile out of which the Israelites will emerge and the anticipated conclusion to the journey as per God's promise. Second, death prohibits Moses from experiencing the promise's fulfillment that is immanently close. He experiences a denial that parallels the textual displacement that characterizes his experience in the desert. As Jean-Luc Marion explains, death itself is a liminal moment that helps to clarify the significance of exile: "The absurdity of death lies not in the putting to death of my life, but in the frustration of meaning, not in the execution of judgment, but in the silence of any judgment. We die—there is nothing unjust or absurd in that. But we die without knowing the truth."[43] At best, one can—as Moses does—catch a glimpse of a *possibility* that exists beyond exile's boundary; this is the anticipated presence that lies at the heart of a liturgical poetics. At the same time, however, such images bring about textual closure. Moses' sudden death leaves the text in a disjointed state, as it overshadows the possibility that stretches out before (and beyond) its exilic viewpoint.

The Pisgah Height thus foreshadows the Last Supper's promise and denial and, therefore, suggests how to read a liturgical poetics. An anticipated presence—which fulfills the liturgical promise—flashes across the text, but the latent exilic parameters therein smother the transcendent possibility towards which the text momentarily opens. This disclosure advances and retreats in a way that transcends and reaffirms the anxiety that defines the human condition. According to Kearney: "This ultimate reference—to a world not merely represented by the text but disclosed by the text—brings us beyond epistemology to ontology. Thus the ultimate horizon of Ricoeur's work remains, from beginning to end, the horizon of being which signals to us obliquely and incompletely: a promised land but never an occupied one. We encounter here a truncated ontology—provisional, tentative,

---

42. It is worth noting that even though the Israelites do subsequently cross into the Promised Land, the stability implied therein does not materialize. Once they occupy this space, the Israelites encounter (and cause) numerous events that reiterate the absence of an Edenic stability.

43. Marion, *Prolegomena to Charity*, 115.

exploratory."[44] This oblique signal becomes the basis for a crucial denial within a liturgical poetics. The intimacy with which the Promised Land comes into view, and then disappears by virtue of Moses' death,[45] prefigures the crucial irony that destabilizes the Last Supper narrative. Jesus' liturgical promise must suffer the weight of absence that his death will bring. Similarly, Moses glimpses briefly how God's promise will be fulfilled, but this momentary presence does not override the death that reiterates the exilic conditions that precede (and extend beyond) this moment. As Kearney notes by linking his allusion to Pisgah with Ricoeur, "it is not sufficient to describe meaning as it *appears*; we are also obliged to interpret it as it *conceals* itself."[46] The Pisgah Height thus provides an important prelude to the disruption that characterizes the Last Supper and, therefore, reiterates that the text cannot extend beyond the liturgical promise's not–yet.

Emily Dickinson's Exilic, Erotic Reading of the Pisgah Height

Emily Dickinson draws on the Pisgah narrative several times in her writing, perhaps most clearly in J597 ("It always felt to me – a wrong"). This poem begins at the moment described above: "It always felt to me—a wrong / To that Old Moses—done— / To let him see—the Canaan— / Without the entering—."[47] Dickinson injects the opening stanza with a sense of deep irony. The moment wherein Moses glimpses the Promised Land is wrong, the error that dislocates the story's narrative arc. Significantly, however, Dickinson softens the denial that Moses experiences by marking off the wrong as done. She implies but does not state the wrong's cause, a point she emphasizes by setting off the key term with a dash. She thus characterizes Moses as absorbing the denial's strain without naming explicitly that the wrong is Moses' death. Moreover, she does not capitalize wrong, which

44. Kearney, *On Paul Ricoeur*, 4.

45. An important note of clarification is needed. The Promised Land itself obviously does not disappear; the Israelites eventually cross into the area that Moses sees briefly. The point in this brief discussion is to identify a crucial liturgical dynamic, namely the erasure of the condition that transcends exile. Moses' specific experience indicates a latent textual dynamic that will manifest itself more clearly during the Last Supper and, more importantly, when Jesus encounters Mary in John 20.

46. Kearney, *On Paul Ricoeur*, 16. I discuss in more detail Ricoeur's analysis of metaphor and how this affects the notion of a liturgical poetics below (see chapter 3).

47. J597, lines 1–4.

constitutes a significant departure from her normal habit of capitalizing nouns in her poetry and, therefore, soothes the promise's denial that Moses endures.

The poem's second stanza extends this softer conception of Moses' death; the speaker indicates a willingness to accept what this moment of denial entails for surprising reasons. Dickinson writes: "And tho' in soberer moments— / No Moses there can be / I'm satisfied—the Romance / In a point of injury—."[48] As the speaker steps back from Pisgah to process the implications of the moment s/he feels to be wrong, her/his language develops a curiously erotic tone. The poem responds to the denial that Moses experiences by discovering in the midst of that injury a satisfaction that tantalizes the reader.[49] Though this poem could easily follow a trajectory from the first stanza and dwell on the slight Moses receives, Dickinson engages the narrative's instability in a capacity that finds in Moses' exile an invitation to a strange, seductive hope. By situating the poem within this disjointed moment (emphasized particularly by the line break between lines 7 and 8), the poem clings to the promise that stretches out beyond the text. The denial and the satisfaction described in the second stanza emerge simultaneously as Moses' death marks a definitive closure. Despite the implications present in the wrong that Moses experiences, then, Dickinson finds satisfaction in the injury, a condensation that recognizes the complex liturgical coherence between erotic and deathly images.[50]

48. Ibid, lines 5–8.

49. Lines 13–14 anticipate this moment in a surprisingly positive tone: "On Moses— seemed to fasten / With tantalizing Play" (J597). Diehl recognizes the liturgical implications in Dickinson's poetry, which in this particular example emerge clearly. Diehl writes: "Her poems move less between the natural world and the self than between a projected view of the possibilities that lie beyond death and the frustrations of consciousness confined to his world" (*Dickinson and the Romantic Imagination*, 184). Despite recognizing the liminal context that is crucial to Dickinson's liturgical poetics, Diehl's analysis does not emphasize the liturgical implications present in this poem and, more broadly, throughout Dickinson's work. Dickinson is very much interested in the boundary between the world and a possible beyond, but, contrary to Diehl's claim that Dickinson is frustrated, I counter that Dickinson recognizes *through* the necessary frustration of the promise's denial the text's ability to endure the displacement that precedes and follows this crucial moment.

50. I disagree with James McIntosh's reading of this poem, which argues that "[a] sense of God's injustice may well stem from her reading of the whole story of the wandering of Moses and the tribes in the Books of Exodus, Numbers, and Deuteronomy" (*Nimble Believing*, 101). Dickinson is certainly aware of the irony that unfolds at Pisgah, but McIntosh's reading does not account for either the softening of the wrong that Moses

In Dickinson's writing, thresholds relate the text intimately to a desired possibility *beyond* the boundary the threshold implies. In J421 ("A Charm invests a face"), Dickinson utilizes the image of a veil in this capacity:

> A Charm invests a face
> Imperfectly beheld—
> The Lady dare not lift her Veil
> For Fear it be dispelled—
>
> But peers beyond her mesh—
> And wishes—and denies—
> Lest interview—annul a want
> That image—satisfies—[51]

The veil situates this poem, both thematically and liturgically, within an exilic context. The other lies intimately close, yet at the same time the veil ensures that this other remains beyond the image's (and therefore the poem's) boundaries. The other can only be seen through the veil; as a result, the text's exilic parameters both encourage and deny the speaker's desire for this other. The veil conveys, then, both the speaker's intimacy with and displacement from the face wherein Dickinson locates the liturgical anticipation's fulfillment. This possibility emerges precisely because the veil can accommodate this paradoxical encounter with the other.

Such disjointed contexts occur frequently in Dickinson's writing. As she wrote to Judge Otis Lord, four years before her death, "we both believe, and disbelieve a Hundred times an Hour, which keeps believing nimble."[52] Commenting on this letter, John Robinson notes: "Once again we encounter [Dickinson's] mistrust of stable states, as if stability falsified or as if it excluded something."[53] In J421, this dislocation proves to be alluring, so much so that the speaker refuses to disrupt the image, despite a deep desire to lift the veil and see clearly the other's face. The break between stanzas emphasizes this point; the speaker reiterates the desire to gaze at the other *only* through the threshold that separates the two. The speaker's willingness to accept a restricted and restricting gaze indicates clearly Dickinson's liturgical focus in this poem. She addresses directly the veil's underlying irony,

---

experiences (in Dickinson's eyes) or the erotic capacity in which J421 develops. As I am arguing, Dickinson interacts with this narrative in a more complex manner in order to lift out the implications of exile.

51. J421, lines 1–8.

52. L750.

53. Robinson, *Emily Dickinson*, 142.

namely that it opens the text to an image that will fulfill the speaker's desire while simultaneously ensuring that the other's satisfying presence remains outside of the text. The veil distorts, yet it is through this distortion that the speaker glimpses the other. Crucially, the speaker is cognizant of what is at stake in the displacement insofar as the veil marks both desire and denial. It sustains the speaker's anticipation and, in so doing, it prohibits the text from experiencing its implied fulfillment. In the end, the poem can accommodate this paradox because Dickinson refuses to permit the text to cross over the boundary that the veil establishes.

Importantly, Dickinson calls attention to the veil's specifically erotic contours. In the final line, "That image" can function in two different capacities. On the one hand, the phrase can refer reflexively and specifically back to the veil and, in so doing, extend the speaker's desire to see the other's face. On the other hand, it can refer more broadly to any image. This latter possibility also sustains the speaker's desire, but in a subtly different way. Any image within the text's exilic parameters lacks the definitive presence that would satisfy the desire at hand. This second reading, then, reiterates that the specific image of the veil affords a symptomatic example of a broader textual dynamic that Dickinson utilizes frequently: thresholds mark both displacement and possibility. By ushering her readers into this kind of space, Dickinson constructs an image that withstands the inevitable denial of desire.

The result that Image causes is Dickinson's characteristic ambiguity. Robert McClure Smith recognizes that this density is an important feature of Dickinson's work: "there is no more powerful reader stimulus in her canon than the continually frustrated attempt to detect and fix on a missing center when there are always only possible options available. In essence, Dickinson's is an aesthetics of frustration: the potential for reader enchantment is in precise relation to that reader's inability to attain the satiated fulfillment of his or her hermeneutic desire."[54] In refusing to satisfy the desire that her structuring images imply, Dickinson thus offers a liturgical poetics that is distinctly exilic. In J421, Dickinson draws on Exodus to emphasize that the veil denies the speaker by displacing the other's presence. Similarly, in Exodus 34 Moses must put on a veil after speaking with God in order to dull the glow on God's face.[55] For Dickinson, the veil becomes that which distances the speaker from the desired other. In so doing she recalls

54. Smith, *The Seductions of Emily Dickinson*, 6.
55. See Exod. 34:29–35.

the passage in Exodus 33 that precedes the need for the veil in Exodus 34. In response to God's command to leave Sinai (tellingly, as a mountaintop threshold), Moses asks to see God and God responds:

> Moses said to the Lord . . . "Now if I have found favor in your sight, show me your ways, so that I may know you and find favor in your sight. Consider too that this nation is your people." He said, "My presence will go with you, and I will give you rest." And he said to him, "If your presence will not go, do not carry us up from here. For how shall it be known that I have found favor in your sight, I and your people, unless you go with us? In this way, we shall be distinct, I and your people, from every people on the face of the earth." The Lord said to Moses, "I will do the very thing that you have asked; for you have found favor in my sight, and I know you by name." Moses said, "Show me your glory, I pray." And he said, "I will make all my goodness pass before you, and will proclaim before you the name, 'The Lord'; and I will be gracious to whom I will be gracious, and will show mercy on whom I will show mercy. But", he said, "you cannot see my face; for no one shall see me and live." And the Lord continued, "See, there is a place by me where you shall stand on the rock; and while my glory passes by I will put you in a cleft of the rock, and I will cover you with my hand until I have passed by; then I will take away my hand, and you shall see my back; but my face shall not be seen."[56]

In the midst of his exile, Moses voices a desire to experience God's stabilizing presence, a request that God satisfies in part. Moses can only experience God's presence as an absence because God's face must remain hidden. Despite the proximity with which God passes by Moses, God will not satisfy fully Moses' desire. This refusal informs the veil in J421, as it emphasizes that the other's face must remain obscured.[57] The veil thus indicates that the

56. Exod. 33:12–23.

57. As Judith Farr notes, "Dickinson's poems about eternal life and love establish the fact that for her the face symbolizes the quintessence of personality" (*The Passion of Emily Dickinson*, 16). The face, then, constitutes an eschatological stability beyond the text's displacement, an anticipated presence that Dickinson routinely denies in her writing. Seeing the other face-to-face remains the fulfillment of a promise that, like Moses' view of the Promised Land, cannot be experienced. Thus, Dickinson alludes not only to the Exodus narrative in J421; she also draws upon Paul's statement about heaven in 1 Corinthians: "For we know only in part, and we prophesy only in part; but when the complete comes, the partial will come to an end . . . For now we see in a mirror, dimly, but then we will see face to face" (1 Cor 13:9–10, 12). As in Exodus, the image of a face-to-face meeting symbolizes God's stabilizing presence. Similar to the Exodus narrative,

other's presence can only be anticipated from within the speaker's exile, a condition that ensures the absent of the other's stabilizing presence.

Another variant of this trope occurs in J398 ("I had not minded—Walls—"), which similarly establishes the veil as a boundary between the speaker and the other's stabilizing presence. The initial "Walls"[58] that the speaker does not mind frame this poem with obvious irony; despite their restrictive connotation, the speaker still hears the other's call.[59] The poem unfolds as the speaker voices desire for this other, who is absent: "A limit like the Veil / Unto the Lady's face—/ But every Mesh—a Citadel—/ And Dragons—in the Crease—."[60] The visually permeable but physically prohibitive boundary inverts the connotations of the Wall that separates the speaker from the desired other. The walls permit the other to be drawn intimately close to the speaker, while the veil—which connotes qualities that are mirror opposites of a wall's normal connotations—alters significantly the capacity in which the speaker approaches the other. The poem concludes with an image that unravels this disjunction into the dash's endless pause. Describing the veil as a citadel connotes an ironic space wherein the (divine) other might finally be present. Given the dragons that lurk, however, the stability implied therein quickly dissolves (the veil's delicate mesh would do little to keep those dragons at bay). The friction between J398's initial and final symbolic coordinates thus reiterates the text's exilic parameters. Dickinson relocates the wall's connotations in the veil, a move that serves to emphasize the intimacy with the other whom the speaker desires, while at the same time emphasizing that the other must remain absent.

The Body's Dual Liminal Symbolism: Sex and Death

Several important concerns emerge from these Dickinson poems, which help, in turn, to clarify how the theme of exile informs her liturgical poetics. She uses liminal imagery to indicate why exile must be acknowledged

---

Paul makes clear that a desire to see God's face emerges from within exilic parameters, which necessarily deny this anticipated eschatological stability. Dickinson utilizes this trope frequently to articulate her liturgical hope to transcend death. See also J461 ("A Wife—at Daybreak I shall be—"), which similarly draws on the image of a face-to-face meeting to indicate a transcendence of the speaker's exilic condition.

58. J398, line 1.

59. "And far I heard his silver call / The other side the Block—" (J398, lines 3–4).

60. J398, lines 13–16.

before liturgical hope can emerge. The text must anticipate a stabilizing fulfillment of the promise (and, therefore, desire) in full recognition of its displacement. It is only though the text's consequent displacement that an anticipated presence can be conceptualized as a not-yet. More specifically, liminal images bring the text into intimate proximity of exile's boundary, which in turn enables an extension of the text beyond its inevitable closure. At the same time, these liminal contexts amplify the strain that the coming textual collapse generates. Moreover, the glimpses of the promise's fulfillment aggravate the force with which the erasure of this anticipated presence subverts the text. As discussed above, for example, Moses' death shatters the textual momentum that builds throughout the story of the Israelites' journey; it punctuates the denial that the text exhibits when the Promised Land unfolds before him.[61]

These salient features indicate further points to consider. The liminal qualities of sexuality and death afford particularly incisive ways to emphasize a liturgical poetics' governing dynamics. The thematic consonance between sex and death indicates how the body anticipates and, therefore, lacks the stability that these experiences suggest. Sex and death are two of the body's most significant experiential possibilities and, moreover, crucial moments that a text cannot contain in a sustained capacity. Whether describing an orgasm or the moment life ceases, the reader must recognize that these experiences conclude with a total collapse. Sexual climax immediately plunges the text back into a state of desire, while death prohibits necessarily any embodied desire or fulfillment. Within a liturgical poetics, the inherent denial of desire—be it to experience ecstasy or to transcend death—precludes the anticipation that opens the text towards eschatological readings.

61. The denial of the promise as it is about to be fulfilled is a crucial theme within a liturgical poetics. Moses' experience foreshadows another, more striking example of this dynamic in John 20, when Jesus tells Mary not to touch him, even though his presence in the garden suggests the fulfillment of the Last Supper's liturgical promise. Despite the text's suggestive glimpse of the promise's anticipated fulfillment, within the text this satisfaction must remain absent. Moses never enters the Promised Land, just as Jesus will not permit Mary to touch him. Both Moses and Mary, then, never move beyond the text's not-yet. What materializes before them is the already departing presence that holds the text open to the eschatological fulfillment that they glimpse briefly before suffering denial's closure. This not-yet—the denial of the promise—recalls the lost originary presence to which exile anticipates a return by reiterating that this hope is possible only by enduring exile's displacement. At the same time, a return remains implicit and, therefore, the denial ensures that the text remains open towards an eschatological presence in the form of fulfilled desire.

Shared liminal contours link images of death and sexuality, which suggests why poets like Dickinson and Donne recover the erotic body from the Last Supper narrative. As a new temple, Jesus' body escorts the text into intimate proximity with a boundary (death) that closes the text. In turn, his body provides a point around which readers can anticipate the stability that comes with the promise's eschatological fulfillment and endure its necessary denial. In particular, the body as the locus of sex and death conveys both the deep desire that informs a liturgical poetics, as well as the displacement that prevents such desire from being satisfied within the text. The ability to convey both of these salient features suggests how the body enables the text to accommodate the paradoxical qualities of desire and denial thus comes into clear focus. These images—located in the body's erotic potential and impending death—provide the conduit through which the text can open towards the promise's fulfillment. The erotic body's symbolic possibilities can sustain this simultaneity into order to imagine transcendence as the text's necessary collapse occurs. As Donne and Dickinson realize, the text's latent instability must be affirmed in this capacity. Both depict what Jesus makes clear during the Last Supper: a denial of desire must be endured at the end of any liturgical poetics if the body is to open the text to an eschatological reading that fulfills the promise.[62]

The thematic consonance between sex and death clarifies how a liturgical poetics accommodates an important theological point. Blanchot suggests that perhaps the central paradox that emerges within exile is that "the work must be the unique clarity of that which grows dim and through which everything is extinguished—that it can only exist where the ultimate

---

62. Blanchot emphasizes death's inevitability as crucial for understanding the paradox that defines exile: "it is not at all difficult to hold that death is true. Death always takes place in a world, it is an event of the greatest world, an event which can be located and which gives us location" (*The Space of Literature*, 96). As mentioned in the previous chapter, death is not an event that can be experienced. Rather, it is a moment that always stands just outside of any possible experience, which clarifies why liminal proximity to death within a liturgical poetics is crucial. Though the text cannot account for the moment of death, it can, through the body, relate intimately to this moment; to recall Lacoste, death places humanity under house arrest. Consequently, Blanchot articulates the possibility and limit that brackets any text in light of death's presence: "one must be capable of satisfaction in death, capable of finding in the supreme dissatisfaction supreme satisfaction, and of maintaining, at the instant of dying, the clear-sightedness which comes from such a balance" (*The Space of Literature*, 91). This is precisely what Jesus accomplishes in marking his own death as the moment of liturgical disclosure. The paradox that his body's closure indicates this new possibility enables a glimpse from within exile to a possibility beyond.

affirmation is verified by the ultimate negation—this requirement we can comprehend, despite its going counter to our need for peace, simplicity, and sleep."[63] Blanchot's words identify a crucial feature of a liturgical poetics; such texts are defined by an inevitable closure and it is only through this point that the liturgical promise's fulfillment can be disclosed. The body's dual symbolic possibilities accommodate this simultaneous desire and denial because thematically the decisive moment that caps either sexual desire or death's inevitable approach appears in the text only as an absence that marks an impossible presence. Images of the erotic body within such a context thus provide the ability to "understand it intimately, as the intimacy of the decision which is ourselves and which gives us being only when, at our risk and peril, we reject . . . being's permanence and protection."[64] This textual intimacy, made possible through the erotic body, allows the text to subvert its own displacement. The boundary that marks exile can, when experienced intimately, be re-imagined, even if it cannot be crossed. A liturgical poetics is able through the very image of death's definitive nature risk a refusal of a different kind. Within intimate proximity to death, a liturgical poetics emerges when the text—marked by the eroticized body's ability to anticipate a significant climactic moment—permits the reader to imagine that which is absent as present.

A liturgical poetics, then, anticipates a *possible* presence within exile by recalibrating the text's latent instability. As such, any liturgical poetics will treat displacement not as a total absence from but rather a journey towards stability. The lack of a stable center can be embraced as a necessary departure rather than total dislocation. According to Lacoste, it is when the text approaches its limits that the text can envision the promise's fulfillment: "[that] architecture can be used to thwart *symbolically* and in the mode of anticipation, both the historical reasons for 'building' and for 'dwelling' and the reasons for our 'worldly' not-being-at-home is no small matter."[65] Two salient features emerge in the possibility that Lacoste outlines. First, the response to one's exilic condition remains a symbolic response; the image itself does not and cannot override the context in which it is established.[66]

63. Blanchot, *The Space of Literature*, 46.

64. Ibid.

65. Lacoste, *Experience and the Absolute*, 37.

66. I use throughout this project the adjectival term 'liturgical' to describe the response that imagines from within exile a possibility beyond exile. I will resist the noun liturgy, which connotes an actuality that remains impossible within the exilic parameters that govern a liturgical poetics.

As such, the text's symbolic "building" and "dwelling" paradoxically occur in a "no where,"[67] even it anticipates a not-yet. The second salient feature returns yet again to the Heideggerian temple. Though unstable, these images afford a temporary point around which others can gather to articulate liturgical hope.[68] Consequently, death's essential displacement ceases to be the final reality to which we can reconcile ourselves. The temple, then, enables the text to anticipate the stabilizing presence that, Clark suggests, "[is] an experience that takes consciousness and language to the limits of their possibility; an encounter, either sexual or traumatic, which is too immediate to be mediated by language and thus remains heterogeneous to the very narratives which it sets in motion."[69] In the bodily temple, desire meets in its own denial a trauma that erases the momentary stability that the liturgical promise suggested therein anticipates. In order to renew the now collapsed anticipation of the promise's fulfillment, the text must pass through its unavoidable exilic condition and its own inevitable erasure to extend beyond the sudden closure that occurs when the temple is destroyed.

A Liturgical Poetics: The Poet's Role

Given the instability that defines the text, a question bears asking: what is the poet's specific role in a liturgical poetics? Heidegger answers insightfully: "Poets are mortals who, singing earnestly of the wine-god, sense the trace of the fugitive gods, stay on the gods' tracks, and so trace for their kindred mortals the way toward the turning."[70] Liturgical poets are acutely aware of their own displacement, which motivates them to articulate hope in the liturgical promise. They stand apart from the "mortals [who] are hardly aware and capable even of their own mortality. Mortals have not yet come into ownership of their own nature. Death withdraws into the enigmatic. The mystery of pain remains veiled. Love has not been learned. But

---

67. Lacoste, *Experience and the Absolute*, 54.

68. When discussing Ricoeur, Jasper provides helpful insight into this point: "Ricoeur describes the significance of the word 'God' as the point of convergence that gathers together all the referents which issue from the many partial discourses in the biblical canon: it is at once 'the co-ordinator of the varied discourses and the index of their incompleteness the point at which something escapes them'" (Jasper, *The Study of Literature and Religion*, 94).

69. Clark, *Derrida, Heidegger, and Blanchot*, 85.

70. Heidegger, "What Are Poets For?" 92.

the mortals *are*. They are, in that there is language."[71] Language is the (non-) place wherein Heidegger locates mortality; liturgical poets, then, accept a dual displacement insofar as it is through language that they affirm their exilic condition and imagine what might lie beyond death's destabilizing boundary. A poet must admit displacement; s/he must accept beforehand that any desire to transcend exile will be denied.

Heidegger's analysis of Hölderlin's "The Ister," helps to clarify the poet's role in articulating a liturgical poetics. According to Heidegger, the poet is best suited for recognizing and incorporating textual instability in a capacity that is distinctly liturgical insofar as the text simultaneously reveals and conceals. In discussing "The Ister," Heidegger emphasizes the hermeneutical limits of understanding a text, while at the same time recognizing what meaning is accessible amidst such dislocation: "*What* the river does, therefore, not even the poet knows. The poet nevertheless knows its activity, its flowing; what the poet does not know is what is decided in this flowing. The flowing river as known poetically is the one that is."[72] Heidegger continues: "Whatever is their own is that to which human beings belong and must belong if they are to fulfill whatever is destined to them, and whatever is fitting, as their specific way of being. Yet that which is their own often remains foreign to human beings for a long time, because they abandon it without having appropriated it . . . because it is what most threatens to overwhelm them."[73] The poet's role, then, is to step into the river-in-process in order to trace the river's journey towards its own erasure. This threshold, when the river empties into the ocean, is the simultaneous moment of closure and disclosure. The poet recognizes this transition as the point wherein the text opens towards a new, alternative condition that while related to its exilic identity signals transcendence.

Heidegger treats the river in a way that parallels Blanchot's characterization of the text as exilic. The river, like the text, finds itself within a process that concludes with its own erasure. The river "is simultaneously vanishing and full of intimation in a double sense. What is proper to the river is thus the essential fullness of a journey. The river is a journey in a singular and consummate way."[74] The essential fullness that Heidegger identifies in this journey is, paradoxically, defined by an emptiness in the context of the pro-

71. Ibid., 94.

72. Heidegger, *Hölderlin's Hymn "The Ister,"* 20.

73. Ibid., 21.

74. Ibid., 30.

cess that is unfolding; the river-in-process will never stabilize the text. The river, then, mirrors humanity's own dislocation. Consequently, Heidegger states: "Journeying determines our coming to be at home upon the earth . . . To put it more clearly: the river is that very locality that is attained in and through the journeying."[75] The poet understands that the river's journey undercuts the text's stability, which in turn reinforces humanity's exilic condition. At the same time, the poet must recognize that releasing him/herself into an unstable context parallels the river's journey towards a conclusion that through its closure announces the moment of disclosure. As it empties itself into the sea, the river ceases to be in process.[76]

Poets, therefore, must endure textual displacement in releasing themselves and their readers into exile's futile journey towards a temple that, once reached, will deny the very locale (the here) it posits. In response to humanity's displacement, poets thus "convert the parting against the Open and inwardly recall its wholesomeness into a sound whole . . . [they] sing the healing whole in the midst of the unholy."[77] The poet guides the reader into and through the text's dislocation in order to encounter the temple as an extension of the liturgical promise. By anticipating a presence that remains absent, the temple echoes Heidegger's discussion of the bridge: "[the bridge] proves to be a location, and does so *because of the bridge*. Thus the bridge does not first come to a location to stand in it; rather, a location comes into existence only by virtue of the bridge. The bridge is a thing; it gathers the fourfold, but in such a way that it allows a site for the fourfold. By this site are determined the localities and ways by which a space is provided for."[78] Heidegger's analysis acknowledges exile's displacement in order to recognize how an image coordinates the text despite its displacement. The example of the bridge simplifies the role that the temple plays. The end result of these images is to provide a momentary counterweight—the anticipated presence's not-yet—to the unceasing displacement between the here and there.[79]

75. Ibid., 31

76. Heidegger concludes that the river's process is a "coming to be at home" (*Hölderlin's Hymn "The Ister,"* 49). This is, in "essence" (ibid., 42), how the river parallels the human condition as being-towards-death.

77. Heidegger, *Hölderlin's Hymn "The Ister,"* 137.

78. Heidegger, "Building Dwelling Thinking," 152.

79. Heidegger uses the term "dwelling" to describe the importance of such symbolic coordinates, even if those coordinates inevitably shift: "Dwelling . . . is the *basic character* of Being in keeping with which mortals exist" ("Building Dwelling Thinking," 158). I

The poet thus constructs the temple within exile, all the while aware that the temple rests on the anticipation of an impossible presence. The poet cannot, therefore, conclude a textual journey through exile, but s/he can endure a journey resigned from the outset to indefinite displacement. This antecedent failure recalls Jesus' initial command during the Last Supper; to engage a text in this capacity requires a doing. The text's instability must be traversed in order to reach the point wherein it opens towards an eschatological reading beyond its inevitable closure. Jesus' command to be remembered draws others towards the new bodily temple that emerges deep within exile. The unavoidable tension at these liminal moments—apparent, for example, in the presence of a deep irony—indicates what is at stake when articulating the liturgical promise. Jesus' body makes clear the temple's simultaneous closure and disclosure that relates humanity's exilic condition to the eschatological promise that he announces.

Excursus: A Liturgical Poetics as a Theological Doing

This paradox demands a brief methodological excursus. As discussed previously, within a liturgical poetics no definitive hermeneutical conclusions are possible insofar as a latent error undermines the text. Consequently, the body's exilic condition always substantiates and threatens the its own symbolic possibilities within a liturgical poetics. Carl Raschke articulates an important distinction that informs the notion of the body as a symbolic temple in light of these conditions. To use Raschke's term, the poet (and the reader) must traverse the text's exilic space by thinking theologically. This term conveys why the distinction is important: *"Inquiry* means a searching and a questing/questioning that does not glide and ramble across the surface of things, but *dives into their very depths*. Questioning in the latter sense comes to be the utmost aim."[80] The authors mentioned thus far share

---

have treated Heidegger's argument transitively in this chapter in order to indicate the literary implications of the temple within a liturgical poetics. Heidegger summarizes in more depth the relation between the image, space, and dwelling as follows: "The making of such things is building. Its nature consists in this, that it corresponds to the character of those things. They are locations that allow spaces. This is why building, by virtue of constructing locations, is a founding and a joining of spaces. Because building produces locations, the joining of the spaces of these locations necessarily brings with it space, as *spatium* and as *extension*, into the thinly structure of the buildings. But building never shapes pure 'space' . . . Building puts up locations that make space and a site for the fourfold" ("Building Dwelling Thinking," 156).

80. Raschke, *Theological Thinking*, vii.

this willingness. They recognize that they must recover the command that follows Jesus' liturgical promise—the doing—as a precondition for traversing the exilic text. Only by descending into the depths, that is, by thinking theologically, can the body function as a temple within the text's exilic parameters.

Thinking theologically is, then, a journey that can only proceed after the acknowledgement that signposts will not be available. The clear hermeneutical pathway that theology often attempts to stake out is, then, a mirage, a promise of stability that is denied at the moment it emerges. In the texts that this project considers, the apparent meandering will come into focus as a central feature of the critical foundation upon which this study rests. Boundaries between texts and disciplines will inevitably blur, but this is an unavoidable consequence of recovering the body as the liturgical promise's locus. In exile, actual bodies are "wayfarer[s who] finds himself [or herself] in a state of liminality, which is to say that both the starting and resting points of his [or her] wanderings are neither evident nor perspicuous."[81] Enduring the text's exilic condition to anticipate a stabilizing presence—which is always implied when one speaks of exile—demands the recognition that a necessary denial of hope will always occur, which limits definitively the body's symbolic capacity.

At its core, then, this project suggests a hermeneutic that operates within exile's constraints. A residual uncertainty constitutes part of the journey; the "adventure"[82] of thinking theologically must admit that within an exilic context, one will never encounter a sustained textual presence. As Raschke argues, an effective hermeneutic "serves to recommission the theological odyssey, to liberate it from the vapid stance of apologetics and to imbue it with a sense of adventure. The viator is always looking out for the promised land beyond the horizon."[83] When discussing the liturgical promise, an important corollary must be reiterated once again: the adventure is difficult because it will, in the end, fail. Paradoxically, the body in general and the erotic, sexualized body in particular emerge as a liturgically valuable resource only because it conveys a desire that appears simultaneously with that desire's denial. This point echoes the collapse that Moses experiences at the Pisgah summit, the endless night, and the veil that forever obscures the other's stabilizing presence.

81. Ibid., 15.
82. Ibid., 16.
83. Ibid.

At the point of textual closure, Raschke's model meets its limit. Thinking theologically can only usher the adventurer towards this boundary. Once there, the reader must recognize the demand that Jesus makes in the Last Supper once more. In order to catch a glimpse of what might lie beyond death, one must undertake a theological *doing*, a poiesis, in order to endure the absence that inevitably smothers the text's anticipated face. Theological thinking enters into the textual instability that cannot experience the promised eschatological presence, but this approach does not account for experiencing the denial that follows the point at which the promise emerges and disappears simultaneously. Raschke's concept thus fails to endure fully the text's displacement. Consequently, thinking theologically does not provide a critical approach that accounts for the total displacement that punctuates a liturgical poetics. A theological doing, on the other hand, endures the text's unavoidable collapse in order to renew the anticipation of the stabilizing presence that in the end must be denied. As a result, theological doing enables the text to regenerate readings that anticipate the fulfilled promise's eschatological stability.

3

Liturgical Decay and Rebirth

Therefore, to be possess'd with double pomp,

To guard a title that was rich before,

To gild refined gold, to paint the lily,

To throw a perfume on the violet,

To smooth the ice, or add another hue

Unto the rainbow, or with taper-light

To seek the beauteous eye of heaven to garnish,

Is wasteful and ridiculous excess.[1]

AS A LITURGICAL POETICS STRETCHES TOWARDS ITS OWN CLOSURE, IT must endure the strain of its own instability. In the Sermon on the Mount, Jesus uses an odd image to encourage humanity in the midst of this context: "Consider the lilies of the field," he tells the crowd, "they grow; they neither toil nor spin, yet I tell you, even Solomon in all his glory was not clothed like one of these. But if God so clothes the grass of the field, which is alive today and tomorrow is thrown into the oven, will he not much more clothe you—you of little faith?"[2] By focusing on a simple flower, Jesus both affirms that human life constitutes a uniquely valuable concern for God and, at the same time, underscores the instability that defines the human condition. God's commitment to the lilies does not override the fate that awaits them: a yearly death. The crowd must recognize that even in their simple existence the lilies mirror humanity's instability. The lilies, then, should be

1. Shakespeare, *King John*, 4.2.9–16.
2. Matt 6:28–30.

considered both in their promise and their demise. Jesus reiterates, therefore, the dynamics at work in a liturgical poetics by pointing to the lilies as a mirror of humanity's own instability.

Shakespeare's "Sonnet XCIV" takes seriously the imperative to consider the lilies. The poem's sestet develops the duality present in Jesus' commandment:

> The summer's flower is to the summer sweet
> Though to itself it only live and die;
> But if that flower with base infection meet,
> The basest weed outbraves his dignity:
>> For sweetest things turn sourest by their deeds:
>> Lilies that fester smell far worse than weeds.[3]

Shakespeare concludes this poem in a way that lays bare the inherent dislocation that defines the lilies. Though he initially affirms the flower's sweetness, this appealing characteristic exists only when one isolates the specific context of summer from the inevitable seasonal progression that governs the text. In considering the lilies, Shakespeare suspends initially these temporal parameters and finds sweetness only in summer, but this bracketing cannot remove the latent decay that will eventually materialize. The flower's sweetness emerges only within a context that is isolated from its inevitable death, a reading that is untenable within an exile. Shakespeare thus reveals the error that displaces the text, which in turn subverts the commandment that, on the surface, engenders hope.

The lilies, like humanity, are always susceptible to an infection. The image's ground, which permits the flowers to grow and, therefore to release their sweet fragrance is, crucially, the site of its decay. In their potential to become weeds the lilies undermine further their function as loci of God's concern. "Sonnet XCIV" therefore exposes the latent dislocation that through the lilies displaces the comforting explanation that Jesus offers to the crowd. Shakespeare calls attention to the reality that Jesus does not mention: the lilies' (and by extension, humanity's) impending death. He then concludes "Sonnet XCIV" by yoking his consideration of the lilies to a more complex theological matrix. The deeds that substantiate the shift from a lily to a weed echo a sinful displacement from God. Consequently, Shakespeare emphasizes the worries that saturate the human condition, a

---

3. Shakespeare, "Sonnet XCIV," lines 9–14.

stress that links the text firmly back to Jesus' commandment. Any momentary sweetness will exhibit simultaneously the decay that lies in the lilies' roots.[4]

The lilies, then, demonstrate crucial features of a liturgical poetics outlined in the two previous chapters. Specifically, they subvert the promise of a stabilizing, divine presence. Belief in this presence sustains a liturgical poetics, but, at the same time, it invites the denial of hope that deconstructs the text. Any reading that endures the latent decay that awaits the lilies emerges only when the point at which this impending dissolution becomes pronounced, which indicates in turn how the text begins the process of regeneration despite its closure. The lilies, thus considered, convey to the reader the cyclical nature of liturgical hope by virtue of the death towards which the they inevitably progress. This dynamic echoes the necessary displacement that frames the Last Supper's liturgical promise; Jesus' body announces an eschatological presence that his impending death delays indefinitely. The promise that Jesus offers during the Last Supper thus predicates its promissory character on a necessary absence. As a result, the bread and wine become anticipatory gestures that cannot transcend the text's boundary. This latent denial within the promise casts the text (and its liturgical derivatives) into a cyclical rereading that subverts continually the hope it enables. The promise's fulfillment never arrives, a denial that echoes the cyclicality that leads to the lilies' blossoming and decay. In both instances, then, Jesus establishes a liturgical context with an image that anticipates necessarily an eschatological stability and reveals the text's coming failure to experience the presence that has been promised.

The cyclicality that characterizes these images thus emphasizes simultaneously the disruption that defines exile, as well as the anticipated fulfillment of the liturgical promise. Any comfort that the lilies convey must be understood in the context of the instability that characterizes their

---

4. Shakespeare continues this line of thought in the next sonnet: "How sweet and lovely dost thou make the shame, / Which, like a canker in the fragrant rose, / Doth spot the beauty of thy budding name! / O, in what sweets doest thou thy sins enclose!" ("Sonnet XCV," lines 1–4). Though a different flower indicates a different point of emphasis, these lines develop further the inherent dislocation present in "Sonnet XCIV." Whereas the lily symbolizes the fundamental decay that lies beneath an outward beauty, the rose's fragrance recovers the beauty lost in the transition from lily to weed. Importantly, "Sonnet XCV" recalls this beauty in the overtly erotic tone that characterizes the Shakespearean Sonnets and, therefore, establishes a thematic parallel with the liturgical poetics described in the previous chapters. The flower's bud entices the speaker (and, by extension, the reader), both in its fragrance and, of course, its heavy sexual symbolism.

cycle of decay and regeneration. Thus, they are, like Jesus' body, an image that functions ironically, which in turn reiterates the reality to which a liturgical poetics responds: death's finitude. At the same time, however, this stress generates through a necessary instability the anticipation of that which the text lacks. These two modes of discourse recover the underlying realism that gives rise to hope in the first place. As embodied, humans are defined by a latent instability, but the lilies make clear within this unstable condition that death need not be the only point to which the human condition can be oriented. The lilies convey alongside their impending decay the latent capacity for rebirth, when, once considered, calibrates the text to alternative (eschatological) readings.

Shakespeare's Cyclicality and the Pauline Rebirth

These cyclical contours parallel a significant feature of Pauline thought. In his First Letter to the Corinthians, Paul establishes the body as a fulcrum between death and an eschatological rebirth. Significantly, the promise that enables this transition requires death:

> Fool! What you sow does not come to life unless it dies. And as for what you sow, you do not sow the body that is to be, but a bare seed, perhaps of wheat or of some other grain. But God gives it a body as he has chosen, and to each kind of seed its own body. Not all flesh is alike, but there is one flesh for human beings, another for animals, another for birds, and another for fish. There are both heavenly bodies and earthly bodies, but the glory of the heavenly is one thing, and that of the earthly is another.[5]

Paul portrays the body as displaced in its embodied and theological capacities. The former reflects the inescapable death that defines the human condition, while the latter expresses the sinful death that informs Paul's theological matrix. In this second instance, the body constantly experiences a death that sin perpetuates, which, when it occurs, emphasizes humanity's dislocation from God. The actual, bodily death marks the impossibility of the body's eschatological restoration without the liturgical promise Jesus provides, while the sinful death displaces continually the hope that Paul finds in Jesus' resurrection.[6] In both cases, Paul characterizes the body in terms that derive from humanity's Edenic displacement. Consequently, the

5. 1 Cor 15:36–40.

6. See 1 Cor 15:20–28.

body exhibits an error that Paul understands as a specifically theological rupture. This sinful error casts the body into a cyclical death and rebirth, a dynamic that, like the lilies, balances any liturgical hope with the denial of that hope.

For Paul, the body is the locus of humanity's displacement, as well as the mark of the liturgical promise that enables humanity to transcend its death. As Peter Brown argues: "A weak thing in itself, the body was presented as lying in the shadow of a mighty force, the power of *the flesh*: the body's physical frailty, its liability to death and the undeniable penchant of its instincts toward sin served Paul as a synecdoche for the state of humankind pitted against the spirit of God."[7] Importantly, Paul recognizes in his analysis of the body a displacement ground in the Fall and a corrective response to emerges during the Last Supper. The body is the locus of humanity's exile and, therefore, the locus for anticipating an eschatological body that experiences God's eternal presence. Brown notes that Paul "set [the body] firmly in place as a 'temple of the Holy Spirit.' It was a clearly visible locus of order, subject to limits that it was sacrilegious to overstep. It belonged to the Lord."[8] Brown's analysis makes clear, then, how Paul understands the body's paradoxical nature within a specifically liturgical context.

Despite the anticipated eschatological condition that Jesus' body promises, Paul cannot overlook the exilic parameters that define humanity's condition. In contrast to the hope he finds in Jesus' bodily temple, Paul summarizes the disruptive implications that this promise generates within exile: "I die every day! That is as certain, brothers and sisters, as my boasting of you—a boast that I make in Christ Jesus our Lord."[9] The body is in its sinfulness the locus for a repeated theological death as it progresses towards its actual death. The hope that emerges in Paul's reading of the body, then, approximates the cyclical nature that informs "Sonnet XCIV." Any rebirth immediately moves towards a subsequent (sinful) death. Paul hints at this cyclicality when he asks rhetorically: "'Where, O death, is your victory? Where, O death, is your sting?'"[10] Paul can question death's sting in theological terms, but as an embodied (and forever sinful) person, he must die.[11] When Paul affirms that he dies to sin every day, he implicitly affirms

7. Brown, *The Body and Society*, 48.

8. Ibid., 51.

9. 1 Cor 15:31.

10. 1 Cor 15:55.

11. In a quote commonly (though incorrectly) attributed to Shakespeare, the different emphasis becomes apparent: "Death where is thy sting? Love, where is thy glory?"

the unsustainability of the hope he finds in his rebirth from sin. From the moment this rebirth occurs, Paul moves towards death again, which traps him in a cyclicality that undermines his rhetorical challenge to death.

This textual (and theological) instability underscores how Shakespeare reads the Pauline conception of the body; the answer to Paul's question lies in the question's obvious irony. Death's sting is, paradoxically, the question. In "Sonnet LXXVI," Shakespeare makes this point clear: "So all my best is dressing old words new, / Spending again what is already spent; / For as the sun is daily new and old, / So my love still telling what is told."[12] Corporeality is a journey that progresses constantly towards an unavoidable death, which in turn subverts the hope Paul locates in Jesus' bodily temple. Shakespeare will speak of hope, but he also refuses to deny the parameters that demand such hope in the first place. Decay and death retain a sting that all bodies must endure.[13]

Similarly, Shakespeare's lilies in "Sonnet XCIV" indicate the twofold implications that emerge in Jesus' commandment to consider the lilies. First, he stresses humanity's embodied condition—and thus its exile—that demand the liturgical promise his body signals. Second, because of the body's exilic reality, one must acknowledge the temporal implications of this liturgical paradigm. The promise offered projects the body-as-symbol as a spatial consideration beyond the text in temporal terms. Stated differently, anticipating Jesus presence after his death qualifies a specifically spatial image in a temporal, or rather eschatological, capacity. Similarly, during the Last Supper Jesus conveys the promise in a symbolic capacity, but as the basis of an eschatological statement these images require an anticipatory element—a temporal expectation—to imagine the promise's fulfillment.

In "Sonnet VI," Shakespeare dwells on this theme in more elusive language: "Then what could death do if thou shouldst depart, / Leaving thee living in posterity?" (lines 11–12). In a rhetorical capacity similar to Paul's famous address to death, Shakespeare focuses on the separation that death causes. Importantly, this disjunction does not ignore death as a necessary consideration for the embodied speaker (and his lover). At the same time, love counters this dislocation through the extension of the bond between the speaker and the lover to whom the poem is addressed. The effect (and here Shakespeare echoes Paul clearly) is to acknowledge the text's instability and to traverse this condition by recovering a renewed (erotic) desire for the lover.

12. Shakespeare, "Sonnet LXXVI," lines 11–14.

13. See, for example, "Sonnet LXV": "O, how shall summer's honey breath hold out / Against the wreckful siege of battering days, / When rocks impregnable are not so stout, / Nor gates of steel so strong, but time decays?" (lines 5–8).

The promise remains something to be fulfilled at an indeterminate point in the future.[14]

Deconstruction and Ungrounding the Text

A liturgical poetics' cyclicality echoes an important textual claim that underscores much of Derrida's deconstructive writing. Julian Wolfreys summarizes the point well. With Derrida, Wolfreys writes, "One can never *finally* read or claim to have read a text in its entirety. One must continue carefully to read and reread, because the act of reading is always marked by an ever-receding horizon. It is always to come."[15] The text's displacement refuses to sanction a definitive reading. Exile, then, not only provides a metaphor for humanity's condition, when read alongside Derrida it also conveys the foundational textual displacement at the heart of his deconstructive apparatus. Exile implies a return, but within such a condition this locale is necessarily absent. As the reader traverses the text's exilic space, s/he journeys towards this impossible destination. According to Hart: "Derrida's main point is that the condition of possibility of an interpretation is also and at the same time its condition of impossibility for totalising a text."[16] Within a liturgical poetics, totality is both the object of desire and, therefore, that which subverts the text in its entirety. The journey through exile thus mirrors the text's constant shifts; in both cases, this movement frustrates hermeneutical efforts. According to Derrida, "The *representamen* functions only by giving rise to an *interpretant* that itself becomes a sign and so on to infinity. The self-identity of the signified conceals itself unceasingly and is always on the move."[17] When reading the Last Supper through this critical approach, one recognizes the displacement that results inevitably from conceptualizing the text as exilic. Without a stable hermeneutical anchor, the text can only suggest as it conceals, a dynamic that counters the liturgical promise's hopeful tenor.

---

14. Though I discuss both the temporal and spatial implications in this chapter, the analysis that follows will focus primarily on the spatial implications that a Pauline cyclicality generates within a liturgical poetics. To examine fully how temporality functions within a liturgical poetics would require an extensive analysis that the current project cannot offer due to the scope of the particular argument at hand.

15. Wolfreys, *Derrida*, 8.

16. Hart, *The Trespass of the Sign*, 113.

17. Derrida, *Of Grammatology*, 49.

Derrida thus abandons metaphysical stability in favor of an unhinging that, paradoxically, locates any (possible) meaning in displacement. Robert P. Scharlemann suggests that this release can sustain the text despite its instability: "it becomes clear why, despite the connotations of the word *destruction*, this regressive analysis is not intended to wipe out the tradition but to recall what it was about."[18] In clearing away the impossible stability that a metaphysics assumes, Derrida's critical apparatus clarifies what is at stake in the recollection that Scharlemann describes. By establishing his body as a temple to anticipate the liturgical promise's fulfillment, Jesus enables the recovery that Scharlemann identifies. This clarifies, for Scharlemann, an important point: "Forgetting the symbol of the otherness of God is, in this way, a counterpart to forgetting the question of the meaning of being."[19] In questioning the promise's meaning as it emerges and retreats, Scharlemann focuses on the paradoxical character that defines both the capacity in which Jesus' body enables hope, as well as the theological calculus that clarifies what the body indicates, namely that "the otherness of God—God's being God by being other than deity."[20] By reframing the liturgical promise in these terms, Scharlemann thus locates how the body accommodates the open textual meaning(s) that Derrida generates through a deconstructive reading of metaphysics. Scharlemann states: "So the word *God* makes it possible for a subject or an object to be the sign-reality that is God's presence, the otherness that is there in the naming."[21] Jesus' body deconstructs the notion of the temple's stability in favor of the (absent) otherness that Scharlemann describes in naming the divine other. When God is not God, therefore, the symbolic temple becomes the image that enables the text to anticipate God's eventual presence as fully God.

Untethered from hermeneutical stability, a liturgical poetics is thus able to deconstruct the theological restraints that orthodoxy uses to uphold to the metaphysical structures that Derrida challenges. The effect is to displace meaning, but only in its ability to posit a presence that Derrida prohibits by abandoning any textual center. This development reasserts the gap between humanity's exilic condition and its lost originary stability. The text, now devoid of a stabilizing core, enables paradoxically a more intimate way to traverse the space between the lost center and its unstable outer

---

18. Scharlemann, *Inscriptions and Reflections*, 34.

19. Ibid., 40.

20. Ibid.

21. Ibid., 49.

edge. Such familiarity builds on what Gianni Vattimo labels "a rediscovery of the finitude that is constitutive of existence."[22] A renewed emphasis on humanity's exilic condition, which settles in the textual gaps that Derrida opens, constitutes an "ungrounding"[23] that characterizes the liturgical trajectory of both Donne and Dickinson. They do not lose sight of the implied (theological) origin, a presence that their liturgical poetics, ungrounded from orthodox constraint, anticipates. In fact, their willingness to traverse the (non-)space that unfolds once removed from a displaced center actually sharpens their ability to recover the hope that underscores Jesus' promise as articulated from within the text's exilic parameters.

The Derridean Trace and the Liturgical Body

Derrida emphasizes the textual dynamic at play in exile's implied origin through the notion of the trace, which signifies "not only the disappearance of origin—within the discourse that we sustain and according to the path that we follow it means that the origin did not even disappear, that it was never constituted except reciprocally by a no origin, the trace, which thus becomes the origin of the origin."[24] Derrida substitutes for any originary possibility the trace that marks the impossibility of such an origin's textual presence. The trace is thus defined by the origin's absence, which, Derrida explains, "*amounts to saying once again that there is no absolute origin of sense in general. The trace is the difference* which opens appearance [*l'apparaître*] and signification."[25] Derrida's analysis, then, reiterates the text's instability by reminding the reader that what suggests a textual presence is, actually, a mark of absence. This subversive dynamic ensures that the text remains unstable and open to subsequent readings.

According to Derrida, this openness underscores the extent to which a Western metaphysics fails to recognize a deep paradox in its dominant liturgical paradigm. He writes:

> The subordination of the trace to full presence summed up in the logos, the humbling of writing beneath a speech dreaming its plentitude, such are the gestures required by an onto–theology determining the archaeological and eschatological meaning of being

22. Vattimo, *The Adventure of Difference*, 5.

23. Ibid., 4.

24. Derrida, *Of Grammatology*, 61.

25. Ibid., 65.

as presence, as parousia, as life without difference: another name
for death, historical metonymy where God's name holds death in
check . . . Only infinite being can reduce the difference in presence.
In that sense, the name of God, at least as it is pronounced within
classical rationalism, is the name of indifference itself.[26]

The goal described here is consistent with the argument above, but Derrida calls specific attention to the concerns that the notion of exile makes
clear. Jesus' promise to share a future meal with the disciples generates a
textual (and liturgical) instability insofar as his body marks this eschatological possibility only by virtue of announcing his impending absence. The
future (the not-yet) must be anticipated, which exposes the impossibility of
the promise's fulfillment. Jesus' body, then, condenses the implied origin's
impossible presence within the text, which reveals the absence at the heart
of a liturgical poetics. As Hart argues, the sign thus serves to remind the
reader that the text's space is "No longer in harmony with God, [and thus]
this world becomes a chiaroscuro of presence and absence; everywhere one
looks, there are signs of a divine presence that has withdrawn and that reveals itself *only* in those signs."[27] The promise emphasizes that to anticipate
the recovery of an originary presence is to foreground the trace's dislocating influence. As the locus for this textual interplay, moreover, Jesus' body
stresses the total instability that death brings to all textual (and actual)
bodies.

In marking the exilic parameters that confine the text, the trace exhibits an ironic character: it anticipates a presence by calling attention to an
absence. In the specific promise that Jesus offers during the Last Supper, the
body is a trace insofar as it anticipates a specifically eschatological presence
that contrasts directly with death's immanent effect. This crucial displacement subverts the hope that the promise generates. Derrida's trace makes
clear the deconstructive effect that Jesus' body brings to the Last Supper
narrative even as it is the locus for the liturgical promise. The body thus in-
stitutes a textual failure by virtue of the trace's absence. Moreover, this hol-
lowness ensures that the promise's fulfillment must be delayed indefinitely.

26. Ibid., 71.
27. Hart, *The Trespass of the Sign*, 4; my emphasis.

Différance and Liturgical Hope

Much hinges upon a single letter in Derrida's textual analysis. Specifically, the term différance conveys the capacity in which the sign establishes a textual void. In basic terms, Derrida explains that the sign "represents presence in absence."[28] When presence is not possible—and within a liturgical poetics, this is always the case—the sign steps in, but, in so doing, it extends the absence of the thing it signifies. In the wake of this failure to make present what it implies, the sign ensures that: "When we cannot grasp or show the thing, state the present, the being–present, when the present cannot be presented, we signify, we go through the detour of the sign."[29] Read against the Last Supper, Derrida identifies the displacement that Jesus generates when he locates the liturgical promise in his body. The sign's detour becomes the circuitous bypass that deconstructs the text's eschatological trajectory. The promise of a stabilizing destination thus calls attention to the impossibility of reaching this point, which collapses the journey that the sign paradoxically initiates. The sign anticipates a presence that it actively deconstructs in announcing this expectation.[30] Consequently, the image that establishes the promise leaves a contrail as it traverses the text, a trace that reiterates the absent originary presence and, therefore, extends the text's displacement. Stated differently, Jesus' promise to the disciples denies necessarily the stability the promise's fulfillment would bring. Jesus' body, then, is, in Derrida's words: "Always differing and deferring, the trace is never as it is in the presentation of itself. It erases itself in presenting itself, muffles itself in resonating, like the a writing itself, inscribing its pyramid in différance."[31] The irony is that the new, symbolic temple is already destroyed.

The sign's elusive character reiterates the paradoxical identity of any liturgical poetics. When the body extends the liturgical promise, it simultaneously calls attention to the body's destruction, a cessation that thickens the textual and liturgical instability that death establishes. In this sense, any

28. Derrida, *Margins of Philosophy*, 9.

29. Ibid.

30. Similarly, when Jesus commands the crowd to consider the lilies an implicit absence becomes apparent, a shift Shakespeare recognizes clearly in identifying the cyclical decay that marks the lily as bound within death's horizon (see chapter 3).

31. Derrida, *Margins of Philosophy*, 23. Clark offers a helpful clarification on this point: "The instant, which never quite *is* in the sense of being present, becomes thus assimilable to Lyotard's model of a *presentation* that can never be represented without, by the same movement, being effaced or *situated*. Its occurrence is thus never quite *present*" (*Poetics of Singularity*, 57).

liturgical poetics must conclude with a closure. As the Last Supper makes clear, Jesus must cease to be present if his body is to become the new, symbolic temple. At the same time, it is through this closure that the image discloses an eschatological reading, which the sign's absence anticipates as a not-yet presence. According to Wolfreys, this announcement through erasure can emerge only through the displacement that Derrida assigns to the trace: "the very trace of being returning, always in other words, as the attestation of the unbearable circulation of being that the literary makes possible to glimpse."[32] Jesus' body may announce its own death as it stands in for that which is desired[33], but this latent dislocation enables the text to be read as anticipating a stabilizing presence. As with the cyclical dynamic at work in Paul's reflection on the body, the specific textual capacity of the bodily temple is to anticipate and deny the promise's fulfillment. Because différance characterizes the text from the outset, no permanent closure is possible; the implied origin remains absent, but the trace ensures that subsequent readings can anticipate this presence. The cycle starts again with each new reading, during which potential rereadings similarly advance and retreat. This destabilizing effect cements as impossible the promise's fulfillment, but the inverse is that such closure permits a new disclosure, which is precisely the paradox that Jesus' body accomplishes through the absence that death generates.

The bodily cycle of death and rebirth thus provides a second spatial metaphor that functions within a liturgical poetics. Like the exilic metaphor that structures the text's anticipatory journey, the repeated closure and disclosure within a liturgical poetics serves an important deconstructive function. As it revolves along the exilic journey's linear axis, the text's cyclicality intensifies the displacement that prevents a stabilizing presence from materializing. Any momentary glimpse of the fulfilled promise dissolves as the cycle spins. The effect is ironic; it subverts the moment in which the text opens into eschatological readings. Despite its hermeneutical disruption, this liturgical dynamic advances the text insofar as the transition from death to rebirth (and back to death) legitimizes the anticipation that will never be fulfilled. Despite its inevitable dissolution, then, the text's cyclicality sustains the liturgical promise by anticipating anew the not–yet presence that will finally provide stability.

32. Wolfreys, *Derrida*, 140.

33. In Derrida's words, the metaphor "always carries its death within itself" (*Margins of Philosophy*, 271).

In light of the necessary textual instability that his analysis identifies, Derrida cautions against totalizing meaning. Because the text remains open through the trace's interplay (and absence), no hermeneutical conclusions can be firmly established and, furthermore, the textual properties that enforce this prohibition also refuse to rule out alternative readings. According to Derrida, "No one inflection enjoys any absolute privilege, no meaning can be fixed or decided upon. No border is guaranteed, inside or out."[34] Consequently, one cannot speak of a closed text; one can only indicate the point at which a text experiences its closure. This occurs at the moment when the sign's supposed presence is exposed as an absence.[35] As Clark points out, the cyclical nature of the trace within the text limits possible readings. Each reading remains singular, which, he explains, requires that "any interpretation of a text must, in so far as that text is genuinely singular, include within itself the mark of its own finitude."[36] The text must unfold as an exilic space, a precondition that both displaces meaning and obligates the reader to resist claims to pinpoint as much. The implied origin within exile remains the trace, which is itself a trace of the original *différance*.[37] This cyclicality describes the trajectory of a liturgical poetics insofar as the beginning comes only after the end. "Always," Derrida emphasizes, "from the outset, the movement of lost presence already will have set in motion the process of its reappropriation."[38] Even when the symbolic and textual parameters that govern an image demand closure, as is the case with Jesus' body, there always remains the anticipation of a possible presence beyond the sign's erasure.

The Exilic Trace and Liturgical Cyclicality

The trace's effect mirrors humanity's exilic condition, which conceptualizes textual space in a capacity that reiterates displacement insofar as any image exhibits at its core a paradoxical duality. Implied within exile is a return, yet such a return always remains textually impossible, which guarantees that

34. Derrida, "Living On," 64.

35. Hart emphasizes this point: "It is important to recognise that the second claim is not that a sign *does* change its meaning if repeated but that a sign's meaning is always *open* to change" (*The Trespass of the Sign*, 13).

36. Clark, *Poetics of Singularity*, 49.

37. See Hart, *The Trespass of the Sign*, 124ff.

38. Derrida, *Margins of Philosophy*, 72.

the text must endure its instability. There is, in the end, no escape from this cycle. Similarly, the trace, which marks an originary disjunction, reiterates the crucial, stabilizing feature that the text necessarily lacks: a real (textual or liturgical) presence. Derrida emphasizes this point: "Presence, then, far from being, as is commonly thought, *what* the sign signifies, what a trace refers to, presence, then, is the trace of the trace, the trace of the erasure of the trace. Such is, for us, the text of metaphysics, and such is, for us, the language which we speak."[39] The sign that marks the promise also erases the promise, an absence that forces the unavoidable closure that a liturgical poetics must endure. However, the impossible presence that the sign anticipates within a liturgical poetics also holds the text open to a renewed anticipatory reading. Consequently, the sign's failure to establish a presence reiterates that no reading can erase all traces of the implied return that remains implicit in humanity's exilic condition.

Derrida provides a critical apparatus that unhinges texts from stable hermeneutical moorings. The command to consider the lilies, then, is not so simple, for if one undertakes this seriously, one recognizes the displacement that lies where one seeks stability. Shakespeare treats the lilies in full recognition that the promise contained therein will be denied, which recalls the initial disjunction at the bodily temple's (absent) origin.[40] To consider the lilies is to place oneself consciously within exile in full recognition of the parameters that must govern any consequent experience of the text. Shakespeare understands this disruptive reality, which he adapts within "Sonnet XCIV" to invert the ease with which Jesus suggests hope can be found by considering the lilies. In so doing, Shakespeare acknowledges the dislocation that emerges within an endless cycle of hope and denial. As a result of this textual dynamic, vertigo takes hold, which disorients further the endless emergence and erasure of meaning. Despite this condition, however, Derrida demands that one engage the text's space on its own terms: "Wherever one is, one must take responsibility for that. This is what is announced whenever one says 'I.'"[41] This I, who would anticipate the liturgical promise's fulfillment, must traverse, therefore, an "abyssal topography of a being, which always where it is, is nevertheless nowhere

---

39. Ibid., 66.

40. When considering Derrida, one must remember constantly the tension between what appears to be present in the sign and the obvious absence that sign marks. See Jasper, *The Study of Literature and Religion*, 119ff.

41. Quoted in Wolfreys, *Derrida*, 133.

as such, other than in spatio-temporal différance that one can glimpse as having been always already shadowed in those motion-signs of *becoming* and *between*. Thus *one* always becomes other again and again, and this takes place, to reiterate the point, *where one is*."[42] This is the challenge that frames the commandment to consider the lilies. The image emerges out of (and into) a textual nowhere, yet, paradoxically, it remains the conduit through which the text anticipates the not-yet presence that will stabilize the text. This possibility, traced by its own erasure, denies what it suggests. In Derrida's words, "The mode of inscription of such a trace in the text . . . is so unthinkable that it must be described as an erasure of the trace itself. The trace is produced as its own erasure. And it belongs to the trace to erase itself, to elude that which might maintain it in presence. The trace is neither perceptible nor imperceptible."[43] Any anticipated presence is, then, possible only because of its paradoxical character, which recalls and amplifies the dislocation that affects the text (and the human condition). Meaning is only possible—and denied—in the no more that announces a further not-yet, the point at which the image folds back on itself. As Derrida stresses, the only hint of the image's presence is its disappearance.

A Liturgical Poetics as Distinct from Negative Theology

This paradoxical character reiterates humanity's condition as beings-towards-death, a trajectory that Jesus traces in his embodiment. In order to substantiate the liturgical promise that his body symbolizes, he must extend that body towards—and then endure—death's closure. As the liturgical promise's sign, the body thus invites the conclusions that Derrida's analysis produces insofar as it exhibits textually a coextensive presence and absence. In light of this dynamic, a liturgical poetics seems to parallel a negative theology. As Derrida describes it, a negative theology "consists of considering that every predicative language is inadequate to the essence, in truth to the hyperessentiality (the being beyond Being) of God; consequently, only a negative ("apophasis") attribution can claim to approach God, and to prepare us for a silent intuition of God."[44] The apophatic tradition frames the journey towards the divine with the suggestion that language ceases to function when the divine is finally present. In light of this paradigm,

42. Wolfreys, *Derrida*, 139.

43. Derrida, *Margins of Philosophy*, 65.

44. Jacques Derrida, "How to Avoid Speaking: Denials," 74.

Derrida's summary describes the text's inadequate ability to accommodate a divine presence, which stresses the impossibility of that presence within the text.

Understanding the trace as exilic characterizes the text as displaced rather than inadequate. As Derrida points out, the textual instability in question indicates how:

> [the] economy [of a negative theology] is paradoxical. In principle, the apophatic movement of discourse would have to negatively retrievers all the stages of symbolic theology and positive predication. It would thus be coextensive with it, confined to the same quantity of discourse. In itself interminable, the apophatic movement cannot contain within itself the principle of its interruption. It can only indefinitely defer the encounter with its own limit.[45]

The difference between a liturgical poetics and a negative theology lies primarily in the text's displaced character. Whereas a negative theology must retraverse symbolic inadequacy as it journeys towards the invisible core that is God's absence, a liturgical poetics follows a trajectory away from any such hermeneutical marker. In other words, a negative theology turns inward in response to its textual limitations, while a liturgical poetics accepts this boundary by moving towards it at the outset. This reorienting opens the text to the liturgical promise's eschatological fulfillment. Unlike the total absence that characterizes the divine other in a negative theology, a liturgical poetics anticipates a stabilizing divine presence.

The crucial moment wherein the text folds back on itself is, then, the liturgical promise's paradoxical locus. This collapse establishes a threshold that imagines a transcendent condition despite the text's inability to cross this boundary. Amidst the dislocation that defines both the text and humanity's exilic condition, this threshold marks off a momentary space that can orient the text towards stability, even if the consequence of doing so is its own erasure. Herein lies the paradox that is crucial to the body's symbolic capacity in a liturgical poetics; this dynamic clarifies why recognizing and thus consciously working within the parameters that exile imposes is a crucial difference between a negative theology and a liturgical poetics. In "How to Avoid Speaking: Denials," Derrida argues that one must mark off such a moment, even if that moment cannot be sustained: "The place is only a place of passage, and more precisely, a threshold. But a threshold this time, to give access to what is no longer a place. A subordination, a

45. Ibid., 81.

relativization of the place, and an extraordinary consequence; the place of Being. What finds itself reduced to the condition of a threshold is Being itself, Being as a place. Solely a threshold, but a sacred place, the outer sanctuary (*parvis*) of the temple."[46] All texts are predicated on a latent instability. However, it is precisely within this disorienting context that Derrida describes how a threshold materializes. Within exile, the body establishes the threshold wherein Being's erasure opens towards a renewed presence. This is the place of closure, which, in its ironic and inevitable collapse, discloses new readings. The Last Supper's narrative and symbolic logic illustrates this point. Jesus' body, which must be broken, becomes the sign that indicates the moment in which death can be transcended. Through its impending destruction, the body becomes a temple, the place around which people can gather in the midst of their own exilic journeys to anticipate an eschatological arrival at a stabilizing destination.

The Symbolic Body and the Impossibly Possible

In light of Derrida's critical framework as discussed above, the body's particular function within a liturgical poetics derives from its paradoxical nature as a symbolic temple. To state that the body extends a liturgical promise to the point of textual closure is to cast the body as a being-towards-death. This is the irony that permits the body-as-sign to transcend the endless cycle of presence and absence. In *Corpus*, Jean-Luc Nancy provides a helpful summary of what is at stake when considering the body as a symbolic temple:

> The body is the Living Temple—the life as Temple and the temple as Living, the one touching the other as a sacred mystery—only by achieving absolutely the circularity that founds it. It is necessary that sense be embodied, in itself and eternally, for the body to make sense—and reciprocally. Thus, the sense of 'sense' is bodily, and the sense of the 'body' is sensed. Within this circular reabsorption of sense, any established signification is immediately wiped away [. . .]. The body is the organ of sense, that is, the organ (or *organon*), absolutely (can also say here: the system, the community, the communion, the subjectivity, the finality, etc.). The body is, therefore nothing less than the auto-symbolization of the absolute organ. Unnamable as God, never exposed to an exterior understanding . . . unnamable in addition to comprising an intimate texture-of-self

46. Ibid, 121.

towards which every philosophy of the 'body proper' exhausts itself ('what we call the flesh, this internally worked over matter, nameless in any philosophy'—Merleau-Ponty). God, Death, Flesh: the trinity of every onto-theology. The body is an exhaustive combinatory, the common assumption of these three impossible names, before which all signification trembles.[47]

Nancy identifies clearly how the body collapses and sustains the "nexus of these three impossible names: God, Death, and the Living Flesh."[48] Jesus' symbolic body thus enables the "transformation of the divine is neither death nor Life, nor even the figure of God, but rather the incarnation of all three senses of the divine within the sense of the body."[49] Derrida's explanation of the threshold comes into focus in the wake of Nancy's astute analysis. The body provides a threshold wherein different elements can touch one another. By enabling such a touch, the body thus carries the text through its own instability to the point—the liminal threshold[50]—from which the impossible hope becomes possible.[51] Moreover, the point of touching establishes the threshold that relates the text to its eschatological fulfillment while simultaneously upholding the boundary between any such condition and the text's nonnegotiable exilic parameters.

Possibility is a crucial concept within liturgical poetics, a point of emphasis that Derrida draws out in his analysis. To speak of the possible is, paradoxically, to recognize the impossibility that underscores the dynamics at work within the text. Thresholds enable the text to relate to a condition beyond its dislocation: "The identity of *this* place, and hence of *this* text,

47. Quoted in Lambert, "Untouchable," 373–74.

48. Lambert, "Untouchable," 369.

49. Ibid., 370.

50. Liminality is a crucial descriptor of the threshold as Derrida describes it. The term brings disparate elements into proximity while sustaining their originary and necessary *différance*: "A tangent touches a line or a surface but without crossing it, without a true intersection, thus in a kind of impertinent pertinence. It touches only one point, but a point is nothing, that is, a limit without depth or surface, untouchable even by way of a figure" (Derrida, *On Touching*, 131).

51. Derrida describes how the body is able to provide this critical, liminal space within a Western liturgical framework: "all the Gospels present the Christic body not only as a body of light and revelation, but, in a hardly less essential way, as a body *touching* as much as *touched*, as flesh that is touched-touching. Between life and death. And if one refers to the Greek word that translates this touching, which is also a divine power and the manifestation of God incarnate, one can take the Gospels for a *general haptics*. Salvation saves by touching, and the Saviour, namely the Toucher, is also touched: he is saved, safe, unscathed, and free of damage. Touched by grace" (*On Touching*, 99–100).

and of *its* reader, comes from the future of what is promised by the promise. The advent of this future has a provenance, the event of the promise . . . But the place that is thus revealed remains the place of waiting, awaiting the realization of the promise. Then it will take place fully."[52] The body provides such a place within a liturgical poetics; it signals a promise of something that has not come and, moreover, cannot permeate the text's boundary. The body must undergo death, yet as the Last Supper makes clear, this same image symbolizes the promise that death will be transcended.

The event—in this case the images of bread and wine which set forth and break down the liturgical promise they convey—anticipates what cannot be present within the text. Even though the promise's fulfillment is, therefore, delayed indefinitely, the notion of impossibility does not prohibit the anticipation of such a fulfillment. Kearney clarifies what is at stake in this Derridean paradox: "For an event is only possible in so far as it comes from the impossible. An event (*événement*) can only happen, in other words, when and where the 'perhaps' lifts all presumptions and assurances what might be and lets the future come as future (*lassie l'avenir à l'avenir*), that is, as the arrival of the impossible."[53] By accepting instability—that is, by accepting the textually impossible presence that the body signals— a liturgical poetics anticipates a presence that through its latent dislocated condition orients the text towards an eschatological stability. Kearney continues: "The 'perhaps' thus solicits a 'yes' to what is still to come, beyond all plans, programs, and predictions. It keeps the ontological question of 'to be or not to be' constantly in question, on its toes, deferring any last word on the matter."[54] During the Last Supper, the body announces a promise that cannot be fulfilled, yet at the same time this body establishes a threshold wherein a fulfilling presence can be anticipated. In order to do so, as Kearney recognizes, the impossible must remain impossible, which is to say it must remain a promise that has yet to come. Such impossibilities, then, open the text to future rereadings, which in turn sustain the promise through its denial.

52. Derrida, "How to Avoid Speaking: Denials," 117–18.

53. Kearney, "Deconstruction, God, and the Possible," 298–99. See also Kearney, *The God Who May Be*, 93–99.

54. Kearney, "Deconstruction, God, and the Possible," 299.

The Metaphor of the Body:
Both What Is and What Is Not

Within a liturgical poetics, the image of the body stresses the text's exilic parameters.[55] Like Heidegger's temple, the metaphor's function is not to cement meaning, but, rather, to suggest a recognizable pattern that Paul Ricoeur calls an "event of discourse."[56] Even though it is "fleeting and transitory," the event "can be identified and reidentified as 'the same.'"[57] The cyclicality that resists fulfillment in a liturgical context exhibits a textual rhythm that despite its fleeting nature enables a familiarity with the dynamics that ultimately subvert the text. Ricoeur is clear in labeling the metaphor[58] as an event that the reader cannot override the underlying textual instability at hand: "the trouble created is as great as the advantages gained . . . For a word to have more than one meaning is, strictly speaking, a synchronistic—

55. Graham Ward summarizes well how the metaphor's properties induce the reader to enter willingly into a displaced space. Because they remain open, Ward argues, metaphors: "do not fix meaning and so they cannot, therefore, become the object of idolatry. Their inherent instability of reference keeps meaning open, tentative and iconoclastic. They articulate and generate a surplus of meaning. By calling for interpretation, metaphors draw the reader into an engagement with the world they configure" (*Theology and Contemporary Critical Theory*, 8). The paradox, then, characterizes how the text unfolds. Significantly, this process resists the notion of textual stability; meaning must arise within and through dislocation. Ward thus calls attention to the metaphor's pivotal role within a poetics, as it must, in Janet Martin Soskice's words, remain "extendable" in meaning (*Metaphor and Religious Language*, 94). This extension belies the openness that frustrates the reader as s/he is drawn into the text's disorienting space. Though Soskice rightly identifies the notion of extendibility as crucial to a metaphor's function, her analysis focuses too heavily on the metaphor's role in "disclosing" new meaning (*Metaphor and Language*, 89). She does not discuss fully how the implications of extendibility follows a necessary textual closure. The point is not that we can "say very little" (96) because of the extended plurality of meanings but, rather, that the dislocation that marks any meaning enables us to say both everything and nothing. On this point, see Ricoeur, *The Rule of Metaphor*, 112ff.

56. Ricoeur, *The Rule of Metaphor*, 80.

57. Ibid.

58. Ricoeur provides a broad range of constituent textual parts in his analysis: "one must begin with this point: an entire statement constitutes the metaphor, yet attention focuses on a particular word, the presence of which constitutes the grounds for considering the statement metaphorical" (*The Rule of Metaphor*, 97). Insofar as Ricoeur recognizes that the displaced effects discussed below function at various levels throughout the text, I equate the notion of metaphor and the label of image. Both terms capture the basic textual feature that Ricoeur analyzes and, moreover, the destabilizing effects that this concept produces are apparent at different textual strata.

it is *now*, in the code, that it signifies several things."[59] The metaphor functions in a way that necessarily displaces meaning, a deconstruction that counters the simultaneous absence and presence that the metaphor announces. This (paradoxical) binary marks the event of discourse, which due to its latent instability constitutes an openness that resists hermeneutical clarity.[60] Moreover, the specific metaphor at hand does not fix a textual presence. Rather, it signals possible meanings, none of which can withstand the text's latent instability.

Ricoeur's analysis of the metaphor converges on the same internal difference that characterizes Derrida's deconstructive apparatus. The stability that an originary presence implies ultimately exposes through its absence the text's dislocation. In discussing how metaphors emerge, Ricoeur indicates this destabilizing paradigm: "[a metaphor's] displaced meaning comes from somewhere else; it is always possible to specify the metaphor's place of origin, or of borrowing."[61] By locating part of a metaphor's meaning beyond the text, Ricoeur highlights how the metaphor functions. It initiates the deconstructive process that makes clear an important textual feature: any implied origin is already a borrowing. The metaphor by definition signals something other than itself; in fact, the metaphor is "doubly alien."[62] All presence is borrowed and, therefore, not actually present.[63] Any familiarity with a particular metaphor ultimately focuses attention on the further displacement that it produces. Metaphors that imply stability turn out to be examples of the text's inherent instability.

In the context of the argument at hand, Ricoeur's analysis emphasizes how the text displacement characterizes the human condition. Inside the text's boundaries, the metaphor suggests a familiarity that both is and is not; the presence implied ultimately indicates a textual absence. Ricoeur summarizes this point clearly:

---

59. Ricoeur, *The Rule of Metaphor*, 142. I bracket the term event from many of the associations that this term invites in contemporary Continental Philosophy. In the present argument, the term event indicates the appearance of a metaphor (the image) that initiates the destabilizing effect of describing the signifying present as absent. For more on this point, see Ricoeur, *The Rule of Metaphor*, 148.

60. Kearney, *On Paul Ricoeur*, 8.

61. Ibid., 20.

62. Ibid.

63. Ibid.

[this] critique only helps us to recognize the assumptions and commitments of one who speaks and uses the very *to be* metaphorically. At the same time, it underlines the inescapably paradoxical character surrounding a metaphorical concept of truth. The paradox consists in the fact there there [sic] is no other way to do justice to the notion of metaphorical truth than to include the critical incision of the (literal) "is not" within the ontological vehemence of the (metaphorical) "is."[64]

Ricoeur's caution parallels a liturgical poetics' instability. Anchored in a body, the liturgical promise lays bare humanity's exilic condition as beings-towards-death. The bread and wine anticipate the promise's fulfillment beyond the text, a delay that stresses from the outset the disruptive function that all metaphors bring to the text. The bread and wine, then, identify but never provide the promise's fulfillment by virtue of marking a textual absence.[65] Through the metaphor's borrowing the promise remains a not-yet, a crucial feature of a liturgical poetics that the bread and wine reveal.

Having discussed these salient concerns, it is time to reconsider yet again the lilies in order to recognize how the textual instability described above affects specifically a liturgical poetics. Metaphors generate possible readings, which, for Derrida, push the text towards the threshold that marks an outer limit:

The imagination attains a limit, reaches a shore whither it can *come only in not coming about*. It thus tends toward that which it can only *hold out to itself without giving itself to hold*, and still without touching; whereby it becomes what it is by essence, imagination, possibility of the impossible, possibility without power, possibility auto-affecting its essence of a nonessence. It is not what it is—the imagination. It is touched, in a movement of withdrawing or retreating to the fold, at the moment it touches the untouchable. The imagination confines without confining itself to itself.[66]

The imagination recognizes the importance of thresholds, which mark the limit to which the author can extend the text. J. Hillis Miller adapts the image of the shore in a way that clarifies the above passage from Derrida: "At the edges, the text collides with that which lies beyond like two

64. Ricoeur, *The Rule of Metaphor*, 302.

65. This displacing effect parallels significantly the theological debates concerning the Eucharist during the Reformation. I discuss the specific relevance of this point in my analysis of Donne (see chapter 4).

66. Derrida, *On Touching*, 106.

thunderclouds colliding in a narrow valley, or like a great wave crashing on the shore. This annihilation, nevertheless, is not complete since the violent collision leaves always a trace, a remnant, foam on the shore."[67] The metaphor stains the text, a rem(a)inder of the now absent presence that it indicates. The trace—the foam—attests to both to the text's crucial absence and the hope that despite its immediate dissolution the image can anticipate a future presence. Derrida emphasizes that the reader must accept the impossibility of any such presence, as the image marks the point at which the text folds back on itself. The liturgical promise located in the bread and wine announces, then, both Jesus' impending death and the indefinite delay that death will bring to bear on the promise's fulfillment.

Emily Dickinson's Specific Reading of the Lilies

Derrida helps to clarify what, precisely, constitutes a liturgical poetics. The need to accept that the text must deny necessarily what it desires suggests how texts anticipate the liturgical promise's fulfillment. Specifically, the parameters discussed in the first part of this chapter distinguish poets such as Donne and Dickinson, who develop a liturgical poetics, from the non-liturgical Romantic Movement, which constitutes the primary literary epoch that separates Donne and Dickinson. As an immediate successor to Shakespeare, Donne was certainly aware of Shakespeare's poetry.[68] Donne draws upon the cyclical imagery that Shakespeare develops. Similarly, Dickinson recognizes the significance of poetic displacement and, in a lineage that reaches around the Romantics and back to Donne, she extends the implications of exile to the very edge that Derrida describes.[69] The com-

67. Miller, "The Critic as Host," 191.

68. Frances Austin asserts that Donne's work is very much grounded in Elizabethan language and ideas (*The Language of the Metaphysical Poets,* 6), but Donne departs from Shakespeare with a particular emphasis on "intimate language" (30). As I will discuss in the following chapter, Donne's intimate texts recover from the Last Supper the body's significance for a liturgical poetics. This move situates his writing within a more overtly "physical" (*The Language of the Metaphysical Poets*, 39), which is to say bodily, textual space.

69. It is important to note that Dickinson, like Donne, read Shakespeare extensively. In fact, concerning Shakespeare, she was uncharacteristically direct. According to Páraic Finnerty, Dickinson purposefully emphasized Shakespeare's significance: "[she] made her devotion to Shakespeare very clear—as if it were something she wanted her contemporaries, and perhaps posterity, to know about her" (*Emily Dickinson's Shakespeare*, 3). For an extensive analysis of how Shakespeare influenced Dickinson, see Finnerty, *Emily Dickinson's Shakespeare*, 95–139.

mon denominator between each of these authors is the willingness to situate their respective writings within the exilic displacement that predicates a liturgical poetics.

This project will thus reconsider the lilies. Jesus' command clearly struck a cord with Dickinson, who, near the end of her life in 1884, told Mrs. Frederick Tuckerman: "the only commandment I ever obeyed—'Consider the lilies.'"[70] That Dickinson identified with this commandment should not surprise; in her writing, flowers frequently symbolized "the eternal."[71] Dickinson recognizes clearly what is at stake in Jesus' commandment and she situates her writing within the lilies' cyclical displacement. In so doing, she recognizes the inevitable death and regeneration that characterize the lilies and, therefore, she anticipates a renewed hope to counter the dislocation that otherwise collapses the text. Paradoxically, then, Dickinson captures the displacement that defines the flower's cyclical existence when she affirms so clearly the commandment to consider the lilies.[72]

In addition to exhibiting a latent instability, the lilies also suggest how to respond to death. When read as personified, the lilies exhibit an important quality that counters their condition: they endure their displacement. The ability to undergo repeatedly the oscillation between death and rebirth indicates how to respond to a liturgical poetics' necessary denial. As Dickinson realizes, the lilies capture both the closure that death brings and how this decay initiates the text's eschatological disclosure. Through their endurance, then, the lilies accomplish the extension of the liturgical promise in the face of the text's (and humanity's) exilic dislocation. While humanity does not, of course, regenerate in the same capacity of the lilies, when read through the Pauline framework discussed above, the lilies enable Dickinson (and her readers) to anticipate within a liturgical poetics' exile the promise's fulfillment.

In J1047 ("The Opening and the Close"), Dickinson outlines these specific implications. In so doing, she indicates how she understands the displacement that defines Jesus' commandment:

---

70. L904.

71. Farr, *The Gardens of Emily Dickinson*, 23.

72. Dickinson would certainly have been aware that lilies are perennials and thus would be fully aware of the lily's annual cycle through life, death, and rebirth.

The Opening and the Close
Of Being, are alike
Or differ, if they do,
As Bloom upon a Stalk.

That from an equal Seed
Unto an equal Bud
Go parallel, perfected
In that they have decayed.[73]

From the outset, this poem exhibits a strong sense of dislocation, which casts the specific image of a flower into the paradoxical nature of a liturgical poetics' cyclicality. Dickinson conflates two significant coordinates— the opening and the close—to elide the space between birth and death. Even that which distinguishes one possible point from another bleeds into a singular image: the flower, which signifies the dislocation that the text cannot escape. More simply, the flower's character establishes this poem as distinctly exilic. This textual dynamic recalls the lilies that on the surface afford hope insofar as they signal God's care for the world.[74] In Dickinson's conception, however, the text cannot sustain this hope. She punctuates the final stanza with that which awaits all flowers (and all people): death. The moment-towards-death, will, of course, reappear with each subsequent rereading, which emphasizes how the lilies' cyclicality prohibits textual stability. At the same time, Dickinson recognizes that this repeated anticipation and erasure prohibits the text from concluding definitively with the flower's death. The poem's final decay bends the text back to the initial opening and, therefore, balances the flower's inevitable death with a reliable counterweight: the lilies' rebirth.

The capacity in which Dickinson deploys the image of the flower in J1047 mirrors the Pauline cycle outlined in 1 Corinthians 15. In a letter to her childhood friend, Abiah Root, Dickinson indicates that she is aware from early in her writing of the symbolic possibilities within the lilies' lifecycle. As she reflects upon a friendship that has grown distant, Dickinson recalls the flower's cyclical nature to express hope: "Abby, I often see, oftener than at sometimes when friendship drooped a little. Did you ever know that a flower once withered and freshened again, became an

73. J1047, lines 1–8.

74. According to Farr, Dickinson "saw in the garden, with its cycle of birth, decay, death, and rebirth, an idea that rendered heaven plausible" (*The Gardens of Emily Dickinson*, 93).

immortal flower—that is, that it rises again? I think resurrections here are sweeter, if may be, than the longer and lasting one—for you expect the one, and only hope for the other."[75] Dickinson's injects a subtle duality into the trope of the flower in a way that emphasizes the interpretive challenges and opportunities that emerge as a result of an image's latent instability. Her language draws her friend into an intimate proximity in order to reflect on the possibility that still exists for their friendship's rebirth, despite the distance that prompts Dickinson to send the letter. In speaking about this strained friendship, Dickinson clearly expresses hope for reconciliation, but she also recognizes that this hope can only be voiced out of a dislocated context. The flower, which stands for their friendship, will, if "freshened again," produce an even stronger bond than before. The risk, of course, remains that the friendship/flower may be mortally damaged, which would in turn disrupt the cyclicality that enables a rebirth after death. Despite the optimism in her letter, then, Dickinson admits explicitly this other possibility. Though she will hope for a rebirth, she knows that a drooping flower indicates a sickness from which the flower may not be able to recover.[76]

In her letter to Abiah Root, then, Dickinson condenses the commandment to consider the lilies and the salient features of a liturgical poetics to indicate the importance of endurance given humanity's exilic condition. The lilies suggest in this case how humanity's displacement reveals the underlying dynamics that govern a liturgical poetics. They orient the text towards the uncertainty that defines any embodied experience, be it a waning friendship or death's finitude. Regardless of the particulars, the point that Dickinson conveys to her friend is the capacity of a liturgical poetics not only to anticipate a coming (eschatological) rebirth, but also the need to recognize in the lilies' endurance a liturgical poetics' nascent communal implications. The lilies are the temple that provides a gathering point, which, once considered in its liturgical capacity, speaks to the exilic condition that the two friends share. Dickinson's letter, then, outlines the development of the community that grows out of the lilies' cycle of death and rebirth. When considering these lilies, Dickinson thus makes clear to

75. L91.

76. Elsewhere, Dickinson elaborates on the flower's symbolic possibility contained with the cyclical balance between hope and denial. See, for example, J339 ("I tend my flowers for thee—"), which similarly utilizes the image of a flower to convey desire for an absent other.

her friend that they share the dislocation of a fading relationship, which, if endured, can open into a birth.[77]

Dickinson incorporates the lilies in a capacity that exhibits the features that Derrida ascribes to the trace.[78] She recognizes the duality of rebirth and death, which underscores the displacement that such images generate. Elsewhere, Dickinson speaks to the absence that marks a former presence, a clear example the Derridean trace. For example, in J1202 ("The Frost was never seen—") Dickinson deploys the image of a flower in a different capacity. Here, the flower does not symbolize a Pauline possibility within the cycle of death and rebirth; rather, it reveals the constant threat with which death haunts life. Importantly, in J1202 death's effects emerge only through the consequences that follow its departure from the text; its now absent presence is recognizable in the trace its leaves on the flowers: "The Frost was never seen— / If met, too rapid passed."[79] The crucial moment in which death arrives cannot be contained within the text, but, like the foam on the shore, the rem(a)inder of such a passed presence is distinct: "The Garden gets the only shot / That never could be traced."[80] The frost recalls death insofar as it reminds the reader that the hope promised in a flower's rebirth remains subject to the fate that all flowers (and all humans) must contend with; death can subvert the flower's (liturgical) rebirth at any moment. Significantly, efforts to identify this disruptive presence in the text will fail, a task that is, Dickinson emphasizes, "Our Vigilance at waste."[81]

The frost (as a trace) disrupts and establishes the text's crucial presence-as-absence in a way that emphasizes the textual instability that this image causes. In the wake of death, marked (absently) by the frost,

---

77. In this project's conclusion I discuss the development of the liturgical community in more depth. However, in keeping with the methodological decisions vis-à-vis the project's literary character, I limit this discussion to the faint outlines that emerge within a liturgical poetics and avoid, therefore, an extensive theological reflection on the nature of the community.

78. Cristanne Miller states directly the extent to which Dickinson's poetry anticipates the critical apparatus that Derrida articulates. According to Miller, "Dickinson's use of 'Difference' here and in "There's a certain Slant of light" [J258] uncannily anticipates Jacques Derrida's idea of *différance* and of negative deconstructive interpretation. Using Derrida's language, one might say of Dickinson's poems generally and of these poems in particular that they do not acknowledge a center of meaning" (*Emily Dickinson*, 102).

79. J1202, lines 1–2.

80. Ibid, lines 11–12. The frost's effect on the flower forms the basis of J1624 ("Apparently, with no surprise,"), which I discuss in chapter 5.

81. J1202, line 10.

"Unproved is much we know— / Unknown the worst we fear— / Of Strangers is the Earth the Inn / Of Secrets is the Air—."[82] Unlike the letter to her friend, here Dickinson calls attention to the difficulty of finding one's way through a text wherein death subverts the images that anticipate regeneration. This is the dislocation that marks humanity's exilic condition, a point of emphasis that Dickinson reiterates in the poem's conclusion: "To analyze perhaps / A Philip would prefer / But Labor vaster than myself / I find it to infer."[83] To make sense of humanity's exile and the implications conveyed through this image constitutes an impossible task. Through her reference to Philip, Dickinson emphasizes the text's dislocation. As Jesus describes his impending departure in John's gospel, Philip demands that Jesus clarify his obscure words: "Philip said to him, 'Lord, show us the Father, and we will be satisfied.'"[84] The request emerges within a context that refuses answers, a condition, a textual gap that characterizes both the capacity in which Jesus speaks to his disciples, as well as the dislocation that the frost causes in J1202. Philip searches for clarity in a condition wherein any answer is impossible.[85] Dickinson sympathizes with such a desire, but she admits and accepts that such a Labor is beyond her capacity. Instead she, like her readers, must accept the paradox that characterizes a liturgical poetics. The speaker cannot ignore the frost's trace; the frosted flowers speak to death's effect. J1202, then, recalls the liturgical paradigm established in the Last Supper. The broken body establishes a promise that rebirth may yet be possible, but this disclosure emerges only through the closure that death brings to the text.

Differentiating Emily Dickinson from Romanticism

The frost in J1202 provides a helpful point to clarify what distinguishes Dickinson (and a liturgical poetics in general) from Romanticism. By frequently situating her poems within the unstable cycle of death and rebirth, Dickinson locates hope in the liturgical promise's fulfillment alongside a corresponding denial. This disjunction complicates a reading of Dickinson

82. Ibid, lines 13–16.

83. Ibid, lines 19–20.

84. John 14:8.

85. Jesus replies to Philip in a way that emphasizes this point: "Jesus said to him, 'Have I been with you all this time, Philip, and you still do not know me? Whoever has seen me has seen the Father. How can you say, "Show us the Father"?' (John 14:9).

that seeks to align her with the Romantic suggestion that the text grants access to a transcendent, stabilizing truth. As Dickinson makes clear, no grounding center is possible because of humanity's exilic condition; the text remains, always, an unstable space, antecedently devoid of what the Romantic Movement pursues. The very nature of Dickinson's liturgical poetics frustrates through its oscillations any stabilizing textual presence; the quest for a center runs strongly against the grain of the text's (and humanity's) latent dislocation. As such, within the text's exilic parameters, Dickinson is clear that a return to stability can only be implied; it can never be realized within any text because exile always refuses the presence of an originary stability. Having established this definitive quality of Dickinson's liturgical poetics, a brief analysis of Romantic poets who parallel Dickinson to some degree will clarify why Romanticism does not cohere with her literary and theological concerns.[86]

The frost in J1202 offers a helpful starting point to distinguish Dickinson from the Romantics, a link that Joanne Feit Diehl establishes in *Dickinson and the Romantic Imagination*. Specifically, Diehl argues persuasively that in J1202, Dickinson responds directly to Coleridge's "Frost at Midnight."[87] From the outset,[88] one can detect a significantly different tone in the way Coleridge characterizes frost. Unlike Dickinson, Coleridge reflects quietly on the frost's presence:

> Only that film, which fluttered on the grate,
> Still flutters there, the sole unquiet thing.
> Methinks its motion in this hush of nature
> Gives it dim sympathies with me who live,
> Making it a companionable form,[89]

---

86. As Diehl states succinctly, a clear difference in approach marks the break between Dickinson and Emerson, her immediate precursor, as well as the broader Romantic tradition. Speaking to the difference between Emerson and Dickinson, Diehl writes: "Whereas Emerson extols the power of the Eye, Dickinson is more absorbed but what she cannot see" (*Dickinson and the Romantic Imagination*, 10). This distinction will become apparent in the analysis that follows.

87. See Diehl, *Dickinson and the Romantic Imagination*, 51ff.

88. Lines 1–2 of "Frost at Midnight" establish a serene frame for the rest of the poem: "The frost performs its secret ministry, / Unhelped by any wind" (Coleridge). Whereas Dickinson's frost is already absent from the text, Coleridge permits his speaker to experience the frost's presence within the text.

89. Coleridge, "Frost at Midnight," lines 14–18.

To some degree, Coleridge's frost suggests humanity's exile; it marks a liminal space that obscures some hidden secret.[90] Despite these similarities, however, Coleridge does not utilize the frost to anticipate a stabilizing presence. Whereas Dickinson's frost announces a displacement, Coleridge's frost establishes a transcendent presence—a companionable form—within the text. More simply, Coleridge's frost stabilizes the text. George P. Landow helps to clarify the distinction between Coleridge and Dickinson's liturgical characterization of the frost: "the interchange between his mind and nature constitutes the entire poem, which usually poses and resolves a spiritual crisis."[91] For Coleridge, the frost resolves the speaker's spiritual crisis through a presence that in Dickinson's poem is wholly untenable.[92] For her, the frost marks an absence that unsettles the spiritual mind. The displacement that the frost causes in J1202 is, then, noticeably absent from Coleridge's "Frost at Midnight."

For Coleridge, the frost indicates a broader, natural transcendence to which the text grants access. The frost's revelation suggests a stable core that Dickinson's own theological understanding of humanity's displacement cannot allow. Whereas Coleridge affirms the text's ability to usher the reader into a natural, transcendent, and stabilizing condition, Dickinson is equally direct in denying any stability within the text. This denial locates her within the Last Supper's legacy; the text can only accommodate the denial of what must be a distinctly eschatological condition. Herein lies another key difference between Dickinson and Coleridge. The latter's transcendent reading of nature is by virtue of its accessibility still ground in the material, embodied experience.[93] Dickinson, on the other hand, recognizes

90. "'Tis calm indeed! so calm, that it disturbs / And vexes meditation with its strange / And extreme silentness. Sea, hill, and wood, / With all the numberless goings–on of life, / Inaudible as dreams!" (Coleridge, "Frost at Midnight", lines 8–12).

91. Landow, *Victorian Types, Victorian Shadows*, 221.

92. Diehl summarizes well how the frost differentiates the two poets. For Coleridge, the frost is "a productive benign, natural force, [which] pursues its religious task of forming icicles in silence. Dickinson responds: the frost evades one's attempt to view it; its presence is witnessed only by what it destroys" (*Dickinson and the Romantic Imagination*, 52). Though Diehl does not extend her analysis to address the concerns that emerge when evaluating the difference between Dickinson and Coleridge through Derrida's critical apparatus, she rightly states the effect of this analysis: "'A stranger in a strange land,' [Dickinson] is left only with the results of a nature she can neither pursue nor comprehend" (53).

93. Coleridge's reading of nature must be situated in the context of his broader intellectual interests, as well as the context in which he pursued his role as a philosophical

this condition as that which separates humanity from the eschatological fulfillment of the liturgical promise's anticipated transcendence. Whereas the frost for Coleridge reveals a divine truth to the speaker, for Dickinson the image reiterates the displacement that prohibits the text from accommodating any stabilizing presence. Coleridge permits a transcendent reading that for Dickinson can only be anticipated by virtue of the displacement that the frost marks, which in turn demands that the text anticipate that which Coleridge readily incorporates into "Frost at Midnight." Dickinson, then (like Donne before her), conceptualizes the relationship between the text and the transcendent in a liturgical capacity that retains the basic parameters of the Last Supper narrative. Her refusal to engage in the easy access to a stability that surpasses the speaker's embodiment reflects an

---

poet (see McFarland, *Coleridge and the Pantheist Tradition*, xxiii–xl). Jasper offers a helpful summary of the capacity in which Coleridge's poetry addressed specifically religious concerns: "The Poet's task is a religious one. Poetic inspiration lays upon him the prophetic burden of mediating divine revelations to mankind. Coleridge's vocations as poet and theologian are therefore inseparable, and each is regulated by the discipline of the critic and the philosopher" (Jasper, *Coleridge as Poet and Religious Thinker*, 19). This portrait highlights both the similarities and differences between Coleridge and Dickinson. On the one hand, both explore through writing the interchange between humanity's condition and the notion of a divine presence. In the context of the point at hand, it is important to emphasize the critical approach that Jasper ascribes to Coleridge insofar as this background unhinges Coleridge from the more orthodox theological sympathies that inform Dickinson's liturgical poetics (the same distinction applies to Donne as well).

In light of this distinction, it is helpful to mention McFarland's study of how Coleridge relates to the Pantheist tradition. Specifically, McFarland explains: "for pantheism, all things are conceived as really one . . . [and] there is no reason to prefer one to the other, or for aligning or arranging them in any special way, or for regarding any existing alignment as more than temporary and advantageous" (*Coleridge and the Pantheist Tradition*, 275). Though Coleridge was not, strictly speaking, a pantheist (*Coleridge and the Pantheist Tradition*, 127ff.), he converged in his Romantic understanding of the natural world—a fact evident in "Frost at Midnight"—on a pantheist mindset. According to McFarland, "for pantheism either matter is conceived as an appearance of spirit, or spirit as an extension of matter" (275). In the present discussion, this intellectual parallel refines the distinction I am making between Dickinson and Coleridge. The extent to which the natural world and a spiritual plane can overlap indicates the crucial difference between Dickinson and her Romantic predecessors. Unlike Coleridge, who permits the natural world and a universalizing spirituality to comingle, Dickinson is rigid in her separation of the natural (i.e., human) condition as thoroughly exilic and the eschatological presence that her theological mind anticipates. Crucially, she does not accept that the natural world can provide a point of entry into a transcendent alternative to humanity's displacement. Theologically, this is clear; as embodied, Jesus must die, which projects the fulfillment of the liturgical promise beyond any natural (or textual) anticipation of the stability implied therein.

understanding of the human condition that departs from the Romantic legacy. She retains the Last Supper's basic structure vis-à-vis humanity's dislocation from God and, therefore, the basic liturgical calculus that Jesus enables through the promise he locates in his body.[94] Dickinson's specific conceptions of how the text speaks to humanity's condition filters through the text's exilic parameters, a framework that excludes necessarily the revelation that Coleridge suggests in "Frost at Midnight."

This discrepancy appears more forcefully near the end of "Frost at Midnight." As the speaker ponders the frost, s/he speaks to the sleeping child in language that makes clear the notion of exile does not predicate the text. Though the speaker acknowledges that the child "shalt wander like a breeze / By lakes and sandy shores, beneath the crags / Of ancient mountain, and beneath the clouds,"[95] such wandering traverses a space structured by the assurance of reaching a destination. The child will encounter *within* its wandering: "The lovely shapes and sounds intelligible / Of that eternal language, which thy God / Utters, who from eternity doth teach / Himself in all, and all things in himself."[96] Nature reveals a truth that stabilizes the journey. This spiritual clarity—accessed through the natural world—is a hallmark of the Romantic vision and it is this characteristic that distances Dickinson from Romanticism. Coleridge recalibrates the natural world in a way that glosses over the dislocation that Dickinson takes as given. As the defining characteristic of the human condition, the world's exile is the problem; it cannot, as Coleridge suggests, provide the spiritual insight that

---

94. The consistency with which Donne and Dickinson keep intact the basic parameters of the Last Supper's theological framework reveals that despite their deconstructive readings of orthodoxy, they never depart completely from the foundation of an orthodox liturgical paradigm. According to Dom Gregory Dix, the Last Supper narrative inaugurates a liturgical framework "the underlying structure is always the same, and this standard structure or Shape alone embodies and expresses the full and complete Eucharistic action for all churches and all races and all times" (*The Shape of the Liturgy*, xii). Dix adds that the term liturgy "covers generally all that worship which is officially organised by the church and which is open to and offered by, or in the name of, all who are members of the church" (*The Shape of the Liturgy*, 1). Dickinson (like Donne before her) falls within this inclusive reading of the basic liturgical paradigm that emerges from the Last Supper. She would disagree with Dix's stress on the institutional organization of this tradition insofar as her liturgical poetics, like Donne's, seek to expand the limited (and limiting) institutional readings of the initial narrative. However, she never abandons the underlying structure that Dix identifies and, therefore, she remains on some level committed to the orthodox tradition that she deconstructs (the same can be said, of course, about Donne).

95. Coleridge, "Frost at Midnight," lines 54–56.

96. Ibid, lines 60–63.

the child can grasp. Coleridge violates, then, the hermeneutical limits that frame the text and, therefore, glosses over death as the crucial feature of the natural world that informs Dickinson's liturgical poetics.

The frost, then, calls attention to the deeper theoretical (and theological) divide between Dickinson and the Romantics. In *"Kubla Khan" and The Fall of Jerusalem: The Mythological School in Biblical Criticism and Secular Literature 1770–1880*, E. S. Shaffer articulates well the concerns that inform Coleridge's writing, which in turn clarifies further the distinctions between Dickinson and the Romantics. Beginning with Milton, Shaffer identifies a search for a cohesive poetic narrative that provides an idyll, a unified—or, at the very least, unifying—core. She writes: "Even major epics, major in length, scope, and intention, tended to have an idyllic core. Schiller spoke of idyll as one of the most characteristic forms of modern poetry, praising Milton's depiction of Adam and Eve as the finest example of it. Its excellence depending not simply on 'primaeval communion with the springs of Being', but on suggesting the progress, refinement, and end of Being as well."[97] The initial displacement develops into the pursuit of the stabilizing idyll, a literary goal that the Romantics recalibrate in a nontheological capacity. Consequently, the posited idyll differentiates the Romantic text from the tradition of a liturgical poetics, which maintains from the outset the impossibility of an idyll by virtue of the text's latent dislocation.[98] The result for Coleridge, Shaffer suggests, is to pursue an idyll that transcends historic and religious particulars: "Instead of standing in the deist manner for all forms of mystification that obscure the simple, natural, and universal content of Christianity, the Mystery is a fully developed rite that acts as an historical synthesis of paganism and Christianity, and supplies the dramatic expression of the meaning of 'tautegory.'"[99] Contrary to a liturgical poetics, Coleridge's condensation softens both the exilic conditions that define

---

97. E.S. Shaffer, *"Kubla Khan" and The Fall of Jerusalem*, 96.

98. In discussing Coleridge's "Oberon," Shaffer articulates clearly how displacement does not totalize the text within this Romantic quest for unity: ""Eden is never wholly lost in this poem—that is the reward of Noah—but as the Deluge comes, Eden perforce takes new forms" (*"Kubla Khan" and The Fall of Jerusalem*, 113). A liturgical poetics recognizes the absolute break from Eden that is presupposed within the Judeo-Christian creation narrative. This initial displacement structures subsequent narratives insofar as it demands a textual closure as the point at which the text can open towards—but never encounter—the kind of stability that an idyll brings.

99. Shaffer, *"Kubla Khan" and The Fall of* Jerusalem, 149.

humanity's condition as beings-towards-death, as well as the transcendence that Jesus' embodiment promises in response to that condition.[100]

In another of Coleridge's poems, "The Rime of the Ancient Mariner," the consequences of refusing a theological transcendence mark a further difference between Romanticism and a liturgical poetics. Despite a cyclicality that is similar to the dynamics discussed at the beginning of this chapter, the old man's tale simply does not open towards an eschatological restoration. At the poem's conclusion, for example, Coleridge hints at this possibility: "Since then, at an uncertain hour, / That agony returns: / And till my ghastly tale is told, / This heart within me burns."[101] If the speaker (and the reader) takes the old man's words at face value, then he (and they) can entertain the possibility that the tale enables the old man to anticipate a release from the destabilizing experience on which he dwells; perhaps his heart does burn with a desire to transcend his pitiful condition. Coleridge, however, exposes in the end that any such anticipation is not authentically liturgical. In the final stanza, the speaker who listens to the old man reveals that the old man's tale does not constitute a true liturgical poetics: "He went like one that hath been stunned, / And is of sense forlorn: / A sadder and a wiser man, / He rose the morrow morn."[102] This remark indicates a different cyclicality because the old man will eventually tell the same story to another person. The vulnerability he shows in calling on God as the ship drifts towards the shore[103] becomes a recycled tale, devoid of any disclosure. Whereas the cyclicality that characterizes the lilies balances the text's closure with an anticipated rebirth, Coleridge's old man will make up the next morning, head to the bar, and repeat his tale in hopes of a redemption that he knows the constant retelling (and rereading) of the poem will never

100. Shaffer argues that this development constitutes a "leveling of Christianity to mythology, [which] is the triumph of Christian apologetics: for now Christ is endowed with an historical reality again, the Incarnation is the be taken at face value, the bread and wine are not symbols but the flesh and blood of Jesus" (*"Kubla Khan" and The Fall of Jerusalem*, 140). Limiting Jesus' life to an historical occurrence and taking the Incarnation at "face value" obscures—or eliminates altogether—the symbolic transcendence that Jesus' life and death establish within a theological matrix. To define Jesus solely as an embodied person is to situate him entirely within humanity's exilic condition (which erases the paradoxically implications of the theological underpinnings vis-à-vis Christianity's central theological claim) and, therefore, to discount the liturgical promise that he speaks during the Last Supper.

101. Coleridge, "The Rime of the Ancient Mariner," part VII, lines 70–73.

102. Ibid, lines 110–13.

103. Ibid., part VI, lines 57ff.

provide. Coleridge himself subverts the redemptive moral that underlines Christianity's liturgical paradigm. In response to Mrs. Barbauld's famous complaint that "The Rime of the Ancient Mariner" lacks a moral, Coleridge responds: "in my own judgment the poem had too much; and that the only or chief fault, if I might say so, was the obtrusion of the moral sentiment so openly on the reader as a principle or cause of action in a work of pure imagination."[104] Coleridge, then, resists the anticipated change in the old man that a liturgical poetics would gesture towards with each rereading.

Coleridge's response to Mrs. Barbauld establishes the presence of irony in "The Rime of the Ancient Mariner," but its effect is distinct from how irony functions within a liturgical poetics. Whereas the ironic closure of a liturgical poetics is simultaneously the moment that discloses an eschatological rereading, in "The Rime of the Ancient Mariner" irony ensures that no such disclosure can take place. As the cyclicality of the poem's structure becomes apparent, the reader expects the old man's tale to orient the text towards a regeneration of hope in response to his endurance of a dislocating experience. In this crucial moment, however, Coleridge subverts this expectation by conveying through irony that no such transition takes place. The renewal that occurs with each rereading does not extend the text towards an eschatological stability; rather, Coleridge's irony undermines the irony that affects a liturgical poetics.[105] The old man's tale approximates a liturgical cyclicality in order to destabilize a text that on the surface offers a hopeful response to the displacement that irrigates his story.

Distinguishing Negative Capability from a Liturgical Poetics

John Keats presents a more difficult Romantic precursor from which to differentiate Dickinson's work.[106] In a famous letter, Keats suggests the notion of Negative Capability as characterizing his poetry. This concept parallels many of the salient features of humanity's exilic condition and, therefore, how a liturgical poetics' responds to this displacement. Writing to his brother in 1817, Keats explains that Negative Capability is a "quality went to form a Man of Achievement especially in literature & which Shakespeare

104. "Samuel Taylor Coleridge (1772–1834)."

105. In this capacity, "The Rime of the Ancient Mariner" parallels Nietzsche's myth of eternal recurrence. See my discussion of how Nietzsche deconstructs a liturgical poetics (chapter 6).

106. See Diehl, *Dickinson and the Romantic Imagination*, 68.

possessed so enormously—I mean Negative Capability, that is when man is capable of being in uncertainties, Mysteries, doubts without any irritable reaching after fact & reason."[107] In aligning the ability to endure uncertainty with Shakespeare, Keats indicates that he understands what is at stake in the cyclicality that structures Shakespeare's poetry. The ability to situate one's work *within* this instability is a crucial feature of liturgical poetics. Through this textual dynamic, Keats echoes a crucial feature that reaches back to the Last Supper narrative.

While Negative Capability echoes the displacement that characterizes a liturgical poetics, when one analyzes poems in which Keats examines the effects that he ascribes to Negative Capability, one can recognize the extent to which Negative Capability does not constitute a liturgical poetics.[108] The natural world provides a mutual point of comparison between Keats and Dickinson, which in turn indicates how her work diverges from the notion of Negative Capability. In "Ode to the Nightingale," Keats begins by conveying the uncertainty that defines Negative Capability: "My heart aches, and a drowsy numbness pains / My sense, as though of hemlock I had drunk."[109] Such is the effect the nightingale's song has on the speaker. The sound induces a serious condition, one that casts the speaker towards the uncertainty that his inevitable death—marked in the song of this "immortal Bird"[110]—brings about. The speaker's response is insightful: "Now more than ever seems it rich to die, / To cease upon the midnight with no pain, / While though art pouring forth thy soul abroad / In such ecstasy!"[111] As the poem's organizing image, the bird's song thus fixes for the speaker a moment that reconciles his human condition with the inevitable death that the nightingale's presence indicates. As a result, the speaker resigns himself to the "sod"[112] that marks an impending burial. Through the first six stanzas, then, Keats maneuvers his speaker through a space defined by death. In this capacity, his Negative Capability echoes the concerns that would come within a liturgical poetics that through its recognition of humanity's exilic condition reconciles the text to a permanent displacement.

---

107. "Keats' Negative Capability."

108. Despite his helpful study on Dickinson and the Romantics, Richard Brantley misses the mark on this point. See Brantley, *Experience and Faith*, 10–15.

109. Keats, "Ode to a Nightingale," stanza I, lines 1–2.

110. Ibid, stanza VII, line 1.

111. Ibid, stanza VI, lines 5–8.

112. Ibid, stanza VI, line 10.

Despite this thematic parallel to a liturgical poetics, "Ode to a Nightingale" retreats from a point wherein Negative Capability plunges fully into the text's exilic implications. The poem cannot endure the destabilizing effect that the bird's song brings, a fact evident in the final stanza wherein the speaker cries "Adieu! adieu! thy plaintive anthem fades."[113] This valediction brings about a closure that does not establish conditions that convey fully the exilic implications of the nightingale's presence. As the nightingale leaves, the text does not close back on itself in the cyclical totality of a Derridean openness that discloses an eschatological rereading. Rather, the text recedes into a question of the whether the encounter occurred in a dream.[114] The uncertainty of the encounter prohibits, then, the closure that a liturgical poetics requires to disclose hope. The result, Harold Bloom states, is a unifying effect: "What Keats so greatly gives to the Romantic tradition in the *Nightingale* ode is what no poet before him had the capability of giving—the sense of the human making choice of a human self, aware of its deathly nature, and yet having the will to celebrate the imaginative richness of mortality."[115] The optimism Bloom finds in "Ode to a Nightingale" reflects the Romantic expectation that nature affords transcendence. A bird, free in its natural beauty, subverts the implications of death that appear at the poem's outset, which in turn implies a transcendence of the instability that death would otherwise bring to the text. Through the nightingale's departure, then, the text slides into a stability that for a liturgical poetics cannot materialize. Keats strengthens this retreat by suggesting that the encounter with the nightingale was just a dream, a move that distances the text further from its initial reminder of the death that no one can avoid. Keats does not, then, endure fully the displacement that he mentions when describing Negative Capability. The poem's conclusion thus avoids the displacement that the speaker can never transcend, which in turn reveals the difference between the Romantic Movement and a liturgical poetics.

In examining the human condition, then, Keats posits a transcendent unity within the natural world, a notion captured in Shaffer's notion of the idyll. In this capacity, Keats diverges clearly from a liturgical poetics. Whereas the nightingale's song indicates a transcendence of humanity's natural displacement, Dickinson resists any such stability in what Richard E. Brantley calls a "more process- than goal-oriented mode of seeing,

113. Ibid, stanza VIII, line 5.
114. Ibid, stanza VIII, lines 9–10.
115. Bloom, "Keats and the Embarrassments of Poetic Tradition," 520.

believing, and imagining."[116] In contrast to "Ode to a Nightingale," for example, Dickinson in J314 ("Nature—sometimes sears a Sapling") reiterates that humanity cannot outpace its latent instability because everyone must die. Nature, Dickinson declares bluntly, actively denies the idyll that Keats posits; she reminds her readers that nature "Sometimes—scalps a Tree—."[117] The tree affords, then, an example of nature's dislocation: "Fainter leaves— / to Further Seasons— / Dumbly testify— / We—who have the Souls— / Die oftener—Not so vitally—."[118] The image of the Tree functions in a parallel manner the cyclical displacement that Dickinson establishes through flowers. The tree in its natural cycle points to the seasons that characterize both death and rebirth. In J314, Dickinson does not indicate whether the leaves are newly sprouted with spring, or changing colors as they pass into autumn. In leaving out this detail, she stresses yet again the displacement that characterizes the natural world. Moreover, she links this dynamic overtly with the death that humans face. Unlike seasonal waxing and waning, death sometimes signals a definite closure, even in the natural, regenerative cycle. By confronting and accepting death's finitude, Dickinson (unlike Keats) uncovers a disclosure that death can be transcended, but this release remains outside of the text. The final line of J314 makes clear that the tree's death is extended endlessly by virtue of its place within a natural, destabilizing cyclicality. At the same time, however, the poem hints that death is not the overriding condition that affects this tree; a latent vitality counters the repeated death that the tree must endure. The tree, then, allows the text to endure the displacement that affects the natural world, which in turn enables the disclosure of a rebirth that overcomes an unavoidable death. Thus, she stretches the text to its unavoidable collapse, a commitment to displacement that Keats shies away from as he bids the nightingale adieu.[119]

The Thematic Link between John Donne and Emily Dickinson

Given the breakdown of Dickinson's apparent similarities with the Romantics, this chapter will conclude by linking her work back with a kindred liturgical spirit: John Donne. In J1593 ("There came a Wind like a Bugle"),

116. Ibid.

117. J314, line 2.

118. J314, lines 5–8.

119. See Derrida, "Living On," 66–70.

Dickinson hints at two poetic traditions—a liturgical poetics and the Romantic Movement—in a way that indicates which lineage she privileges. She concludes the poem with a telling reflection on the instability that characterizes the natural world:

> The Bell within the steeple wild
> The flying tidings told—
> How much can come
> And much can go,
> And yet abide the World![120]

Dickinson examines directly the Romantic privileging of nature as the locus of revelation. More specifically, the pealing bell's tidings allude to the nightingale's song from the trees. Dickinson thus situates J1593 in the natural context that for Keats reveals transcendence.[121] In keeping with "Ode to a Nightingale," she affirms the natural rhythms of life and death that the bird's song connotes. Death affects continually the natural world, a point Dickinson makes in language that echoes the cycle of death and rebirth. In this capacity, Dickinson signals her disagreement with Keats through a single word: abide. Whereas the nightingale departs, J1593 concludes by enduring the displacement that the natural world's oscillations cause. Importantly, this abiding accommodates the death that ultimately comes to everything in the natural world. Unlike Keats, who does not force his speaker to account for his own death, Dickinson confronts the latent instability within the natural world, which in turn enables her to conceptualize this displaced context as a space wherein the text can anticipate regeneration. It is only by abiding death that the natural world can transform into a temple that discloses an anticipated transcendence.[122]

The reference to the bell alludes to both Keats and Donne and, therefore, provides a fulcrum between the Romantic Movement and a liturgical poetics. In "Ode to a Nightingale," Keats describes how the bell affects his speaker: "Forlorn! the very word is like a bell / To toll me back from thee to my sole self!"[123] These lines punctuate the analysis offered above. The

120. J1593, lines 13–17.

121. Dickinson also explores this theme in J324 ("Some keep the Sabbath going to Church—").

122. The natural world, then, becomes through its displacement a temple in the Heideggerian sense. As discussed, Dickinson is finely tuned to the natural coming and going, a point evident in her strong links to the commandment to consider the lilies.

123. Keats, "Ode to a Nightingale," stanza VIII, lines 1–2.

speaker's "forlorn" cry conveys a sense of exile, displaced amidst "tears amid the alien corn,"[124] yet the bell enables the text to belie its latent displacement. In contrast, Donne utilizes the sound of the bell to emphasize the death that displaces all of humanity. At the beginning of "Devotion XVII: Nun Lento Sonitu Dicunt, Morieri," Donne reflects on the sound of a bell as it speaks to his (and humanity's) displacement: "Now, this bell tolling softly for another, says to me: Thou must die."[125] The bell marks death's unavoidable arrival, which, unlike Keats, Donne confronts directly. He accepts what the ringing indicates; he, like everyone, must die. Paradoxically, then, the bell engenders a nascent community, which, like the Last Supper's promise, marks the disclosure of an eschatological condition wherein death will be transcended. Thus, Donne finds in death's inevitability a reason for hope despite the instability that the bell indicates: "Another man may be sick too, and sick to death, and this affliction may lie in his bowels, as gold in a mine, and be of no use to him; but this bell, that tells me of his affliction, digs out and applies that gold to me: if by this consideration of another's danger I take mine own into contemplation, and so secure myself, by making my recourse to my God, who is our only security."[126] The paradox with which Donne concludes this passage situates the image of the bell squarely within a liturgical context. Though death's effect is certain, the closure that the bell marks enables Donne to anticipate an eschatological stability by linking his shared exile with the ecclesial element of the promise that Jesus speaks during the Last Supper.[127]

The hope Donne finds even as the text emphasizes death echoes the sentiment that Dickinson conveys in J1593. Uncertainty pervades her poem, which yokes the text to the displacement that Donne describes. Moreover, her willingness to endure the bell's destabilizing announcement refuses the natural transcendence that Keats suggests. Through their mutual endurance, then, Donne and Dickinson exhibit a symptomatic feature of a liturgical poetics: recalibrating the text's displacement as a disclosure of an eschatological release from the natural world's instability. Donne and Dickinson find in the bell a closure that becomes the basis for opening the text towards the stabilizing transcendence that will release humanity from

124. Ibid, stanza VII, line 7.

125. Donne, *Devotions Upon Emergent Occasions*, 102.

126. Ibid, 103–4.

127. See the conclusion for a more extensive discussion of a liturgical poetics' ecclesial implications.

its exile by virtue of a theological restoration that only God's eschatological presence can provide.

Just as Dickinson tells Mrs. Tuckerman that she takes Jesus' commandment seriously, Donne makes clear that he, too, considers the lilies in full recognition of the instability that characterizes their cyclical nature. In a sermon preached on Easter, Donne mediates on a two rhetorical questions from the Psalms that bring into focus the consequences of humanity's exilic condition: "Who can live and never see death? Who can escape the power of Sheol?"[128] The answer, of course, is no one. Despite the displacement his questions emphasize, Donne finds in the lilies a reason to hope that everyone's unavoidable death can be transcended. He tells his audience:

> The contemplation of God, and heaven, is a kinde of burial, and Sepulchre, and rest of the soule; and in this death of rapture, and extasie, in this death of the Contemplation of my interest in my Saviour, I shall finde my self, and all my sins entered, and entombed in his wounds, and like a Lily in Paradise, out of red earth, I shall see my soule rise out of his blade, in a candor, and in an innocence, contracted there, acceptable in the sight of his Father.[129]

In the face of the psalmist's rhetorical reminders of the fate that awaits him, Donne returns to the lilies and, therefore, to the symbol that anticipates God's eschatological presence in the midst of humanity's exile. Death awaits, but this does not prevent Donne from believing the promise that Jesus locates in his similarly destabilized body. Consequently, Donne is able to anticipate the fulfillment of the promise—in erotic terms no less—despite the instability that marks every body. He indicates a possibility beyond the decay that haunts the lilies by re-imagining their unavoidable and therefore destabilizing cyclicality as a continual rebirth. In so doing, he accepts and recalibrates the death he cannot escape and extends the text towards that which he desires but cannot experience within his exilic condition. Donne, then, returns to Jesus' broken body as symbolically coherent with the lilies that Jesus commands the crowd to consider, a link that Dickinson echoes in her own consideration of the lilies.

---

128. Ps 89:48.

129. John Donne, "Sermon No. 1," 42–43.

4

John Donne's Dying Body

In the Lord I take refuge; how can you say to me,
"Flee like a bird to the mountains;
for look, the wicked bend the bow,
they have fitted their arrow to the string,
to shoot in the dark at the upright in heart.
If the foundations are destroyed,
what can the righteous do?"[1]

THE BODY'S BROKENNESS RUNS AGAINST THE GRAIN OF THE ANTICIPATED
stability that underwrites a liturgical poetics. When he preaches on Psalm
11 before King James I, Donne indicates how this instability generates
doubt. God's refuge is not a given; to anticipate God's security is to undertake a significant risk amidst a dislocated context. As embodied beings,
humanity is unhinged from the stability that the divine refuge provides, a
reality that Donne takes seriously. He uses the psalmist's rhetorical doubt to
articulate the challenge discussed at the end of the previous chapter. What,
Donne asks through the psalmist's words, if God's presence never arrives
to overcome humanity's instability? In offering answers to this question,
Donne situates his message to the king directly within the exilic parameters
that characterize a liturgical poetics. Far from being secure in faith, Donne
conveys exile's effect by stressing the psalmist's concern: anticipating God's
presence must endure the doubt that pervades humanity's exilic condition.

Donne, then, undertakes a journey that risks the indefinite extension of God's absence to suggest paradoxically that hope can emerge despite humanity's latent instability. Donne tells the king (and the rest of the

1. Ps 11:1–3.

audience): "Goe still the same way to him, by Water, by repentant *Teares*: And remember still, that when *Ezechias* wept . . . God saw *his Teare*, His Teare in the *Singular: God* sawe his first teare, every severall tere: If thou thinker *God* have not done so by thee, Continue they teares, till thou finde hee doe."[2] Donne echoes the previously discussed Easter sermon wherein he considers the lilies by focusing on an image that in stressing God's absence destabilizes the text. The tears provide the locus for anticipating God's presence, but they do also mark the displacement that must be endured. Like the lilies, traversing the cycle's closure becomes the basis for anticipating anew a stabilizing presence. At the same time, the tears reiterate that God is absent from the text. Donne has in mind the condition described the Book of Revelation wherein God's eschatological presence affords permanent stability: "And I heard a loud voice from the throne saying, 'See, the home of God is among mortals. He will dwell with them; they will be his peoples, and God himself will be with them; he will wipe every tear from their eyes. Death will be no more; mourning and crying and pain will be no more, for the first things have passed away.'"[3] When God dwells with humanity, the need to cry out will cease. God's presence will wipe away the tears that indicate God's absence and, therefore, humanity's exilic condition. The stability that God brings will fulfill the promise that Jesus utters during the Last Supper. In both cases, the anticipated presence arrives, which satisfies the hope that death will not be the final word on the human condition. The tears, then, span imaginatively the space between humanity's exile and God's absence beyond the text, which establishes a threshold wherein the text relates intimately to God. The tears mark off the liminal space[4] that sustains hope despite the instability that subverts the text. They establish the inescapable and unstable reality of humanity's

2. Donne, "Sermon 3," 92.

3. Rev 21:3–4. As will be mentioned throughout this chapter, Donne's strategy—in this case incorporating imagery from Revelation to anticipate the liturgical promise's fulfillment—reappears in a similar capacity in Dickinson's poetry. See Doriani, *Emily Dickinson*, 92ff.

4. It is important to note that in addition to the Revelation allusion, Donne also refers to Jesus' experience in Gethsemane, which traditionally understands that in his prayer Jesus weeps (it is important to note that tradition does not match the text). These tears link the Gethsemane experience firmly to the liminal space wherein Christianity's liturgical paradigm develops. Traditionally, Jesus' tears emphasize the suffering and death that are inescapable as he speaks to God. Though Jesus knows his fate in unavoidable, he still expresses a deeply liturgical hope, namely that he can transcend that which he faces immanently. See Matt 26:36–45 and Mark 14:32–42.

impending death and, therefore, reiterate the text's instability, even as they anticipate the divine presence that will overcome this condition.

A Delicate Balance: John Donne's Literary and Theological Identities

Donne confronts the doubt that the psalmist voices and, in response, he molds his sermon to address the displacement that indicates God's absence. He accepts, then, that the text must unfold in a manner consistent with humanity's exile. More specifically, God's absence reflects humanity's dislocation as a result of the Fall. In examining the deeply rooted personal and theological concerns about death in this context, Donne strikes a fine balance between his literary and theological identities. He develops his writing against the backdrop of the shift from a late-medieval Catholic to a Protestant theological matrix in post-Reformation England. Despite his embeddedness within this transition, however, he both affirms and challenges the limits of his theological milieu as he probes with a delicate pen the displacement that is still a common denominator between the two traditions. Donne's work thus traverses a narrow ridge between distinct historical, cultural, and theological developments, none of which can be treated in isolation in reading his work as a liturgical poetics.

As a prominent member of England's new ecclesial structure, Donne exhibited orthodox tendencies that obscured the departure that his writing undertakes from his outward theological identity.[5] Despite the emphasis within his milieu on standardizing the English Church's fledgling institutional (and cultural) identity, Donne does not fit easily into smooth theological categories. On the contrary, his writing indicates the extent to which he occupied the fringes of the shifting theological boundaries of his day. Donne's social and physical struggles only aggravated his tense relationship with institutional orthodoxy, a strain that ultimately enabled his liturgical poetics to develop. On this point, Blanchot is helpful to understand how

---

5. There is much critical discussion available concerning Donne's preferences towards Catholic or Protestant theology. I will avoid this discussion in the current project by affirming that Donne exhibits elements of both traditions. The specifics of his systematic theology do not alter fundamentally an examination of his liturgical poetics. The question of Donne's specific theological identity—like other critical faultlines—ultimately obscures the analysis I offer. This is not, of course, to suggest that these critical discussions are irrelevant, but, rather, to emphasize the need for a different critical angle when examining a liturgical poetics.

Donne's context informed his writing: "writing, in the heart of the distress and the weakness from which it is inseparable, again becomes a possibility of plentitude, a road without any goal at the end, but capable perhaps of corresponding to that goal without any road leading to it which is the one and only goal we must reach."[6] As he navigated a variety of uneven and ever-shifting circumstances, Donne turned to the text as a way to make sense of the displacement of which he was acutely aware. He found a basis for enduring these challenges in the context that Blanchot describes as the only congruent response to the human condition: writing. More specifi-cally, Donne recognizes the particular capacity of the Last Supper narrative to speak to the concerns that preoccupied his mind. He understands how a liturgical poetics accommodates both his dislocation and a simultaneous anticipation of an eschatological condition wherein he will transcend the rupture that death causes. He believes in Jesus' liturgical promise, a faith he exhibits by unhinging his writing from the outwardly stable coordinates that his ecclesial role posits. As a result, he opens his writing towards the possibility that Blanchot locates within the displacement that envelops writing.[7]

A liturgical poetics' paradoxical character did not escape Donne. He develops his writing in this capacity in order to counter the inability of his institutional orthodoxy to assuage his concerns about death. The need to endure closure in order to open into an eschatological disclosure is, for Donne, an important motivation in emphasizing the body as the sign of Jesus' liturgical promise. Ironically, the Last Supper's destabilizing textual properties sanction the theological paradigm that this promise engenders. Donne, then, immerses himself in this tradition—defined by its instabil-ity—in order to blend his theological concerns with his writing. A latent instability provides the connective tissue between these influences, which Donne recognizes as mirroring the personal, bodily instability that con-tinually unsettled his mind. As a result, he lifts out from the Last Supper the dynamic whereby Jesus' body establishes a promise that anticipates a return to God's presence. Accomplished through the writing that emerges from within distress, Blanchot characterizes what is at stake when a writer like Donne enters the text's instability: "in precisely this terrible state of self-delusion, where he is lost for others and for himself . . . His feeling

6. Blanchot, *The Space of Literature*, 62.

7. See my discussion above concerning the poet's role in constructing a liturgical poetics (chapter 2).

profoundly destroyed is the first intimation of the profundity which re-places destruction with the possibility of the greatest creation."[8] The Last Supper provides the basis for this transition; in death, the body endures a closure that enables the text to undergo an eschatological disclosure. The creative blending of the literary and theological capacities in which the Last Supper speaks to his exile enables Donne to develop a liturgical poetics. Through this writing, he is able to traverse the instability that, because of death, no one can transcend.

As he navigates the theological context of his day, Donne never loses sight of exile's paradoxical implications for humanity. He focuses his imaginative gaze on the latent instability that underscores the psalmist's lament. Specifically, death weighs heavily on Donne's mind, which pro-duces an almost myopic focus that rejects a simplified theological balm as he confronts his embodied reality. In response to death, the simplistic an-swer—to have faith in his God—does not provide the stable counterweight that Donne desires, even if his privileged position within the Church of England demanded such an outward confidence. He realizes the yawning doubt beneath an orthodox faith and humanity's exilic condition, yet he is also aware that he can respond to this fissure only within and through his ecclesial role. This subversive doubt both frightens and interests Donne, a tension in which he submerges himself throughout his writing. The goal, never present and never fixed in Donne's writing, is the journey towards the undetermined but unavoidable encounter with death in order to anticipate humanity's restoration to a prelapsarian stability. Though the text can never transcend the cause of displacement, it can endure the consequent instabil-ity and, therefore, anticipate the stability that a union with God will bring.

As a normative critical concern, death does not in itself constitute a novel point of entry for analyzing Donne. In this chapter, however, the sa-lient concern is how he responds to death in a capacity that acknowledges its consequences while at the same time maintaining hope that death's rup-ture can be transcended. Literarily and theologically, one cannot overstate the influence death exerts on Donne's work. He is aware of this problem and he responds by refusing to wait passively for death's unavoidable ar-rival.[9] To do so, he departs from a simplistic theological response—one that assumes the liturgical promise's fulfillment—to death in order to confront

8. Blanchot, *The Space of Literature*, 62–63.

9. This approach anticipates Dickinson's own poetic recalibration of how humans can relate to their inevitable death (see chapter 5).

his fear of the body's split from the soul. Thus, he develops a liturgical poetics by lifting out of his orthodox context Jesus' displaced body as an, anticipatory sign that speaks directly to the locus wherein death's effects are manifest clearly. As a result, when struggling against death's finitude Donne finds in the Last Supper narrative the basis for a textual disclosure of the eschatological condition that will unite body and soul with God. This is the not-yet that enables Donne to sustain his hope in a promissory note that his institutional context cannot provide.

Situating John Donne's Liturgical Poetics within His Cultural Context

The salient concerns in Donne's cultural context inform significantly any attempt to analyze his liturgical poetics. In his recent book *Liturgy and Literature in the Making of Protestant England*, Timothy Rosendale argues that literature afforded an interpretive space to process the theological, ecclesial, and literary fissures that opened in the wake of England's break from Rome.[10] Specifically, Rosendale describes the Book of Common Prayer (BCP) as textual space that sought to balance the consequences of: "two enormously potent, and potentially contradictory, sixteenth–century conceptual entities: the early modern nation and the Protestant individual. This synthesis is worked out *hermeneutically*; the constantly renegotiated balance between individual and community, authority and conscience, pivots around a newly stressed faith in the power of representations and their interpretation to articulate and transform the relations of human and divine."[11] Rosendale articulates well the common thread in these various concerns—the hermeneutical implications of how the sign was to be understood in a liturgical context[12]—that Schwartz addresses through close readings of multiple writers from this crucial period in *Sacramental Poetics at the Dawn of Secularism*. The crucial connective tissue at the dawn of secularism is, for Schwartz, the role of the sign, both within the obvious theological questions concerning the Eucharist, as well as the related shift in how poetry afforded an opportunity to suggest alternative possibilities for

10. The argument in the previous section coheres with Rosendale's characterization of Donne's milieu as unprecedented. However, Rosendale does not account adequately for the specific theological tension that Donne carries over from his early Catholicism.

11. Rosendale, *Liturgy and Literature in the Making of Protestant England*, 8.

12. Ibid., 103.

understanding the sign. Rosendale and Schwartz both focus on the causal relationship between the English Reformation and the literary explosion that followed. Despite this similarity, however, each stresses a particular aspect of this literary epoch, which in turn prevents either analysis from maintaining the crucial balance that Donne strikes between this literary milieu and the still strong theological influences that he incorporates into his writing. Rosendale, like Schwartz is quick to project onto Donne a nascent secularism/modernism; they read his deconstructive literature as an unmooring from his theological past. Donne, however, does not keep pace with this projection and any distance he exhibits from the orthodox theologies of his day indicate his privileging of humanity's exile. The new literary avenues that he wanders provide the opportunity to recalibrate a still medieval theological response to death.

Rosendale rightly recognizes, however, that the BCP permitted the hermeneutical liberties that Donne takes when incorporating the Last Supper's theological legacy into the post-Reformation literary landscape. However, Rosendale conceptualizes this effect in a way that too quickly departs from the still present theological filtering of the human condition through its relationship to God. For example, Rosendale states early in his analysis: "The Prayer Book was, in short, designed to fix the problems that the English Bible caused, to stabilize a historical moment in which inspiration threatened to run amok. But by also incorporating the radical individualism implicit in Protestantism, it sought to become a complex textual matrix of identity that held in productive tension both the imperatives of the hierarchical nation and the prerogative of the evangelical soul."[13] The key point that Rosendale stresses—the supposed radical individualism and the consequent textual matrix for individual identity—does not translate into a proto–modern evangelism. Further, the radical individualism that Rosendale ascribes to Donne glosses over the still flickering medieval assumptions that inform Donne's writing. More importantly, Donne's nascent relationship with the literary freedom that the BCP sanctions does not override his underlying concern about death as a consequence of the Fall. Stated differently, Donne very much explored the BCP's new interpretative possibilities within reach of the traditional theological beliefs that preceded the English Reformation. For example, post-Reformation theological and literary developments did not alter Donne's medieval preoccupation with what happened to the body and soul after death. Despite Rosendale's

13. Ibid., 5.

attempts to fast-track Donne towards a modern individualism, the fact remains that Donne situated his writing against a theological backdrop that
Rosendale is anxious to declare bygone.

While Schwartz offers a skillful reading of shifting hermeneutical
fault lines in her treatment of English Literature's towering figures from the
post–Reformation era, she, too, misreads the extent to a pre-modern theological mindset informs Donne's writing. Her oversight emerges specifically because of her overly heavy literary analysis. By tilting her argument
so obviously towards Donne's literary persona, Schwartz miscalculates how
deeply Donne embeds his writing within his theological beliefs. Schwartz's
willingness to bracket Donne's theological background from her analysis
constitutes a dismissal of the crucial balance that Donne strikes between
these two facets of his work. Consequently, her study falls short in its attempt to situate Donne accurately within the specifically theological developments concerning the eucharistic symbols. In turn, she does not speak
sufficiently to the sign's complex role within the Eucharist's *liturgical* framework. As a result, Schwartz does not recognize what is at stake in Donne's
literary corpus, despite her accurate argument that Donne's concerns for
the sign were crucial to his project. By reading Donne's work as a liturgical
poetics, one can recognize clearly that Schwartz does not characterize the
sign's shifting liturgical role accurately in her book. The shortcomings of
the term sacramental—despite semantic similarities with the notion of liturgical poetics—fail to capture the extensive influence that the specifically
theological understanding of humanity's displacement generates within
Donne's writing.

Moreover, in conceptualizing the sign as sacramental, Schwartz suggests, like Rosendale, that Donne heralds the arrival of a secular world.
While this development takes place eventually, Donne is hardly a secular standard-bearer. If anything, he exhibits the still valued influence of
pre–Reformation theological beliefs. Consequently any secularism that
Schwartz wants to ascribe to Donne (as well a fledgling individualism)
grates against Donne's understanding of himself (and humanity) as defined by the expulsion from Eden. This antecedent condition not only
emphasizes the theological backdrop against which Donne writes, it also
maintains a strong sense that humanity's condition is understood through
a shared awareness of exile. This initial dislocation from God establishes
the parameters that determine the sign's specific function within the Last
Supper, as well as the liturgical legacy that follows. Donne clings to the sign

as a locus for Jesus' promise to be present at an eschatological banquet. In failing to address fully this theological framework, Schwartz does not account for the initial, Edenic displacement or the sign's role as anticipating a return to humanity's absent originary stability. This oversight hinders her analysis of Donne insofar as it does not extend her reading of the sign into the theological context that underscores the crucial shift in understanding the sign's liturgical function.

At the outset of her book, Schwartz problematically defines sacramental in terms that connote the very interpretation of the Eucharist that the reformers rejected and, consequently, she offers a reading that does not parallel the subtle *theological* re-imaginings within the canon that she examines. Schwartz writes that a sacramental poetics: "signifies more than it says . . . [it] creates more than its signs, yet does so, like liturgy, through image, sound, and time, in language that takes the hearer *beyond* each of those elements."[14] Her definition requires the text to experience the presence that the sign promises. Two problems immediately emerge in light of this claim. The first has been made clear; within a liturgical poetics: the text cannot accommodate the eschatological presence that the sign indicates. Schwartz, however, insists that the sign brings about the promise's fulfillment. As a result, her analysis violates the exilic conditions out of which the sign emerges, as well as the theological divide that the sign does not cross.[15] Her claim thus runs counter to the necessary absence that Jesus' promise—as a textual and theological not-yet—demands. Donne is consistent in treating the sign in accordance with the delay that lingers after Jesus' establishes the eucharistic signs; their promissory character necessarily prohibits the extension beyond the text that Schwartz posits. Her reading thus suggests a textual stability—stretching the text to the beyond—that a liturgical poetics denies. Moreover, she does not account for the theological framework that makes clear the impossibility of transcending humanity's exile from within the text. Donne, in his liturgical poetics, upholds both the literary and theological displacement that characterizes the sign and, as such, endures the instability that typifies a liturgical poetics.

Schwartz's misreading results largely from her failure to acknowledge that Donne's theological mindset does not cohere with the proto-modern

---

14. Schwartz, *Sacramental Poetics at the Dawn of Secularism*, 7.

15. Jesus makes clear the divide between humanity's exile and his eschatological presence when he explains to Mary in John 20 why she cannot touch him. For more on this point, see chapter 6.

label she is anxious to affix to his writing. Donne exhibits strong vestiges of medieval theological beliefs, which affect significantly how he understands the sign's role within a liturgical poetics. More importantly, his theological assumptions supersede any literary analysis of his writing. The specifically eucharistic sign still functions as a response to Jesus' liturgical promise, which, for Donne, casts the text as anticipating an eschatological presence that is still absent. This distinction indicates the link between Donne and a pre-Reformation theology. As the sign of a liturgical promise, Jesus' body opens the text towards an eschatological presence that remains absent and, therefore, precludes the extension to a beyond that Schwartz permits the sacramental poetics to undertake. For Donne, the sign does not transcend the text, but, rather, reiterates the embodied context that generates the eucharistic signs. More specifically, the sign indicates simultaneously death's immediacy and the liturgical promise that death will be transcended by virtue of Jesus' eschatological presence.

The sign's role, then, is to accommodate through its linguistic function the theological displacement that informs the eucharistic bread and wine. This development must be understood in the specific context that understands humanity's exile as the result of its expulsion from Eden. In tinkering with the sign's role in post-Reformation England, Donne expands how a text can endure the protracted absence that the sign anticipates; the eschatological fulfillment of the promise remains absent by virtue of the sign's paradoxical character. Jesus' death—as a specifically embodied event—condenses this delay into both a textual and a theological absence, which in turn enables the anticipation of the promise's fulfillment through its necessary denial. This indefinite not-yet resists the reading that Schwartz suggests insofar as it refuses to pre-empt the body's material (and textual) exile in order to sanction a proto-modern reading of Donne. Schwartz, then, offers her analysis of the sign's changing role in post-Reformation England at the cost of the complex relationship between Donne's personal theological mindset and the orthodox expectations of his ecclesial environment. The eucharistic signs remain for Donne embedded in humanity's exile, which is a necessary consideration if the sign is to function theologically as an anticipation of a coming eschatological presence. In the end, Donne's theological beliefs prove to be incongruent with the reading Schwartz offers, a friction that becomes more pronounced as she narrows her argument.

When addressing the Eucharist specifically, Schwartz invites the aforementioned criticism of her sacramental poetics. She casts various rereadings of the eucharistic signs and their literary outgrowth in a way that does not cohere with Donne's reading of the sign as the basis for his liturgical poetics. For example, Schwartz states that at the turn of the Seventeenth Century, the Eucharist "turned into a commemoration of a sacrifice rather than a re-enactment, a commemoration of a moment in the distant past."[16] Schwartz rightly distances new readings of the Eucharist from the Catholic stance that the signs transform into Jesus' actual body and blood, but, as mentioned in the previous paragraph, she moves too far too quickly. The pace of her argument ultimately recalibrates how Donne understands the sign in a way that bends the sign back towards its prior Catholic interpretation.

As a result of her retreat to a simplified liturgical framework, Schwartz suggests a sketch of Donne that is not tenable. Donne's Catholic residue informs the theological (and textual) boundaries of his writing; what occurs within that space is a deconstructive reading of the simplistic, orthodox readings that mirror Schwartz's understanding of the Eucharist. Donne's concern is how death separates the body from the soul. It is to this reading of humanity's condition that Donne's writing responds on the basis of the eucharistic signs' bodily nature. The loosening literary guidelines for responding to this fear mark the shift that Rosendale attributes to the BCP. Donne shows nascent signs of the anthropological transition that on the basis of this hermeneutical shift matures into a modern (and secular) mindset, but it is crucial to understand Donne held firmly to the assumption that humanity was and is displaced from Eden, which in turn gives rise to Donne's anticipation of an eschatological presence that will restore humanity to a prelapsarian stability. Schwartz, like Rosendale, thus discounts the extent to which Donne's theological reading of the human condition compels his the textual response to death that his liturgical poetics offers.

Because she glosses over the theological backdrop against which Donne explores the sign's function, Schwartz fails to recognize within the text the consequent tension that the eucharistic sign's paradoxical character generates. Specifically, this sign's eschatological implications endure the promise's delayed fulfillment because of the body's capacity to anticipate anew this not-yet presence through its experiential possibilities. Herein lies a final point of emphasis: Schwartz does not account fully for the Last

---

16. Schwartz, *Sacramental Poetics at the Dawn of Secularism*, 57.

Supper as the narrative precursor to how Donne understands the sign. The consequences for failing in this regard are apparent, as Schwartz does not discuss the vital point made clear in the symbolic implications of Jesus' body. His body *cannot* transcend death; its promise emerges by virtue of the necessity that as an embodied being Jesus must die. His body can only disclose an eschatological promise if the text mirrors the closure that death brings.

Death's Destabilizing Influence on John Donne's Writing

For Donne, death is perhaps *the* concern to address (and fear), both literarily and theologically. He believed fully that death marks the moment in which his body and soul are separated[17] and, consequently, he conceptualizes death as a devastating rupture. His writing responds to this inevitable dislocation by turning to the promise that Jesus speaks during the Last Supper. When addressing death, then, Donne situates his writing within a cycle of hope and denial, which, as is true of all liturgical poetics, runs counter to the stability implied in Schwartz's suggestion that Donne considers the union of body and soul to be possible in the here and now. Donne's work, when read as a liturgical poetics, makes clear that any stabilizing presence that is still to come and, therefore, must remain necessarily beyond the text's reach by virtue of humanity's continued displacement. For Donne, the Last Supper does not transcend death; it promises that Jesus' death will enable the anticipation of this transcendence. In the wake of this promise, then, all anticipation remains bound by exile and, as a result, the text is for Donne a matter of faith.[18]

By drawing on the displacement that characterizes the Last Supper narrative and its precursor, the story of humanity's expulsion from Eden, Donne frequently situates the text at a point wherein its collapse is immanent. As the reader moves through Donne's corpus, s/he recognizes the

17. See Targoff, *John Donne, Body and Soul*, 1–25.

18. In his famous final sermon, "Death's Duel," Donne asserts that his humanity depends on the union of his body and soul: "for the union of the body and soul makes the man, and he whose soul and body are separated by death as long as that state lasts, is properly no man" (*Devotions upon Emergent Occasions and Death's Duel*, 163). Death, then, is not the moment Donne will reunite with God in heaven; death is the moment in which Donne's humanity may be lost forever. This concern filters through Donne's work in a way that draws him repeatedly back to the Last Supper's promised eschatological stability, which, for Donne, indicates the eternal, stable union of his body and soul.

harsh linguistic and experiential reality that death brings to his writing. As a result, Stanley Fish argues that the text is: "beyond the aid that discursive or rational forms can offer . . . [and the text] becomes the vehicle of its own abandonment."[19] Donne's writing often concludes by sounding a note of displacement. By predicating his writing on death's inevitability, Donne recovers a salient concern within the Last Supper that frames the notion of a liturgical poetics. He makes clear the need to accept that death prevents the liturgical promise from being fulfilled. The definitive quality Donne recognizes in death is the way in which it disrupts human life and, moreover, its ironic subversion of the promise that anchors the Last Supper narrative. Insofar as he accepts these linguistic, culturally, and ultimately theological challenges, Donne thus embraces the isolating effect that death renders within a text. By affirming death as an unavoidable feature of embodied existence, Donne grounds his writing in humanity's post-Edenic exile in order to anticipate despite this dislocation the fulfillment of the Last Supper's liturgical promise.

Eden as the Source of Spatial and Temporal Displacement

Space and time emerge as consequences of the theological mindset that informs Donne's writing, which, paradoxically, emphasizes the problems that materialize when casting Donne too readily as a proto-modern mind. The problem can be seen, for example, in *John Donne, Undone*, wherein Thomas Docherty argues that temporality results from the displacement that death causes: "Temporality, a 'fall' into secular history, is the corollary of this spatial displacement; and the human now lives in and through time and change, through difference, rather than in a hypostasized realm of 'eternal verities; or transcendence, totalizing identity."[20] Docherty's analysis

19. Fish, *Self-Consuming Artifacts*, 3. Though Fish recognizes an effect that parallels exile's influence, his causal reading suggests an individualism that projects Donne into a post-Enlightenment rationality. He, like Schwartz, fails to ground his analysis fully in Donne's theological beliefs.

20. Docherty, *John Donne, Undone*, 8. In *Literature and Sacrament: The Sacred and the Secular in John Donne's Poetry*, DiPasquale's reading of Donne dovetails with Schwartz's notion of the sacramental in a way that challenges Docherty's reading: "But his [Baumin's] conclusion that these poems are informed by a poststructuralist 'Poetics of Absence' is distortive" (DiPasquale, *Literature and Sacrament*, 5). DiPasquale's denial of the distortion at the heart of Donne's work seemingly reflects her dislike of the "phallo-centric certainty of religion and theological discourse" (ibid., 4) that she finds in Docherty's reading of Donne. There can be little argument that Donne's work exhibits

here converges on the balance that defines Donne's poetry, but it demands qualification in light of the claim that Donne's understanding of displacement is secular. Death does mark the point at which this fall begins in a bodily sense, but for Donne this concern filters through the theological narrative of the Fall. Docherty's analysis, like Schwartz's, fails to account fully for human's condition in light of its expulsion from Eden. Temporality indicates the absence of Eden's stability; no longer in possession of eternal life, humanity endures time as the progression of life towards death. This theological understanding reveals the latent qualities of Donne's writing that resist the overtly secular reading that Docherty suggests. The effect is to identify an important feature of Donne's work, but to do so in a way that fails to account for the capacity in which Donne's texts take shape as specific responses to his theological assumptions. Time and space thus converge in the event of death as a consequence of humanity's exile from Eden; the initial parameters are, therefore, distinctly theological in nature. Donne conceptualizes the displacement that Docherty describes in terms of exile because there exists, always, an implied yet absent theological origin. The spatial and temporal parameters that govern humanity's displaced condition characterize, then, an absence from God's eternal presence in Eden.

Humanity's displacement emphasizes the extent to which Blanchot's notion of exile and Derrida's notion of différance can inform a reading of Donne, which in turn clarifies why his work constitutes a liturgical poetics. The challenges of language preclude a reading of the text as stable, which in turn dislocates the author and reader as they traverse the text's space. When writing within or about this condition, Donne draws on the

---

an overt phallo-centrism, but DiPasquale's dismissal of Docherty solely because he affirms these contours in Donne's work belies her later alignment with Judith Scherer Herz, who "points out, Donne's poems resist attempts 'to impose a unity, to make [them] yield single, albeit complex readings'" (DiPasquale, *Literature and Sacrament*, 25–26). Three important points are necessary at this point. First, DiPasquale cannot avoid the implications that Donne's work resists stability, which, contra Schwartz, lies at the heart of his liturgical poetics. Secondly, Donne's complexity denies a definitive reading, which as will be discussed in the next chapter, is a hallmark of Dickinson's poetry; in fact, her liturgical poetics builds upon Donne's phallo-centric project, which indicates the third point to mention at this junction. Too often the bodily implications within a liturgical poetics invite an overly hasty, gendered analysis of Donne's writing. Donne's phallo-centric liturgical poetics coheres with Dickinson's own poetic project, a link that, as will be discussed in chapter 6 forms the foundation for defending Donne, Dickinson, and other liturgical poetics that locate hope on/in the body. For an example from DiPasquale's own work in which Donne's gendered poetics affirms an exilic dislocation, see DiPasquale, *Literature and Sacrament*, 102ff, and Donne, "Goodfriday 1613."

spatial and temporal consequences of humanity's expulsion from Eden to unsettle the text as it anticipates a stabilizing presence. He knows that the liturgical promise's fulfillment cannot occur because the text will inevitably collapse under exilic pressures. Similarly, the reader cannot engage and thus pass through the text's displacement without experiencing the closure that recalls humanity's inevitable death. The consequences of the Fall, then, govern the text, which indicates in turn that God's anticipated presence will result in a specifically eschatological condition that restores humanity to its Edenic stability.

These exilic parameters in Donne's work echo Heidegger's understanding of the human condition as being-thrown, which helps to clarify further how Donne incorporates the latent instability that results from the Fall into his writing. In response to its displaced condition, Heidegger writes that for humanity: "poetry first causes dwelling to be dwelling. Poetry is what really lets us dwell. But through what do we attain to a dwelling place? Through building. Poetic creation, which lets us dwell, is a kind of building."[21] The need to dwell indicates a desire for an originary stability that, for Donne, is God's eternal presence in Eden. Space and time mark a continual displacement; humans must dwell because they have been released from their divine foundation into a condition that establishes the absence of the stability that defined humanity's Edenic experience.[22] For Donne, to dwell is to anticipate God's restorative presence, which will allow humanity to transcend the spatial and temporal experience that marks God's absence. This transcendence of death is the hope that Donne draws from the Last Supper's promise, which echoes Heidegger's reading of humanity's search for stability: "The region of secureness must first be shown to us, it must be accessible before hand as the possible arena of conversion. But what brings us a secure being, and with it generally the dimension of security, is that daring venture which is at times more daring than Life itself."[23] Donne recognizes in the Last Supper narrative the crucial paradox that Jesus' body discloses the possibility of transcending death by undergoing death as the full extent of humanity's dislocation from God. The bread and wine thus signal both a definitive closure of the liturgical promise and, therefore, the disclosure of the eschatological condition that will provide humanity with its lost secureness. The body's paradoxical role as a sign of this anticipated

---

21. Heidegger, ". . . Poetically Man Dwells . . .," 213.
22. Heidegger, "What Are Poets For?," 114–16.
23. Ibid., 123–24.

presence provides a temple, which, as discussed previously, opens the text towards a reading beyond its exilic boundaries.[24]

Of course, Donne's reliance on the Last Supper narrative differs from Heidegger. Still, a strong thematic resonance links Donne with Heidegger's claim that to dwell is to seek stability through writing. Heidegger may not be talking about God as Donne is, but the motivation he identifies for seeking stability offers a helpful critical tool for recognizing how Donne draws on Jesus' body as a temple to anticipate a restoration to Edenic stability. Like Heidegger, Donne refuses to suspend humanity's dislocated condition because, ironically, this condition provides the textual foundation from which Donne anticipates the fulfillment of the liturgical promise. To combat the constant destabilizing effect that humanity's displacement generates, Donne attempts to arrest momentarily the endless sliding away from stability that death brings. In this capacity, Donne's writing becomes, according to Docherty, a "scene not of stable meaning but rather of precisely the opposite: change of meaning."[25]

Bracketing Temporality to Articulate Liturgical Hope

The reality of time (and its consequences for embodiment's spatial considerations) cannot be escaped, an irony to which Donne often stakes his texts. In "A Lecture upon the Shadow," one finds a symptomatic example of how Donne symbolically arrests time in order to anticipate God's stabilizing presence. The poem's opening lines announce the need to halt time if the speaker is to envision a release from both the Fall's spatial and temporal consequences:

> Stand still, and I will read to thee
> A lecture, love, in love's philosophy.
> These three hours that we have spent,
> Walking here, two shadows went
> Along with us, which we ourselves produced.[26]

24. Crucially, however, Donne always does so in full recognition that his texts cannot transcend their own exilic preconditions. Thus, he recalls Heidegger's qualification that humanity can only dwell paradoxically (i.e., in full admission of its continued displacement): "Mortals dwell in that they initiate their own nature-their being capable of death as death-into the use and practice of this capacity, so that there may be a good death. To initiate mortals into the nature of death in no way means to make death, as empty Nothing, the goal" (Heidegger, "Building, Dwelling, Thinking," 148–49).

25. Docherty, *John Donne, Undone*, 9.

26. "A Lecture upon the Shadow," lines 1–5.

There is a precondition for hearing the speaker's insights about love: the other in the poem must cease to move. This command's spatial implications establish a firm yet disjunctive requirement; stopping is, of course, temporally impossible. The lecture that follows thus generates friction as the speaker attempts to bracket the text's latent displacement. This "entropic deviation" is "misleading," argues Docherty, insofar as it casts the supposed lecture as misdirection.[27] Docherty thus argues that Donne's goal is to delay the lovers' consummation.[28] This point emerges at the climactic moment in the lovers' walk continues at exactly noon: "Except our loves at this noon stay, / We shall new shadows make the other way."[29] The speaker traces the lovers' journey towards a precise moment through the shadows that accompany them. The shadows connote death, or "decay" as Donne later says,[30] which establishes the destabilizing condition that results from God's absence. The one exception comes at noon, when shadows cease to exist; at just this moment the lovers will occupy a shadow-less text wherein they can envision a love free from the disruption that death brings. This anticipated point is deeply ironic, of course, insofar as "after noon, is night."[31] Donne suggests, then, a release from death that cannot be sustained. This crucial moment cannot last, a reminder of the temporal progression that after the Fall cannot be halted.

The poem's title is ironic. The topic of the lecture needs no clarification insofar as death's effects are clear. The lecture that would otherwise open the text towards stability becomes a reminder of the exilic parameters that the text (like the lovers) cannot escape. Time does not and cannot stop and, therefore, the lovers cannot experience the transcendence that occurs only at noon.[32] The instant in which the sun casts no shadows will disappear immediately; by the time the lovers (and the reader) are aware of

27. Docherty, *John Donne, Undone*, 102.

28. Ibid., 102–3.

29. "A Lecture upon the Shadow," lines 14–15.

30. Ibid., line 26.

31. Ibid.

32. As Docherty points out, the text is never authentically in the moment; the moment will always be a rereading, a "necessary 'betrayal' of the text itself" (*John Donne, Undone*, 101). Thus, the moment that Donne tries to fix is "always deferred" (ibid., 94), which links the poem firmly back to the Last Supper's liturgical promise. The text imagines a stabilizing presence, but the fulfillment of this promise cannot be sustained within the text. Though he does not discuss this dynamic with sufficient depth, Docherty does converge on the indefinite delay that is, for Donne, a crucial feature of a liturgical poetics.

this moment's implications, the shadows will be back as the sun—as time's marker—progresses. The shadows mark an important closure insofar as they indicate the resumption of the temporality that characterizes humanity's displacement. Rather than establish through their absence a stabilizing presence, they become in their presence a reminder of stability's absence. Noon is not, then, a release but rather an ironic reiteration of humanity's instability, a condition punctuated by the shadow as a sign of death. Moreover, the presence of death recalls humanity's ironic expulsion *into* time, which in turn recalls the crucial theological framework that informs the poem. Even the moment that seemingly conveys stability will always be undercut by the temporal progression that ushers the lovers towards their death. This inevitability invites into the text what Donne fears about death: the separation of body and soul. The speaker's initial exhortation to stop thus folds in on itself; the requisite conditions for a liturgical lecture become a reminder that death is the only point at which time will stop.

Displacement and the Erotic in John Donne's Writing

While the lovers in "A Lecture upon a Shadow" anticipate a union, they ultimately signal the permanent dislocation that death brings, a theme Donne echoes in "Twicknam Garden." In this poem, the speaker enters into a garden that Donne characterizes from the outset in disruptive and subtly erotic terms: "Blasted with sighs, and surrounded with tears, / Hither I come to seek the spring, / And at mine eyes, and at mine ears, / Receive such balms, as else cure everything."[33] Donne's speaker seeks a rebirth amidst the "sighs" and "tears" that convey his displaced condition. In contrast to these details, the speaker encounters a spring that connotes a baptismal restoration as a counterweight to his exile. The hoped-for restoration clarifies this displaced condition as sinful and, therefore, anticipates a return to God's eternal presence. The spring thus signals a cleansing of sin as a return to Eden's stability, a definitive reminder that the text unfolds within a specifically theological framework. Moreover, such restoration parallels the fulfillment of the Last Supper's promise insofar as that, too, anticipates a presence that will transcend the displacement that death brings to the human condition.

The dual presence of sin's displacement and a recovery from this condition overlaps thematically with the Pauline cycle of death and rebirth,

33. "Twicknam Garden," lines 1–4.

which in turn draws attention to the specifically embodied condition that frames the speaker's experience. The spring identifies the text as a liturgical poetics insofar as it connotes a stabilizing restoration. At the same time, the hope that the spring suggests cannot override sin's pervasive effect as the speaker traverses a garden that reminds him of the Edenic garden's prelapsarian stability; his presence in Twicknam garden emphasizes his absence from Eden. The rest of the first stanza reiterates that this sinful displacement is inescapable: "But O, self traitor, I do bring / The spider love, which transubstantiates all, / And can convert manna to gall."[34] The speaker associates himself with Adam as the initial traitor; consequently, the spring's cleansing effect becomes something that the speaker cannot experience insofar as he must endure his exilic condition. The fact that the speaker cannot actually undergo the restoration that the spring offers reiterates that the text's garden is as an exilic space. The promised restoration, then, is predicated on a denial of what the spring offers. At the beginning of the second stanza, the speaker reiterates that he is trapped within this destabilizing context: "'Twere wholesomer for me, that winter did / Benight the glory of this place / And that a grace frost did forbid / These trees to laugh, and mock me to my face."[35] The speaker's sin permeates his existence to the point that he recognizes his helplessness to overcome it. The frost[36] glazes the ground that would otherwise permit a symbolic rebirth to bloom, yet another reminder of the displacement that characterizes humanity's sinful condition.

The garden not only serves as a foil to Eden's prelapsarian stability, it also casts the poem in a distinctly erotic mold. The garden's suggestive context recalibrates the speaker's displacement when he encounters two other lovers: "Hither with crystal vials, lovers come, / And take my tears, which are love's wine."[37] Whereas the poem begins with the speaker's anticipation of the spring's restorative cleansing, his final encounter with the lovers transforms the expectation of stability into an experience of exclusion. The lovers, already linked, exhibit a bond that prohibits the speaker's inclusion

---

34. Ibid., lines 5–7. See Exod 16.

35. "Twicknam Garden," lines 10–13.

36. As is frequently the case, details in Donne writing emerge again under Dickinson's steady hand. Dickinson was certainly aware of Donne's writing and often mirrors his imagery. See Banzer, "'Compound Matter': Emily Dickinson and the Metaphysical Poets," 417–33.

37. "Twicknam Garden," lines 19–20.

and, therefore emphasize further his displacement. Donne reuses the same word—Hither—to contrast the speaker's initial hope for the spring's restorative effect with the lovers' arrival, a comparison that makes clear the anticipated cleansing will not occur. The lovers intensify the speaker's displacement by removing the tears that in the first stanza anticipate God's presence from within his exile. The implication is that the vial is also able to contain the spring's cleansing water, while the speaker, in lacking such a container, must continue without this restorative balm. At the same time, however, the lovers' wine alludes to the Last Supper. As such, the speaker's exclusion from the lovers' union is not only a closure that re-establishes the text's exile; it also renews hope that a stabilizing presence will come eventually.

When the lovers transform the speaker's tears into wine, they mirror the miracle Jesus performs in John 2. The allusion both establishes liturgical anticipation that is consonant with John's characteristic delays. Jesus prefigures his actions at Cana with his initial response to the lack of wine: "My hour has not yet come."[38] The subsequent change from water to wine is thus contained within an indefinite delay, an effect that Donne brings to bear on the speaker in "Twicknam Garden." In hinting at what is to come—and even providing a little taste—Jesus establishes that humanity's restoration must wait. As a result, the speaker remains dislocated from the lovers' restorative union because there remains a necessary theological delay. Transforming the speaker's tears into wine announces an exclusion that is present in John 2 and becomes manifest clearly in John 20 when Mary must endure the indefinite delay that Jesus' presence establishes.

"Elegy 20: Love's War" offers another example of how the anticipation that precedes the two lovers' encounter signals simultaneously an eventual textual collapse and the fulfillment of the Last Supper's promise. This poem magnifies the thematic and textual displacement present in "A Lecture upon the Shadow" and "Twicknam Garden" through a more pronounced erotic conceit. In this capacity, "Elegy 20" indicates more precisely how Donne's recovers Jesus' body as the promise's locus; the body is tuned to accommodate the promise's simultaneous anticipation and denial. The poem begins by yoking two lovers together in response to conflict: "Other men war that they their rest may gain, / But we will rest that we may fight again."[39] Sex is a different kind of warfare, one that parabolically demands more from

---

38. John 2:4.

39. "Elegy 20: Love's War," lines 33–34.

its participants because it condenses the cycle of desire, fulfillment, and deflation within the exilic parameters that characterize the human condition. Whereas war brings about a definitive end (most of the time), the lovers' sexual war results in battles that must be fought repeatedly. Their desire, if fulfilled, results in the loss of the pleasure. The erotic body, then, cannot fulfill any liturgical promise insofar as it cannot sustain the moment that signals the conflict's end. Theologically, the lovers relate in a way that recalls in a different capacity the Pauline cycle of death and rebirth.[40] Consequently, the text's erotic framework anticipates the very thing it suggests should be avoided in satisfying the lovers' desire: "Here let me parley, batter, bleed, and die."[41] By conflating the destructive encounter of warfare with sexual climax, Donne enriches and problematizes the body as the liturgical promise's locus.

The lover's in "Elegy 20" die as their bodies move towards a resolution by absorbing the damaging effects that come with war's violence; the "thrusts, pikes, stabs, yea bullets hurt not here."[42] At the same time, these images exhibit a sexual rhythm that concludes with a similarly strong bodily awareness of these effects through the collapse that follows orgasm. Donne's point, then, is that a clear, climactic erasure links the closure that the body experiences in sex and death. By conflating war and sex, moreover, "Elegy 20" locates rebirth in the body that dies, which in turn situates the metaphor within the theological calculus that Donne lifts out of the Last Supper narrative. Like Jesus' death, the body transcends the destruction that war's violence brings about: "shall I not do then / More glorious service, staying to make men?"[43] This final image mirrors the bodily temple that Jesus establishes through his own death. A hint of hope, conveyed

40. DiPasquale identifies a similar trajectory in Donne's "La Coruna," which, she argues, draws on Pauline thought: "Particularly relevant to the poem's Eucharistic function is Romans 13:11, 'now is our salvation nearer'" (*Literature and Sacrament*, 66). This contrasts with A. B. Chambers' work, which, DiPasquale notes, suggests "The most sensitive criticism of . . . ["La Coruna"] who has convincingly demonstrated *La Coruna*'s relationship to the endless cycle of the liturgical year" (59). DiPasquale's analysis rightly identifies that Donne's texts extend towards a point (or moment) that implies stability. Moreover, she astutely recognizes the cyclical concerns that inform "La Coruna," which indicate a pattern to Donne's liturgical poetics. However, DiPasquale fails to emphasize sufficiently the displacement that prohibits the text from transcending humanity's exile in a specifically liturgical context.

41. "Elegy 20: Love's War," line 30.

42. Ibid., line 38.

43. Ibid., line 46.

through a rhetorical question, anticipates a divine, stabilizing presence—an eschatological tryst—that finally releases the lovers from the endless cycle of fulfillment and collapse that defines love's war.

The Erotic Body's Anticipation of a Divine Presence

Donne's rich imagery in "Elegy 20" offers a symptomatic look at how erotic contexts inform his liturgical poetics. Specifically, he often characterizes intimate moments between lovers through tense, even violent imagery. As a man who feared the destruction that death brings to the body and, moreover, his eschatological anticipation of God's presence by separating the body from the soul, Donne's use of the body's erotic capacity emphasizes his awareness of humanity's displacement. However, the texts that Donne constructs through such metaphors ultimately permit him to anticipate an eschatological union of body and soul. In turn, the body provides the basis from which Donne responds—via the Last Supper narrative's paradoxical and theological use of Jesus' body—to death. The specifically erotic body thus links Donne's writing with the Last Supper through Jesus' own anticipation of an eschatological presence as his body progresses towards death. Like the Last Supper narrative, Donne's texts frequently progress towards the satisfaction of desire, which in turn creates a void when this expectation is denied. Donne's use of the body, then, extends the anticipation of God's eschatological presence by virtue of the displacement that the body cannot overcome.

Donne, establishes intimacy to characterize the liturgical tension between anticipation and denial. An example of this textual dynamic occurs in "The Sun Rising." The poem begins at daybreak with two lovers resting after spending a night together. When the sun's light enters the room, the text experiences a strong interruption, to which the speaker responds: "Busy old fool, unruly sun, / Why dost thou thus, / Through windows, and through curtains call on us? / Must to they motions lovers' seasons run?"[44] The sunlight announces that the previous night's liaison is over, a moment that the speaker clearly does not want (for Donne, this kind of desire tends to dislike interruption). The sun is, quite simply, unwelcome; its presence jars the lovers' satisfaction. In so doing, the sun refuses the speaker's attempts to bracket the moment in a way that resists its inevitable closure. The speaker knows the previous night's dalliance is over, but his injunction against the

44. "The Sun Rising," lines 1–4.

sun expresses a longing for a recovery of a now absent intimacy. The sun's effect, though disruptive, thus refigures the poem's tone, which, as Robert Detweiler argues in *Breaking the Fall: Religious Readings of Contemporary Fiction*, is precisely what a metaphor should do. Read through Detweiler's argument, the sun serves "through the conjoining of dissimilar images . . . to conceive a new, often more complex, often strange and tentative image that acts as a probe for establishing a deeper and more encompassing view of our reality."[45] Stated simply, the sun's intrusive presence marks the transitional moment between the lovers' sexual encounter and the prohibition of continuing this experience. Importantly, this closure establishes the text's liturgical dimension. The sun concludes the previous' night's rendezvous, but it also enables a renewed desire for the lovers to anticipate a future dalliance. The sun's interruption, then, paradoxically extends the desire that precluded the scene that it interrupts.

The speaker is disappointed, to be sure, but his initial address to the sun enables a subsequent reflection on the implications of the sun's interruption. By the end of the poem, the speaker understands the sun not as an intrusive outsider, but rather as an accepted (even if, paradoxically, still excepted) presence: "Since thy duties be / To warm the world, that's done in warming us. / Shine here to us, and thou art everywhere; / This bed thy centre is, these walls, thy sphere."[46] The sun now forms a bond between the lovers that transcends mere sexuality. It affirms their shared humanity by virtue of their mutual displacement. The interruption thus exhibits the telling irony of a liturgical poetics. The sun announces a simultaneous closure and disclosure. The end of the lovers' intimacy—a textual collapse that echoes both death's finality and, of course, the lovers' mutual climax—paradoxically becomes the basis for extending their desire through the closure that the sun causes. Donne, then, compensates for the rupture by reframing the moment as one in which the speaker becomes aware that the sun's presence in the room transforms an absent intimacy into an anticipated reunion.[47] The sun's disruption, which is felt acutely in the lovers' bodies, opens the text towards a theologically suggestive climax even as they are reminded continually of the cyclical, erotic displacement that frames any

45. Detweiler, *Breaking the Fall*, 21.

46. "The Sun Rising," lines 27–30.

47. Of course, the pun on sun and son points to a trinitarian universality, which ultimately sanctions the lovers' encounter.

and all of their intimate encounters. Every sunrise necessarily awaits a sunset, which, for the lovers, anticipates the fulfillment that the night brings.

The irony is that the sun's interruption preserves the intimacy between the lovers by enabling them to anticipate the recovery of a now absent satisfaction. This effect provides what Detweiler calls a "probe toward new patterns of knowledge that offer us greater choices of what we might believe, how we might respond."[48] Consequently, Detweiler explains, such images allow the speaker's mode of knowing to "expand into a mode of *trustful* interacting, in which the risk-taking is made to pay off."[49] The speaker's initial, frustrated response gradually shifts to recognize how the sun's ironic effect—the renewal of desire—opens the text towards (eschatological) re-readings from within the text's displacement. The transition echoes Detweiler's discussion of *Gelassenheit*. The term connotes "'releasement' or 'abandonment,'"[50] which characterizes the sun's arrival and, moreover, emphasizes the exilic parameters that subsequently destabilize the text. When the speaker addresses the sun in confrontational terms, his words mark the collapse of the text's intimacy. Thus, the speaker experiences a dislocation wherein a shared sexual experience does not demand the response that Detweiler describes; before the speaker addresses the sun, no response is required. Consequently, one finds that another, paradoxical connotation of *Gelassenheit* describes the space between the conclusion of "The Sun Rising" and subsequent rereadings of the sun's initial interruption. According to Detweiler, the term also suggests "relaxation, serenity and nonchalance, a condition of acceptance that is neither nihilistic nor fatalistic but the ability—and it may be a gift—to move gracefully through life's fortunes and accidents, or to wait out its calamities."[51] This subtle overlapping emerges at the end of "The Sun Rising" when the speaker's frustration towards the sun's sudden presence gradually recognizes the renewed desire that emerges within (and despite) the sun's initial displacement.[52]

The capacity in which "The Sun Rising" condenses the dual meanings of *Gelassenheit* illustrates how Donne's writing builds upon the cyclicality that characterizes a liturgical poetics. As the poem is read and re-read, the text's lack of stability mirrors Derrida's deconstructive theological analysis.

48. Detweiler, *Breaking the Fall*, 22.

49. Ibid., 27.

50. Ibid., 35.

51. Ibid.

52. See Detweiler, *Breaking the Fall*, 44.

The lovers' oscillating desire and displacement convey through the consequent textual instability the exile that defines the human condition. Importantly, they experience this dislocation corporeally, which echoes the displacement that characterizes the Last Supper narrative. The body thus provides the basis for incorporating Donne's theological mindset into the lovers' bedchamber. The overlap between the lovers' bodies and Jesus' body opens into a well-known biblical text: "And though one might prevail against another, two will withstand one. A threefold cord is not quickly broken."[53] In "The Sun Rising," the sun's presence ultimately dissolves the lovers' individuality, a rupture that becomes the locus for a stabilizing union with God. The sun thus fuses the Last Supper's liturgical promise and the lovers' anticipation of a restored intimacy. Through the conduit that the erotic body provides, the shared feature of an unmet expectation strikes a balance between the overt eroticism that characterizes the poem and the deeper theological concern about humanity's displacement from God.

Confronting death, or identifying moments wherein a rebirth is possible, constitutes an important connective tissue in Donne's writing. This "redemptive potential"[54] identifies in Donne's work a threshold between his frequently eroticized texts and the anticipation of God's stabilizing presence. As Detweiler explains, "[the threshold's] liminality is more concerned with the process of change than with its product; it stresses the *difference* that constitutes change, and encourages cultures to celebrate that difference rather than making it the object of anxiety or idolatry."[55] The arc of "The Sun Rising" illustrates this point well. The speaker is caught in the text's transition, isolated from the now absent climax that precedes the poem and the unrealized but still anticipated recurrence of the liaison. The threshold thus calls attention to the Last Supper's overarching paradox; its liminality conveys the cyclicality of desire and denial that the text cannot transcend. The promise that the body establishes must be extended—but never fulfilled—insofar as any hint of satisfaction cannot outlast the text's coming collapse.

The challenge that Detweiler recognizes is, therefore, crucial. If the speaker in "The Sun Rising" relapses into frustration in response to the sun's interruption, then the text will slide back into the dislocation that defines the first sense of *Gelassenheit* without glimpsing—however briefly—the

53. Eccl 4:12.
54. Detweiler, *Breaking the Fall*, 50.
55. Ibid., 56.

stability that the second reading of *Gelassenheit* anticipates. In order for a disclosure to emerge, the speaker must endure the text's closure. This stability remains, however, a not-yet presence that must be anticipated through subsequent cycles of closure. Irony announces its presence through this indefinite delay, which establishes further thematic parallels between "The Sun Rising" and the Last Supper narrative. Through this subversive presence, however, the text resists a total closure; the speaker is able to extend his anticipation of a future reunion through his endurance of the inevitable closure that marks the retreat of the stability that is disclosed.

Much like the lovers in "The Sun Rising" can anticipate anew the fulfillment of their desire when they are jarred out of their intimate context, in "Elegy 8" two (potential) lovers experience an implied satisfaction in the absence of sexual activity. The speaker makes clear at the outset the paradoxical effect of desire that is denied: "Come madam, come, all rest my powers defy; / Until I labor, I in labor lie."[56] As he initiates his seduction, the speaker condenses the poem's specific sexual context and its liturgical anticipation. The difficulty of convincing her to accept his advances emphasizes the displacement that is present at the poem's outset, yet this instability becomes the basis for anticipating a new(born) condition. As he endures the separation that precludes fulfillment, the speaker transforms his efforts into the anticipatory experience of childbirth. The implication is clear: overcoming labor's difficulty is possible through the implication of the still absent result of new life.[57]

The union he desires exposes what is absent: the stability that awaits when humanity is restored to God's presence. The lovers' bed becomes in this anticipation a sacred space that functions as Jesus' body does in the Last Supper; it is "love's hallow'd temple."[58] As a space that imagines a release from exile, this temple anticipates her bodily presence, which in turn suggests the eschatological fulfillment that will be approximated if the speaker's seduction is successful. The heaven her body will bring is decidedly erotic[59] and the result is apparent in this anticipation's effect on

56. "Elegy 8," lines 1–2.

57. There is certainly space to critique Donne's decision to highjack childbirth as a way to seduce a woman, but such critiques would do well to affirm the obvious irony at work in the comparison. The more important liturgical point to recognize in this image is the reference to humanity's fallen condition. The labor of childbirth is, of course, a consequence of humanity's expulsion from Eden (Gen 3:16).

58. "Elegy 8," line 18.

59. Ibid., lines 20–21.

his body. His desire extends his body separation towards the release that the temple anticipates, an effect that is evident in the way her heavenly presence sets "the flesh upright."[60] The speaker's erection is a necessary step before the climactic satisfaction that will permit the union he desires, yet in its visibility it remains separate from the other whom the speaker desires. Liturgically, this bodily image stands for the condition that the heavenly consummation will bring about if the seduction succeeds. The speaker's rising flesh anticipates in sexual climax a reunion of body and soul that, as discussed previously, underwrites Donne's liturgical poetics.

The Erotic Body's Risk

While Donne's lovers endure the text's latent instability, at times their response to the text's displacement can become problematic. Occasionally, the violent character of sexual activity emerges as a significant consequence to the erotic apparatus that Donne employs. These difficulties emerge forcefully in one of Donne's most famous poems, "Holy Sonnet XIV." The speaker implores God to be present in a capacity that problematizes the erotic overtones that characterize the request: "Batter my heart, three-personed God; for, you / As yet but knock, breathe, shine, and seek to mend; / That I may rise, and stand, o'erthrow me, and bend / Your force, to break, blow, burn, and make me new."[61] Ramie Targoff describes the "craving for personal renewal from God" as characterizing Donne's Holy Sonnets, a thematic point that "reaches its climactic expression in Holy Sonnet XIV."[62] Targoff's language identifies the sexualized framework within which this poem unfolds, which through its implied, climactic moment conveys a regenerative experience that enables the speaker to traverse the text's instability. However, this dynamic functions on the basis of a sexually aggressive God. The point at which God begins to batter the speaker's heart thus morphs into a troublesome climax. The speaker's plea, then, is both powerful and scandalous; it resolves through God's aggression the concern that Donne feels concerning the rupture that death brings.[63] Consequently,

60. Ibid., line 24.
61. "Holy Sonnet XIV," lines 1–4.
62. Targoff, *John Donne, Body and Soul*, 120.
63. Targoff states: "Donne's petition . . . hovers on the edge of something that on the whole horrified him throughout his life: the possibility of persona annihilation" (*John Donne, Body and Soul*, 121). Targoff's language captures the liturgical texture of Donne's

the text calls to God in a way that assumes a passive and therefore vulnerable posture. Read through the poem's erotic first lines, the speaker invites God's stabilizing presence in the form of an intimate violation, a shift that Targoff describes as a shift from "military to erotic" images.[64] Like "Elegy 20," this alteration clarifies the relationship between sexuality and violence. The former places its participants in vulnerable positions as they wait for the latter's destabilizing (and occasionally devastating) effects.

"Holy Sonnet XIV" concludes on this note. Donne writes, "Take me to you, imprison me, for I / Except you enthrall me, never shall be free, / Nor ever chaste, except you ravish me."[65] The passivity invited in the poem's opening lines becomes an erotic submission to God's overt sexualized authority. Even though the speaker is violated, he cannot resist the allure that such encounters exhibit. The plea to be battered becomes a request to be victimized and this conflation of power and sexuality situates Donne's speaker in a dangerous place. The body becomes something for God to possess and, potentially, abuse, which challenges the theological backdrop to this sonnet. God's stabilizing presence is not simply the extension of the notion that God is love. Rather, in "Holy Sonnet XIV," God's presence borders on the predatory.[66] To be chaste, to be made whole in the capacity that

---

poetry well. The sexual language may be scandalous, but it also moves Donne away from institutionalized theological conceptions of God. He challenges the reader to imagine God in a capacity that ultimately results in the intimacy and reassurance about his fate that he desires.

64. Targoff, *John Donne, Body and Soul*, 123.

65. "Holy Sonnet XIV," lines 12–14.

66. Yeats' "Leda and the Swan" provides another example of the risk Donne runs insofar as a sexual dynamic between a divine other can transition from an implicit inequality to overt sexual abuse. "Leda and the Swan" denies the feminine body the capability to resist the sexual encounter that unfolds. More specifically, the erotic risk that characterizes the body becomes in "Leda and the Swan" an exploitation. He suggests that Leda's victimhood frames her body's sexuality (W. B. Yeats, "Leda and the Swan"). Consequently, the poem suggests that the divine other's abuse of Leda predicates her own sexuality, which in turn prohibits Leda from conceptualizing the event on her own terms. As a result, the text cannot open towards an eschatological stability (and in this capacity, "Leda and the Swan" does not constitute a liturgical poetics). Yeats does not commit to this reading (lines 14–15), but the mere possibility that rape can obscure the benefits of conceptualizing a relationship with the divine other as sexual is, clearly, problematic. This potential violation illustrates clearly the possible consequences of the narrative arc in "Holy Sonnet XIV." Yeats' poem, then, indicates a further possibility on the spectrum that characterizes the sexual dynamic in "Holy Sonnet XIV." Though Donne balances the risk in "Holy Sonnet XIV" in a way that does not permit the text to descend into the deeply problematic implications that emerge in "Leda and the Swan," "Holy Sonnet XIV"

Donne desires demands that the speaker be ravished. As Detweiler argues, such tension within a metaphorical encounter with God is risky: "Sexuality can be exploited and abused by those wishing to gain power, but the price they pay is to engage in writing and sexuality as acts of compulsion rather than to experience them as acts, shared willingly, of revelation and love."[67] The plea to be battered must be voluntary, but the notion of chastity—as pure and pursued—refuses a simple glossing over of how Donne conceptualizes God's anticipated presence. This tension in "Holy Sonnet XIV" recalls a distinction made earlier in this chapter: Donne's theological mindset exhibits an element of compulsion. Donne's residual medieval theology thus emerges within the charged, destabilzing context of "Holy Sonnet XIV." Humanity is compelled to respond to its exile when it acknowledges that its condition lacks an originary stability. Read through the speaker's chastity, this compulsion takes the shape of a voluntary submission as the cost of anticipating God's restorative presence. Chastity, then, functions in a dual capacity. It marks the speaker as distinct from God and it establishes a context wherein God and the speaker move towards a union. As a liturgical poetics, moreover, the notion of chastity establishes an ironic streak throughout this narrative framework. Given humanity's exilic condition, the reader might expect God to be the chaste lover and the speaker to be the ravishing party. Donne, however, inverts such expectation in order to emphasize the paradoxical capacity in which the body provides the locus for anticipating God's presence.

The speaker's request to submit his body to God's ravishing enables "Holy Sonnet XIV" to anticipate a divine presence that will stabilize the speaker's displacement. The mysterious tension between the two connotations of *Gelassenheit* thus emerges in the speaker's dangerous position during "Holy Sonnet XIV." Through his plea, the speaker anticipates the rupture of body and soul that awaits in the moment of death. Insofar as the text foreshadows this moment, the speaker finds fulfillment in the risk that Donne's overtly sexual imagery accommodates. The willingness to be ravished indicates, then, an important qualifying allusion in conceptualizing God as sexually aggressive: God's own dangerous passivity in Jesus' embodiment. "Holy Sonnet XIV" incorporates through the body's risk the

---

raises serious concerns that I will discuss in more detail in chapter 6. For more on the problematic sexual dynamic between the divine and the (female) human, see Warner, *Alone of All Her Sex*, 35.

67. Detweiler, *Breaking the Fall*, 142.

crucial disruption that characterizes the Last Supper narrative. Just as Jesus becomes the victim of overt violence, Donne's speaker submits to a violation in order to enable the liturgical promise's fulfillment. As a result, the speaker clarifies what happens in the liturgical context that such images marks out.[68] By emptying himself of control over his body, the speaker of "Holy Sonnet XIV" enters into a mysterious, erotic exchange with God. Submission to God is the text's necessary doing, a bodily anticipation that enables the text to open towards the release from exile that God's presence will bring.[69]

Balancing the Body's Symbolic Hope and Its Death

In his *Devotions*, Donne enriches the body's symbolic role within the context of a liturgical poetics. Written as he suffered an illness that brought him close to death, *Devotions* illustrates the extent to which Donne longed to trust that his body and soul would reunite in an eschatological context. In "Metuit: The Physician Is Afraid," Donne exhorts the reader to pray in a similar capacity as "A Lecture upon a Shadow": "Pray in thy bed at midnight, and God will not say, I will hear thee to-morrow upon thy knees, at thy bedside; pray upon thy knees there then, and God will not say, I will hear thee on Sunday at church; God is no dilatory God, no froward God; prayer is never unseasonable, God is never asleep, nor absent."[70] Just as the

68. According to Detweiler, such moments occur with "the collapsing of metaphor into metonymy, or the convergence of the symbolic and literal action" (*Breaking the Fall*, 133).

69. Despite my dissonance with Schwartz's work, I agree with her claim that Donne takes the Eucharist "to the bedroom" (*Sacramental Poetics at the Dawn of Secularism*, 87). Overt eroticism is a hallmark of Donne's work and, moreover, it is crucial as Schwartz points out to the way in which he articulates a new possibility of how the sign functions in this context. However, she reads Donne's erotic poetics as concerned with "communion—between body and soul, man and God, and human lovers—[which] is achievable in *this* world and in *this* time" (ibid, 89). Here, then, Schwartz's argument runs dangerously close to the kind of reading Donne (and others) consciously altered. The notion of actuality suggested in this passage is precisely the kind of hermeneutical interpretation of the eucharistic signs that does not appear in Donne's work. The eschatological presence that fulfills the liturgical promise remains beyond the text. The eucharistic signs are linked thematically with Donne's erotic contexts through this emphasis on the not-yet present stability that God's presence will bring. A liturgical poetics, in the bedroom or the upper room, point to a moment that forever lies beyond the text and is thus never achievable in this world.

70. Donne, *Devotions*, 34.

midday sun casts no shadow, the stroke of midnight constitutes a threshold that brackets temporality's cyclical disjunction. At the stroke of midnight, Donne encourages prayer because, he suggests, in this still moment God responds to prayer. At the same time, the need to pray reiterates God's absence; midnight remains another moment within the temporal cycle that frames humanity's exile. Midnight, then, simultaneously acknowledges the condition that threatens a rupture between body and soul, as well as the anticipation of a presence that will transcend death's finitude. It is thus during the text's closure that Donne claims God will hear prayers.[71] The problem, however, remains the same; Donne's text cannot escape the instability out of which prayers arise. Though God might hear prayers at midnight, the moment will pass before the prayer can be uttered, which in turn reiterates the instability that characterizes the human condition.

This paradox frames Donne's entire reflective process in *Devotions*. When he falls ill, he must face acutely the reality that death precludes an eschatological possibility to which the text opens. He establishes this urgency within the first lines of *Devotions*: "Variable, and therefore miserable condition of man! this minute I was well, and am ill, this minute. I am surprised with a sudden change, and alteration to worse, and can impute to it no cause, no call it by any name."[72] On either side of the precise moment that Donne uses to anticipate God's presence, he recognizes oppositional experiences that deny his hope. He stresses that the body can shift between different conditions with ease, a volatility that indicates the unstable nature of humanity's exile. This continual variation will always preempt the body's ability to function as a liturgical sign, which in turn emphasizes the latent displacement that frames the Last Supper's liturgical promise. Significantly for Donne's project in *Devotions*, death constitutes the only recognizable coordinate within exile. As with midnight, or noon, such moments continue to pass on the page, a progression that reiterates the text's (and humanity's) displacement.

71. It is important to recognize the extent to which Donne draws upon the biblical tradition to accent his language. God's willingness to respond to prayer recalls a nadir for the Israelites in Egypt (see Exod 2:24). Moreover, Jesus exhorts his followers to pray with confidence that God will answer prayers (see Luke 18:1–17). Donne's point, then, is to emphasize that God relates intimately to the isolated moment of midnight. The imagery of the new day figures strongly in focusing the text on midnight. This liminal moment signals that time will move towards light, or rebirth.

72. Donne, *Devotions*, 3.

This oscillation between promise and denial hints at the solution that forms the subtext of Donne's writing. Across different formats, Donne employs a consistent theological framework to inform how his writing anticipates an eschatological condition that transcends his embodiment. The body's displacement is a given; all attempts to escape death bend back to humanity's initial expulsion from Eden. As Fish explains, in Donne's writing "The reader-hearer will pass through doors only to find himself in the room he has just left. Sequence will not be the generator of meaning, but the marking off of discrete areas within which the audience will or will not make contact with the one true meaning, as its great author permits."[73] The purpose of writing within these parameters is, for Donne, to imagine a space wherein a stabilizing presence will fulfill the promise Jesus speaks during the Last Supper. Donne's willingness to engender this hope despite the anticipated presence's necessary absence captures the reason why his writing constitutes a liturgical poetics. More specifically, by situating his work within a cycle of desire and denial he purposefully leads readers (and indeed himself) towards the always-absent originary presence, but he does so in order to orient the text through its closure towards the disclosed, eschatological presence that has been promised during the Last Supper. In this capacity, death becomes not the point at which life concludes, but rather as the moment in which the possibility emerges that beyond death waits the God in whom Donne believes.[74]

73. Fish, *Self-Consuming Artifacts*, 42.

74. In DiPasquale's analysis, the various capacities in which Donne uses an erotic context to examine the eucharistic signs converge in "The Flea." This characterization marks the emergence of a link to the Last Supper: "Elevating a flea's consecrated blood, he celebrates a sexual Eucharist within the jet cloister of an insect's exoskeleton" (DiPasquale, *Literature and Sacrament*, 173). Like Dickinson's J465 ("I heard a fly buzz when I died"), the insect establishes an anticipatory element that resists the coming textual collapse. Consequently, Donne's flea (and Dickinson's fly) enables the text to approach death's closure in hopes that a transcendence of death is possible. The flea functions, then, as a gathering point for the separate but intimately close lovers; it provides the temple that enables their potential liaison to transcend imaginatively their mutual displacement. Just as Jesus' body provides the basis for anticipating an eschatological release from death's disruption, the flea opens the encounter between the lovers towards a reading of their erotic encounter as a liturgical poetics.

Because it contains both the blood of both lovers, the flea's body counters a negative understanding of the their (potential) sexual activity. The speaker is clear that permitting a further mixture of bodies would extend the stabilizing effect that the flea suggests: "This flea is you and I, and this / Our marriage bed, and marriage temple is" ("The Flea," lines 12–13). The text progresses towards a sanctioned union that not only provides a stabilizing response, but also does so (the speaker insists) in a capacity that upholds

Anticipating God's Presence in John Donne's Writing

As he confronts death, Donne clings to the hope that God's eternal presence will be realized after death. The strain of this belief in the shadow of death increases as the text extends towards the moment that offers resolution to Donne's concerns. In "Holy Sonnet III," Donne makes clear the text's inability to resolve this tension: "and my race / Idly, yet quickly run, hath this last pace; / My span's last inch; my minute's last point."[75] Donne offers both

---

the connotations that sexual activity should occur in specific contexts. Any dissonance between the speaker's advance and the eucharistic character of their sexual act recalls the jarring effect that Jesus' own death generates in the context of offering the liturgical promise during the Last Supper (see DiPasquale, "Receiving a Sexual Sacrament," 350–61). The eschatological condition to which this tension opens the text is reason enough for the seduction at hand. Consequently, the two must become one in sharing their blood sexually if they are to substantiate the promise that the flea offers through its eucharistic body to their shared exiled condition.

The speaker's erotic desire thus casts the potential liaison at hand as a theological event. As such, the poem's irony becomes apparent; any climax that the speaker achieves will, like the flea, encounter necessarily its own collapse. As a result, the stability that the flea's body suggests is still governed by the parameters of humanity's exile. The flea is the fulcrum that accommodates both the body's necessary instability and the sign that this instability will be overcome. More simply, the flea is a mirror for Jesus' own death, which substantiates the initial promise spoken during the Last Supper. As DiPasquale notes, the effect is that "the reader of the poem . . . decides the lady's final answer in the white space following the third stanza" (*Literature and Sacrament*, 175). DiPasquale recognizes that the flea's body—like Jesus'—brings the lovers into proximity of an act that will anticipate in its symbolic capacity a restoration to a prelapsarian stability. The flea's demise parallels the paradox at work in Jesus' own paradoxical death, which provides the theological atonement that enables an eschatological reunion with God. In other words, the flea encapsulates the basic core of Donne's theological mindset as it informs his liturgical poetics.

"The Flea" is symptomatic of the balance Donne strikes between his literary and theological identities. A cursory glance at "The Flea" suggests a parodic reading of an orthodox theological context. A close analysis, however, unearths the deep theological roots in "The Flea." In its fragility, the flea approximates the atonement that Jesus' death provides. The dissonance between Jesus' crucifixion and the lover's argument about the flea indicate how Donne uses irony to establish a textual point of simultaneous closure and disclosure. The flea's death ultimately speaks to the rupture of body and soul that unsettles Donne. By aligning the flea's body with the eucharistic signs, then, Donne draws upon the body's erotic capacity to convey his hope that the atonement provided in the bodily temple's destruction will be fulfilled. "The Flea" thus reiterates an important liturgical consideration: death is forever present and it is through the body that this finitude is confronted. Moreover, this encounter brings about a necessary closure that paradoxically discloses the eschatological transcendence that Jesus promises.

75. "Holy Sonnet III," lines 2–4.

spatial and temporal metaphors to characterize the text as it approaches the threshold of life's end. The puns are obvious; this is a decidedly sexualized way of understanding the end of his life. At the same time, by foregrounding the end of life as an extension of his erotic body, Donne reveals the strength that defines his liturgical desire. Death does not soften the text as it approaches the climactic moment in which the body is released from its exile. Importantly, no anticipation can escape the rupture that death brings. Donne never loses sight of the fact that the crucial moment that the text anticipates will "instantly unjoint / My body and soul."[76] In confronting this reality despite the fears he could never escape, Donne is able to gesture towards the God he hopes to encounter after the moment in which death severs the body from the soul. In that instant, he confesses he does not know if he will "see that face."[77]

This desire for the restorative stability that Jesus promises lies at the heart of Donne's liturgical poetics. More specifically, according to Fish enduring the displacement that death generates is a distinguishing characteristic of Donne's work: "[his work is] continually pointing away from itself, calling attention to what it is not doing (and indeed could not do), proclaiming not only its own insufficiency, but the insufficiency of the frame of reference from which it issues, the human frame of reference its hearers inhabit."[78] Donne's writing is a wandering that locates the corrective response to humanity's instability in the eschatological context to which Jesus' body opens the text (even if the text cannot progress to this point). For Donne, it is from within its sinful displacement that humanity is compelled to have faith in the Last Supper's promise. The text remains defined through God's absence as a result of humanity's expulsion from Eden. This indefinite displacement seeks through its desire to return to God's presence an eschatological cleansing of sin's effects. The eucharistic promise to accomplish this restorative effect is a theological element that Donne lifts out of the Last Supper narrative and situates within his writing. More specifically, he locates in the body both the displacement that death brings to all bodies and the disclosure that Jesus' own encounter with death enables. Even though God must remain absent, the bodily temple is thus able to

---

76. Ibid., lines 5–6.

77. Ibid., line 7. The image of God's face as a mark of humanity's release from exile is a trope that Dickinson similarly adapts in her liturgical poetics.

78. Fish, *Self-Consuming Artifacts*, 42.

anticipate a condition wherein God's presence will provide a release from exile into an eschatological stability.[79]

Donne's liturgical poetics thus draws upon and challenges his theological background. He accepts the instability of humanity's embodiment, but he also finds within the body a basis for rejecting simplified, orthodox understandings of the body. His reading of the Last Supper locates in the body a paradoxical hope insofar as Jesus' body promises a stability that restores humanity to God's presence. These theological assumptions bind Donne to the late medieval tradition that understood the eucharistic promise to respond to the specific instability that characterizes humanity after the Fall. On the basis of this theological platform, Donne constructs a liturgical poetics that thrives on the irony that the body's symbolism injects into a text. As a result, the body is not simply the locus wherein humanity's dislocation from God is manifest clearly; it becomes the paradoxical image that enables Donne to anticipate an eschatological reunion with God. Donne, then, responds through the body to the challenge posed by the psalmist in the face of death. In so doing, he develops an intimate, textual temple wherein the body's erotic capacity enables his readers to endure their dislocation in light of Psalm 11's conclusion: "the Lord is righteous; he loves righteous deeds; the upright shall behold his face."[80]

---

79. This liturgical framework situates Donne's imaginative readings of the body within an established theological tradition, namely the understanding that God is immutable and that humanity, by virtue of its dislocation from God, is mutable. Significantly, the body's condition is not antecedently mutable; the consequences of being cast into temporality subject humanity to a condition from which they were immune in Eden. Examining the effects that the body endures is a frequent concern in the literature of Donne's era. Shakespeare, for example, frequently reads the erotic relationship between the speaker and a beloved through the filter of the body's decay as time progresses (see, for example, "Sonnet XVIII"). For more on the theological anchors of this concern, see Augustine, *Confessions*, book XII); and Aquinas, *Summa Theologiae*, part I, question 9.

80. Ps 11:7.

5

Emily Dickinson's Indefinite Desire

He brought me to the banqueting house, and his intention
toward me was love. Sustain me with raisins, refresh me with apples;
for I am faint with love. O that his left hand were under my head,
and that his right hand embraced me![1]

LIKE DONNE, DICKINSON FREQUENTLY DRAWS ON THE BODY TO ADDRESS
a preoccupation with death. The body is, for Dickinson, subject to the
rhythms of the natural world. This instability is the result of death's inevitability, a dynamic Dickinson makes clear in J749 ("All but Death, can be
Adjusted—"):

> All but Death, can be Adjusted—
> Dynasties repaired—
> Systems—settled in their Sockets—
> Citadels—dissolved—
>
> Wastes of lives—resown with Colors
> By Succeeding Springs—
> Death—unto itself—Exception—
> Is exempt from Change—[2]

The majority of the images in J749 move from instability to stability; as
such, the text suggests that even a shattered life can be restored to vibrancy.

---

1. Song 2:4–6. All biblical quotations in this chapter come from the King James Version of the Bible, which is the text with which Dickinson would have been intimately
familiar. Roger Lundin states succinctly: "In her adulthood, the only source that Emily
Dickinson quoted more often than Shakespeare was the King James Bible" (*Emily Dickinson and the Art of Belief*, 197).

2. J749, lines 1–8.

Dickinson, then, emphasizes the possibility of recovery, redefinition, or rebirth. Significantly, she casts this hope in terms that she knew well. Her interest in horticulture—its cycles, its successes, and its failures[3]—provides an important symbolic reservoir from which she draws to examine the regeneration that the natural world—always subject to death—can undergo. The invariable rebirth that spring brings to the flowers in her garden, as well as the lives that these flowers symbolize,[4] inject J749 with an anticipatory energy that echoes Donne's lovers' desire.

Death runs counter to this optimistic tone. It is a presence that literally and figuratively brackets the examples of regeneration that J749 provides. Death is the *only* thing that cannot be adjusted; it is the one thing that does not change. Dickinson, then, subverts the ability of the natural world to renew life by calling attention to the specific capacity in which humanity (as part of that world) is excluded from a natural rebirth. As such, death is the singular exception to hope and it has the initial and final say in J749. This consistent pressure mirrors, in turn, a preoccupation in Dickinson's own life against which she constantly struggled.[5]

The thematic link between death and rebirth in J749 establishes the exilic parameters that inform much of Dickinson's poetry. Her outward concern with death and the capacity in which her texts respond to this unavoidable reality casts her writing in the mold of a liturgical poetics. In characterizing Dickinson in this capacity, the consistency with which she treats death is manifest in how she utilizes the garden and its derivative

3. Patrick J. Keane describes Dickinson's relationship to her garden in terms that anticipate the liturgical discussion that unfolds throughout this chapter: "Gardener as well as poet, Emily Dickinson was acutely aware of seasonal transition, often using the flowers and plants in her essentially 'perennial' garden as parables of the life-death cycle, even as reaffirmations of, or, more often, challenges to, a providential theodicy" (*Emily Dickinson's Approving God*, 116).

4. According to Judith Farr, Dickinson "always acknowledged a symbolic identity between herself and her flowers" (*The Gardens of Emily Dickinson*, 72), a symbolic trope that Dickinson often extends to others as well.

5. There is no shortage of biographies on Dickinson that mention this fact. McIntosh summarizes nicely the centrality death has in Dickinson's poetry: "Moreover, always in the background of her affirming messages is her anxiety about death. While she may need to unknown hauntedness of nature or the unknown mysteriousness of god to stimulate her poetic expression, death is the terrifying unknown that challenges all faith and all expression" (*Nimble Believing*, 71). For a helpful overview of Dickinson's life and writing, see Richard B Sewall's *The Life of Emily Dickinson*. See also Robinson, *Emily Dickinson*: "Dickinson uses that energy to stage a drama of the soul as it struggles to bridge the unbridgeable gulf between the reality of death and the promise of salvation" (125).

imagery in her writing. She frequently examines the garden as a specific site for death's destabilizing effects, which aligns her poetry through specific biblical texts with the liturgical promise spoken at the Last Supper. The garden's latent cyclicality affords the symbolic resources to anticipate a transcendence of death, even as it subverts the text's optimistic tone. This dynamic echoes the Last Supper and frames, therefore, how Dickinson draws on this narrative to structure her liturgical poetics. Through these intersections Dickinson eroticizes the text in order to recast death's closure in a way that discloses the stabilizing presence of the other, a feature that the different biblical gardens upon which she draws have in common.

Emily Dickinson's Theological Context

Though it is beyond the scope of the current argument to discuss in detail the historical context surrounding Dickinson's relationship with her Calvinist roots, it is important to stress that the analysis that follows will resist an over-simplification of her theological identity.[6] Frequently, biographical projects and literary analyses reduce Dickinson's theological mindset to caricatures that do not recognize the intellectual dexterity that she brought to her relationship with her Christian heritage. This is a crucial oversight that tends to miss the extent to which these theological reflections inform her writing. Often, Dickinson's Calvinist background is painted with inaccurate colors. For example, in discussing Dickinson's appreciation of nature, Barton Levi St. Armand states: "[nature] gave the summer day a whole new liturgical significance. The earthly paradise supplied all of the High Church ritual, all of that sacerdotal wealth of embroidered vestments, gleaming vessels, and heady incense, that Puritanism had denied her, reared as she was within the wintry confines of the New England meetinghouse."[7] St. Armand is considered a major figure in Dickinson scholarship, yet he sees in Dickinson's theological mind a reaction against Puritanism (already a significant alteration from the Calvinism that more recent scholarship ascribes to Dickinson[8]) that conflates Dickinson's fascination with nature

---

6. There are excellent biographies that succeed to some degree in addressing the issue. See, for example, Roger Lundin, *Emily Dickinson and the Art of Belief*; and McIntosh, *Nimble Believing*.

7. Quoted in Aliki Barnstone, *Changing Rapture*, 14.

8. I find that Magdalena Zapedowska's article "Wrestling with Silence: Emily Dickinson's Calvinist God," argues well how Dickinson's broad understanding of God exhibits Calvinist overtones. Many are quick to assume Dickinson exhibits the Puritan

and a high–liturgical sensibility. Moreover, St. Armand links this simplified religious[9] character too closely with Dickinson's Romantic predecessors. As has been discussed and as will become clear, Dickinson departs noticeably from the Romantic Movement's readings of nature as a transcendent gateway. The natural world is, for Dickinson, a dislocated context in which humanity exists, a condition that provides the basis of her unstable liturgical poetics.

By simplifying the theological character of Dickinson's poetry, St. Armand strips away the theological complexity with which Dickinson examines death. For example, he (like many other critics) casts her social withdrawal as a complete separation from her cultural context—particularly the theological nuances of her day—a reading that is, at best, simplistic. Her extensive correspondence indicates that she was well tuned to the world around her. Moreover, her social isolation was a calculated feature of her poetic persona.[10] The tendency to caricature Dickinson based on this constructed identity ultimately obscures her deep concern with theological matters, a quality that emerges clearly when reading her poetry and letters as a liturgical poetics. Dickinson, like Donne, embedded her writing in a theological context and, moreover, understood the Fall as theological basis for humanity's dislocation.[11]

---

background of her ancestors. This stereotype indicates the problem that lies in the simple confusion between the two common terms ascribed to Dickinson: Calvinist and Puritan. Though related, they are distinct as per their specific theological and historical developments (something one would expect scholars to realize when ascribing a label to Dickinson). Even if her family were devoutly Puritan, the label would still ignore the two hundred years of influence that the particular Christian context in Massachusetts exhibited in the nineteenth century.

9. I use the term religion consciously to indicate a further discrepancy between St. Armand's reading and what I consider to be Dickinson's theological exercise in her poetry. St Armand equates Dickinson's relationship with her Christian tradition with behavioral tendencies, a move that glosses the theological reflection that she clearly undertakes in her writing.

10. Though it is beyond the scope of this project to discuss at length Dickinson's social withdrawal, I do suggest that her isolation constitutes a conscious layer of her larger poetic project. Specifically, she understands the role of poet as necessary to mold the liturgical coordinates of her work to enable singular readings that outline possible communities in the capacity that a Heideggerian temple affords a coordinate around which such participants can gather. She exhibits a clearly liturgical bent insofar as she understands the poet's role as a conduit for anticipating a transcendence of humanity's dislocated condition.

11. Dickinson's relationship with Isaac Watts is but one clear example that she engaged the theological milieu of her day. Though her use of Watts' meter is accepted

Emily Dickinson's Liturgical Poetics

Before analyzing the capacity in which Dickinson draws upon biblical gardens, it will be helpful to clarify the claim that she is a deeply liturgical poet. Lacoste is helpful in this reading of Dickinson insofar as he stresses death as a structuring concern of the human condition. Humans, as subjects, are capable of addressing this fixed boundary; Lacoste uses the word "horizon"[12] to describe this definitive condition of humanity's dwelling[13] in the world. The word choice is important, as it emphasizes that life is a movement–towards–death and that this progression unfolds within a spatial framework. By orienting the human response to death through this metaphor, Lacoste emphasizes that any response—or approach—to life's horizon experiences simultaneously "the form of the world [that] exercises [influence] over the I."[14] The world's influence is recognizable in a specifically corporeal capacity[15] that must be recognized if the text is to respond to humanity's latent instability.

The world exercises an influence that makes clear the body's inevitable decay and eventual death. Dickinson captures this destabilizing effect in J378 ("I saw no Way—The heavens were stitched—"). This poem offers a clear example of how Dickinson orients her writing to confront—and ultimately be smothered by—death. The poem, then, is symptomatic of her liturgical poetics:

> I saw no Way—The heavens were stitched—
> I felt the Columns close—
> The Earth reversed her Hemispheres—
> I touched the Universe—
>
> And back it slid—and I alone—
> A speck upon a Ball—
> Went out upon Circumference—
> Beyond the Dip of Bell—[16]

---

as "parodic" (Wolosky, "Rhetoric or Not," 214), it seems unlikely that she would have mastered the Watts' metrical rhythm well enough to engage in extensive satire without engaging the hymns' content.

12. Lacoste, *Experience and the Absolute*, 10.

13. See Heidegger, "Building, Dwelling, Thinking," 141–60.

14. Lacoste, *Experience and the Absolute*, 12.

15. Ibid., 13.

16. J378, lines 1–8.

The first line frames what follows with a definitive statement; an antecedent failure frames the speaker's journey towards death's horizon. Consequently, s/he recognizes that there is no escape through the sky, which closes the place that implies a release from the world's instability.[17] The only reality to which the speaker can reconcile her/himself is death's continued reminder that s/he is trapped within the body's progression towards death. This boundary—what Dickinson terms "Circumference"[18]—marks the text's limit, a point from which the speaker can only slide back into the feeling of dislocation that characterizes the world. In this regression, however, the speaker reconfigures the text as liturgical. What is at stake in this poem is not the ability to tear through the boundary that is stitched shut, but rather the implicit recognition that the speaker's condition is "the possibility of being *symbolically* absent from the world and earth, not so as to give the impression of death, but to *make manifest* a dimension of life that is neither worldly nor earthly."[19] Circumference's boundary remains a threshold that though it cannot be crossed offers, paradoxically, a counterweight to the displacement that the world makes manifest. Though the speaker is aware that s/he cannot transcend these exilic parameters, the sliding away enables an alternative reading. The stitches indicate that the closure is not permanent, which extends the speaker's initial desire to traverse Circumference through the (repeated) sliding back into exile.

Even though the stitched heavens establish a boundary that predetermines the failure of the speaker's anticipatory journey, J378 is instructive as a common framework in Dickinson's writing whereby the reader must traverse the text in full awareness of an antecedent closure. In his analysis of this poem, Fred D. White recognizes what is at stake in this dynamic: "There may exist an infinity of possible realms—Heaven itself among them—that beckon to be explored, but they never can be *escaped* into. The speaker can never venture beyond 'circumference,' the word in this context effectively conveying the paradoxical human predicament of being both free and confined: free to explore while at the same time

---

17. As Lacoste writes, the goal is not to remove humanity from the reality of life on earth (*Experience and the Absolute*, 37), but rather that it "is very much from within our location, and not by abstracting from it, that we must inscribe the modes of a relation to the absolute" (ibid., 34). Dickinson clearly situates the absolute beyond the Circumference. For the sake of clarity, however, I will reserve discussion of this specific relationship until later in this chapter.

18. See Gribbin, "Emily Dickinson's Circumference," 1–21.

19. Ibid., 39.

confined by the inescapable forces of gravity, mortality, and the limitations of individual human perception."[20] Dickinson clearly utilizes the text to respond to death's finitude. What matters, then, is how she recalibrates the ways in which her speaker undertakes her/his journey in order to situate and sustain the poem's presence at Circumference. As a result, Dickinson conceptualizes death's effect not as a preemptive denial, but rather as a threshold that despite its denial anticipates a transcendent condition on the other side of Circumference. The effect is a self-absolution that is rekindled with each rereading of the text. This poetic re-sowing becomes apparent in J883 ("The Poets light but Lamps—"):

> The Poets light but Lamps—
> Themselves—go out—
> The Wicks they stimulate—
> If vital light
>
> Inhere as do the Suns—
> Each Age a Lens
> Disseminating their
> Circumference—[21]

Dickinson deploys the image of "Circumference" to link her role as poet with the broader exilic implications of Circumference in J378. The cyclical rereading of the text that generates a tension exists most strikingly at the limit of Circumference and she endures this instability through her reconfiguration of how humanity relates to the prohibition that this boundary upholds.

To indicate her persistence in response to death, Dickinson suggests that a peculiar kind of light fills the gap between the text and Circumference's boundary. The image recalls Blanchot's understanding of the text as a solitary space, a conception that characterizes Dickinson's writing as a liturgical poetics: "It is light which is also the abyss, a light one sinks into, both terrifying and tantalizing . . . Whoever is fascinated doesn't see, properly speaking, what he sees. Rather, it touches him in an immediate proximity; it seizes and ceaselessly draws him close, even though it leaves him absolutely at a distance."[22] In J883, the speaker's solitary journey shortens the textual radius. As a result, Dickinson reimagines the speaker's inevitable,

---

20. White "Emily Dickinson's Existential Dramas," 95.

21. J883, lines 1–8.

22. Blanchot, *The Space of Literature*, 33.

continued failure to transcend death's boundary as a promissory denial. The effect on the reader is, as Blanchot notes, subversive; any anticipation must slide away as it approaches Circumference. As James McIntosh recognizes, this repeated denial at Circumference is symptomatic of how Dickinson understands death (as Circumference), and, importantly, her relationship to that space: "Dickinson resorts openly to contradiction to exhibit the paradoxical nature of what goes on at circumference."[23] Circumference is alluring and Dickinson uses this effect to traverse a space that leads to an inevitable closure. Still, she escorts her readers to this point in order to disclose what might lie beyond Circumference.

A Liturgical Reimagining of Death

Dickinson is willing to accompany her readers to Circumference and, in so doing, she highlights the subversive effect this progression brings to the text. J390 ("It's coming—the postponeless Creature—") captures death's pervasive effect on the human condition:

> It's coming—the postponeless Creature—
> It gains the Block—and now—it gains the Door—
> Chooses its latch, from all the other fastenings—
> Enters—with a "You know Me—Sir"?
>
> Simple Salute—and certain Recognition—
> Bold—were it Enemy—Brief—were if friend—
> Dress each House in Crape, and Icicle—
> And carries one—out of it—to God—[24]

Dickinson's idiosyncratic punctuation gives the poem a rhythm of inevitability. Each dash reminds the reader that death's footsteps draw ever closer. This pursuit is relentless;[25] death even reaches into the safety that the speaker's house connotes.[26] Dickinson is clear, then, that death overwhelms the speaker as a totalizing concern that prohibits any respite within the text.[27]

23. McIntosh, *Nimble Believing*, 109.

24. J390, lines 1–8.

25. See J1686 ("The Event was directly behind Him").

26. Blanchot emphasizes this constancy as central when considering a pervasive displacement: "Death exists not only, then, at the moment of death; at all times we are its contemporaries" (*The Space of Literature*, 37).

27. Lacoste describes the human condition as one in which death places humans under "house-arrest" (*Experience and the Absolute*, 12).

By unhinging the speaker from the security that her/his home implies, Dickinson conceptualizes death's influence on the text in exilic terms; there exists from the outset an instability that the speaker cannot escape. No lock or latch can keep death out, which reiterates the destabilizing effect that death brings to the text. The speaker's removal from the house highlights this effect, but this departure initiates a necessary journey away from the displaced center towards Circumference.

Despite the instability it causes, death enables J390 to open towards a transcendence of the speaker's exilic instability. Blanchot emphasizes this point: "death is an important event, but it does not have the paradoxical character of a brute fact bearing no truth. It is a relation to another world where, precisely, truth is believed to have its origin."[28] Consequently, Blanchot explains, "in the great religious systems of the West, it is not a all difficult to hold that death is true. Death always takes place in a world, it is an event of the greatest world, an event which can be located and which gives us a location."[29] In J390, death's unrelenting approach conveys an unavoidable dislocation. Once the speaker is thus unhinged from the home's refuge, s/he is released towards death. Importantly, this transition permits the speaker to recalibrate death's arrival. As death carries the speaker away, s/he realizes that s/he is approaching a threshold that despite its destabilizing effect is the boundary between the text's exile and the possibility of an eschatological presence beyond Circumference. The effect is to transform the reality (death) that stitches the heavens shut (in J378) into a permeable border that can be crossed imaginatively by enduring the text's closure.

In Dickinson's writing, then, the notion of exile clarifies how death affects the human condition. Blanchot provides a helpful description of considering Dickinson in this capacity: "[the poet] does not belong to truth because the work is itself what escapes the movement of the true."[30] Dickinson, then, is displaced within her own texts, an instability that mirrors death's arrival in J390. A poem is lived in exile from the stability of the implied origin and though it exposes a text's latent instability, this framework responds to the absent movement of the true by re-imagining the text's dislocation as a journey towards a stabilizing presence. In this condition, the poet experiences "dissatisfaction,"[31] which manifests itself as an anticipated

28. Blanchot, *The Space of Literature*, 96.
29. Ibid.
30. Ibid., 237.
31. Ibid.

recovery of the implied origin and, ironically, a recognition that no origin can be recovered within the text's exile. In other words, Dickinson's writing constitutes a liturgical poetics in its attempt to recast death's effect as a threshold that opens the text towards an eschatological restoration to a stabilizing origin.[32]

An Erotic Exile: Courting Death

Dickinson often eroticizes the context in which her speakers relate to death, a strategy that enables the anticipation of a release from exile. As an amorous figure, death permits the speaker to glimpse a transcendent reality from the midst of its intimate destabilizing of the text. In J712 ("Because I could not stop for Death—"), this characterization and its effects occur clearly when death is transformed from an invasive threat to an erotic suitor:

> Because I could not stop for Death—
> He kindly stopped for me—
> The Carriage held but just Ourselves—
> And Immortality.
>
> We slowly drove—He knew no haste
> And I had put away
> My labor and my leisure too,
> For His Civility—[33]

This death is different. He responds kindly to the speaker's inability to stop, which establishes a bond with the speaker despite death's effect. The result is that she can resign herself to the journey towards her life's end. Death's presence thus ceases to be a boundary at the end of life and becomes a threshold that opens towards an eschatological release. Crucially, this threshold relates the speaker's exilic condition to her release through an erotic relationship with the cause of her displacement. The speaker's anticipated destination, then, casts the poem's journey as a movement towards a specifically erotic fulfillment. This narrative arc ensures, however, that the anticipated, climactic release will never come because the speaker must

---

32. J721 ("Behind Me—Dips Eternity—") presents Dickinson's clearest conception of the liminality that defines her poetic space as exilic and, consequently, liturgical. See also J615 ("Our journey has advanced—"): "Retreat—was out of Hope— / Behind—a sealed Route— / Eternity's White Flag—Before— / And God—at every gate—" (lines 9–12).

33. J712, lines 1–8. Though my analysis will focus on J712, Dickinson utilizes this conceit in a less developed capacity in J1445 ("Death is the supple Suitor").

endure the entire ride; death must have its say before the speaker can cross into what awaits beyond the destination of this journey. As an erotic other, death thus indicates the simultaneous extension and denial of desire that characterizes a liturgical poetics. In conceptualizing a transcendence of death as yielding to its courtship, Dickinson links J712 to the Last Supper's similarly erotic structure wherein Jesus must encounter death in order to extend the liturgical promise.

The speaker in J712 never reaches its destination; she is suspended at the threshold she hopes to cross. She can only glimpse, then, her eschatological release, an ironic reminder that any disclosure comes only by virtue the closure that death brings. The final lines of J712 make this point clear: "Since then—tis' Centuries—and yet / Feels shorter than the Day / I first surmised the Horses' Heads / Were toward Eternity—."[34] Eternity lies just beyond the text, which leaves to speaker (and the reader) to anticipate the journey's unrealized conclusion. The final dash emphasizes that the journey can only continue and, therefore, can never reach the destination that materializes before the speaker. No reading of the poem will encounter anything beyond the dash; every reading will be resigned to its indefinite extension.

The erotic undercurrents in J712 are significant, as they reveal a more pervasive symbolic construct that appears frequently in Dickinson's poetry. In J712, Dickinson eroticizes the text's exilic parameters, which opens the text towards an eschatological fulfillment of the desire that emerges out of death's courtship. More specifically, the eroticization of death in J712 helps to clarify a frequent image elsewhere in Dickinson's poetry: the garden. In her study *The Passion of Emily Dickinson*, Judith Farr identifies the garden's erotic space as crucial to Dickinson's larger poetic—and therefore liturgical—project. Recognizing Dickinson as descending from the Romantic tradition, Farr states: "Love, as in the case of the great romantics, allowed her to glimpse and record the relation between this world and the next."[35] Farr offers a useful critical apparatus to recognize how the body's erotic capacity opens the text towards the experience of a stabilizing presence. In J249 ("Wild Nights—Wild Nights!") this destination is Eden:

34. J712, lines 21–24.

35. Farr, *The Passion of Emily Dickinson*, 247. See also J695 ("As if the Sea should part")

Wild Nights—Wild Nights!
Were I with thee
Wild Nights should be
Our luxury!

Futile—the Winds—
To a Heart in port—
Done with the Compass—
Done with the Chart!

Rowing in Eden—
Ah, the Sea!
Might I but moor—Tonight—
In Thee![36]

A clear, erotic desire emerges out of the text's exile, a charge that brackets the its latent instability. The result is the speaker's deeply erotic progression towards the recovery of a lost origin. Dickinson tends not to punctuate her lines, so the exclamation point in the first line conveys strongly the erotic energy that frames the poem. This energy enables the speaker to navigate these nights without a Compass or a Chart, a clear indication that her desire is strong enough to endure the instability that characterizes every Wild Night.

In addition to its obvious erotic context, J249's specific images underscore how the speaker's desire is liturgical. For example, the journey on/through the sea is, according to Farr, "a multivalent symbol that could stand for eternity, or terror, or sexuality."[37] In J249, the emphasis is clearly on the overwhelming sexual connotations of the sea,[38] which lace the speaker's erotic journey with eschatological implications. Consequently, in the third stanza Dickinson shifts the image; the sea becomes Eden, the specific origin from which humanity has been displaced. The mooring that the speaker desires thus condenses the fulfillment of an erotic desire with a recovery of Eden's stability. This destination becomes, then, an absence that structures J249 as a liturgical poetics. As Smith points out, such a conclusion captures "that Dickinson's is frequently a poetics of absence, I would suggest

36. J249, lines 1–12.

37. Farr, *The Passion of Emily Dickinson*, 202. Farr clarifies the specific associations gardens have for Dickinson viz. the relationship between Dickinson's poetic space and the possibility of eternity: "she saw in the garden, with its cycle of birth, decay, death, and rebirth, an idea that rendered heaven plausible" (*The Gardens of Emily Dickinson*, 93).

38. See L750: "I cannot tell how eternity seems. It sweeps around me like a sea."

that absence ultimately serves preserve in its evocation of that which is missing."[39] In poems such as J249, the text's exilic parameters anticipate an eternal possibility through recognition of the fulfillment's impossibility. Smith's word choice is telling. Dickinson does not merely indicate the absent, eternal other through her language; she evokes and sustains it through a specifically erotic desire for that other's presence.

Dickinson can be cast as an asexual hermit, a charge that her biography supports. However, despite the probability that she was never sexually active, her writing makes clear that her lack of sexual experience does not preclude the erotic nature of her liturgical poetics. On the contrary, the extent of the erotic contours in Dickinson's poetry must be emphasized here. Rebecca Patterson does well to call attention to this aspect of Dickinson's poetry: "There is, on the contrary, no more erotic poetry in the English language . . . Death is eroticized, pain is eroticized, religion is eroticized . . . Expressed in a slight different way, she has but two subjects, which are in fact one subject—an eroticized death and what might called a thanatized eros."[40] Though parabolic in her language, Patterson does affirm the pervasive eroticism in Dickinson's poetry. Specifically, Patterson captures the central thematic tension that characterizes J249. Death and eros commingle to the point that the text can be described as an eroticized thanatos, or, in Patterson's language, the thanatized eros. In either case, this erotic element configures the text as liturgical insofar as it condenses eros and thanatos into a singular image, which provides the basis for anticipating the absent divine other. Moreover, the overlapping of death and eros recalls the body's crucial function within a liturgical poetics. The satisfaction implied just beyond the text—the Eternity that the speaker in J712 glimpses—emerges only when the text relates intimately to its own closure. Erotic satisfaction thus indicates the anticipated transcendence that will permit the speaker to see the divine other face-to-face.[41]

Eden: The Biblical Roots of Emily Dickinson's Gardens

Having discussed the erotic nature of Dickinson's poetry, the analysis at hand can return to the tension between absence and presence that Smith identifies. In Dickinson's poetry, Eden is frequently the destination that

---

39. Smith, *The Seductions of Emily Dickinson*, 111.

40. Patterson, *Emily Dickinson's Imagery*, 30.

41. See also J263 ("A Single Screw of Flesh").

the speaker's release from exile will lead to. Jack Capps provides a helpful starting point for considering Eden as the context of a restored stability: "Eden is one of the most meaningful of symbols. It implies the supernatural bliss of prelapsarian existence."[42] Though Dickinson frequently uses Eden to characterize a lost origin, she does not treat this garden in the simplistic terms that Capps suggests; a more complex symbolism is at work. As Farr notes, the garden had a particular, personal significance for Dickinson. In fact, the window looking out from her room literally merged the garden with another presence: "Indeed, the garden and the cemetery were more than vaguely related in her mind, the dead being described in her mature poems as flowers or bulbs that would arise at a brighter time and season."[43] As the absent origin, Eden provides a point of reference wherein death did not affect humanity. As such, Eden provides Dickinson with a theological framework to conceptualize death. In seeking to return to Eden, then, her speakers exhibit a desire for a theological transcendence of death, which will result in humanity's return to God's presence. God becomes, therefore, the desired other that anchors the erotic contexts in which Dickinson constructs her liturgical poetics.

The Garden of Eden thus fuses death's exilic implications and the stability that a transcendence of this condition will provide. In his recent book *Emily Dickinson's Approving God: Divine Design and the Problem of Suffering*, Patrick J. Keane undertakes an extensive analysis of J1624 ("Apparently with no surprise"), which affords a symptomatic look at how Dickinson draws on the garden to anticipate a return to an Edenic stability. In J1624, Keane points out, the poem's central moment is "the destructive . . . impact of frost upon a flower,"[44] a clear stress on the fate that death marks for all life. For Keane, the symbolism is unmistakably a central tenet of Dickinson's use of garden-based imagery: "For Dickinson, a lifelong expert gardener as well as a poet, the central issue of theodicy—what to make of suffering and death and possible rebirth in an ordered world presided over by a supposedly providential and loving God—was seasonally enacted

---

42. Capps, *Emily Dickinson's Reading 1836–1886*, 31. Farr echoes this point: "As a mature poet, in a striking group of love poems, she chose 'Eden,' the lost garden of pure natural delight, as a symbol for romantic ecstasy" (*The Gardens of Emily Dickinson*, 12).

43. Farr, *The Gardens of Emily Dickinson*, 19. For more biographical information on Dickinson's personal garden, see Farr, *The Gardens of Emily Dickinson*, 1–12. Given Dickinson's commitment to her own, garden, the rich symbolic resources of this familiar environment allow her to expand the metaphor of the garden as recovered origin.

44. Keane, *Emily Dickinson's Approving God*, 26.

year after year in her own beloved garden."[45] In light of the flower's behead-
ing, Lacoste's emphasis that all liturgical imaginings occur from within
exile emerges clearly. The garden in J1624 is both the site of continual rebirth in the face of death and the inevitable subversion of this regenerative
condition. Accordingly, any desire for Eden calls to mind necessarily the
displacement that Eden, now lost, generates within the human condition.

Smith sees the garden's complex imagery as indicative of Dickinson's
larger poetic project. The garden is the site of death, as well as rebirth.[46]
Thus, Smith argues: "In this context, the word's connotations best capture
the dangerous sexiness of an embedding that blurs thanatos and eros, annihilation and eroticism, experiences of loss of self that end in embalmings.
Seduction (*seducere*) is a leading both on and in, an ambiguous experience of risk, promising mastery while demanding submission, perilous, yet
requiring the seducee to suspend awareness of the peril."[47] If Dickinson's
gardens are treated as merely sensuous, then one misses the theological
implications that these references import into her writing. Eden is not just
a paradise; it is the sight of a theological death, the result of a complex
seduction that clearly interested Dickinson from an early age.[48] More importantly, as Smith argues, Dickinson likely read the story of Eve through
a post-Miltonic framework.[49] The act of seduction in Eden is streaked
with textual properties that mirror the uneven exilic space of the poems in

---

45. Ibid., 33.

46. Smith notes that, often, the central event in Dickinson's garden poems is "pol-
lination" (2). This clearly erotic dynamic echoes what Alicia Ostriker calls the "palpable
eroticism [of J211]. . .and the thoroughly orgasmic [J249]" ("Re-playing the Bible," 64).
When reading Dickinson, the symbolic release of orgasm and the release of death thus
overlap. This thematic parallel reinforces the ties between Dickinson's gardens as places
of liturgical anticipation and the necessary denial of this desire that must occur. Patterson's language holds; in Dickinson's liminal spaces, one can speak of either a thanatized
eros or an eroticized thanatos.

47. Smith, *The Seductions of Emily Dickinson*, 5.

48. In her letter to her friend Abiah Root, written at the age of sixteen, Dickinson
states "I have lately come to the conclusion that I am Eve. You know there is no account
of her death in the Bible" (L 9). It is important to emphasize that even as a young woman,
Dickinson already associated Eve with both death and a transcendence of death.

49. In her one year at Mt. Holyoke Seminary, Dickinson "was expected to leave with
as thorough a knowledge of *Paradise Lost* as she had of the King James Bible" (Smith, *The
Seductions of Emily Dickinson*, 26).

which Dickinson utilizes Eden to symbolize an anticipated context that will restore humanity's stability.[50]

Once again, death and life commingle in a complex way, which calls attention to the capacity in which Dickinson problematizes the symbolic resources that the garden offers. In turn, this suggests that Dickinson draws upon biblical gardens more subtlety than has been recognized in critical examinations of how Dickinson references Eden. As the lost origin that now indicates humanity's cyclical instability, Eden helps Dickinson to establish the paradoxical dynamics that characterize her liturgical poetics.[51]

Emily Dickinson's Erotic Garden: The Song of Songs

Eden is not the only biblical garden that informs Dickinson's writing. In *The Erotic Word: Sexuality, Spirituality, and the Bible*, David M. Carr recognizes that the Bible's many gardens share an underlying thematic consistency, which, he explains, is distinctly erotic. Carr writes: "In the world of the Bible, gardens (and vineyards) are places where lovers meet to make love."[52] One such garden that clearly informs Dickinson's writing provides the context for the most overtly erotic book in the Bible: the Song of Songs. In this garden, Carr notes that "The man and woman never actually 'make it' in this poem. Yet, here, as at so many other points in the Song of Songs, the poetry tantalizes us with the probability of their embrace."[53] This gap is significant. Just as Dickinson's speaker in J712 can only glimpse Eternity (as the fulfillment of her anticipation/desire), the lovers in the Song of Songs never experience the crucial, climactic moment that their narrative arc implies. In Songs 8:3, for example, the female speaker says, "His left

---

50. Smith writes, "the word 'seduction' is marvelously scored with contradiction: it alludes to notions of conquest and captivation while relying on expressions of consent or acquiescence; it compresses charm and fascination with bribery and coercion; it conflates delight and pleasure with wrongs and betrayals" (12). In this capacity, Dickinson recognizes that a liturgical poetics' erotic implications frequently introduce the possibility of abuse within the intimate space that such texts demarcate.

51. Regardless of the garden in question, Farr offers the following general claims about the symbolism of flowers in Dickinson's writing: "the death of her plants always mirrored human death to Dickinson; they were mystical events to her" (*The Gardens of Emily Dickinson*, 90); and "Finally, it is no exaggeration to claim that flowers . . . had spiritual significance for Emily Dickinson" (ibid, 132).

52. Carr, *The Erotic Word*, 13.

53. Ibid., 115.

hand should be under my head, and his right hand should embrace me."[54] The woman suggests a moment that either precedes or follows the lovers' consummation of their relationship.[55] The erotic framework thus brings the lovers into proximity while maintaining a separation. As Carr describes the text, "the Song constantly approaches their lovemaking and fades away, or teases with double entendres. It stokes the first of erotic imagination, getting explicit enough to get the flames burning, yet not dousing them with the water of description."[56] This intimacy is central to the garden in Song of Songs and, moreover, it establishes a thematic link between this garden and a liturgical poetics. In the Songs garden, that which anticipates a presence ultimately establishes a textual absence. This dynamic echoes the Last Supper narrative because it mirrors the parameters of Jesus' promise: a presence is announced only through an absence.

By refusing to depict the lovers' implied consummation, the Song of Songs conveys desire in anticipation of a conclusion that the text will not provide. This is a significant denial because it echoes the impossibility of transcending the text's displacement. Moreover, given its erotic contours, the text is paradoxically strengthened by this refusal to bring the narrative to its implied conclusion. In Song 5, the speaker's desire endures the other lover's absence: "I am come into my garden, my sister, my spouse: I have gathered my myrrh with my spice; I have eaten my honeycomb with my honey; I have drunk my wine with my milk: eat, O friends; drink, yea, drink abundantly, O beloved. I sleep, but my heart waketh; it is the voice of my beloved that knocketh, saying, Open to me, my sister, my love, my dove, my undefiled; for my head is filled with dew, and my locks with the drops of the night."[57] Two details in this passage warrant specific mention. First, the woman begins her story by mentioning that she enters into the garden. Thus, the thematic ties that Carr mentions are easily identifiable from the outset. Secondly, this locale sustains the erotic energy by stressing the male lover's absence. It is within this displaced context that the absent lover is called into proximity: "I rose up to open to my beloved; and my hands dropped with myrrh, and my fingers with sweet smelling myrrh, upon the handles of the lock. I opened to my beloved; but my beloved had withdrawn himself, and was gone; my soul failed when he spake; I sought him, but I

---

54. Song 8:3.

55. Carr, *The Erotic Word*, 149.

56. Ibid., 116.

57. Song 5:1–2.

could not find him; I called him, but he gave me no answer."[58] As he knocks at the door, the male lover announces his approach to the woman's bed-chamber while simultaneously reiterating that he has not yet arrived. The door establishes a threshold between the lovers that provides an intimate context through which they can relate while also prohibiting their mutually anticipated union. This denial intensifies their mutual displacement, which, paradoxically, both extends and undermines their intimacy. The door is a boundary that neither can cross, a refusal that predicates the lovers' desire on their inability to experience the threshold brings into focus.

The lovers' unfulfilled anticipation identifies the crucial denial that establishes the Song of Songs as a liturgical poetics. Their inability to fulfill their desire constitutes a central theme throughout the Song, which in turn ensures that the lovers cannot transcend their displacement. In her commentary on the Song of Songs, J. Cheryl Exum identifies this absence as central to the Song's erotic contours: "Throughout the Song, speech embodies desire by calling bodies into being and playing with their disappearance in an infinite deferral of presence. Conjuring seeks to make immanent through language what is absent, to construct the lovers as 'real' (that is, present before us) and endow them with meaning."[59] The Song's lovers fail to obtain what they want. The effect, Exum notes, is that "Desire in the Song is always on the brink of fulfillment, and has an urgency about it."[60] In light of Exum's analysis, the lovers' failure to satisfy their desire constitutes a paradoxical closure insofar as they endure a mutual absence throughout the text. As a result, their denied desire opens the text to repeated readings in anticipation of the expected but not-yet dénouement that readers infer. Because desire never experiences satisfaction, it continues, endlessly, without suffering the collapse that follows sexual climax.[61]

Following humanity's expulsion from Eden, the Songs garden provides an erotic space that anticipates a stabilizing union. As a result, the two gardens' shared erotic contours highlight what is at stake in the denial

58. Song 5:5–6.

59. Exum, *Song of Songs*, 7.

60. Ibid., 11.

61. In this capacity, the Song of Songs converges with Derrida's insistence that images mark and are marked by *différance*. As Exum notes: "Its resistance to closure is perhaps the Song's most important strategy for immortalizing love. Closure would mean the end of desiring, the silence of the text, the death of love" (*Song of Songs*, 12). In the Songs' garden, one returns repeatedly to that which all liturgical poetics indicate but never attain: a stable center that does not strain against textual *différance*.

of satisfaction that characterizes the Song of Songs. In J663 ("Again—his voice is at the door—"), Dickinson draws on the Songs garden to frame an encounter between lovers:

> Again—his voice is at the door—
> I feel the old *Degree*—
> I hear him ask the servant
> For such an one—as me—
>
> I take a *flower*—as I go—
> My face to *justify*—
> He never *saw* me—in *this* life—
> I might *surprise* his eye!
>
> I cross the Hall with *mingled* steps—
> I—silent—pass the door—
> I look on all this world *contains*—
> Just his face—nothing more![62]

The poem's opening word subverts everything that follows. The missed encounter that Dickinson alludes to from the Song of Songs occurs yet again, which announces the inevitable denial of the desire that is about to unfold (and, moreover, that has already occurred). Upon hearing her lover's voice, the speaker goes to the door, flower in hand.[63] Her motivation for approaching this threshold—her face to justify—is distinctly liturgical. She seeks from her lover the absolution contained in the theological notion of justification. If he would only look upon her face, she would obtain the restorative, stabilizing assurance that the gaze implies. The theological language thus equates satisfied desire with a restored Edenic stability. The lover, then, is not just anyone. Though never identified, the theological implications of the lover's gaze indicate that Jesus is the lover.[64] Seeing this

---

62. J663, lines 1–12.

63. The flower that the speaker brings to the door connotes two important points. First, Dickinson accents the source for this poem's imagery: the garden from the Song of Songs. Moreover, as Farr notes, flowers "seem to her the best emblems of the eternal" (*The Gardens of Emily Dickinson*, 23). Thus, the flower brought to the door emphasizes both the lover's absence (though he is intimately close) and the recovery of stability that the lover's presence would provide.

64. See J317 ("Just so—Jesus—raps—"), which reverses the narrative flow: "Just so—Jesus—raps— / He—doesn't weary— / Last—at the Knocker— / And first—at the Bell. / Then—on divinest tiptoe—standing— / Might he but spy the lady's soul—" (lines 1–6). Dickinson's pun on justification strikes the delicate balance between absence and

(divine) lover face-to-face will satisfy the speaker's desire for a restored stability, which links the anticipated return to an Edenic condition with the erotic absence that characterizes the Songs garden.

A distinct theological tenor is, therefore, present as the speaker antici-pates her lover's presence. When she reaches the door, the point at which she can finally fulfill her desire, she finds only the trace of her lover's depar-ture. The erotic framework in J663 therefore parallels the expected consum-mation that never occurs in the Songs garden. This unfulfilled desire thus circles around to the denial contained in the poem's first word. The antici-pated satisfaction that the erotic context suggests disappears when, in the final stanza, the speaker laments: "I'd give—to live that hour—*again*—."[65] The poem's narrative arc never encounters the eschatological fulfillment that Jesus' presence (as the divine lover) would provide. Dickinson echoes, then, the unfulfilled promise from the Last Supper to indicate through Je-sus' absence the subversive effects that the exilic condition in question has upon the lovers' anticipation in J663.

Displaced Desire and Liturgical Hope

Dickinson recognizes and utilizes to great effect the implications of unful-filled desire in the context of a liturgical poetics. As Roger Lundin argues, because she was "a romantic poet whose imagination had been fed by Christian images of splendor, Dickinson found it sweeter to imagine sat-isfaction that to taste it."[66] Lundin's analysis is accurate, even if he does not recognize these implications as specifically liturgical in their anticipated fulfillment of desire. He does, however, build upon this point in a telling manner: "Dickinson liked to dwell upon the relationship between intense affection and its missing object."[67] In this regard, Lundin does not link the implications of unfulfilled desire with the complex intertextuality that

---

presence that the door enables in both Songs and J663. In addition to identifying the lover as Jesus, J317 also emphasizes the theological association of Jesus' death—conveyed in the image of the bell—with the justification that the female lover seeks in J663 and receives in J317.

65. J663, line 26.

66. Lundin, *Emily Dickinson and the Art of Belief*, 117. It is important to note that in using the term "romantic" to describe Dickinson, Lundin does not align her with the Romantic poetic movement. Rather, he conveys with this description the erotic contours that her poetry exhibits.

67. Lundin, *Emily Dickinson and the Art of Belief*, 247.

Dickinson's references to biblical gardens generates. These influences calibrate frustrated desire as a liturgical response to humanity's expulsion from Eden, which in turn clarifies further what it is that Dickinson articulates by focusing on the lovers' denied consumation. The continued separation that prevents their satisfaction mirrors humanity's continued dislocation from God. The Songs garden anticipates the lover's arrival in this context and, therefore, conflates satisfied desire with the eschatological stability that Jesus' presence will provide.

Through the image of the door, Dickinson draws on the Song of Songs to bring the lovers into intimate proximity while ensuring that they never experience the satisfaction that the text implies. Dickinson utilizes this displacing conceit to convey through the lovers' continued separation a liturgical possibility in J1055 ("The Soul should always stand ajar"):

> The Soul should always stand ajar
> That if the Heaven inquire
> He will not be obliged to wait
> Or shy of troubling Her
>
> Depart, before the Host have slid
> The Bolt unto the Door—
> To search for the accomplished Guest,
> Her visitor, no more—[68]

The soul, just like the door in Song 5, becomes the locus for anticipating the divine lover's presence by marking his absence from the text. The speaker must be ready to embrace the erotic, divine other before the Host[69] departs from this space. The image that conveys this possibility adds a sense of urgency to the liaison that unfolds; the sign that the moment will be lost is overtly sexual. The Bolt that would lock the Door and thus deny the two lovers the chance to see one another is an obvious euphemism for, respectively, men's and women's genitalia. Should this definitive action come to pass, the door would be closed and the lover would be a visitor no more. Importantly, the door exhibits the irony that characterizes a liturgical poetics. The consummation that the locked door represents also constitutes a strengthening of the barrier that keeps the lovers separate. The erotic image

68. J1055, lines 1–8.

69. Dickinson's wordplay is, once again, surprisingly clear in its reference, even if the subsequent meaning is not so. The "Host" is the male lover, Jesus, who is present through his absence (marked by the eucharistic host/body), which links again the poem to the Last Supper's liturgical promise.

emphasizes, then, that the lovers' desire both sustains the text despite their mutual absence while simultaneously emphasizing that the lovers will not be able to cross the threshold that will permit the fulfillment of their desire. The door's bolt and lock thus mirror Jesus' absence following his announcement of the Last Supper's promise.

Intimate, Distant Desire: The Garden in John 20

The continued separation that the door ensures alludes to a third biblical garden in John 20 wherein Mary Magdalene encounters Jesus after his resurrection.[70] When Mary arrives at the garden and speaks to the angels, her language echoes that of the woman in the Song of Songs longing for her lover.[71] The implications of this textual link become clear when Jesus tells Mary that she must not experience the fulfillment that she—as a lover— anticipates: "Jesus saith unto her, Touch me not; for I am not yet ascended to my Father: but go to my brethren, and say unto them, I ascend unto my Father, and your Father; and to my God, and your God."[72] Despite the desire that surges through Mary when she realizes that Jesus, whose presence seemingly fulfills the promise made during the Last Supper, is so near she could touch him, the text is strict in its denial. Jesus' words are definitive; Mary cannot touch him. Moreover, the command implies that Mary should not even want to touch him, which reiterates the closure that the encounter causes. As he does during the Last Supper, Jesus emphasizes that his presence only announces that he is about to depart.

Jesus' command not to touch his body exhibits the paradoxical nature that defines a liturgical poetics. Mary's gesture anticipates the divine lover's presence that Jesus promised during the Last Supper. At the same time, his response reiterates that she cannot transcend the exilic context out of which

70. Carr writes, "After Jesus' crucifixion, John says that Jesus' body is anointed with 'myrrh and aloes.' As Raymond Brown notes, this is an unusual combination of spices. Aloe is not typically used in burials. The same combination, however, myrrh and aloe, does occur in Song of Songs 4:14. They are the last two spices mentioned in the man's description of his lover as a garden of spices" (*The Erotic Word*, 163).

71. "'They said to her, 'Woman, why are you weeping?' She said to them, 'They have taken away my Lord, and I do not know where they have laid him'" (John 20:13). Carr writes of this passage: "Mary's implicit query to the angels at the tomb about where Jesus is recalls the woman of the Song of Songs asking if the guards of the city have seen her love" (*The Erotic Word*, 164).

72. John 20:17.

she reaches. This is the crucial link between Dickinson and the garden in John 20. This exchange marks Jesus' paradoxical emergence and retreat in the garden. Derrida recognizes what is at stake during this encounter in *On Touching—Jean-Luc Nancy*. He links the image of the touch's liminality with his argument that such thresholds both bring possibilities into proximity and assert the fundamental *différance* that prohibits any originary stability for those who touch. Derrida writes: "Touching, in any case, thus remains limitrophe; it touches what it does not touch; it does not touch; it *abstains* from touching on what it touches, and within the abstinence retaining it at the heart of its desire and need, in an inhibition truly constituting its appetite, it eats without eating what is its nourishment, touching, without touching."[73] The touch signals both desire in its awareness of its own dislocation and, consequently, the necessary exilic denial that any touch must endure; to touch is to trace an impossible origin (Eden, in this case) that must remain absent. Importantly, this complex symbolic play occurs at the most intimate of thresholds wherein: "limit, *limit itself*, seems deprived of a body. Limit is not to be touched and does not touch itself; it does not let itself be touched, and steals away at a touch, which either never attains it or trespasses on it forever."[74] The body's capacity to relate intimately to an/other body allows the text to oscillate between an almost and a not-yet fulfillment, which summarizes well the paradoxical closure and disclosure that Jesus announces when he situates liturgical hope in his own body during the Last Supper.

The touch, then, links Dickinson's lovers and gardens to the desire Mary conveys through her gesture. In turn, these associations reiterate the cyclical dynamic that dislocates the text. The imperative not to touch underscores the liturgical not-yet that emerges from the Last Supper narrative and comes into focus in John 20. The anticipated stability that Jesus promises cannot be fulfilled within the context of humanity's exilic condition. Consequently, Jesus responds to Mary in a way that makes clear the need to withdraw her gesture, which in turn extends indefinitely the desire that precluded her reach. She must not cross the boundary that separates her from Jesus. This prohibition reminds Mary that the body's closure in death must be upheld if the liturgical promise is to extend through Jesus' departure.[75]

73. Derrida, *On Touching*, 67.

74. Ibid., 6.

75. This point indicates that Dickinson, like Donne, does not reject entirely the

The Body's Desire as a Liturgical Locus

Jesus' appearance in John 20 establishes a threshold that, to recall Derrida, establishes (and maintains) the text's différance. Jean-Luc Nancy echoes the need to occupy this intimate space without transgressing its exilic boundaries: "He speaks in order to say that he is there and that he is leaving immediately. He speaks in order to say to the other that he is not where he is believed to be; he is already elsewhere, while nonetheless being present: here, but not right here. It is up to the other to understand. It is up to the other to see and hear."[76] Jesus' presence, then, should not be read as a fulfillment. Rather, he reiterates to Mary the necessary departure that he cites during the Last Supper as a condition of his liturgical promise. Through this paradox, however, he establishes that his promise will be fulfilled in the future, which, in John 20, demands that he refute Mary's reach. Thus, he upholds a liturgical poetics' ironic requirement that any anticipation of the promise's fulfillment will be denied within the text.

In John 20, Jesus' body makes clear this paradox. Nancy writes: "To touch him or to hold him back would be to adhere to immediate presence, and just as this would be to believe in touching (to believe in the presence of the present), it would be to miss the departing [*la partance*] according to which the touch and presence come to us."[77] The departure, Nancy emphasizes, enables the text to accommodate the necessary denial that Jesus absence generates. The meeting in John 20 highlights this indefinite displacement, something Mary realizes only after she reaches out to touch him. Jesus' physical presence holds open the textual space in question long enough for Mary to act on her desire and, therefore, to realize that her desire must be denied. This rejection materializes in a specifically corporeal capacity, which strengthens the link between John 20 and the garden in the Song of Songs. The desired body structures the erotic context out of which the liturgical promise materializes, which enables the simultaneous closure and disclosure that distinguishes a liturgical poetics.

Dickinson thus recognizes the crucial textual and theological dynamics that emerge when Mary learns that her desire to touch Jesus must remain unfulfilled. In drawing on both the garden in Song of Songs and

---

orthodox theological beliefs that her liturgical poetics deconstructs. Despite her creative liberties in adapting the narrative in John 20, Dickinson adheres to the underlying theological logic, a sign that she does not reject completely her own theological tradition.

76. Nancy, *Noli Me Tangere*, 11.

77. Ibid., 15.

John 20, Dickinson establishes that the text's erotic framework enables an endurance of its latent instability in order to anticipate the divine presence that will restore humanity's prelapsarian stability. In J1257 ("Dominion lasts until obtained—"), Dickinson clarifies how the image of touch both suggests and stifles this eschatological fulfillment: "Dominion lasts until obtained— / Possession just as long— / But these—endowing as they flit / Eternally belong."[78] The speaker echoes Derrida's account of the touch in its ability to anticipate but never achieve stability. Dominion and Possession suggest momentarily that which exilic texts anticipate: the recovery of Eden's lost stability. At the same time, Dickinson underscores the text's denial of any such fulfillment. Satisfaction belongs to an eternally stable space outside the text.

In the second stanza of J1257, Dickinson builds on this paradox. In so doing, she both holds together and disperses the liturgical desire for stability: "How everlasting are the Lips / Known only to the Dew— / These are the Brides of permanence / Supplanting me and you."[79] Dickinson imagines fulfillment as a kiss that never occurs. The effect is clear; satisfying desire is only possible beyond the text, a fact that becomes clear through the image's erasure. This absence strengthens the link between Dickinson's use of the Song of Songs garden and Mary's encounter with Jesus in John 20. As Diehl notes, unfulfilled desire constitutes the crucial theme in J1257: "The lesson is clear: anticipation surpasses fulfillment and so should be preserved."[80] Importantly, Diehl's analysis parallels how Derrida understands touch. The absent kiss in J1257 implies an/other who has already departed the text. The consequent, unfulfilled desire expressed therein sustains the text at this intimate threshold. J1257 thus coheres with Derrida's explanation of how the touch functions as: "the experience of the border and of overflowing, the trembling apprehension of that which, *touching* on the border, at once goes overboard and remains at the border, holding out and holding back, retaining itself or abstaining, on the border."[81] The unrealized kiss withholds from the reader what it implies, namely the satisfaction of desire and, by extension, the stability that the divine other provides.

Unfulfilled desire is a crucial theme that Dickinson lifts out of the biblical gardens and the Last Supper throughout her writing. The presence of

78. J1257, lines 1–4.

79. Ibid., lines 5–8.

80. Diehl, *Emily Dickinson and the Romantic Imagination*, 95.

81. Derrida, *On Touching*, 109.

a garden indicates the absence of the other who would satisfy the speaker's desire. The other's absence structures the text as a dislocated space. For example, the opening lines of J484 ("My Garden—like a Beach—") anticipate an alternative to the speaker's exile: "My Garden—like a Beach— / Denotes there be—a Sea—."[82] The allusion to the garden opens the text to an absent, anticipated eschatological stability. Though the speaker longs for this condition—and the transcendence of death implied therein—Dickinson stresses that a textual return to Eden is impossible; the sea remains distinct from the garden. Herein lies the reason behind her use of the garden from the Song of Songs and John 20. Unlike Eden, this garden is a place where lovers and Dickinson's readers can reach towards the erotic other and endure the closure this anticipation inevitably encounters when the gesture is refused. The garden setting thus conveys through a specifically erotic context a commitment to the promise that Jesus makes during the Last Supper. Dickinson acknowledges that the conditions of the promise deny necessarily any fulfillment, which affirms the exilic parameters that govern the text as a liturgical poetics. The erotic body, then, provides the basis for enduring the indefinite separation that characterizes the biblical gardens that Dickinson draws upon in her writing.

To read Dickinson's corpus as a liturgical poetics, one must accept that denial is the only possible conclusion to erotic desire that materializes in her gardens. However, this closure paradoxically enables a counterweight to death's inevitability, namely that through its denial the desire for the divine other can anticipate anew its satisfaction. The body's effect that she recovers from the Last Supper narrative in the form of Jesus' promise is, for Dickinson, the cyclical desire and denial that disrupts the text as it promises a recovery of humanity's prelapsarian stability. In the end, all desire must remain grounded in exile, which predicates any intimate glimpse of the other on that other's absence. The divine lover, then, extends desire by ensuring that:

> Ungained—it may be—by a Life's low Venture—
> But then—
> Eternity enable the endeavoring
> Again.[83]

---

82. J484, lines 1–2.
83. J680 ("Each Life Converges to some Centre—"), lines 17–20.

6

The Body and Betrayal

Jesus said to her, "Woman, why are you weeping? Whom are you looking for?" Supposing him to be the gardener, she said to him, "Sir, if you have carried him away, tell me where you have laid him, and I will take him away." Jesus said to her, "Mary!" She turned and said to him in Hebrew, "Rabbouni!" Jesus said to her, "Do not hold on to me, because I have not yet ascended to the Father. But go to my brothers and say to them, "I am ascending to my Father and your Father, to my God and your God."[1]

FOR DICKINSON, THE THEOLOGICAL PARAMETERS THAT JESUS' BODY GEN-erates in John 20 enable rereadings despite the text's closure. His appearance reveals only partially the theological implications that govern his encounter with Mary. One can forgive Mary, then, for not knowing that she cannot touch Jesus. In the wake of the previous days' events, this encounter wholly disrupts her mourning. It is only when Jesus speaks her name that Mary suddenly faces the possibility that Jesus' death did not subvert the promise he made in the upper room. Her desire to touch Jesus expresses a deeply felt trust in that promise. Nearly overwhelmed, she extends her hand to the edge of her displacement; she reaches out to confirm the presence that emerges before her. In response, Jesus refuses the gesture to remind Mary that she cannot touch him because he must depart to ascend to God and thus to transcend the exilic context in which this meeting takes place. This theological requirement leaves her to anticipate his return—an event cast indefinitely into the future—wherein he will stay with her and permit her touch.[2] This garden, then, continues the theological arc that begins with

---

1. John 20:15–17.

2. There are readings of John 20 that challenge this summary. Specifically, the theological nature of Jesus' rebuke frequently provides the stepping off point for analyzing the

humanity's expulsion from Eden. In order for humanity to be restored to God's presence, Jesus must fulfill the theological requirements of his atoning death by ascending to God.

In *Noli Me Tangere*, Titian portrays this moment with details that echo the capacity in which Dickinson adapts this scene in light of the theological requirement that Jesus mentions. Titan situates Mary at Jesus' feet as she looks up longingly, not at his face, but at his body. Her hand follows her gaze, though on a slightly lower plane; Titian stops the reach just before her hand can grasp Jesus' robes. In response, Jesus swings his hips away from her as he gathers the object of her desire with his right hand.[3] His left hand holds a gardening tool, which stands erect at an acute angle. Each of these details infuses the painting with distinctly erotic overtones. The robes around Jesus' groin have gathered in a way that implies Jesus has an erection when he encounters Mary. The slant of cloth matches that of his

---

scene, a critical decision that analyzes this passage in significantly different terms. While my own analysis does not preclude these readings, it does emphasize what is at stake in this text as a liturgical poetics, which in turn accents particular features. This does not, of course, deny that John 20 constitutes a significant theological text. Rather, the point is to stress that my reading, like this project, emerge from a distinctly literary methodology, a critical decision that knowingly brackets points of emphasis that would otherwise produce a different reading than I offer here.

3. There exists a distinct possibility that Botticelli's *The Annunciation* (1489/90) influences Titian's *Noli Me Tangere* (c. 1514), which enriches how Titian depicts the encounter between Jesus and Mary. Botticelli's painting captures another crucial moment wherein Jesus' embodiment begins. Botticelli thus prefigures the theological paradigm that structures how Titian portrays John 20, a link that highlights the erotic contours that characterize Jesus' embodiment. Specifically, *The Annunciation* implies an orgasm. Everything about the angel in Botticelli's painting suggests as much. His gaze and his reach extend towards Mary's loins. The traditional lily stands erect to the point that one questions why the heavy flower's head does not cause the stem to bend beneath gravity's pull. To punctuate the point, a tree bisects the angel's figure in a way that, though hidden, places the trunk squarely within a plane that includes the angel's crotch.

Given the continuity between Mary/Jesus and the angel/Mary, it is suggestively possible that Titian was aware of Botticelli's work. Jesus mirrors almost exactly the body language that Mary exhibits, which in both cases emphasizes the body's erotic capacity. At the same time, Mary's actions in *The Annunciation* indicate a denial that Titian draws upon in characterizing Jesus' own refusal in John 20. Similarly, Botticelli's angel provides the outline for Titian's Mary. Both supplicate themselves before an erotic other and their gestures convey strong desire for this other's body. The similarities between the two paintings thus link the point at hand in this chapter to the embodiment that enables Jesus to undergo his restorative death. Importantly, this continuity emphasizes the inherent erotic outline that enables Jesus to establish his body as the temple wherein an eschatological return to God's presence can be anticipated.

tool, which in this parallel capacity emphasizes the phallic image that the tool represents. To compete the scandalous scene, one notices that Mary's hand is open in such a way that the (possible) erection would fit into her palm perfectly. Everything about Mary's gesture announces that her desire is deeply erotic, which in turn informs how Titian depicts Jesus' response. His head remains roughly in line with Mary. His eyes are closed. His hips and his hand—both of which return the viewer's gaze to the loincloth—indicate that his denial is similarly cast in an erotic capacity.

Titian, then, condenses the specific analysis from the previous two chapters into this crucial anticipatory scene. He emphasizes the paradoxical nature of Jesus' (erotic) body. His presence in the garden lures Mary to act as though their encounter is about to fulfill the promise spoken at the Last Supper. At the same time, Titian upholds Jesus' denial, which affirms the theological parameters that Jesus extends through his withdrawal. His presence cannot be sustained; his appearance to Mary does not (yet) transcend the exilic context in which they meet. The point is, then, theological at its core insofar as Jesus' cites in his denial a theological necessity that he must depart from the garden. The promise cannot be fulfilled and Mary should not act as thought it has been. This destabilizing explanation mirrors the impending departure that Jesus announces during the Last Supper, which, like John 20, establishes that the promise will extend along a specifically theological axis.

Jesus' Erotic Body

On this point, Leo Steinberg's book, *The Sexuality of Christ in Renaissance Art and in Modern Oblivion*, affords a helpful analysis of the context out of which Titian's painting emerges.[4] The mention of Jesus' genitals is taboo. To depict them in a way that privileges the body's erotic capacity runs against the grain of Western orthodox thought, which consistently seeks to downplay this part of humanity's embodied condition. If a depiction of Jesus as

4. I cite Steinberg's book in full recognition that his work has generated serious debate amongst scholars—many of whom disagree with his argument—from the disciplines of both art history and theology. The book's second edition provides insight into these critical arguments in response to Steinberg's analysis, as well as his replies. The decision to incorporate Steinberg into this project is not a move to claim his thesis as normative, but, rather, to mirror the process whereby Donne and Dickinson draw on the erotic body to deconstruct orthodox guidelines for understanding the theology that emerges from Jesus embodied life.

fully embodied disrupts a more staid liturgical understanding of this resurrection appearance, then Steinberg's analysis is well taken when it comes to Renaissance painting: "We are left with a paradox: Renaissance artists and preachers were able to make Christian confession only by breaking out of Christian restraints."[5] On the topic of Jesus' penis, however, Steinberg converges on the point at which Titian overlaps with Donne and Dickinson: "no Christian artist, medieval or Renaissance, would have taken this long-fixed convention for anything but a sign of erotic communion, either carnal or spiritual."[6] Steinberg recovers the implications that are deeply embedded within Jesus' body as the sign that promises an eschatological presence. Steinberg continues: "to profess that God once embodied himself in a human nature is to confess that the eternal, there and then, became mortal and sexual. Thus understood, the evidence of Christ's sexual member serves as the pledge of God's humanation."[7] Such claims frequently meet with derision, but Steinberg's argument affords significant ballast in response to such criticism. As a symbol that anticipates an eschatological presence, Jesus' body must be *fully* embodied, a requirement that marks off space for artists and writers to deploy the image of Jesus' specifically erotic body, as Titian does in *Noli Me Tangere*. The hint of an erection, then, substantiates that Jesus' body will sustain the liturgical promise established during the Last Supper.

As a liturgical locus that emerges from within humanity's exilic condition, Jesus' body in its fully embodied capacity accommodates the analysis that Steinberg suggests.[8] In *The Sacred Body*, David Jasper offers

5. Leo Steinberg, *The Sexuality of Christ in Renaissance Art and Modern Oblivion*, 73. I would like to emphasize that Donne wrote during the Renaissance's zenith. As such, he follows suggestively the epoch in art that Steinberg describes, which could well have informed how he injects a distinct and disruptive eroticism in his poetry. As discussed in chapter 4, the occasionally coarse contours in his writing belie a more nuanced attempt to balance his innovative liturgical poetics—born substantially through the recovery of the erotic body as a liturgical resource—and his orthodox theological position.

6 Steinberg, *The Sexuality of Christ in Renaissance Art and Modern Oblivion*, 5.

7. Ibid., 15.

8. Again, it is important to distinguish between a theological analysis and a literary analysis on this point. In discussing Jesus' embodiment and presence, I am not undertaking an extensive examination of the Eucharist. Rather, I am focusing on the textual implications that follow from Jesus' materiality insofar as he establishes his body as a sign. As an organizing metaphor that focuses the text's response to death from an embodied context, exile conveys the thematic and textual instability that describes humanity as beings–towards–death. Moreover, to examine John 20 as a text (which, as discussed above, convey important theological points) does not link the analysis at hand to the

a significant contribution in defense of this claim. At the outset, he under-scores that the body is crucial to any liturgical analysis: "it can finally only be enacted in the *full* realization of the body here and now, and it is only in such enactment that theology itself is finally real."[9] Within a liturgical poetics, this point cannot be overstated. Jesus indicates clearly the central-ity of his body; it conveys the liturgical promise that underpins the Last Supper narrative. This symbolic point of emphasis substantiates the critical approach that both Steinberg and Jasper undertake, yet, as both argue, such readings frequently run counter to orthodox standards. Jasper summarizes well the consequences of a refusal to treat Jesus' body as fully embodied: "In theology's obsession with the body in all its imperfections, its ancient sus-picion of bodily functions and it corseting of what is regarded as acceptable bodily behavior, the mystery of the incarnation has been radically reversed. What needs to be recovered is a genuine and radical hermeneutics of the body, freed from the deathly impositions that have been laid on it and freed to be the proper temple of the soul with which it is one, embracing the soul but more deeply embraced by it."[10] When read alongside the notion of a liturgical poetics, Jasper's comments make clear that the body's imperfec-tions cannot be avoided when analyzing Jesus' body as a liturgical sign. These imperfections and their symbolic manifestation ultimately permit the body to accommodate the Last Supper's paradoxical implications. All symbols are imperfect in the sense that they exhibit a latent instability; they suggest a presence that is, textually speaking, not present. This inevitable displacement is exposed when Jesus—having transcended death—refuses Mary's touch. The exilic parameters (theologically and textually) that pro-hibit Jesus from allowing Mary's gesture emphasize the divide between

---

aforementioned theological debates concerning the Real Presence during the Eucharist. Rather, Jesus' unsustainable presence in John 20 indicates a textual and symbolic impos-sibility, namely that he cannot be present because the text's unstable properties ensure a departure. The theological necessity for this departure thus mirrors the textual dynamics at hand and this congruence is a crucial feature of a liturgical poetics.

9. Jasper, *The Sacred Body*, 2; my emphasis. Jasper's analysis differs from my own insofar as he stresses the tradition of the aestheticized body within Christianity's litur-gical tradition, while the liturgical poetics suggested in this project follows a different critical trajectory. Jasper's analysis focuses on theological texts as his entry point into his examination of the body. My point of emphasis, however, lies in the body's erotic capacity within a specifically literary capacity, which is manifest, for example, in Donne's bedchambers or Dickinson's gardens. As a result, the theological claims I make concern-ing the body diverge from the aesthetic tradition upon which Jasper focuses.

10. Jasper, *The Sacred Body*, 23.

them insofar as Jesus' bodily presence is not fully present to Mary's because she remains displaced in exile.

Titian's *Noli Me Tangere*, then, conveys the symbolic complexity that unfolds in John 20 by recognizing fully the implications of Jesus' resurrected appearance in the garden as a definitively embodied presence. Titian thus captures the paradoxical encounter that sustains Mary's hope despite Jesus' departure. On this point, Jasper affords a helpful reading of the symbolic implications of this body. In reaching back to a new symbolic paradigm as articulated during the Last Supper, Jesus' body subsequently serves "to show the body of the Word made flesh, however, and to invite its ingestion, is to enter a far more complex and liturgical world of presence and absence of the unity of body and soul in a profound silence that is beyond the mere constructions of language, and still capable of utterance in a language that is strange and even violent."[11] Herein one finds an image that anticipates the way in which both Donne and Dickinson recover the Last Supper's erotic undercurrents. First, the corporeal symbolism refuses attempts to scrub away the body's erotic identity; John 20 is a distinctly erotic scene. This, in turn, spotlights the second important point: erotic textures lace the Last Supper[12], the crucifixion, and the subsequent Resurrection appearances. Finally, the liturgical paradigm that unfolds and thus the new temple that Jesus' body establishes relies on his condition as fully embodied. At the moment when Mary's desire is tantalizingly close—Jesus' body is there to touch, to fulfill the promise he made previously—the text must collapse because Jesus must refuse Mary's gesture. The entire scene suggests that Mary's hope will be fulfilled, yet the nature of Jesus' resurrected body ensures that Mary's desire is denied. She must be cast back into the displaced condition out of which she reaches.

The Body's Necessary Betrayal in a Liturgical Poetics

Quite simply, Jesus denies Mary, a refusal that through its closure opens the text to her continued anticipation of the promise's fulfillment.[13] This

11. Ibid., 117.

12. According to Detweiler: "The celebration of the Eucharist is, after all, at heart an intensely erotic act that marks both the presence and the triumph of the scandalised and transformed body, and one might inquire how this moment shapes the centre not only of Christian–defined redemption but of Western culture" ("Torn by Desire: Sparagmos in Greek Tragedy and Recent Fiction," 73).

13. Mary's attempted touch establishes a threshold that brings into proximity the

dynamic reiterates the divide between Mary's still exiled body and the transcendent nature of Jesus' resurrected body. This, Nancy argues, constitutes what is at stake when Jesus responds to Mary's desire: "*Noli me tangere* is the word and the instant of relation and of revelation between two bodies, that is, of a single body infinitely altered and exposed to both in its fall [*tombée*] as well as in its raising."[14] Crucially for Mary, this moment occurs when her body is intimately close to Jesus', but Mary cannot cross the divide based on the theological limitations that govern this encounter. Her touch would, if permitted, preempt the liturgical promise established during the Last Supper, which in turn would offer an impossible stability within her exilic condition. The theological divide that governs this space must be upheld. His eschatological presence lies beyond humanity's exilic condition, which, in turn, qualifies his presence in John 20 as momentary insofar as the promise can only be extended by virtue of his absence. Until he departs from his (paradoxical) presence within exile, Jesus cannot permit an embodied touch. The irony of his words is clear in its disruption. Jesus is present, yet this presence is the basis for denying that which his appearance suggests to Mary.

When he summarizes the implications of this moment, Nancy identifies a distinct contour in the symbolic nature of Jesus' erotic body: "That is why this place can only be a place of vertigo or of scandal, the place of the intolerable at the same time as that of the impossible. This violent paradox is not to be resolved; it remains the place of a gap that is as intimate as it is irreducible: 'Don't touch me.'"[15] Nancy's conclusion uncovers a fundamentally important element within any liturgical poetics: betrayal. Jesus' erotic body does not merely deny desire; it marks a necessary betrayal that must occur in order to uphold the liturgical promise. Jesus draws Mary into an intimate space in order to tell her that her desire cannot be fulfilled. In describing the moment as paradoxical, Nancy revisits what is at stake in promise that Jesus articulates during the Last Supper. The bodily signs enable the anticipation of an eschatological condition wherein the body is

---

desire to transcend her exile with the presence that would provide this release. The body's ability to touch conveys desire as it simultaneously upholds her exile. As Derrida explains: "the experience of the border and of overflowing, the trembling apprehension of that which, *touching* on the border, at once goes overboard and remains at the border, holding out and holding back, retaining itself or abstaining, on the border" (Derrida, *On Touching*, 109). See also Derrida, *On Touching*, 99–100.

14. Nancy, *Noli Me Tangere*, 48.

15. Ibid., 52.

longer bound by death. However, as Jesus makes clear in both the Last Supper narrative and John 20, the promise is conveyed in a way that actively deceives.[16] The encounter thus exposes the element of betrayal that is latent in the text; Jesus' presence distorts Mary's understanding of the promise. Crucially, if the text is to open towards an eschatological reading, it must accommodate this moment of betrayal.

The near touch in John 20 highlights the anticipated presence that characterizes liturgical desire, but this occurs only at the cost of a necessary betrayal. In Mary's gesture, one finds strong echoes of Derrida's conception of touching: "Paradoxical implications, then. The tact of a caress, thus turned toward *this* untouchable inviolability (the femininity of the Beloved *as* the irresponsible infancy of the young animal), according to the face beyond the face, also plays with death, and not only with death as the absence of life or the negative absence of whatever it may be, but with murder. Death at one's fingertips—that is what the movement of the hand is."[17] There exists throughout a liturgical poetics an unavoidable risk. The body's erotic possibilities demand that it be exposed to its own cessation. In reaching out towards Jesus, Mary places her hope in what his body represents, but (her own) death continues to block her from the satisfaction she expects. Moreover, the body that would fulfill her desire—having signaled a promise to do so—is simultaneously what must reject her gesture. Mary's hope is denied, clearly, yet Derrida permits other possible readings of how Jesus' refusal to permit Mary's reach relates to death. Though Jesus responds with a necessary denial, Mary's exilic condition prefigures this theological necessity. Her displacement from God demands her continued separation from Jesus. The theological explanation that Jesus offers need not be understood as a prohibition, but rather as a reminder of the conditions that frame their encounter. Derrida thus helps to clarify the crucial exilic error that undermines Mary's desire, which in turn reiterates the theological implications that Jesus' response mentions. His death, now passed, requires the betrayal that his response to Mary makes clear.

The theological requirements at hand, then, prohibit Mary from understanding fully that Jesus' actions are necessary.[18] The reason for denying

16. See Jasper, "Evil, Betrayal and the Sacred Community."

17. Derrida, *On Touching*, 88.

18. The point of view in this passage is crucial to understanding the claim that a betrayal is necessary. By virtue of his coming ascension to God, Jesus is aware that his actions in the garden are not a betrayal, but rather the next step in fulfilling the promise he lays out during the Last Supper. Mary, however, does not know the full theological

Mary's touch is so rigid that Mary should not even try to reach out to Jesus. However, the fact that she does reach towards him reveals that she is still bound by her exile, which explains why she does not recognize the theological dynamics at hand. Nancy clarifies this point:

> The verb *nolo* is the negative of *volo*: it means "Do not want." In that, too, the Latin translation displaces the Greek *mē mou haptou* (the literal transposition of which would be *non me tange*). *Noli*: do not wish it; do not even think of it. Not only don't do it, but even if you do do it . . . forget it immediately. You hold nothing; you are unable to hold or retain anything, and that is precisely what you must love and know . . . Love what escapes you. Love the one who goes. Love that he goes.[19]

The necessary betrayal reveals a further paradoxical feature of this scene. The theological requirement that Jesus must depart is in its refusal an extension of the promise, which by virtue of its impending absence carries the promise through the text's coming closure. Mary cannot know this beforehand (and the fact that she does not initially recognize Jesus suggests as much), but because she confronts the betrayal she is subsequently aware that her expectations were misplaced. As a result, her desire can endure Jesus' departure because through his denial Jesus ensures that the promise is still on the table. The refusal of her touch does not reveal fully the theological framework that structures this encounter; she remains, always, within her displaced condition.

The Erotic Body as the Site of Liturgical Risk

Jean-Luc Marion's recent book, *The Erotic Phenomenon*, provides a critical apparatus that helps to clarify what is at stake in Jesus' denial of Mary. By examining John 20 through Marion's work, the extent to which his betrayal constellates a liturgical poetics becomes apparent. Within an exilic context,[20] the power of the erotic body to bring a text into intimate proxim-

---

unfolding of which she is a part, so she still experiences Jesus' response as a denial. A liturgical poetics is a response from within humanity's exilic condition. As such, the claim that Jesus' denial is a betrayal is legitimate insofar as it stresses Jesus' actions as perceived from exile.

19. Nancy, *Noli Me Tangere*, 37.

20. Marion summarizes the human condition as "radically finite" (*The Erotic Phenomenon*, 55). Consequently, he suggests that the erotic self (necessarily embodied) thus affords "the phenomenological necessity of a radical reduction to the given—of the

ity with a possibility beyond that condition materializes: "in order to love *myself* (or at least claim to do so), I must acknowledge myself as a radically finite self . . . I must trace a limit—my own—beyond which this 'out there' can appear in its exteriority, but on this side which I occupy a territory that is finite, and therefore unquestionably mine."[21] The body provides a threshold that brings the divine other close to the text, while simultaneously restricting any touch between the two. Mary's gesture makes clear, then, a "claim as much to a radical finitude (in demand of an assurance from out there) as to positive infinity (accomplishing the assurance from out there)."[22] Jesus' body is the new temple, yet this bodily temple can only invite desire, as it must refuse to fulfill this desire. Consequently, the bodily (and thus the liturgical) satisfaction that Jesus' appearance connotes reveals unmistakably and necessarily the paradoxical context in which this intimate encounter takes place.[23] As a threshold, the body both draws Mary forward and prohibits her advance.

By appearing to Mary, Jesus predicates her hopeful gesture with an impending betrayal. The result is, ironically, the sudden erasure of the fulfillment that his presence implies. The consequences are devastating; they cast her rejected desire squarely back into its finitude. Marion is helpful on this point: "To naturalize in effect signifies the embalming of a cadaver, in order that it may be conserved as an object and give the illusion of remaining there in person, while in fact it belongs to death."[24] The resurrected body's presence demands that another cadaver occupy the tomb—the mark

---

erotic reduction of the *ego* of the lover, to the advance, and finally to the flesh in glory" (*The Erotic Phenomenon*, 129). Importantly, this condition blurs the lines between "self-hatred" and "self-love" (ibid., 54), which problematizes any erotic context. Yet again, the inherent displacement that marks the human condition prohibits a definitive transcending of the condition. Any self-love that advances towards an/other beyond the boundary that death poses, the erotic reduction (see Marion, *The Erotic Phenomenon*, 70–76 and 82–97) cannot escape the limit that its own question admits: "a temporal anteriority flows from the very structure of this question, which always signifies, 'Does anyone *out there* love me?' and implies aiming at an endpoint that is radically exterior to that which an actual love awaits, that is to say, an other" (ibid., 43). When examining Mary's encounter with Jesus, her gesture brings this inherent discord into focus. Her advance cannot pass through the boundary that exists within the intimate space that she must occupy in order to act on the possibility that her love for this other might transcend her condition.

21. Marion, *The Erotic Phenomenon*, 55.

22. Ibid.

23. Marion resists to some extent the play that the text in John 20 permits; he labels such encounters "formal contradiction[s]" (*The Erotic Phenomenon*, 55).

24. Marion, *The Erotic Phenomenon*, 115.

of death's finitude—in order to extend the Last Supper's promise. The erotic contours of Mary's encounter in the garden thus anticipate the death that prefigures her necessary experience of betrayal. The faith that her action indicates is shattered when she experiences the only possible conclusion to this meeting. Any illusion of life in this garden—at least from Mary's perspective—cannot obscure the reality that the transcendence for which she hopes has deceived her. The resurrected body's presence can only mark an absence; Jesus' appearance emphasizes the death that awaits the one who reaches out for him in totalizing, climactic desire.[25]

The paradoxical nature of Jesus' appearance in John 20 constitutes a betrayal, then, due to the disruptive effect it intensifies. When Mary reaches out to Jesus, his response emphasizes that their liminal intimacy must remain "irreducible to the other."[26] This necessary separation breaks apart the threshold that brings them together. Marion's emphasis on the divide between erotic bodies thus echoes the theological divide that Jesus maintains: "the aporia of eroticization, which immediately distinguishes what it joins."[27] This divisiveness constitutes the moment of betrayal insofar as Jesus' appearance draws Mary closer, only to deny her as she acts in accordance with that which his presence suggests. Mary, subsequently betrayed, immediately finds herself in an intimate proximity to total denial instead of fulfilled desire. As a result, the parallel nature of betrayal and anticipation becomes apparent. According to Marion, this similarity "does

25. The text of John 20 does not mention how Mary reacts to Jesus' denial. However, it is important to note that Marion extends the image of the metaphor in a capacity that recalls the displacement—and its cyclical implications as experienced within a liturgical poetics—that characterizes John 20: "One does not die of love—that's the horror. One starts over again with love, just as one 'starts a new life'—that's the horror. If we survive the end of eroticization, then love does not have the rank of an absolute" (Marion, *The Erotic Phenomenon*, 156). This point links the image of the orgasm back to the liturgical poetics at hand. Specifically, in the wake of the orgasm the lover returns to the initial point of desire through a sudden collapse. The horror that Marion describes points to the inescapable cyclicality that the erotic body signifies within a liturgical poetics. The crucial moment must cease totally; closure and disclosure once again unfold simultaneously as the text collapses amidst its anticipation.

26. Marion, *The Erotic Phenomenon*, 176. The theme of the orgasm continues to thread its way through Marion's analysis. Due to the irreducibility of the flesh, Marion states clearly: "each climaxes alone, although each gains full enjoyment from the other, and the crossing of the flesh never merges or exchanges it" (ibid., 176–77). Derrida echoes this point when describing the textual properties of such liminal spaces: "Above all, nobody, no body, no body proper has ever touched—with a hand of through skin contact—something as abstract as a limit" (*On Touching*, 103).

27. Marion, *The Erotic Phenomenon*, 177.

reach the other as individual (and me, too)—in this sense, it [betrayal] is incontestably equivalent to the erotic reduction. However, it only succeeds by destroying the flesh of the other and my own at the same time: in this sense, it does travel the path of the lover, but in the opposite direction."[28] Nancy's analysis echoes this point; Jesus' appearance is a disappearance that leads the text (through its collapse) away from the threshold that suggests the promise will be fulfilled.

Marking Betrayal and Fulfillment: The Kiss in Gethsemane

Jesus' appearance in John 20 sustains the liturgical promise he first announces at the Last Supper, but only by denying Mary what she so desperately desires. In this narrative, Marion's argument emerges forcefully. Jesus' body exhibits an erotic capacity that within a liturgical poetics introduces simultaneously two textually similar possibilities: fulfillment and betrayal. Jesus makes clear in his response to Mary the ironic inversion at work. The desire to touch transforms the threshold that his body establishes into an ever-widening gap that reiterates the very exilic condition his presence transcends. On this point, Derrida is helpful: "To be sensitive to touch, feel contact, and to sense, is to *consent*. The sense of touch is first of all, like the sense of every sensation, a sense of consent; it is and has this sense: *yes, to consent*, which always, and in advance, implies transitivity."[29] Jesus consents to be seen and desired, but not to fulfill that desire. As Derrida suggests, this withholding enables the text to continue its anticipation.

Yet again, one finds the inherent paradox that distinguishes a liturgical poetics. The desire that sustains hope within humanity's exilic condition can only endure the text's closure because of a betrayal. In light of this paradox, another significant garden, Gethsemane, illustrates further the crucial role that betrayal plays in a liturgical poetics.[30] In Matthew's account, the

---

28. Ibid., 178. Derrida's analysis of the touch dovetails strongly with Marion's analysis. Derrida writes: "A tangent touches a line or a surface but without crossing it, without a true intersection, thus in a kind of impertinent pertinence. It touches only one point, but a point is nothing, that is, a limit without depth or surface, untouchable even by way of a figure" (*On Touching*, 131).

29. Derrida, *On Touching*, 246.

30. The Synoptic Gospels all frame the Last Supper narrative by indicating Judas' impending betrayal (see Matt 26:14–16; Mark 14:17–18; Luke 22:3–4). Paul's liturgical framework in 1 Corinthians follows this pattern: "the Lord Jesus on the night when he

reader finds an image that mirrors Mary's reach in John 20: Judas' kiss.[31] As his lips touch Jesus, Judas marks Jesus' body as the site of an unfolding betrayal. Several details in this vignette warrant mention. First, the capacity in which Judas identifies exhibits clearly erotic overtones. Second, Judas' betrayal meets with the consent that Derrida recognizes as maintaining the text's transitivity; it is important to note, however, that in Gethsemane, Jesus permits Judas' touch. As Judas kisses him, Jesus responds: "'Friend, do what you are here to do.'"[32] Though inflected differently, Jesus' response to Judas parallels his rejection of Mary in John 20. In both cases, an erotic act meets with a response that enables the betrayal at hand to occur. Unlike Mary, however, Judas is able to touch Jesus because Jesus does not prohibit this act. In Gethsemane, Jesus is fully embodied and, consequently, the theological requirement that prohibits Mary's touch has not been activated. Consequently, Jesus does not need to deny Judas kiss, an act that escorts the text towards the closure that Jesus' death brings.

Marion is clear that the erotic body demands a kenotic advance towards the other.[33] He writes, "The lover *bears everything*. Indeed, by definition, the other owes no reciprocity whatsoever to the lover."[34] In John 20, Mary certainly bears everything in response to Jesus' denial, but in Gethsemane, Jesus endures the consequences of betrayal. The one who loves and the one who betrays converge and it is within this moment that the consequences of bearing everything come into sharp focus. Such a lover can say within this condition: "I eroticize myself and I climax by abandoning myself to the automatic eroticization of my flesh by the flesh of the other, above all by doing nothing, by allowing everything to be done in me without me—the same goes for the other."[35] Consequently, Jesus advances

---

was betrayed took a loaf of bread, and when he had given thanks, he broke it and said, 'This is my body that is for you. Do this in remembrance of me'" (1 Cor 11:23–24). John's gospel is unique insofar as it calls attention to the garden as the locale for significant encounters immediately before (John 18) and immediately after (John 20) the account of Jesus' death (John 19).

31. "While he was still speaking, Judas, one of the twelve, arrived; with him was a large crowd with swords and clubs, from the chief priests and the elders of the people. Now the betrayer had given them a sign, saying, 'The one I will kiss is the man; arrest him.' At once he came up to Jesus and said, 'Greetings, Rabbi!' and kissed him" (Matt 26:47–49).

32. Matt 26:50.

33. See Marion, *The Erotic Phenomenon*, 106–35.

34. Ibid., 85.

35. Ibid, 141.

as the lover in his kenotic, erotic self. In Gethsemane, this advance reveals how the body provides the locus for the betrayal in order to substantiate the promise made during the Last Supper.

Reading Bodies as Liturgical Loci

The above discussion calls attention to the inherent risk that the erotic body brings to the text insofar as it is the locus for a liturgical poetics' necessary betrayal. Though the authors in this study mark this betrayal in different capacities, the underlying dynamic is consistent. Betrayal ensures that the liturgical promise remains unfulfilled and, therefore, reiterates the exilic context that characterizes the body. These effects call attention to important considerations when privileging the body as a temple within exile. On this point, Linda Holler offers a helpful stepping off point for addressing the ethical implications of a liturgical poetics' use of the body. She states: "What we call sensual awareness, coming from non-sense to sense is a moral and political act because it restores our ties to the material world and to the consequences of our actions."[36] Betrayal is manifest in the body, which, as Holler notes, is the place wherein the consequences of the act will also emerge. Holler is right, then, to call attention to the ethical implications of a shared embodied existence. Frequently, orthodox readings (both historical and theological) of the body suggest, if not declare outright, a normative sexual binary that invites betrayal in a capacity that overwhelms a text to the point that the body is abused.

At the outset of this excursus, it is important to emphasize the framework against which authors such as Donne and Dickinson develop the body's erotic symbolism. Western theology frequently treats the body's erotic capacity with suspicion. As a result, the erotic body's potential to extend a liturgical possibility through exile can be truncated, which in turn invites skepticism towards the body's (be it Jesus' or any other human's) erotic characteristics. A predominant narrative within the orthodox tradition at hand exhibits a blind spot that Margaret R. Miles clarifies as "a journey to self-knowledge achieved through physical struggle, labor, and pain. The hero's self-knowledge is carnal knowledge, awareness recorded in the body. One who has not experienced limitation and suffering cannot recognize the suffering of others and cannot locate himself in a human

---

36. Holler, *Erotic Morality*, 3.

community shaped by awareness of limitation and mortality."[37] The limited
or absent erotic characteristics in these normative assumptions steer readings of the body towards a culturally masculine paradigm. Consequently,
the culturally feminine body is relegated to the paradigm's edges, if it is
accounted for at all. To respond bluntly to this tendency, women's bodies
experience equally significant suffering, not only as humans in exile, but
also in light of the cultural bias through which a masculine tradition reads
women's bodies.[38] Recording the struggle through exile does not necessarily prohibit the female body from anticipating a release from exile (Mary
makes this much clear), but the social implications for inscribing a woman's
body with such bias identifies an important concern with respect to a liturgical poetics' emphasis on the body. All humans are equally displaced and,
as such, all embodied responses to this condition must endure the same
paradoxical effects of a liturgical poetics' textual dynamics.

The body as a liturgical locus demands, therefore, a constant awareness of the social strata that inform readings within a specific context.
Miles argues convincingly that the Christian record represents women's
bodies as the locus for various conceptions of displacement—"sin, sex, and
evil"[39]—yet such caricatures fail to affirm the female body as capable of
anticipating the eschatological fulfillment that Jesus' body promises. These
associations initiate and sustain a cultural reading that excludes women's

37. Miles, *Carnal Knowing*, 8.

38. Women's shared experience in this capacity is a hallmark of feminist thought and
I affirm its validity as a critique of a pervasive masculine bias in orthodox Western Christianity (and, more broadly, culture). In asserting the legitimacy of this critique, however,
I would like to stress that there exists an implicit normativity in identifying this bias,
namely the shared experience women have within this tradition. Thus, it is important
to resist the relativizing stance that some feminist critiques adopt. For example, Heather
Walton notes that Katie Cannon and Kathleen Sands emphasize particular experiences
rather than a "commonality of women's experience" (*Literature, Theology and Feminism*,
59). Such relativizing comments undermine the legitimacy of a critique that Walton cites
from Alicia Ostriker: "women poets begin to draw maps of the female body, the female
passions, the female mind and spirit, demystifying these mysteries" (quoted in Walton,
Literature, Theology and Feminism 52). These coordinates do not cohere in a capacity
that supports the legitimate critique that feminist seeks to level. Individual experiences
can, of course, influence particular critiques, but to suggest that each individual experience lacks connective tissue between other feminist writings or, more tellingly, between
different genders in a shared human capacity exhibits an unwillingness to examine such
particular claims through their own critical apparatus.

39. Walton, *Literature, Theology and Feminism*, 125.

bodies from the temple that Jesus' body establishes.[40] Consequently, the masculine paradigm that normalizes an orthodox reading of the Last Supper frequently emerges from a physiological point: Jesus is embodied in a male body. However, to translate this physicality as culturally masculine is to orient the subsequent liturgical narrative in a way that subverts the promise as speaking to humanity's exile. Jesus' particularly male physiology is not a politicizing symbol that excludes the female body (and as well as male bodies that do not within a culturally-defined masculine norm) from anticipating the fulfillment that this body signifies. Rather, his body offers the expectation of transcendence to every body.

The importance of avoiding privileged readings based on gender emerges at the very outset of Jesus' embodied experience. Specifically, from the point at which Jesus is conceived two salient features become clear. First, the entire narrative requires a woman's body; Jesus needs a mother if he is to be born as a fully embodied person. This point, however, frequently becomes the basis for locating in Mary's body a dual bias against the body's specifically erotic capacity and, more broadly, against women.[41] Contrary to readings that relegate the female body to a subordinate role, the emphasis on Mary's motherhood affirms that the female body is, like Jesus' male body, crucial to the Last Supper's narrative and theological arc.

Overcoming the Bias Against Women's Bodies

A consequence of emphasizing Mary's virginity in order to uphold a theological construct produced a devastating tendency in how Western Christianity conceptualized the body. Marina Warner writes: "the root of [the problem] was the Fathers' definition of evil. Sexuality represented to them the gravest danger and the fatal flaw; they viewed virginity as its opposite

---

40. Miles argues: "representations do not simply reflect society; they also reproduce cultural attitudes, styles of relationship, and social arrangements" (*Carnal Knowing*, 136).

41. From early in its intellectual history, Christianity's orthodox guardians have ignored this blind spot. Marina Warner describes succinctly the process whereby women's bodies provided a symbolic counterweight to eschatological restoration that Jesus' body promises: "When Augustine, Ambrose, and Jerome endorsed virginity for its special holiness, they were the heirs and representatives of much current thought in the Roman empire of their day. And in this battle between the flesh and spirit, the female sex was firmly placed on the side of the flesh. For as childbirth was woman's special function, and its pangs the special penalty decreed by God after the Fall, and as the child she bore in her womb was stained by sin from the moment of its conception, the evils of sex were particularly identified with the female" (*Alone of All Her Sex*, 57).

and its conqueror, sadly failing to appreciate that renunciation does not banish or overcome desire."[42] Warner captures precisely the bias against the body that a liturgical poetics overturns by drawing on the body's erotic capacity. She emphasizes that the female body's sexuality is just as central a quality as this capacity is for the masculine body, a reality that Mary's virginal identity often obscured. Moreover, the critique against the church fathers' suspicion of sexuality extends to the masculine body as well; traditionally Jesus' embodied experience similarly had to be free of any erotic desire in order to uphold his sinless nature.[43]

Importantly, recovering erotic desire as a positive component of embodied experience must resist the slide back into normative social readings of male and female bodies. Specifically, Warner argues, the underlying bias in early church thought prevented a reassertion of desire as a valuable component of any embodied experience: "Although [the early Church] considered women socially subject to the male, it granted them an identical immortal soul. Women were therefore equal in religion as long as the Christian code was accepted, and that entailed accepting its view of sex and childbirth."[44] Warner's caution substantiates part of what a liturgical poetics accomplishes, namely a deconstructive reading of orthodox paradigms that are biased against bodies in general and women's bodies in particular.

42. Warner, *Alone of All Her Sex*, 50.

43. The criticism leveled against Kazantzakis' *The Last Temptation of Christ* offers a symptomatic example of how suggesting Jesus experienced any kind of sexual desire is anathema in many circles, orthodox and otherwise. Such dismissals are, however, incongruent with Jesus' embodiment. Hebrews 4:15 characterizes Jesus in a capacity that invites the kind of imaginative rereading that Kazantzakis suggests: "For we do not have a high priest who is unable to sympathize with our weaknesses, but we have one who in every respect has been tested as we are, yet without sin." Given the traditional Christian association of sex with sin, the Hebrews passage sanctions the notion that Jesus would have experience sexual temptation, but, at the same time, this crucial component of embodied existence enables the conclusion that Heb 4:15 establishes, namely that Jesus resisted fully such temptations (a purity that draws upon Jesus' ability to resist temptation in the desert; see Matt 4:1–11; Mark 1:12–13; and Luke 4:1–13). Kazantzakis, like Steinberg, recognizes the need to affirm Jesus' fully embodied condition, while at the same time upholding as sinless Jesus' embodiment. Steinberg's analysis, then, stands as an important critical voice to consider fully the implications of locating Christianity's liturgical locus in Jesus body. Such analyses certainly challenge orthodox thought, but they do not subvert the underlying theological paradigm that both orthodox thought and deconstructive approaches to this tradition share. Like Donne and Dickinson, Steinberg recognizes the extent to which one must depart from a sterile orthodox reading of the body to affirm Jesus as fully embodied.

44. Warner, *Alone of All Her Sex*, 72.

Physiological differences do not and cannot privilege one embodied experience over another, a definitive statement that is necessary to challenge the social assumptions that historically have relegated women's specific physiological characteristics and experiences as more vulnerable to the problems that erotic desire connotes within the orthodox paradigm that Warner critiques.[45]

In navigating this important concern, this project's underlying methodology remains the same. The need to rethink the body is consistent in its pitch, even when discussing the obvious inconsistencies in how Western theology tends to read the male or female body. The bias can be traced to Augustine, a legacy which Thomas Laqueur summarizes well: "Thus, after Augustine as before, the body was thought to work much as pagan medical writers had described it. Augustine's new understanding of sexuality as an inner, and ever present, sign of the will's estrangement by the fall did create an alternative arena for the generative body. As Brown says, it 'opened the Christian bedchamber to the priest.'"[46] The problem is grounded in readings that politicize the body in general and, more specifically, the body's erotic capacity. To permit a priest to enter the bedchamber exerts necessarily institutional control over a context wherein individuals relate intimately. The effects of this intrusion make clear the extent to which readings in which women suffer from cultural biases (frequently the extension of institutions) must be resisted. This is a crucial methodological recognition, but it does not negate an analysis that treats women and men as sharing a common, embodied condition. In fact, acknowledging and critiquing the masculine bias inherent in much theological discourse must avoid any formulaic conclusions that preclude a liturgical poetics.[47] Two conclusions may be drawn at this point: the concern about a liturgical reading of Jesus' body that privileges socially the male body is legitimate and, therefore, a text

45. The flip side of Warner's critique, which I discuss in more depth later in this chapter, is that a woman's physiologically specific experiential possibilities cannot be identified as better vis-à-vis a male body's inability to experience this same thing.

46. Laqueur, *Making Sex*, 61.

47. Michèle Le Doeuff claims that she is "convinced . . . that this recognition of the always incomplete and limited character of philosophical effort has advantages, if only that of the hope of finding a new way of thinking philosophically, a way which, unlike so many others, would not be hegemonic" (*Hipparchia's Choice*, 8). Consequently, she cautions that a serious intellectual endeavor must accept the uneven contours of the text: "Instead of wanting to justify our project at all costs, we can admit that an element of non-knowledge unavoidably inhabits any undertaking, including a philosophical one" (ibid., 8).

that posits a shared human condition must reject any paradigm that treats a body as having qualitatively "better" symbolic possibilities than another. Distinctions between men and women *can* matter in structuring a text, but they do not preempt the shared human condition of exile. A common denominator that links all bodies—the inherent erotic capacity for sexuality and desire—should not be categorized and thus organized with implicit or, as is more often the case, explicit value judgments.

Reading the Specific Bodies of John Donne and Emily Dickinson

Laqueur summarizes well the problem that can arise when politicizing (or ignoring) the differences between bodies. He begins by stating: "My goal is to show how a biology of hierarchy in which there is only one sex, a biology of incommensurability between two sexes, and the claim that there is no publicly relevant sexual difference at all, or no sex, have constrained the interpretation of bodies and the strategies of sexual politics for some two thousand years."[48] Bodies clearly have differences and these differences can be utilized to significant effect in the context of a liturgical poetics. However, Laqueur's outline presupposes a denial of difference, which, as discussed below, is not present in this capacity in Donne and Dickinson. For both, specific gendered or physiologically determined readings do not alter the underlying concern with death and, therefore, the liturgical poetics that each constructs. As such, their texts speak to a condition that affects all bodies. In Donne's case, one can easily level criticism that he objectifies women's bodies in a way that affirms a patriarchally grounded sexual politics. DiPasquale illustrates this tendency when she summarizes a telling feminist reading of Donne: "as Judith Scherer Herz points out, Donne's poems resist attempts 'to impose a unity, to make [them] yield single, albeit complex readings.'"[49] Such readings of Donne predicate the politicization of women's bodies in Donne's poetry on the notion of textual unity, which, as discussed in chapter 4, does not hold up when one analyzes a liturgical poetics' textual and theological displacement. Thus, readings that simplify Donne's poetics as a "phallo-centric certainty of religion and theological

48. Laqueur, *Making Sex*, 23.
49. DiPasquale, *Literature and Sacrament*, 25–26.

discourse"[50] handcuff the paradoxical capacity in which the body functions symbolically. Granted, Donne stews his poetry with a noticeable machismo, but to suggest that he is merely trying to build towards a phallocentric pun obscures the source from which he draws out the body as a liturgical resource. This is not to excuse Donne completely from criticism; at times he exhibits the kinds of paradigms that Laqueur finds to be problematic. However, the capacity in which Donne utilizes the erotic body in order to articulate a liturgical poetics offers, in the end, an unexpected ally in the effort to overcome biases against women's bodies. Donne can be accused of many things, but he recognizes and resists the problems of permitting anyone (except God) into his lovers' bedrooms. As such, he recovers the importance of affirming every individual's body's erotic capacity in a liturgical poetics.

Dickinson's poetry brings into sharper focus the risk of politicizing the specifically erotic body within a liturgical poetics. Many critics are quick to adopt feminist readings of Dickinson's poetry. Farr, for example, in discussing J638 ("To my small Hearth His fire came—") makes the claim that there are "characteristic attributes of the male lover as Dickinson recognizes them: abruptness, vehement energy, a forcefulness that invades but sets her in motion, and the permanent faculty to convert a night (associated with the female lover), seen as barren, into noon or day."[51] Though this line of analysis is certainly relevant, reading Dickinson's poetry only through a lens that conceives of every image as a critique of traditional gender binaries obscures the theological considerations in her writing. Consequently, the risk is always present that other salient concerns—such as the use of those same gender binaries to anticipate a transcendence of death—can be lost. Farr recognizes, for example, that: "Noon stands for passionate fulfillment in Dickinson's love poems, but it is also one of her emblems for eternal life."[52] If anything, Dickinson's allusion to Donne's own symbolism in J638 should subvert the notion that she champions a feminist ideology by drawing on a poet who the same feminist critics are, more often than not, happy to dismiss as antithetical to their concerns.

One can find a particularly striking example of how a feminist reading of Dickinson can be problematic in Angela Conrad's *The Wayward Nun of Amherst: Emily Dickinson and Medieval Mystical Women*. In her

---

50. Quoted in Di Pasquale, *Literature and Sacrament*, 4.

51. Farr, *The Passion of Emily Dickinson*, 56.

52. Ibid.

"Introduction," Conrad reveals her agenda when she claims that: "Rather than submit to self-censorship, she cast her work into a mystic tradition which justified a radical female voice of power and passion, as long as it was connected with the Divine."[53] In one respect, this is accurate; Dickinson certainly blazed her own poetic trail. However, to enlist Dickinson's liturgical poetics as a radical female voice of power prohibits Conrad from recognizing the extent to which Dickinson draws on—and therefore permits—certain biblical texts to articulate her liturgical poetics. Thus, when Conrad claims that "the merest of mortals can share in Christ by sharing in his pain—not an intellectual but a bodily pursuit, reserved especially for those with a 'weak intellect,'"[54] she cancels out a crucial point, namely that humanity's *shared* exile is a structuring feature of Dickinson's liturgical poetics. Conrad's initial claims thus force her analysis to pursue an increasingly politicized reading of Dickinson, which results in progressively more problematic claims. For example, Conrad argues that Dickinson drew on women mystics because "They search for God through their bodies. What for some male writers is symbolic, for them must be tangible, bodily."[55] Such claims present two clear problems. First, they dismiss out of hand the aforementioned baseline of a liturgical poetics: that all humans share an embodied, exilic condition. Jesus does not substitute his (erotic) body for the temple in the politicized terms present in Conrad's reading of Dickinson; his body establishes a new liturgical locus without distinctions.[56] Second, Conrad's argument produces self-affirming conclusions that further obscure the shared human condition that underscores Dickinson's liturgical poetics. As a result, her argument ultimately reveals the extent to which drafting Dickinson as a radical feminist voice exhibits the very bias that such voices claim to critique. A final quote from Conrad will make this point clear. Based on the feminist claim to understand the body in a more

53. Conrad, *The Wayward Nun of Amherst*, xv.

54. Ibid., 65.

55. Ibid., 92. The problematic nature of such claims is clear. From the obvious (all textual bodies are symbolic to some degree) to an overt gender binary (Men do only "X" while women do only "Y"), Conrad's reading invites the criticism of any gendered bias that Laqueur lays out.

56. There exists a risk in arguing against culturally politicized conceptions of the body in the capacity that Conrad draws on Dickinson. Her analysis props up the very assumptions that she subsequently dismisses. To assume a gendered binary as the stepping off point for her analysis is certainly legitimate. However, to say that one such pole of the binary is problematic while maintaining at the same time the other pole exhibits a striking critical inconsistency.

"tangible" way, Conrad thus concludes: "Female mystics, with their 'bodily' approach, are physiologically better equipped for both plausible sexual and spiritual union with Christ than are male mystics."[57] As the foregoing analysis makes clear, Jesus' body extends the liturgical promise for all of humanity. Thus, Conrad ultimately reveals the shortcomings of projecting a radical feminism onto Dickinson's writing insofar as this reading glosses over or ignores altogether the implications of Dickinson's liturgical poetics, which she meant, it would seem, for readers of any gender.

57. Conrad, *The Wayward Nun of Amherst*, 94. In addition to the obviously slanted conclusion, I would like to point that the supposedly "better" capacity to commune "with Christ" reveals a further twofold problem. First, such analysis requires the very paradigm it seeks to supplant. Conrad clearly upholds a sexual binary that is precisely the focal point of many a feminist critique. The only difference here is that Conrad inverts which half of the couple is politicized as "better" than the other. By preserving this paradigm as normative, Conrad also preserves a particular definition of gender. That is, her conclusion privileges a *hetero*normative sexuality, which necessarily excludes those who do not cohere with what she defines as better. Thus, alternatives such as a homosexually characterized liturgical poetics—much like the homoerotic narrative in "Until the End of the World"—are not possible. In either case, Conrad typifies the shortcomings of those who would conscript Dickinson into the service of a specifically radicalized feminism.

This strategy frequently finds itself in a critical corner. In response to criticism about *The Sexuality of Christ in Renaissance Art and in Modern Oblivion*, Steinberg confronts a similar attempt to alter the symbolism at work in a liturgical poetics in order to import a feminist paradigm that is, quite simply, not present. Steinberg mentions that Caroline Walker Bynum dismisses his physiological point that Jesus was, historically speaking, male, which means that his embodied experience exhibited a male body. In response, Steinberg notes, "Bynum demurs because she would marginalize Christ's masculinity to make room for androgyny" (*The Sexuality of Christ*, 329). Any such analysis obscures what is at stake in the erotic body's role within a liturgical poetics. As Steinberg claims: "I suggested that the penis restored to the sacred body after centuries of denial signified the sexual potential as such—not to exclude the female, but to acknowledge sex as participant in that human nature which the Incarnation espoused" (ibid., 365). This response summarizes well why one should avoid sexual politics when analyzing the erotic body's role in a liturgical poetics (and indeed within any liturgical context). There is certainly room to critique Steinberg's response as dismissive of Bynum's legitimate concerns. However, positing that Jesus' physiological condition is somehow a normative cultural construct is problematic. As a counter example, to argue that one should disregard Mary's physiology in reading her role as Jesus' mother would be unlikely to receive commendation from Bynum. The point that Steinberg makes in response to Bynum remains, then, defensible (Jesus, it is worth noting, does not speak of his body in a gendered capacity during the Last Supper narrative).

Betrayal as a Distinguishing Feature of a Liturgical Poetics

Enduring betrayal distinguishes the body's unique function within a liturgical poetics. The body condenses the paradoxical desire and denial that Mary encounters in the garden, which, to return to Marion, clarifies how betrayal affects the text in question: "Hatred . . . leaps over this aporia [the denial] without difficulty; more accurately, it frees itself from it without even considering it. For hatred dispenses with the flesh, while love must pass through it."[58] The initial aporia—the simultaneous absence of the erotic encounter's presence—is unavoidable, yet the willingness to pass through this betrayal is the crucial moment wherein the liturgical promise is extended through the text's closure. The hatred Marion describes therefore clarifies how betrayal is a crucial feature of a liturgical poetics.

The need to usher a text up to, and then through the moment wherein the body's desire is denied clarifies why two significant cyclical ideas in literature that otherwise resemble a liturgical poetics do not fulfill the crucial requirement to pass through a moment of betrayal. The first, Keats' "Ode to a Grecian Urn," presents a text that appears to exhibit all of a liturgical poetics' salient features. Situated at an erotic threshold, the poem anticipates but does not permit two lovers to embrace. However, the text never progresses beyond this initial outlay. The speaker does not reach the crucial moment wherein the erotic bodies are most fully exposed—at the moment they meet—to the risk of denial. Just before the moment of possible betrayal, the lovers "Heard melodies [that] are sweet, but those unheard / Are sweeter; therefore, ye soft pipes, play on."[59] There exists, then, a constant delay, but unlike a liturgical poetics that confronts a necessary denial of desire, Keats' poem stops just before exposing these lovers to a textual closure.

Significantly, the speaker in "Ode to a Grecian Urn" addresses the male lover in an attempt to console him in the face of that which will forever wait just beyond the his (and the text's) reach: "Bold Lover, never, never canst thou kiss, / Though winning near the goal—yet, do not grieve; / She cannot fade, though thou hast not thy bliss, / For ever wilt thou love, and she be fair!"[60] The speaker makes clear that the lover has yet to gesture towards the beloved and, therefore, he has not risked denial. As discussed previously, Keats' work is, amongst the Romantics, the corpus that is most similar to a

---

58. Marion, *The Erotic Phenomenon*, 177.

59. Keats, "Ode to a Grecian Urn," lines 11–12.

60. Ibid., lines 17–20.

liturgical poetics, yet "Ode to a Grecian Urn" makes clear that the crucial moment—the point at which one can experience the possibility of transcending the endless cycle of desire and denial—never materializes because the lover never endures betrayal's closure. Thus, despite assurances that his endless love and her eternal beauty will continue, the speaker's consolation precludes the text from undergoing the necessary closure that will provide a liturgical poetics' disclosure. The lovers never reach towards one another in the crucial advance towards satisfying their desire that must be denied.

The second text that parallels the dynamics of a liturgical poetics is Friedrich Nietzsche's *Thus Spoke Zarathustra*. Unlike Keats' "Ode to a Grecian Urn," the myth of eternal recurrence that appears in *Thus Spoke Zarathustra* establishes a point of closure. Consequently, Nietzsche resigns the reader to repeat the same anticipation that will eventually collapse when it encounters its inevitable denial. Nietzsche provides a striking example of this point when Zarathustra discusses a doorway with a dwarf: "Behold this gateway, dwarf . . . It has two faces. Two ways come together here: nobody has ever taken them to the end."[61] This scene unfolds at a threshold, which establishes the necessary context for a transition from closure to disclosure. Zarathustra continues: "This long lane back here: it goes on for eternity. And that long lane out there—that is another eternity. They contradict themselves, these ways; they confront one another head on, and here, at this gateway is where they come together. The name of the gateway is described above it: 'Moment.'"[62] This door is paradoxical; the dwarf cannot walk to the end of both roads that extend away from the door because they unfold in opposite directions. Moreover, the dwarf responds in a way that acknowledges the displacement that this image conveys. The door's label—the Moment—freezes the text temporarily, which enables the dwarf to recognize a fundamental error that generates the paradox at hand: "All that is straight lies . . . All truth is crooked; time itself is a circle."[63] This remark indicates a final similarity with a liturgical poetics insofar as it recognizes in the Moment's paradoxical character the text's inevitable cyclicality that cannot be transcended.

The dwarf thus punctuates a complex exchange in a way that illustrates two salient features of Nietzsche's myth of eternal return. The first links Nietzsche with Romantic thought, which in turn provides the basis

61. Nietzsche, *Thus Spoke Zarathustra*, §13.2.
62. Ibid.
63. Ibid.

upon which one can distinguish the myth of eternal return from a liturgical poetics. Robert A. Yelle suggests that at its core Nietzsche's myth of eternal return is "an attempt to fulfill the promise of a rebirth myth," a search for which "there is precedent . . . in the writings of certain Romantic mythologists."[64] Just as the Romantics sought to access an originary idyll, Yelle argues that in Nietzsche's case: "the cycle of opposites, particularly in the form of the ouroborous or serpent biting its own tail, became for Nietzsche a symbol of the unity of myth and philosophy and the rebirth of the former out of the latter."[65] Yelle's tone captures Nietzsche's attempt to undermine a specifically Christian framework.[66] In a later passage, the extent to which Nietzsche's eternal return destabilizes the text becomes apparent: "your animals know well, O Zarathustra, who you are and must become: behold, *you are the teacher of eternal recurrence*—that is now *your* fate."[67] These remarks counter directly the liturgical paradigm that Jesus articulates. Whereas Jesus' body promises a transcendence of humanity's exile, Zarathustra's message emphasizes that the text can only return to the initial Moment wherein the impossible choice must be made again, a return that intensifies exile's instability. As such, Zarathustra (or anyone else, for that matter) will not—and indeed cannot—imagine a crossing of the threshold that the door establishes. The paradoxical "knot,"[68] if untied, cannot escape the fact that "Souls are as mortal as bodies are."[69] Consequently, the cyclicality that governs eternal recurrence only permits Zarathustra to "come again, with this sun, with this earth, with this eagle, with this serpent—*not* to a new life or a better life or a similar life:—I come eternally again to this self–same life, in the greatest and smallest respects, so that again I teach the eternal recurrence of all things—."[70] Nietzsche's new myth is, then, an

---

64. Yelle, "The Rebirth of Myth?," 179. As discussed in chapter 3, Shaffer recognizes this search as a key component of the Romantics' overall project.

65. Yelle, "The Rebirth of Myth?," 179. The image of the shepherd and the serpent can be found in Nietzsche, *Thus Spoke Zarathustra*, §13.2.

66. The dwarf's response echoes strongly John 14:6, in which Jesus tells his disciples: "I am the way, and the truth, and the life. No one comes to the Father except through me." Such symbolism undermines itself. Any such light ultimately reveals that the truth at hand is its own error, an internal contradiction made apparent in the crooked nature of the path described.

67. Nietzsche, *Thus Spoke Zarathustra*, §13.3.

68. Ibid.

69. Ibid.

70. Ibid.

anti-idyll. In *Thus Spoke Zarathustra*, the origin that the Romantic project seeks to establish turns out to be a hollow shell, trapped in an unbreakable circle: the mark of eternal recurrence.

What Nietzsche describes in this passage thus coheres with the exilic condition that informs a liturgical poetics insofar as the text exhibits a moment of closure. Crucially, however, Zarathustra's lesson about eternal recurrence prohibits antecedently any disclosure. Nietzsche's dual lines of eternity ensure that the dwarf cannot anticipate a transcendent release from the text's instability. The collapse that occurs as a result of this prohibition belies the capacity in which the eternal return cannot, therefore, constitute a liturgical poetics.[71] Nietzsche's goal is to establish at the center of this myth an exile without an implied return (not even Judas has to endure this). The Moment above the door conveys a totalizing notion of betrayal. This breakdown indicates the extent to which Nietzsche critiques a Western theological framework. Whereas the betrayal within a liturgical poetics enables a textual disclosure, Nietzsche is clear that betrayal is, in the end, the only possible conclusion. This moment of closure does not disclose simultaneously a (possible) release from the text's latent instability.

71. The centrality of hope to a liturgical poetics cannot be overstated. Unless the text posits a possibility that is open to all, it cannot be called a liturgical poetics. This distinction prevents a descent towards the hollow circularity that Nietzsche describes in *Thus Spoke Zarathustra*. The text's inability to transcend imaginatively its instability in a way that suggests an/other, hopeful possibility ensures that a liturgical poetics is not classified with texts that do not fulfill this specific requirement. Importantly, this brackets the notion of a liturgical poetics from a descent into mayhem that the central role of betrayal invites. Authors such as the Marquis de Sade could be described as searching for some possibility through their nihilistic eroticism. However, what Nietzsche makes clear in approximating a liturgical poetics in *Thus Spoke Zarathustra* is that a text cannot exhibit only its own circularity if it is to imagine a hope that transcends its own exilic condition.

Conclusion

*For the soul mixes with the wine of God's love the milk of natural affection,
that is, the desire for her body and its glorification. She glows with the wine
of holy love which she has drunk; but she is not yet all on fire, for she has
tempered the potency of that wine with milk. The unmingled wine would
enrapture the soul and make her wholly unconscious of self; but here is
no such transport for she is still desirous of her body. When that desire is
appeased, when the one lack is supplied, what should hinder her
then from yielding herself utterly to God, losing her own likeness
and being made like unto Him?*[1]

BERNARD OF CLAIRVAUX'S DESCRIPTION OF THE SOUL SUMMARIZES WELL
what is at stake in a liturgical poetics. The eucharistic wine mixes with the
soul's deep desire to be reunited with its body. This anticipated reunion is
the Last Supper's promise fulfilled in an eschatological context. However,
as Bernard makes clear, this desire continues because the union has not yet
come to pass. This deep, erotic longing captures the essence of this project's
analysis; Bernard's words anticipate a condition wherein desire, finally fulfilled, establishes an eschatological stability in terms of that the displaced
lovers from the Song of Songs would understand. Importantly, this passage
exhibits an ironic twist: the soul is also displaced by the body's death. The
body, then, is a necessary component of the eschatological condition that
humanity will experience when it transcends its inevitable death.

Bernard is a capstone in the tradition that privileges the body in its full
capacity. Characteristics that are frequently scrubbed away become in his
writing a privileged feature of both humanity's condition and the theological machinations that underpin the narrative surrounding Jesus' restorative
body. In "Sermon 4," for example, Bernard explains God's role as the destination towards which the body progresses by asking rhetorically: "When
therefore we make satisfaction and become reconciled by the re-joining of

1. Bernard of Clairvaux, *On Loving God*, chapter 11.

the cleavage caused by sin, in what better way can I describe the favor we receive than as a kiss of peace?"[2] The kiss that betrays becomes the only possible response to God once humanity experiences God's eschatological presence. What marks the betrayal that leads to Jesus' death becomes for Bernard the appropriate expression of the eternal disclosure that governs the text. "Sermon 4" thus builds upon the way that Bernard characterizes the kiss in "Sermon 3"; the anticipation of the kiss brings the reader intimately close to the other. Bernard considers this approach in the same capacity as the threshold that situates a liturgical poetics intimately close to the moment wherein the liturgical promise's fulfillment can be glimpsed (but never experienced). The kiss is like a knock at the door, which, Bernard claims with confidence, will always be answered.[3] In knocking, one establishes her/his distance from God (the lover), but brings her/his body as closely as possible to the reading towards which this threshold opens. The desire that gestures in knocking will, Bernard explains, achieve the satisfaction it seeks: "It is my belief that to a person so disposed, God will not refuse that most intimate kiss of all."[4] God's eschatological presence is felt in the body's intimate capacity to relate to the other. Having finally crossed the threshold that upholds humanity's displacement from God, the body will (Bernard is clear that this remains a condition that is not-yet) be corporeally aware that death has been transcended. This experience brings the liturgical promise full-circle; the locus of displacement and betrayal becomes the site to which an originary stability is restored.

Donne and Dickinson converge in their own way on this sentiment. They echo what Bernard makes clear: the body's erotic character enables the liturgical promise to endure the displacement of death's closure. Recognizing fully that humanity cannot outpace this encounter, both orient their texts away from any possible center and the stability implied therein and, in so doing, they affirm that within exile any stabilizing presence must remain beyond the text's boundaries. As they progress towards this limit, both Donne and Dickinson deploy images that bring their texts into intimate proximity with the inevitable collapse that exile ensures. Donne and Dickinson thus anticipate a possibility that transcends death, despite the impossibility of any such experience. They endure, then, the necessary closure that marks the point at which a liturgical disclosure occurs, a

2. Bernard of Clairvaux, *On the Song of Songs*, 21.

3. Ibid., 19.

4. Ibid.

trajectory that mirrors the promise that Jesus utters at the Last Supper. This hope is the erotic desire that underscores Bernard's image of the soul that longs for its body. The eternal (re)union that this desire implies captures the imaginative transcendence that links Donne and Dickinson as liturgical poets. For both, the body is the locus for anticipating the promise's fulfillment, just as Bernard states that the kiss will establish God's eternal presence. This is the deep paradox that defines a liturgical poetics. It is *only* the body—something Donne and Dickinson know well—that can convey humanity's deep desire to transcend death and accommodate the denial that any anticipation of this release must encounter.

In recovering the erotic body as a structuring feature of the Last Supper, Donne and Dickinson embark on parallel courses. Separated by historical, literary, cultural, and theological differences, each converges on a salient hope: that death does not bring total closure to the body. Both return to the Last Supper and find in Jesus' body the basis for nurturing hope as an anticipated eschatological release from exile. As Bernard suggests, it is a specifically erotic anticipation that permits the body to endure the death that it cannot avoid. In reading the body in this capacity, Donne and Dickinson undertake a similar deconstructive project. By departing from an orthodox understanding of the body, Donne and Dickinson anticipate through an erotic context that the Last Supper's promise will be fulfilled because this body permits their texts to endure exile's latent instability.

Reimagining the Text

In "The Good Morrow," Donne establishes the erotic body as the threshold that leads to the liturgical promise's fulfillment. Midway through the poem, the speaker describes the breaking of a new day: "And now good morrow to our waking souls, / Which watch not one another out of fear; / For love, all love of other sights controls, / And makes one little room, an every where."[5] The waking souls suggest a new hope for Donne's speaker, but in a way that balances the paradoxical implications that characterize a liturgical poetics. On the one hand, Donne's speaker announces the cyclicality that frames this space as exilic; any hope that awakens with the good morrow experiences at the same moment the beginning of its own closure as the coming night undermines what the new morning announces. At the same time, Donne counters this instability by layering over the body's

5. "The Good Morrow," lines 8–11.

diurnal condition a release from the instability that this framework causes. The speaker imagines, then, the good morrow as an eternal awakening. The text's temporal progression concludes when the body's waking must inevitably cease in its (deathly) sleep.

The souls that awake after death's sleep transcend the displacement that the text makes clear. They emerge within a space wherein fear of separation (in death) no longer governs the intimacy that they share with the body. To emphasize the point, the speaker calls attention to the spatial implications of this moment. The "little room" that hosts these two lovers in their exilic condition becomes an "every where." The split between words is crucial insofar as it emphasizes the totalizing—which is to say eternal—space that their displaced, desiring bodies come to occupy. The room no longer indicates its own erasure (though Donne is aware of the irony in suggesting otherwise). Rather, the good morrow brackets the textual and bodily displacement that undermines the waking that the speaker describes. Through the erotic body, then, Donne recasts the temporal progression that marks humanity's exile as a desire that will transcend the instability that fractures the lovers' intimacy.

In *The Poetics of Space*, Gaston Bachelard conceptualizes how a text like "The Good Morrow" reimagines its exilic instability. Specifically, Bachelard argues that the transition from existing within a displacing temporal cycle to a release from this destabilizing context is the text's specific province: "[it] produces an attitude that is so special, an inner state that is so unlike any other, that the daydream transports the dreamer outside the immediate world to a world that bears the mark of infinity."[6] Any such transposition paradoxically unfolds, of course, within the text's latent displacement, but Bachelard recognizes that this is precondition can be transcended imaginatively. Texts, then, offer a crucial response to humanity's dislocation; within the specific understanding of this instability that a liturgical poetics' exhibits, the implications are more pronounced. The ability to anticipate an alternative to the exile out of which a text emerges is the core dynamic that the temple enables. From this point in the text, a release into stability can be glimpsed even if the temple—like the text—must collapse.[7]

---

6. Bachelard, *The Poetics of Space*, 183.

7. According to Bachelard, "The exterior spectacle helps intimate grandeur unfold" (*The Poetics of Space*, 192). As has been noted previously, the paradoxical implications of a liturgical poetics emerge clearly when considered as Bachelard does here.

A liturgical poetics thrives when the erotic body serves as the temple that discloses (possible) stability beyond the text. Detweiler sketches a critical approach to literature that clarifies what is at stake in the body's ability to provide this glimpse through the intimate proximity to the release that a liturgical poetics anticipates. He writes: "[the] narrative becomes a model for anxious open-endedness and self-doubt that inspires a desire for closure but simultaneously fears and avoids it."[8] Detweiler calls attention to the textual paradox that Derrida identifies: in its closure, a text cannot close completely.[9] For example, despite the release experienced when the souls awake in "The Good Morrow," the body betrays this transcendent possibility by reiterating that only death can unhinge the soul from exile. This lingering rupture reveals, in the end, that the text achieves in its imaginative anticipation "no resolution."[10] In this necessary death, however, the body establishes a threshold whereby a "mystery . . . [which] leaves the celebrant not with a fear of chaos but rather with a sense of satisfaction and fulfillment."[11] Consequently, Detweiler explains, the body houses "Mystery embodied in the liminal language of [a liturgical poetics, which] appears as an ultimate, as a formal inexpressibility of form, that serves paradoxically as a resting point."[12] The mysterious intimacy that the body provides both sustains and subverts its role as a threshold between the text's exile and the transcendence of this condition. The paradox of this duality is felt, always, in the body; as Jesus makes clear in promising an eschatological reunion, the body can only disclose what is to come through the absence that death's closure brings.

Jesus' Erotic Body as a Textual Body

Detweiler's analysis recognizes the crucial role that the erotic body plays within a liturgical poetics. As a temple, Jesus' body establishes a point around which displaced bodies can gather. This temple, then, affords a paradoxical "nexus of sacred text and sacred space."[13] In this dual capacity,

8. Detweiler, *Breaking the Fall*, 15.

9. See Detweiler, *Breaking the Fall*, 45, 126. See also Derrida, *Margins of Philosophy*, 309–11.

10. Detweiler, *Breaking the Fall*, 58.

11. Ibid.

12. Ibid.

13. Ibid., 131.

the body enables an intimacy that sustains the anticipation of an eschatological presence despite the latent displacement that inevitably casts all bodies back into exile. Thus, Detweiler claims that Jesus' body hosts: "A *communitas* of readers, joined at first merely by the fact that they read, can learn to confess their need of a shared narrative . . . that holds in useful tension the doubleness we feel: that we live at once both liminally and in conclusion."[14] The irony of the body's impending death is the solidarity that this instability provides. The Last Supper's promise, then, establishes in its anticipation of an eschatological presence a nascent community that can through its shared displacement endure exile. The body as the sign of a promise, as a text, and as a community of readers permits: "a group of persons engaged in gestures of friendship with each other [to move] across the erotic space of the text."[15] This community's initial outlines emerge as erotic traces that guide readers towards the release that the bodily temple anticipates, even though no constituent part of this textual construct can avoid the collapse that must come.

These hints of a community anticipate an eschatological body that is, in the end, a Body. A liturgical poetics thus speaks not only to the displacement that every individual endures, but also to how this shared bond provides the foundation of a liturgical community. As Jesus explains, the eschatological presence that fulfills the promise will be a banquet, attended by many. The text, then, opens towards a community, an effect that enriches a reading of both Donne and Dickinson. The former reaches across the text through the lovers' bedchamber, while the latter invites the reader to traverse the garden wherein erotic gestures reach out towards this blooming ecclesia. At the same time, Donne's writing makes clear the ease with which the text's instability can undermine the presence that the lovers'

14. Ibid., 190. It is important to note that elsewhere Detweiler echoes the ethical concerns raised in the previous chapter. Specifically, a body that can gather readers is vulnerable to the abuse that any communal space might encounter. Betrayal, then, accompanies any image that establishes a paradoxical temple within exile. Detweiler writes, "Both writing and sexuality can be exploited and abused by those wishing to gain power, but the price they pay is to engage in writing and sexuality as acts of compulsion rather than to experience them as acts, shared willingly, of revelation and love" (*Breaking the Fall*, 142). Betrayal's ability to smother a text's liturgical possibility emerges with full force. Those who do not affirm a shared condition—as beings bound to individual exile—deny the very possibility that confronting betrayal opens. The erotic body thus becomes an object to be abused rather than a symbol that can pass through the shared textual and actual death that betrayal marks within any liturgical text.

15. Detweiler, *Breaking the Fall*, 34–35.

bodies anticipate. Similarly, Dickinson extends the text to the very edges of instability, a strategy that, when coupled with her carefully controlled distribution of her writing stresses the still dislocated nature of the community of readers. In each instance, then, the bodily temple signals a not-yet (but approaching) union that simultaneously destabilizes the body as it links bodies together. By remembering the promise that Jesus locates in his body, readers re-member; they come back together as a communal Body, bound by their shared exile and, consequently, their mutual anticipation of the promise's fulfillment.

The Not–Yet Eschatological Consummation

Despite this anticipation, the text remains subject to the exilic parameters that prohibit the promise's fulfillment. Images that bracket these concerns are, ironically, reminders that the bodily temple must collapse; no body as fully embodied can avoid its inevitable death. Yet again, the paradoxical parameters that govern a liturgical poetics subvert what the text promises. The textual effects that this paradox generates thus reiterate an important theological point: Jesus' body is a threshold that establishes a simultaneous divine presence and absence. As such, the transcendence that Jesus conveys in the garden of John 20 is withheld. As Scharlemann argues, this bodily closure enables the disclosure that emerges within a liturgical poetics: "The end of destruction is the beginning of a retrieval of the symbol of existent deity, lost in theism, and of its attendant conception of the being of God when God is not being God."[16] Scharlemann's analysis captures the tension that Jesus' body generates even as it promises a release from exile. As a temple, it discloses an eschatological presence, but with the provision that the body remains subject to death's destabilizing effects. Scharlemann thus exposes the paradox at the heart of the Last Supper; the body's closure will always preclude its disclosure. Jesus' body is a temple only because it, too, must undergo death to become part of the eschatological Body.[17]

Death thus stands as a constant rem(a)inder of the exilic condition out of which a liturgical poetics emerges. Given that readers must remember

16. Scharlemann, *Inscriptions and Reflections*, 51.

17. On this point, Scharlemann offers clarity: "To forget the otherness, the negation, in God means being oblivious both of the difference that is in the 'I' of 'I am here'—the difference between Dasein and deity—and also of the difference that is in God and that makes it possible for God to be God as other than deity" (*Inscriptions and Reflections*, 41).

the body from within this displaced context, the impossibility of experiencing the promise's fulfillment as embodied beings becomes apparent. Transcendence is only possible after its release—crossing death's threshold—is no longer a relevant consideration. Herein lies the necessary betrayal that characterizes a liturgical poetics; its desire must be predicated on its own denial. John 20 announces this devastating requirement clearly. Jesus' body establishes a space of utmost intimacy and, therefore, provides a threshold at the brink of the promise's fulfillment. As he draws Mary towards his body, however, Jesus also indicates that he can only withdraw in response to her gesture. The reader, then, is left as Jesus leaves Mary, with one option: to leave the intimate textual space and return to exile, sustained only by the promise that has just been denied.

In the end, a liturgical poetics cannot avoid its own necessary closure. Its goal, then, is to endure the extent to which this collapse shatters the hope that Jesus' body offers. In J1737 ("Rearrange a Wife's Affection!"), Dickinson reveals how closely the fate that awaits any body can parallel the hope that the divine other will fulfill the body's desire. Dickinson's speaker announces the burden a crown symbolizes to a wife who must endure when her lover passes "through the Grave."[18] Death prohibits the union that the now absent spouse provides and, as Dickinson makes clear, this separation precludes a specifically bodily desire. Consequently, the wife accepts that she must experience her spouse's death as a denial of her desire. As the text lingers near death's threshold, Dickinson shifts the poem's tone; the fourth stanza proves to be the key for recognizing how a liturgical poetics confronts death's separation in order to sustain hope for an eschatological reunion. Dickinson writes: "Burden—borne so far triumphant— / None suspect me of the crown, / For I wear the 'Thorns' till *Sunset*— / Then—my diadem put on."[19] The crown links the wife's desired reunion and the cause of her separation; it alludes to the crown of thorns that Jesus wears during his crucifixion, which emphasizes the finitude that death brings to all bodies. The burden of separation is not only death, then, but also humanity's separation from God. In wearing the crown's burden, the speaker acknowledges the conditions of exile to which she remains subject.

By enduring what the crown symbolizes, however, the text discloses that the speaker anticipates a reunion wherein the crown's destabilizing implications are transcended. As the sun sets on the speaker's life, the

18. J1737, line 20.
19. Ibid., lines 13–16.

crown transforms into a mark of her eschatological release from death and, therefore, her now divine wifehood. Importantly, Dickinson concludes this transition in terms that echo the erotic union that the speaker desires at the poem's beginning. In wearing the diadem, she is a divine wife, a title that will be consummated in the evening into which the text opens. Moreover, as a divine wife whose crown becomes a diadem, the speaker's spouse is revealed as Jesus. Having endured death, Jesus will fulfill the promise to be present in God's kingdom. Jesus, then, is the king who wears (and has worn) the crown and, moreover, the body who will consummate the speaker's eschatological release from exile.

Dickinson thus condenses within a single image both the denial of hope that exile demands and the disclosure from within these conditions that Jesus' body provides. Importantly, the transition in J1737 remains a release that the speaker can only anticipate. Her lover, having passed through the grave, remains beyond her reach as one who is still alive and, therefore, subject to exile. Like Mary, the speaker never experiences what she imagines. J1737's erotic framework thus conveys through Jesus' absent body the anticipated presence that will fulfill the promise his body extends despite (and because of) his death. The poem ends, therefore, not with the consummation that the speaker's arrival in heaven will (as Jesus' wife) enable, but rather with an anticipation that gestures across the grave. Death still separates the lover in her exile from her beloved, but the crown she wears sustains the promise that she will put on her diadem as the text progresses endlessly "to thee."[20]

---

20. J1737, line 20.

Bibliography

Alvarez, Al. *The School of Donne*. New York: Pantheon, 1961.

Ariès, Philippe. *The Hour of Our Death*. Translated by Helen Weaver. London: Allen Lane, 1981.

———. *Western Attitudes toward Death: From the Middle Ages to the Present*. Translated by Patricia Ranum. The Johns Hopkins Symposia in Comparative History. London: Marion Boyars, 1994.

Aquinas, Saint Thomas. *Summa Theologiae*. Amazon Kindle Edition: Public Domain Books, 2006.

Augustine, Saint. *Confessions*. Translated by R. S. Pine-Coffin. Penguin Classics Edition. New York: Penguin, 1961.

Austin, Frances. *The Language of the Metaphysical Poets*. New York: MacMillan, 1992.

Bachelard, Gaston. *The Poetics of Space: The Classic Look at How We Experience Intimate Places*. Translated by Maria Jolas. Boston: Beacon, 1994.

Banzer, Judith. "'Compound Matter': Emily Dickinson and the Metaphysical Poets." *American Literature* 32.4 (January 1961) 417–33.

Barnstone, Aliki. *Changing Rapture: Emily Dickinson's Poetics Development*. Lebanon, NH: University Press of New England, 2006.

Barthes, Roland. "The Death of the Author." Translated by Richard Howard. No pages. Online: http://evans–experientialism.freewebspace.com/barthes06.htm.

———. *The Pleasure of the Text*. Translated by Richard Miller. New York: Hill and Wang, 1975.

Beaty, Nancy Lee. *The Craft of Dying*. New Haven: Yale University Press, 1970.

Bernard of Clairvaux, Saint. *On Loving God*. Christian Classics Ethereal Library. No pages. Online: http://www.ccel.org/ccel/bernard/loving_god.titlepage.html.

———. *On the Song of Songs I*. Translated by Kilian Walsh. Shannon, Ireland: Irish University Press, 1971.

The Bible: Authorized King James Version. Oxford World Classics. Edited by Robert Carroll and Stephen Prickett. Oxford: Oxford University Press, 2008.

Blanchot, Maurice. *The Space of Literature*. Translated by Ann Smock. Lincoln: University of Nebraska Press, 1989.

Bloom, Harold. *The Anxiety of Influence: A Theory of Poetry*. New York: Oxford University Press, 1973.

———. "Keats and the Embarrassments of Poetic Tradition." In *From Sensibility to Romanticism*, edited by Frederick W. Hilles and Harold Bloom. Oxford: Oxford University Press, 1970.

Botticelli, Sandro. *The Annunciation*. The Metropolitan Museum of Art, New York.

Brantley, Richard E. *Experience and Faith: The Late-Romantic Imagination of Emily Dickinson*. New York: Palgrave MacMillan, 2004.

Brown, Peter. *The Body and Society: Men, Women, and Sexual Renunciation in Early Christianity*. New York: Columbia University Press, 1988.

Bynum, Caroline Walker. *Fragmentation and Redemption: Essays on Gender and the Human Body in Medieval Religion*. New York: Zone, 1992.

———. *The Resurrection of the Body in Western Christianity, 200–1336*. New York: Columbia University Press, 1995.

Capps, Jack L. *Emily Dickinson's Reading 1836–1886*. Cambridge, MA: Harvard University Press, 1966.

Carr, David M. *The Erotic Word: Sexuality, Spirituality, and the Bible*. Oxford: Oxford University Press, 2003.

Cerbone, David. *Heidegger: A Guide for the Perplexed*. New York: Continuum, 2008.

Chambers, A. B. *Transfigured Rights in Seventeenth-Century English Poetry*. Columbia: University of Missouri Press, 1992.

Clark, Timothy. *Derrida, Heidegger, Blanchot: Sources of Derrida's Notion of Practice of Literature*. Cambridge: Cambridge University Press, 2008.

———. *The Poetics of Singularity: The Counter-Culturalist Turn in Heidegger, Derrida, Blanchot and the later Gadamer*. Edinburgh: Edinburgh University Press, 2005.

Coleridge, Samuel Taylor. *The Poetical Works of Samuel Taylor Coleridge*. Edited by James Dykes Campbell. London: Macmillan, 1903.

Conrad, Angela. *The Wayward Nun of Amherst: Emily Dickinson and Medieval Mystical Women*. New York: Garland, 2000.

Cranmer, Thomas. *39 Articles*. No Pages. Online: http://http://www.victorianweb.org/religion/39articles.html.

Cunningham, Valentine. "The Best Stories in the Best Order? Canons, Apocryphas and (Post)Modern Reading." *Literature and Theology* 14.1 (March 2000) 69–80.

———. *Reading After Theory*. Oxford: Blackwell, 2002.

Derrida, Jacques. "How to Avoid Speaking: Denials." Translated by Ken Frieden. In *Derrida and Negative Theology*, edited by Harold Coward and Toby Foshay, 73–102. Albany: State University of New York Press, 1992.

———. "Living On." In *Deconstruction and Criticism*, 62–142. New York: Continuum, 2004.

———. *Of Grammatology*. Translated by Gayatri Chakravorty Spivak. Corrected Edition. Baltimore: The Johns Hopkins University Press, 1997.

———. *On Touching—Jean-Luc Nancy*. Translated by Christine Irizarry. 1st Edition. Stanford: Stanford University Press, 2005.

———. *Margins of Philosophy*. Translated by Allan Bass. Chicago: The University of Chicago Press, 1972.

Detweiler, Robert. *Breaking the Fall: Religious Readings of Contemporary Fiction*. Louisville: Westminster John Knox, 1995.

———. "Torn by Desire: Sparagmos in Greek Tragedy and Recent Fiction." In *Postmodernism, Literature and the Future of Theology*, edited by David Jasper. London: MacMillan, 1993.

Dickinson, Emily. *The Complete Poems*. Edited by Thomas H. Johnson. London: Faber and Faber, 1975.

———. *The Letters of Emily Dickinson*. Edited by Thomas H. Johnson and Theodora Ward. Cambridge, MA: Belknap, 1986.

Diehl, Joanne Feit. *Dickinson and the Romantic Imagination*. Princeton: Princeton University Press, 1981.

DiPasquale, Theresa M. *Literature and Sacrament: The Sacred and the Secular in John Donne's Poetry*. Pittsburgh: Duquesne University Press, 1999.

———. "Receiving a Sexual Sacrament: 'The Flea' as Profane Eucharist." In *John Donne's Poetry*, edited by Donald R. Dickson, 350–61. New York: Norton, 2007.

Dix, Dom Gregory. *The Shape of Liturgy*. London: Dacre, 1970.

Docherty, Thomas. *John Donne, Undone*. Boston: Routledge Kegan and Paul, 1987.

Donne, John. *Devotions upon Emergent Occasions and Death's Duel*. Vintage Spiritual Classics. New York: Vintage, 1999.

———. *The Poems of John Donne*. Edited by E. K. Chambers. London: Lawrence and Bullen, 1896.

———. *John Donne's Sermons on the Psalms and Gospels: With a Selection of Prayers and Meditations*. Edited by Evelyn M. Simpson. Berkeley: University of California Press, 2003.

Doriani, Beth Maclay. *Emily Dickinson: Daughter of Prophecy*. Amherst: University of Massachusetts Press, 1996.

Enright, D. J. *The Alluring Problem (an Essay on Irony)*. New York: Oxford University Press, 1987.

Exum, J. Cheryl. *Song of Songs: A Commentary*. Louisville: Westminster John Knox, 2005.

Farr, Judith. *The Gardens of Emily Dickinson*. Cambridge, MA: Harvard University Press, 2004.

———. *The Passion of Emily Dickinson*. Cambridge, MA: Harvard University Press, 1992.

Finnerty, Páraic. *Emily Dickinson's Shakespeare*. Amherst: University of Massachusetts Press, 2006.

Fish, Stanley Eugene. *Self-Consuming Artifacts: The Experience of Seventeenth-Century Literature*. Berkeley: University of California Press, 1972.

Franke, William. *Poetry and Apocalypse: Theological Disclosures of Poetic Language*. Stanford: Stanford University Press, 2008.

Freud, Sigmund. *The Freud Reader*. Edited by Peter Gay. New York: Norton, 1995.

Gelpi, Albert J. *Emily Dickinson: The Mind of the Poet*. New York: Norton, 1971.

Gribbin, Laura. "Emily Dickinson's Circumference: Figuring a Blind Spot in the Romantic Tradition." *The Emily Dickinson Journal* 2.1 (1993) 1–21.

Hart, Kevin. *Trespass of the Sign: Deconstruction, Theology and Philosophy*. Cambridge: Cambridge University Press, 1989.

Heidegger, Martin. *Being and Time*. Translated by John Macquarrie and Edward Robinson. London: SCM, 1962.

———. "Building Dwelling Thinking." In *Poetry, Language, Thought*, 141–60. Tranlsated by Albert Hofstadter. New York: Perennial Classics, 2001.

———. *Hölderlin's Hymn "The Ister."* Translated by William McNeill and Julia Davis. Bloomington: Indiana University Press, 1984.

———. *Off the Beaten Track*. Edited and translated by Julian Young and Kenneth Haynes. Cambridge: Cambridge University Press, 2002.

———. "... Poetically Man Dwells ..." In *Poetry, Language, Thought*, 201–229. Tranlsated by Albert Hofstadter. New York: Perennial Classics, 2001.

———. "What are Poets For?" In *Poetry, Language, Thought*, 87–104. Tranlsated by Albert Hofstadter. New York: Perennial Classics, 2001.

Holler, Linda. *Erotic Morality: The Role of Touch in Moral Agency*. New Brunswick, NJ: Rutgers University Press, 2002.

The Holy Bible: Containing the Old and New Testaments. New Revised Standard Version. Oxford: Oxford University Press, 1995.

Jasper, David. *Coleridge as Poet and Religious Thinker*. Allison Park, PA: Pickwick, 1985.

———. "Evil, Betrayal and the Sacred Community." Paper delivered at the University of Iowa, April 2010.

———. *Rhetoric, Power and Community: An Exercise in Reserve*. Louisville: Westminster John Knox, 1993.

———. *The Sacred Body: Asceticism in Religion, Literature, Art, and Culture*. Waco, TX: Baylor University Press, 2009.

———. *The Sacred Desert: Religion, Literature, Art, and Culture*. Oxford: Blackwell, 2004.

———. *The Study of Literature and Religion: An Introduction*. 2nd edition. London: MacMillan, 1992.

Jeanrond, Werner G. *Theology of Love*. New York: Continuum, 2010.

Kazantzakis, Nikos. *The Last Temptation of Christ*. Translated by P. A. Bien. New York: Scribner, 1998.

Keane, Patrick J. *Emily Dickinson's Approving God: Divine Design and the Problem of Suffering*. Columbia: University of Missouri Press, 2008.

Kearney, Richard. "Deconstruction, God, and the Possible." In *Derrida and Religion: Other Testaments,* edited by Yvonne Sherwood and Kevin Hart, 297–308. New York: Routledge, 2004.

———. *The God Who May Be: A Hermeneutics of Religion*. Indiana Series in Philosophy of Religion. Bloomington: Indiana University Press, 2001.

———. *On Paul Ricoeur: The Owl of Minerva*. Farnham, UK: Ashgate, 2004.

———. *Strangers, Gods and Monsters: Interpreting Otherness*. New York: Routledge, 2003.

Keats, John. *The Poems of John Keats*. Edited by E. De Selincourt. New York: Dodd, Mead, 1921.

"Keats' Negative Capability." No pages. Online: http://www.mrbauld.com/negcap.html.

Kennelly, Brendan. *The Book of Judas*. Newcastle upon Tyne, UK: Bloodaxe, 1991.

Lacoste, Jean-Yves. *Experience and the Absolute: Disputed Questions on the Humanity of Man*. Perspectives in Continental Philosophy. Translated by Mark Raftery-Skehan. New York: Fordham University Press, 2004.

Lambert, Gregg. "Untouchable." In *Derrida and Religion: Other Testaments*, edited by Yvonne Sherwood and Kevin Hart, 363–74. New York: Routledge, 2004.

Landow, George P. *Victorian Types, Victorian Shadows: Biblical Typography in Victorian Literature, Art, and Thought*. Boston: Routledge and Kegan, 1980.

Laqueur, Thomas. *Making Sex: Body and Gender from the Greeks to Freud*. Cambridge, MA: Harvard University Press, 1990.

Le Doeuff, Michèle. *Hipparchia's Choice: An Essay Concerning Women, Philosophy, Etc.* Translated by Trista Selous. New York: Columbia University Press, 2007.

Lundin, Roger. *Emily Dickinson and the Art of Belief*. Grand Rapids: Eerdmans, 2004.

Marion, Jean-Luc. *The Erotic Phenomenon*. Translated by Stephen E. Lewis. Chicago: The University of Chicago Press, 2008.

———. *Prolegomena to Charity*. Translated by Stephen E. Lewis. New York: Fordham University Press, 2002.

McFarland, Thomas. *Coleridge and the Pantheist Tradition*. Oxford: Clarendon, 1969.

McIntosh, James. *Nimble Believing: Dickinson and the Unknown*. Ann Arbor: University of Michigan Press, 2000.

Miles, Margaret R. *Carnal Knowing: Female Nakedness and Religious Meaning in the Christian West*. Kent, UK: Burns and Oates, 1989.

Miller, Cristanne. *Emily Dickinson: A Poet's Grammar*. Cambridge, MA: Harvard University Press, 1987.

Miller, J. Hillis. "The Critic as Host." In *Deconstruction and Criticism*, edited by Harold Bloom et al. New York: Continuum, 2004.

Nancy, Jean-Luc. *Corpus*. 3rd Edition. Perspectives in Continental Philosophy. Translated by Richard A. Rand. New York: Fordham University Press, 2008.

————. *Noli Me Tangere: On the Raising of the Body*. Translated by Sarah Clift, Pascale-Anne Brault, and Michael Naas. New York: Fordham University Press, 2008.

Nietzsche, Friedrich. *Thus Spoke Zarathustra: A Book for Everyone and Nobody*. Oxford World Classics. Translated by Graham Parkes. Oxford: Oxford University Press, 2005.

Norris, Christopher. *Deconstruction: Theory and Practice*. London: Methuen Young, 1982.

Ostriker, Alicia. "Re-playing the Bible: My Emily Dickinson." *The Emily Dickinson Journal* 2.2 (Fall 1993) 160–71.

Patterson, Rebecca. *Emily Dickinson's Imagery*. Amherst: University of Massachusetts Press, 1979.

Raschke, Carl A. *Theological Thinking: An Inquiry*. Atlanta: Scholars, 1988.

Ricoeur, Paul. *From Text to Action: Essays in Hermeneutics, II*. Translated by Kathleen Blamey and John B. Thompson. London: Athlone, 1991.

————. *The Rule of Metaphor: The Creation of Meaning in Language*. Translated by Robert Czerny et al. New York: Routledge, 2009.

Robinson, John. *Emily Dickinson: Looking to Canaan*. London: Faber and Faber, 1986.

Rosendale, Timothy. *Liturgy and Literature in the Making of Protestant England*. Cambridge: Cambridge University Press, 2007.

"Samuel Taylor Coleridge (1772–1834)." The Free Library by Farlex. No pages. Online: http://coleridge.thefreelibrary.com.

Sewall, Richard Benson. *The Life of Emily Dickinson*. Cambridge, MA: Harvard University Press, 1998.

Scharlemann, Robert P. *Inscriptions and Reflections: Essays in Philosophical Theology*. Charlottesville: University Press of Virginia, 1989.

Schwartz, Regina. *Sacramental Poetics at the Dawn of Secularism: When God Left the World*. Stanford: Stanford University Press, 2008.

Shaffer, E. S. *"Kubla Khan" and The Fall of Jerusalem: The Mythological School in Biblical Criticism and Secular Literature 1770–1880*. Cambridge: Cambridge University Press, 1975.

Shakespeare, William. *Sonnets*. London: Knickerbocker, 1913.

————. *King John*. Oxford World Classics. Edited by A. R. Braunmuller. New York: Oxford University Press, 2008.

Smith, Robert McClure. *The Seductions of Emily Dickinson*. Tuscaloosa: The University of Alabama Press, 1996.

Soskice, Janet Martin. *Metaphor and Religious Language*. New York: Oxford University Press, 1987.

St. Armand, Barton Levi. *Emily Dickinson and Her Culture: The Soul's Society*. Cambridge: Cambridge University Press, 1986.

Steinberg, Leo. *The Sexuality of Christ in Renaissance Art and Modern Oblivion*. 2nd Edition. Chicago: The University of Chicago Press, 1996.

Stubbs, John. *John Donne: The Reformed Soul.* New York: Viking, 2006.

Targoff, Ramie. *John Donne, Body and Soul.* Chicago: The University of Chicago Press, 2009.

Taylor, Jeremy. *Holy Living and Dying: With Prayers Containing the Whole Duty of a Christian; and the Parts of Devotion Fitted to All Occasions, and Furnished for All Necessities.* Elibron Classics Replica Edition. Chestnut Hill, MA: Adament, 2001.

Tertullian. *The Apology of Tertullian for the Christians.* Translated by T. Herbert Bindley. London: Parker, 1890.

Titian. *Noli me Tangere.* The National Gallery, London.

Vattimo, Gianni. *The Adventure of Difference: Philosophy after Nietzsche and Heidegger.* Translated by Cyprian Blamires and Thomas Harrison. Cambridge: Polity, 1993.

Walton, Heather. *Literature, Theology and Feminism.* Manchester, UK: Manchester University Press, 2008.

Ward, Graham. *Theology and Contemporary Critical Theory.* 2nd Edition. London: MacMillan, 2000.

Warner, Marina. *Alone of All Her Sex: The Myth and Cult of the Virgin Mary.* New York: Vintage, 2000.

White, Fred D. "Emily Dickinson's Existential Dramas." In *The Cambridge Companion to Emily Dickinson*, edited by Wendy Martin, 91–106. Cambridge: Cambridge University Press, 2003.

Wolosky, Shira. "Rhetoric or Not: Hymnal Tropes in Emily Dickinson and Isaac Watts." *The New England Quarterly* 61.2 (June 1988) 214–32.

Yeats, William Butler. *The Complete Poems of W. B. Yeats.* Edited by Richard J. Finneran. 2nd Revised Edition. New York: Scribner, 1996.

Yelle, Robert A. "The Rebirth of Myth? Nietzsche's Eternal Recurrence and Its Romantic Antecedents." *Numen* 47.2 (2000) 175–202

Zapedowska, Magdalena. "Wrestling with Silence: Emily Dickinson's Calvinist God." *The American Transcendental Quarterly* (March 2006). Online: http://findarticles.com/p/articles/mi_7008/is_1_20/ai_n28347894/.

Index

www.ingramcontent.com/pod-product-compliance
Lightning Source LLC
Chambersburg PA
CBHW070838030726
47504CB00005B/1147